PRAISE FOR CLAI

'A knockout new talent you shoul[...]

'It really had me gripped.'
   —Marian Keyes, international bestselling author of *Grown Ups*

'The definition of an utterly absorbing page-turner. Richly drawn characters, a compelling plot, and a finale that will keep you guessing.'

   —John Marrs, bestselling author of
   What Lies Between Us and *The One*

'A real nail-biter of a thriller that gets darker and more twisted with every page. If you liked *What You Did*, you'll love *The Push*.'
   —Erin Kelly, *Sunday Times* bestselling author of *He Said/She Said*

'Absorbing, timely, and beautifully written, *What You Did* is a superior psychological thriller from a major talent.'

   —Mark Edwards, bestselling author of
   The Retreat and *Here to Stay*

'I loved this story. The flesh-and-blood characters, dry wit, and brilliant plotting are every bit as enjoyable as *Big Little Lies*.'

   —Louise Candlish, bestselling author of
   Our House and *The Other Passenger*

'A perfectly plotted murder mystery that had me hooked from the first page. Twisty domestic suspense that's perfect for fans of *Big Little Lies*.'
   —Lisa Gray, bestselling author of the Jessica Shaw series

'I haven't flown through a book so quickly in a very long time. It delivers on every single level.'

—Caz Frear, bestselling author of the DC Cat Kinsella series

'What a nail-biting, just-one-more-page-I-can't-put-it-down roller coaster of suspense!'

—Steph Broadribb, author of *Deep Down Dead*

'Smart, sassy, and satisfyingly twisty.'

—Sarah Hilary, author of the DI Marnie Rome series

'Huge fun with some very dark moments and brilliantly awful characters. Excellent, twisty plotting.'

—Harriet Tyce, author of *Blood Orange*

'A brilliantly observed and compelling thriller.'

—Anna Mazzola, author of *The Story Keeper*

'A roller coaster read, full of thrills and one spectacular spill!'

—Liz Nugent, bestselling author of *Skin Deep*

'*What You Did* is a triumph, a gripping story of the secrets and lies that can underpin even the closest friendships. Put some time aside – this is one you'll want to read in a single sitting.'

—Kevin Wignall, bestselling author of
A Death in Sweden and *The Traitor's Story*

'Hitting the rare sweet spot between a satisfying read and a real page-turner, this brilliantly written book deserves to fly high.'

—Cass Green, bestselling author of *In a Cottage In a Wood*

'A meticulous thriller full of twists and false turns.'

—Crime Time

'Creepy and oh-so-clever.'

—*Fabulous* magazine

'A fantastic and intense book that grips you right from the very first line.'

—We Love This Book

'McGowan's pacey, direct style ensures that the twists come thick and fast.'

—*The Irish Times*

'A riveting police thriller.'

—*Woman* (Pick of the Week)

'Taut plotting and assured writing.'

—*Good Housekeeping*

'You'll be desperate to know what happened and how everything will turn out.'

—*Sun*

'An excellent murder mystery.'

—*Bella*

'Plenty of twists and turns keep you hooked.'

—*Crime Monthly*

'With a great plot and brilliant characters, this is a read-in-one-sitting page-turner.'

—*Fabulous* magazine

'A brilliant portrait of a fractured society and a mystery full of heart-stopping twists. Compelling, clever and entertaining.'

—Jane Casey

'A keeps-you-guessing mystery.'

—Alex Marwood

'A brilliant crime novel . . . gripping.'

—*Company*

'A compelling and flawless thriller . . . there is nothing not to like.'

—Sharon Bolton

'Ireland's answer to Ruth Rendell.'

—Ken Bruen

ARE
YOU
AWAKE?

Fiction

The Fall
What You Did
The Other Wife
The Push
I Know You

Non-fiction

The Vanishing Triangle

Paula Maguire series

The Lost
The Dead Ground
The Silent Dead
A Savage Hunger
Blood Tide
The Killing House

Writing as Eva Woods

ARE YOU

YOU

AWAKE?

CLAIRE
McGOWAN

THOMAS & MERCER

Text copyright © 2022 Claire McGowan
All rights reserved.

Published by Thomas & Mercer, Seattle

www.apub.com

Amazon, the Amazon logo, and Thomas & Mercer are trademarks of Amazon.com, Inc., or its affiliates.

ISBN-13: 9781542035378
ISBN-10: 1542035376

Cover design by Heike Schüssler

Printed in the United States of America

ARE
YOU
AWAKE?

Samantha

The room was small and dirty. Bare floorboards gritty with dust. Walls that were maybe cream once, now spotted over with black mould and grease. In places, splashes of something she knew was blood. They had never cleaned it up properly, a fact she couldn't stop thinking about. Windows boarded over, so only a crack of light made it through to tell her what time of day it was. There was a lamp, giving out the faintest glow, and a mattress on the floor where she slept. This was all. Not much. A hellhole, you might even say.

The man stood across the room from her, where she sat cross-legged on the mattress. As she watched, he undid the expensive watch he wore around his left wrist. Her eyes tracked it as he slid it off, set it down on the grimy windowsill with a small chink of metal. He was in dark jeans and a black jumper that she could tell was also expensive. Leather boots, which he now bent to undo, tucking the laces carefully in, setting them aside. He did not speak to her. She did not speak to him either. What good would words do now?

He rolled up the sleeves of the jumper and her heart began to race, gulping away in her chest. She tried to breathe deeply.

It's OK, it's OK.

Panic would not help; it might even get her killed. She just had to stay calm and remember that she was alive, she was safe, for now at least. That was what mattered. He picked up the knife that lay on the windowsill, catching a dull glint of light from the window, then carried it across the room to her, his feet making no sound. They would get covered in dirt, his nice socks. He set the knife on the mattress, where it lay, innocent as a snake. She was frozen, unable to look away.

It's OK, it's OK.

She had to stay calm. But as it began, and her breath stopped in her throat, it was hard. It was very, very hard not to panic, as she felt his strong manicured hands around her neck, the pulse beating hard against his fingers. As his grip tightened, he called her by a name that was not her own.

'*Colette.*'

Mary

'I hate you.' She stared through the bars, rage in her eyes.

'OK. That's not going to change anything.'

'I HATE YOU.'

'Alright, I get the message. Now will you please go to sleep?' In response, Audrey opened her mouth and began to howl.

Mary had encountered parents who seemed to have become entirely deaf to their children's cries. Or not deaf exactly, but undisturbed by them, certainly. More of a resigned *oh look, he's crying again*, than an *oh my God what is that sound I must stop it at any cost*. She herself had never gone deaf to her children, more was the pity. And with two of them, it seemed they could cry in stereo, or in a perfect rota so that if one briefly went to sleep and shut up, the other would wake up and start screaming.

Right now she was standing over Audrey's crib, trying to press her, very gently, back down to the mattress. Audrey had strong little toddler legs, and didn't want to go to sleep. It was morning, she insisted. 'Morning, Mummy!' And she wasn't wrong. It was 4 a.m. and the sky was already grey with light. Mary felt the days never ended at the moment, that they just ran into each other, bleeding round the edges. Her brain never switched off and it was beginning to make her crazy. As in, she actually worried she was going mad, could feel it fritzing at the sides of her mind. How long did you have to be awake before you lost it entirely? Almost three years, that should do it, surely.

In his crib against the opposite wall, Leo tensed in his sleep. Oh God, she couldn't cope if they both woke up, she really couldn't.

'Audrey,' she whispered firmly. 'You have to go to sleep. It's night-time.'

'Morning-time!'

'Come on.' She scooped the hot, angry child out of her cot and carried her to the window. 'Look. There's no one about. It's too early still.' Audrey was two, she had no concept of time. She squirmed in Mary's arms, in her vest and nappy. It was too hot to sleep, too hot and too bright. London intruded even at this hour – it wasn't true that no one was about. Cars went past regularly, and there were even a few people walking down the street. Where to? Mary wondered. Perhaps low-paid jobs like cleaning or opening up a coffee shop. That made her feel guilty. She didn't have to work at all at the moment, she had another six months on her maternity leave for Leo. Jack earned enough to keep them all, even if the flat only had two bedrooms and the kids woke each other up constantly. She should be grateful, rather than filled with resentment that Jack was fast asleep next door, arms thrown over his head, oblivious. Maybe she'd go back to writing down those daily gratitudes, like her friend Francine had suggested, and that would make her a nicer, more pleasant wife and mother. She'd kept up the habit for a few days, then Audrey had ripped out the pages of the expensive notebook and scribbled on them in crayon, and Jack had set down a coffee cup on the cover, leaving a large brown ring.

Bleary-eyed, she stared out of the window, just to look at something that wasn't her flat, the peeling wallpaper where Audrey had picked at it, the struggling child in her arms, gasping and hot against her chest, outraged and not able to say why. They lived opposite the park, and when they'd bought the maisonette flat four years ago it had seemed like a lovely location, more than big enough for a working couple who were always out on weekends. No need for a garden, they agreed, when they had green space so close. Now the park was just somewhere to drag the kids round for ten minutes. She squinted in the half-dawn – something had caught her eye, in the row of houses that overlooked the park, a street at a right angle to Mary's own. Movement of some kind. She tried to catch it again – a glow of light, and the sensation of frantic activity, as if someone was dancing or performing martial arts or something like that. At this time of night? Maybe they couldn't sleep either. For a moment she watched the movement – was it two people? What were they doing? – the mild curiosity cutting through her brain fog a little. Who would be up in the middle of the night, and what were they doing? For a brief second Mary wondered if she should be worried. Was there a suggestion of violence in the moving shadows, thrown against the shuttered window? Maybe she was witnessing something terrible and she wouldn't even realise until she saw it on the news. Or maybe she just watched too many true-crime documentaries on Netflix, since they were the only thing she could focus on without falling asleep.

Then Leo coughed in his sleep and started mewling, and she turned away and forgot all about it.

Tim

The night was so long. Normal people, people who could sleep, just close their eyes and sink into grateful oblivion, they would never truly know how long the night was. How much space there was between midnight and 6 a.m., a time by which it was hardly worth going to sleep, assuming you even could. How many hours to beat yourself up about your every failure and shortcoming. To be stuck with your miserable, wide-awake self, and no escape.

His night usually went like this – midnight, turn off the light. His phone in another room. He knew all the science on blue light and circadian rhythms, he followed the rules. Midnight to half past, read books or magazines by a dim light to soothe his brain into accepting it was night, reduce the production of wakeful hormones. His pillow was spritzed with lavender, his eye mask from a British Airways business-class flight. He had custom-moulded earbuds crammed into each cavity. He'd close his eyes. Play his favourite sleep meditation, a soothing-voiced woman inviting him to imagine a forest glade, though it rarely worked for him. Then it would end and it was time. *Go to sleep.* It was deceiving, the active verb. There was no way to will yourself to sleep. You had to surrender to it, but that was the hardest thing of all. To just wait. He had made his bedroom as dark and cool as he could, but there was still disruption – this was London, after all. Someone at the bins of the flats, almost too late for the morning collection. The swish of a car on the road. The murdered-child shrieks of foxes, which no longer even raised his heart rate. Also, he was really hot. Why was it so hot? He kicked off the covers, then irritably shrugged down his flannel pyjamas. He'd sleep in just pants. Not that he could sleep.

There was a light. Where was it coming from? He'd have to get up and check. He lumbered into the orange-lit kitchen, flooded from the street light outside, and twitched the blinds further shut. He might as well check his phone too while he was there, bathing his face in blue, waking himself up more. Four a.m. How was it 4 a.m. already? It seemed no time had passed. He had to be up in four hours, otherwise he wouldn't sleep the following night either. The familiar anxiety began – four hours was enough, wasn't it? Survivable. He'd be tired, but he could make it through to the next night. It would be fine, but only if he fell asleep right now. The literature said he should get up if he couldn't drop off, read a book for a while. But that would cut into his sleeping time even more. His stomach growled – that was another thing about being up during hours you shouldn't be, you got hungry, and then it was also that keeping you awake.

God. The endless frazzle of his brain. He knew the reason he felt crazy was that parts of it were shutting down, gone to sleep though he was conscious, so he actually wasn't in his right mind. He actually was a little mad. *Just stop, will you? Just stop. Go to sleep, you stupid lump of meat.* Why could he not manage this most basic and automatic of human processes? What was wrong with him? He paused at his kitchen window, and through a chink in the blind was caught in the orange beam of the night-time city. He looked out, simply for something to do, and that was when he saw it. Movement, in the window of one of the houses by the park.

Mary

The next morning – if you could even call it that when you'd barely been to sleep at all – Mary was at the kitchen table trying to force food into both children at the same time. Leo was latched to her left breast, suckling hard with his greedy little mouth. Was it supposed to hurt? On TV it always looked so gentle and blissful. Not like being drained dry by a gaping-mouthed demon. With her other hand she was trying to feed porridge to Audrey, who quite reasonably did not want to eat a hot breakfast when it was already 27 degrees outside.

'No, Mummy! Coco Pops!' She was only allowed Coco Pops at her grandma's – Jack's mother, of course, interfering as always – but the sugary cereal had lodged indelibly in her toddler brain. Often, Mary thought about just giving in, buying them, so her daughter would at least eat something. But she had to hold the line, or the other mothers at Audrey's chi-chi nursery would be sure to judge. Hence the porridge made with organic oats and chopped blueberries, which Audrey was fishing out and throwing on the floor. 'Yuck berries. Yuck, Mummy.'

'Yes, OK, I get it, you hate them.' Leo tugged harder, and Mary gasped in pain, catching Audrey's worried glance. 'It's OK, darling. Leo's just hungry.'

'He's naughty.'

'No – not naughty. He's just little.' She worried about that. Audrey had of course been disturbed by the arrival of her baby brother three months ago, and become fixated on the idea the baby was bad when he cried or threw up or scratched Mary with his flailing hands. She wouldn't hurt him, would she? On those long nights, the two wakeful children crammed into that tiny hot bedroom?

Jack came bumbling in then, catching his thigh on the edge of the dresser and letting out a curse word that Audrey cocked her head at, no doubt storing it away to bring out at the least appropriate moment. 'Ow!' He hopped about for a minute. Let him try giving birth, see how much of a fuss he'd make about a small bruise then. 'God, I'm exhausted. Hardly slept at all.'

Do not punch your husband, do not punch him. 'You looked asleep to me.' Mary took advantage of Audrey's distraction to spoon some porridge into her mouth. Outraged at the trick, she spat it out on to the table. Mary sighed.

'I suppose I got a bit. You?'

'Up most of the night with one or the other. It's too hot for them – will you see about getting an air-con unit today?'

'Huh, some chance! They've been sold out for weeks.'

Mary scraped up another spoonful of porridge. 'I thought I saw something last night. Out the window?'

'Umm?' Jack was staring into the fridge. What was he looking for? The cold air was getting out.

'Some kind of . . . people moving about. Dancing. Or maybe like, I don't know. Violence.'

'Violence?'

'I'm not sure. It was in one of those houses that look on to the park.'

9

'That's too far away to see, surely. You probably imagined it, you're so sleep-deprived.' He cast a vague eye over the table. 'What's there for breakfast?'

'You could finish Audrey's porridge, since she's barely eaten a bite.'

'Um. No. Granola?'

'Run out. I'll try and go today.' The thought of dragging the two children round the supermarket made her want to cry. 'Or you could go on the way home.'

He took some bread from the open packet, spilling crumbs. 'I'll be late today.'

'Again?' He was late so often at the moment, and she was ashamed to admit she counted down the hours until someone else could take responsibility for the children, even for a minute.

'Lots on. Sorry.'

She sighed again. The sound reminded her of her mother, who'd never worked after having her three children. Discontentment. An unhappy marriage stuck in old gender roles. How had she fallen into this too? She was a lawyer. She used to get her nails done, potter about Whistles on her lunch hour. She used to actually have a lunch hour, instead of an extended battle somewhere between eleven to three, depending on naps and when the kids woke up, which usually ended with significantly more food on the floor than in anyone's stomachs. *She won't starve,* her own mother always said about Audrey. *If she won't eat, let her go hungry.* Firmly, Mary stood up – Leo squawked at the sudden movement, clutched to her breast – and took the dish away from Audrey. 'Alright then, no breakfast if you won't eat it.'

Audrey started to cry. Jack's brow furrowed as he extracted his burnt toast from the machine. 'She'll be hungry, Mary.'

'She's fine.'

'Listen to her!'

'She cries like this every ten minutes,' she snapped. 'You'd know that if you were ever here.' Ah, a classic frustrated wife line. Where did they come from? Had she absorbed them before she could even speak? Jack looked pained. A pause. She took a deep breath. 'There's jam in the fridge.'

She sat back down again. Placed the bowl in front of the toddler, who seized the plastic spoon and began to eat with every sign of enjoyment. 'See?' said Jack. 'She was hungry.'

Mary counted to ten, and when that didn't work, just kept on counting until her husband had spread jam on his toast, leaving crumbs and smears everywhere, stuffed it into his mouth in three bites, and ruffled Audrey's hair before running out for the train. An hour crammed up into people's armpits, during the hottest week of the year, followed by more hours in a stuffy non-air-conditioned office working on the world's dullest subject, tax law. Coming home at eight, sweaty and rumpled, the same crowded trains and irate commuters. An hour to himself before bed, if he could stay awake that long.

Lucky bastard, Mary thought, as he slammed the door behind him.

Tim

Stumbling out into the daylight felt like an assault on his senses. Bringing back memories of *that* day, the first spark of light piercing the dark, the terrible hope, and then the worst moments of all, waiting for them to reach him, sure that his air would run out before then, or that the crushing pain in his legs meant he'd bleed to death once moved. He'd seen it on TV medical shows, that sometimes you couldn't feel your wound until they removed the object that was stuck in you, and the blood that was being kept in would rush out and you'd die just when you thought you were saved. He could not bear the thought of that.

All the same, he knew it was important to leave the house and soak up daylight, especially when it was sunny like now. To help calibrate his body clock, and 'enjoy the weather', as Alice would have said. She was obsessed with *making the most of the weather*, having grown up in a country where it wasn't reliable. His father had never understood this – you hid indoors when it was warm, you closed the blinds and doors and kept the heat out. He would mutter to himself seeing Alice sprawled out on a yoga mat on the lawn, face held to the sun, body glistening with oil. But his father was dead six years, and Tim did not want to think about Alice's body – some things were too painful.

Oh. Tim jerked to himself, suddenly aware that he had just woken up, standing on his feet in the kitchen. This happened sometimes. Micro-sleeps, they called it, so fast you didn't register it happening, lasting only seconds. Lethal if you were driving at the time. His brain was so starved of sleep it was shutting itself down. A bad sign. And they were getting longer, too – the other day he'd found himself wandering the aisles at Sainsbury's, a packet of tofu in hand, with no memory of going there. Tim didn't even eat tofu, that was Alice's thing.

He opened his door, checking compulsively that he had his keys, and stepped on to the dirty carpet in the hallway of his flats. This was OK. He wasn't trapped, that had been many months ago. He didn't need to think about Alice, she was gone, separate from him. He only had to think about going out, pushing his feet into old flip-flops and slogging round the park. Suddenly he remembered himself in the night, standing at the kitchen window, almost sleepwalking with exhaustion. He'd seen something in one of the houses overlooking the park, something his brain had not been able to parse. Movement, violent movement, in the middle of the night. That was strange. Deep inside, buried under layers of his own rubble, Tim felt a spark. Interest. The curiosity that drove you as a journalist, to find and uncover. What was going on in that house – was someone being hurt? He hadn't felt the immediate worry that would have sent him to call the police, but there'd been something about it that snagged his attention all the same. He couldn't even say exactly what he'd seen. Tim decided he would try to find out more, and this would give some purpose to his morning shamble, dodging small children and dogs, aware of the disapproving glances the local mums gave him, with his unshaven beard and uncut hair, his rumpled clothes. He knew he was a state. How to explain that none of it seemed to matter? It was hard enough to put the shoes on and find his keys and his phone. Often he didn't even take his phone with him. No one was going to be calling him, no one who mattered anyway. The only person he wanted to hear from would never call him again.

The front hall of the flats was neglected and dusty, post piling up for long-ago tenants, names adrift in London. He opened the front door and winced at the world hitting him – bright sun, the traffic on the road, a lawnmower droning somewhere nearby. The smell of hot rubbish from the bins. Sunlight warm on his skin, both pleasant and unpleasant because it made him remember again. It had been hot that day too. Sweat down his back and on his top lip, clean-shaven back then. Perhaps so people knew that, despite his dark hair and eyes, he wasn't local. He was a Westerner, a reporter. As if that gave you some magic patina of protection. It didn't.

He crossed the road, the sun in his eyes making everything a dazzle. Hordes of children everywhere, drawn as if by magnets under his feet. A barking dachshund approached, tangling its lead briefly around his bare legs. He gasped. 'Sorry, sorry,' said the owner, a harassed man with a baby in a sling. Even that brief contact, the pressure of the cord on Tim's skin, it triggered things. Memories. It was so long since anyone had laid a hand on him.

Usually, he just walked around in circles round the park, perhaps bought a coffee from the organic café where a latte cost four pounds, if he could face the noise of children and dogs inside, the babies flinging food and their parents ignoring them, determined to still lead the same lives they had before reproducing. But today he had a mission – have a look at that house from the night before.

First though, he had to figure out which one it was. There was a row of ten backing on to the park, and it had been somewhere in the middle, but he wasn't sure which house exactly. He'd start with the backs, which were separated from the park by a crumbling brick wall and an iron fence. In between the fence and wall, an overgrown no-man's-land strewn with rubbish and weeds.

The park was a small one, which could be walked around in about twenty minutes. The gates – there were two, one on each vertical side – had signs that said they were locked at dusk, whatever time that was. Around ten at the moment, the height of summer. For Tim, it just meant even fewer hours where sleep might be coaxed from its hiding place. The street with the houses, Cliveden Road, made the fourth side of the park, the other three ringed with railings and trees. Some of the houses, he could now see, had the outlines of old doors leading into the park, half-hidden by ivy and trailing plants. Did any of them still open? There was nothing here that suggested anything odd, and the backs of the four middle houses were largely the same – tall trees in the gardens, slate roofs, chimney pots. Two had burglar alarms fitted to the back of the house, and one appeared to be in the process of renovation – the windows were shuttered with wood panels. But despite that, Tim was almost sure this was the house he'd seen the movement in. He'd have to go round the front and work out which number it was.

He looked up, and the world reeled for a second. There was someone on the roof up there! Sniper. *Sniper!* And all these kids and parents and dogs and . . .

It was a chimney. Of course it was a chimney, because he was in London, not the Middle East, not in a war zone. There were no snipers. And yet his brain did not seem to understand that, would react as if he was likely to be shot or blown up at any moment. He'd thrown himself to the ground the week before when a car backfired, then had to endure all the concerned people crowding round him, asking was he alright, and pretend he'd just tripped, even though he could barely speak, his tongue thick with terror.

Tim suddenly became aware that someone was watching him, as his heart rate stuttered back to normal. He turned, the hairs on his neck prickling. Two women, one in a summer dress that flapped around her ankles and rainbow-striped trainers, and one in shorts and a striped top, were staring at him. Between them they had five children, the older ones on scooters and the younger clutched by the hand or in a pushchair. They also had two dogs. All nine were staring at him as he lurked in the bushes. This was London, so they wouldn't actually say anything, but it made him uncomfortable enough that he turned and rushed away, feeling the back of his neck turn red with shame. It was hard to be a lone man nowadays. Everyone thought you were a danger, when really you might be the one that needed help.

Mary

The morning passed in a blur. Jack had left at eight, and she looked up sometime later and it was already half ten and neither child was bathed or dressed. Audrey was wearing a superhero cape and had porridge in her hair. Mary herself hadn't showered and was wearing her old college hoody and no trousers, dirty white socks of Jack's. Things had gone to pot, and she still needed to drag the kids round the supermarket. She resorted to a trick she often used – stepped into the shower with Leo in her arms, squirming as the warm water fell on him, shielding his face while trying to scrub herself with the other hand. He would shriek the place down if she set him in his cot for a second. Audrey she put on the bathroom floor with some toys, but the toddler kept pulling the curtain aside and trying to get in the shower fully clothed, aware that she had in some way been supplanted by her brother. It was hard. Every day felt like a struggle, every moment, every second. Would it ever just be easy? Could she ever just live, and not think in such strategic detail about washing, eating, sleeping, putting on socks?

She dried herself and the baby, Audrey clinging to one damp leg, then hobbled into the bedroom. She placed Leo on the bed, then her heart skipped as he suddenly bellyflopped right to the edge. 'Leo! You turned over!' He hadn't been able to do that yesterday. Mary felt liquid horror slide through her veins. He'd almost fallen off the bed because she assumed he couldn't. The parameters were always shifting. For a moment she sat down, half-dressed, winded by shock. Imagine if he'd fallen. She'd have had to rush him to hospital, wait about for hours. Perhaps answer questions from social services. He might have hit his fragile head, bled into his brain. Jack would have been called at work, and he'd have looked at her like she couldn't cope. But it was alright. Leo hadn't fallen. She pulled on her jeans with him clutched against her, so tight he began to mewl again. They only wanted to be close, but as soon as they were they wanted independence.

Then, she was almost ready to go when she made the mistake of checking her emails. She was still looped into some work chains, to try and keep in touch. Her boss, Geoffrey – red trousers, Oxford, terrible breath – had sent one titled *Well Done Francesca*. Mary clicked on it, knowing it was masochistic. *After over a year of wrangling, we have successfully completed the Domato divorce settlement, all thanks to the considerable skills of Francesca – champagne in the conference room to celebrate!*

That case had been Mary's – she'd worked on it night and day for almost a year, trying to bring the warring and extremely wealthy former couple to agreement, until three months ago, when she'd had to hand over to her trainee, who was now her maternity cover. Francesca. Twenty-eight. Not even thinking of having children yet. Years left to get herself established, and she'd cracked this case in its final straits, so she would take all the credit. Mary stood in the kitchen for a moment, feeling sorry for herself. They wouldn't want her back. Six more months off work was a long time – her skills would go rusty, they'd rather have someone younger who could think clearly and didn't have porridge on their jacket. Another woman lost to motherhood, a bad feminist, a bad mother too since she'd almost let her child roll off the bed.

A wail from the living room interrupted her spiral – apparently she wasn't even allowed time for self-pity now. Somehow, she got all three of them out the door, trailing reusable bags and jackets, even though it was almost thirty degrees. The car was empty of air, hot with dust, and Audrey began to cry and buck as Mary strapped her into the seat. 'No car! No go!'

'We're going to the shops! You can sit on Thomas!' This was a ride-on Thomas the Tank Engine, cynically located outside the supermarket. Instantly Audrey stopped crying, and Mary wondered with dread if she had a pound in her purse to operate Thomas. The consequences of such a broken promise would be dire. She put Leo in his seat, grateful that he stayed where she left him for now, though clearly those days were coming to an end. And they were off. The car was almost out of petrol, and she remembered Jack had taken it out last two evenings before, supposedly to get milk. He'd been gone a long time, hadn't he? She hadn't really processed it then, because time could lose all meaning in the pre-bath pre-bed vortex. She had just pulled out of her drive and into the road, still musing on this, when someone stepped off the pavement, right in front of her.

Mary's brain was slow. She felt the delay, the half-second drag of her mind telling her foot to slam down. The car was stopping. But not fast enough. The man was still standing there, staring in the other direction, back into the park. She was going to hit him. This was it. She was going to run someone over. Then the car stopped, two inches from his legs. He turned to look at her, and she saw he was wild-eyed, with a thick beard and uncut hair, wearing cargo shorts with lots of pockets, and a hoody despite the heat. She recognised him from somewhere, maybe. For a second they just stared at each other, Mary panting with shock. Audrey was pointing. 'Mummy, the man.'

She rolled down the window, rage hijacking her mind. 'Why can't you look where you're going!'

'Sorry. Sorry.' He had an upper-class English accent, RP. At odds with his appearance.

'I have two kids in the car, we could have been killed!' Hardly, since she'd only been going five miles an hour, but still. Stupid man. Making everything harder when it was already impossible. For the second time that morning she had a sense of doom averted, a shaky relief that made her want to burst into tears. Behind her, another car blew its horn, and Mary realised she'd better move. 'Just watch out,' she snapped at the man, and irritably started her engine, forcing him to stumble out of the way, back on to the pavement. To Audrey, she said, 'That's why we always look both ways,' but Audrey was staring back at the man, sucking thoughtfully on the hem of her summer dress. Mary shouldn't have shouted in front of the kids like that – and at someone who might be a neighbour as well. Too late to fix it now.

Mary put on the radio to try and fill her brain with something else. The lunchtime news. Words. It all seemed to blur into one these days. Brexit. Europe. Crime. People lost and people found, but not as they'd been. She snapped it off again, worried Audrey was taking too much of it in, the panic and fear of the world.

The supermarket was so big. Mary struggled to remember where things were – maple syrup? Wouldn't it be with the jam? No, it was in a random section by the freezers, with ice-cream toppings. This caused her great irrational anger, since it made absolutely no sense. Jack had added lots of things to the list, in his scrawly handwriting. Whey powder? They didn't sell that in Sainsbury's, for God's sake. And what was he doing with it anyway? That was for the kind of bulky man who took lots of selfies at the gym. Jack was a tax lawyer. Her mind raced on – he was trying to get in shape, probably for some new young woman at the office, bright and smiling and not covered in Petit Filous. She would have words with him later. Let him buy his own bloody whey powder, if he wanted it so much.

She moved through the aisles, trying to make her brain focus. Audrey whined for sweets, and Leo filled his nappy in the middle of the bakery department, causing people to move away and cast offended looks in their direction. She couldn't seem to decipher the shopping list. It was all so hard. Was this sleeplessness? Weren't you supposed to be like a drunk when you hadn't slept for even one night? Mary hadn't slept in nearly three years. Or was it baby brain? Had Leo actually sucked some of her out – consumed her brain cells in the womb? Hard to imagine she had once negotiated complex settlements, presented to people in suits, pastries curling up on the conference room table because no one ate carbs. Hard to believe she was even the same person.

At the checkout, Mary's eye was caught by a rack of newspapers. It was years since she'd read one and she barely even watched the TV news, though Jack liked to pretend he still kept up with it. FEARS FOR MISSING SAM was the headline, and as she scanned it, something connected in her brain. She'd heard about this on the radio – a girl was missing, and it was right nearby, less than two miles from where Mary lived. A picture of a teenage girl, pouting and pretty, those thick eyebrows they all had now, blonde hair in a tight ponytail, crop-top showing off the kind of flat stomach Mary would never have again. Something shot through her fog of exhaustion and self-pity – fear? Anger? Recognition? Had she seen this girl before? Whatever it was, Mary snatched up the paper and dumped it on top of her groceries.

www.mystreet.com

29th January, 2019

Post by Jason Abuba

For sale – child's bike. £50 ONO.

Post by Jackie Carmichael

Does anyone know about a house on Cliveden Road – number 16? It's been empty for as long as I've lived here but I saw a sold sign outside it today. Hope there won't be too much building noise or dirt (😡) or sub-dividing into loads of cheap flats!!

> **Reply by Stephen Jones**
> This is good, house was run-down/unsafe and pulling down the values of others in the area. As far as I know not got planning permission for more flats on the site so let's not be too NIMBY about it.

Tim

The world felt malign. That was the word in his head, *malign*. Just a trip across the road, and he'd almost been run over by an angry woman in a car. The edges of reality were sharp. He'd felt this for a long time after it happened. Going into a building he would start to sweat and shake, looking up at the ceiling. Thinking*: That won't hold. If something happens, we'll be trapped in here.* Imagining the inside of the walls, how much grey brick and insulated wiring buildings were made of when they were ripped apart. Feeling it on top of him, the pressure on his chest that only allowed him to take tiny sips of air. Aware all the time it was getting heavier, that soon even the sips would stop and he would die.

But he was better, wasn't he? He was eating and going out in daylight hours and sometimes talking to friends on Skype, though he usually left the camera off so they wouldn't see he hadn't cut his hair or shaved in months. He wasn't sleeping and of course had not written a thing since it happened, but those were not essential either. Anyway, he did sleep sometimes. He must. He didn't recall every single crawling second of the nights, though it sometimes felt that way. Often he would fall hard into oblivion around six, when it was already light and the birds were singing loudly outside, and that hour or so would be the deepest, the most restful and delicious sleep he'd ever had, all the sweeter for its shortness.

Why don't you take some pills, Tim? That had been Alice's advice. Get up, get it fixed. Call a plumber, call a shrink. Buy a book, watch a YouTube video. Take a class. In the end she had simply lost patience with the shakes and insomnia and the refusal to go anywhere that wasn't home. Anyway, the pills didn't work. They knocked you out, like a cosh over the head in a dark alley, and you woke up similarly robbed of something. Like anaesthetic, the same feeling of being unplugged and restarted. That was tempting, yes, but the next day he would never be truly awake, a fogged glass between him and the world. He preferred to keep as much control of himself as he could. Besides, he would struggle even against chemical sleep, his brain desperately fighting to stay alert, as he had then, under the rubble. You sleep, you die. He understood enough psychology to know this was his problem. It just wasn't safe for him to let go. There was no one to keep watch.

When he got home from the park, having narrowly escaped being run over, he brushed dust off his laptop and turned it on. Once this thing had been his lifeline, lugged all over the world, and the moment he flexed his fingers and placed them over the keys, wrists resting on whatever surface was available, he'd felt most himself. He had not typed in months, but his hands remembered how. He'd had a vague plan to look up the house on Cliveden Road, see if there were any recent estate agent listings or planning applications. But instead, in a gush of pathetic warmth, he typed Facebook into the URL bar. He hadn't used it in months either, but the computer remembered his log-in. There were messages and red ticks everywhere, but he ignored them and went to Alice's profile. She'd never unfriended him, so it was all there for him to see. She did not believe in showing unhappiness so there she was, in a running selfie from earlier that day. It jolted him, to realise she was carrying on with her life. In the picture she looked glowing, happy, powerful. *Personal best on the 10k!* It was the park near their old house, where they used to buy coffee and wander round looking at the ducks on the lake, holding hands sometimes. Alice had not been a runner then, used to complain about walking up the steep hill, even. People changed. They went on without you and soon you didn't know them at all. Somehow that thought was so difficult, so unwieldy and sad, that he felt breathless.

He enlarged all her recent pictures and scanned them for any signs of someone in the background, a man's knee, the back of a head. No one. Of course, that didn't mean she wasn't dating. Then he went to his own newsfeed, clicking through the details of near-strangers' lives, their children riding bikes and their holidays and meals out and birthdays, none of it meaning anything, and then his eye was caught by something, a welcome distraction.

HAVE YOU SEEN SAMANTHA? It was a post a few people had shared. A picture of a girl, late teens perhaps, thin and blonde with a high ponytail. She was half-angled away from the camera – a selfie. Not smiling, but eyeing it with something like defiance. Another spark of interest, and a deep rush of gratitude for it. He hadn't lost that along with everything else, then, the need to find out, to burrow, to nose like a beagle. There was a story here.

He clicked on the link and read about the case, realising he had been vaguely aware of it, seen it online or heard snatches on the radio when he wasn't really listening. He recalled seeing this same picture on a poster somewhere, maybe attached to a lamp post or in the supermarket. Samantha Ellis was nineteen and had gone missing in South London a week before. She'd been working in a local nursing home as a carer – he knew the one, it was just a few miles away, and he'd driven past it a few times. She'd left work at three in the morning after her shift, but never made it back to her home in Bexleyheath. Pretty, he supposed. He'd lost the ability to see anything like that. Something in her face that struck a chord, some kind of strength or secrecy. And was there familiarity in the line of her shoulder, the way she looked over it? Had he seen her somewhere? Something . . . he tried to grasp for it like soap in the bath, lost it.

The paper was basically paying Tim to stay away and 'recuperate', if such a thing were possible. But he was still a journalist, and this, a missing girl in his own neighbourhood, was a real story, and for the first time in a long time he felt like chasing its tail, seeing where it led. Maybe because of that spark of recognition, perhaps a trick of his tired mind. Maybe because it was so close. Or maybe he was just desperate for something that took him out of his own brain. Gasping for breath like someone diving into deep cold water, he went into the story.

Mary

'Is there any dinner?'

'What?' Mary looked up from her laptop, dazed. What time was it? Late enough for Jack to be home, obviously. The clock read close to seven, the light fading to golden outside. She'd barely heard a peep from either child in hours, and no wonder – when she glanced into the living room they were both asleep, Leo in his playpen and Audrey on the sofa. She'd entirely missed their bedtime. 'Sorry. I was just – I got caught up doing something.'

'Work?' Jack said it hopefully. She was allowed some 'keeping in touch' days, but so far no one from the office had contacted her, not even to say congratulations on the baby. He knew she was worried about this.

'Kind of.' *No, I was scouring true-crime forums for wild speculations about what might have happened to a missing girl I don't even know.* Since coming home from the supermarket, Mary had gone down a deep, deep rabbit hole on the case from the paper, breaking off only to feed and wrangle the children. Samantha Ellis, a girl she'd barely heard of until that morning, and now knew everything about. Her sister's name. Where her ex-boyfriend worked. What brand of make-up she used. Samantha was nineteen, worked part-time as a care assistant in an old people's home. She lived with her mother, younger half-sister, and stepfather in Bexleyheath, which was less than two miles away. Given the proximity, Mary was surprised the case had largely passed over her head, but then, pretty much the only TV she watched was about an animated talking pig. Here was the story – Samantha had a late shift at the care home, due to finish at three in the morning. Her stepfather had offered to pick her up, but she was happy getting the bus. She'd left work as planned – CCTV stills were available online, showing a small figure, hands shoved in the pockets of a hoody, ponytail swinging. Something so sinister about the night-vision view, but of course you only saw people on those cameras when things had gone terribly wrong, when the person had been lost, come to harm. Stepping into the dark and disappearing. Where was she now? Mary was slightly alarmed at how deep she'd gone – she'd even set up an account on a true-crime forum called The Dark Side, and written a post asking what people thought about the case.

Now she blinked, remembering that her husband was standing in front of her, hungry and miffed, her children unbathed and sleeping on furniture.

'I'm sorry. I can make a stir fry?'

Jack gave a small martyred sigh. 'We'd better order something.'

'Alright. Sorry, I just lost track of time. Didn't get much sleep again.' Her trump card – he wasn't the one existing on Guantanamo Bay levels of sleep deprivation.

'I know. Shouldn't they be in bed now, though?' He'd reached into the fridge for a protein smoothie, which he must have bought himself, since she certainly hadn't. Once he would have had a beer after work, or opened a bottle of wine, poured her a glass. What was going on here? If only she had the energy to worry about it.

Jack ate his lukewarm takeaway pizza in front of *Channel 4 News* on +1, while Mary put the children to bed, then came downstairs. She'd likely be up again in minutes when one of them started to cry. Was it worth starting to watch something, or picking up a book?

She could hardly bear the news these days. Everything seemed an intolerable threat to her children, who'd lived so few days in the world. They'd grow up in a non-European Britain, a world with rising seas and poisoned air and right-wing extremism and bombs at concerts. It didn't seem fair. Leo was three months old. Conceived barely a year ago. Didn't he deserve some time in swaddled comfort, without the fears and terrors of the outside? Audrey picked up on some of it, she knew, the snatches of dread from the TV and her parents' phones.

Jack glanced at her, then back to the news. 'Alright?'

'For now.' Hadn't he once helped with Audrey's bedtime? He'd taken shared parental leave that time too, and she'd felt they were handling it all marvellously. This time he'd gone back to work after two weeks, and seemed to assume it was all her job. Had Jack ever put Leo to bed? Or was it rather that the baby never really went to bed, and was more or less permanently attached to her breast?

'Police are appealing for information on Samantha Ellis, who's been missing from her home in South London for a week now . . .'

Mary's tired attention pricked up at the name. On screen, the reporter stood outside a modest detached house on a cul-de-sac, presumably the family home. So close to them. 'That's the girl who's missing.'

'Mmm.' Jack seemed uninterested.

Her mind raced ahead. Was someone taking girls, pulling them into cars? A question formed in her mind, the same one she and Jack had been circling around for two years – should they move out of London? It seemed inevitable, almost a test of endurance as to how long you could stay in the city once you had two children. Droves of friends had already gone to villages in Kent and Hertfordshire, posted enthusiastically online about quiz nights at the local pub and long muddy walks, getting a puppy soon. Mary had always thought she detected a certain air of making the best of things, justifying their decision. But what point was there being in London when you couldn't go anywhere, and your life consisted of driving to the supermarket and the odd baby group?

A man was on the TV now, middle-aged, in a short-sleeved shirt and slacks, standing outside the same house, reading from a paper. 'We'd like to appeal to anyone who might have seen Samantha, however briefly, however small a hunch you have . . .' On screen it read *John Stokes, stepfather*. The family must be frantic.

She could smell the sweat on Jack, the patina of the Tube in a heatwave. He'd go to bed in an hour and a half and be up at six to start it all over again. Was this living? Wringing the barest moments of joy from it? She opened her mouth to say something about that, comment on the funk they'd fallen into, ask for his help or attention or a date night or a couples counselling session or even just a hug, provided he would shower first, but was interrupted by a strangled cry from upstairs. Leo. She sighed. Waited a second. Jack kept his eyes on the screen, where they were now interviewing a uniformed policeman, greying and distinguished. *'We're growing increasingly concerned for Samantha, and would ask anyone with information to come forward . . .'*

A stand-off. A louder cry. What was the point? Jack couldn't settle the baby anyway, lacking breasts as he did. Mary got up, feeling the effort it took to raise her body, her flesh pulled down by gravity. Dragged herself up the stairs. Audrey was still, miraculously, asleep, her face flushed, her fists curled up near her damp blonde hair. The baby was red and screaming. Wind? She draped him over her shoulder and began to pace, muttering meaningless words. 'There now. You're OK. Mummy's here.' He didn't understand. She was saying it for herself, really. 'Sshh, shh. You'll wake your sister.' Was he sick? The nappy seemed dry and clean. She rubbed his little stomach. The pain of living was etched all over him. 'I'm sorry, baby.'

Usually, Leo would go to sleep again after a while, but tonight he did not. Every time his eyes shut and breathing slowed, she would try to creep to the door and sneak it open, holding her own breath like she was in a heist film. Only to hear the slight choking cry as he woke. Back she'd go to scoop him up, the only way to stop him waking Audrey, who shifted and moaned in her sleep each time. How much time had gone by? She heard Jack turn the TV off and pad up to bed. He hadn't come in to check on her.

'Jack,' she hissed. '*Jack*.'

Finally, he opened the door, moving as stealthily as her. There was nothing they feared more than both children waking up at once.

'All OK?' His voice low in the darkening room.

'Well not really, no. I can't leave him, he keeps waking up.'

'Oh.' He just stood there. Useless.

'Can you at least bring my phone? And a glass of water?'

He did so, and then she heard him brush his teeth and flush the loo, the creak of springs as he climbed into bed next door. When she heard his snores start up, she hated him with a power so strong it shocked her.

The night wore on. Mary crawled into her own bed about one. At 1.22 a.m., Leo woke up howling. She checked his nappy, which was dry, and wearily looked him over for injuries, rashes, signs of meningitis. Was meningitis still a thing? You didn't hear as much about it as you used to. He was fine, just wailing inconsolably, so she took him into their bed, held him against her. The need to sleep was like a physical pain. *Please, please just close your eyes. Please.* Eventually, she must have dozed off, because she jerked awake and he was asleep on her, breathing deeply. Mindful of horror stories about suffocation, she lifted him like a bomb disposal expert and laid him in his cot, crept in beside a comatose Jack.

At 2.10 a.m., Audrey woke up and began shouting loudly for breakfast. Startled awake, Mary ran in to her. Leo was fast asleep but Audrey was sitting up, pointing at the window, which with the street light right outside it was bright as day. 'Darling, it's night-time, not breakfast-time.'

'No night-time, I SEE SUN!' With fantasies about living in a dark and silent cottage, miles from anyone, Mary read a story in a low voice, until Audrey began to droop over her thumb. Mary knew she shouldn't let her suck her thumb, but had not the stomach for the inevitable war it would provoke.

At 2.47 a.m., mere minutes after Audrey had got back to sleep, Leo woke up, yelling for his feed. His nappy was sodden, his little bottom red and sore. She cleaned him up under the growling light of the bathroom, the noise of which woke Audrey. Mary shushed her to sleep with a made-up story about binmen, while feeding Leo, who suckled from her so greedily she winced in pain. She crawled back into bed again beside Jack, who had not stirred once during all of this. For a moment she lay awake, staring at his profile in the grey light. It would be dawn in less than an hour – she could already hear a bird twittering outside. Did she love him? Was it worth all this, the exhaustion, the resentment? It wasn't his fault he didn't wake – and nothing much was to be gained from them both being up, since he had to work the next day and not make mistakes with the finances of very important clients. But still. She would have been less annoyed with him if he'd just share her misery sometimes.

Three fifteen a.m., more howling. It was endless. The time on her phone ceased to make sense. Back in the chair in the kids' room, she clicked in and out of e-books, Twitter, news sites. Reading more on the story of the missing girl, just for something to do. Someone else's pain, to distract from her own unhappiness, exhaustion. Those poor parents. Trying to remember that her children were a blessing, even if they wouldn't sleep.

She carried Leo to the window, to look at him by the street light. No injuries, nothing wrong that she could see. His breathing calmed a little and she kept rubbing, rocking. Her eyes went to the park again, the dark expanse of it among the burning orange street lights. Someone was there! A man, she was sure, poking about in the bushes at the top end of the park. Why was he in there in the middle of the night – didn't the gates get locked? As she watched, he turned his head towards her window, and in the glow of the street light she saw who it was – the man she'd almost run over earlier. What was he doing out there?

Tim

Last week, Tim had tried going to bed very early, so that when it took him hours to drop off he'd still fall asleep at a reasonable hour. But that didn't work, because 8 p.m. in the summer was as bright and noisy as midday. Next, he tried going to bed very late, with the idea that he'd be exhausted and easily pass out. He stayed up till almost three, forcing himself to watch terrible late-night TV even though the lights burned his eyes and he felt his head drooping. All the same, once he lay down on the pillow, he was wide awake, mind racing. He was too hot. He had to open the window, but then it was too noisy, the sound of cars passing and people shouting and foxes screeching making it impossible to sleep. He tried thrusting all but one arm out of the duvet, to cool down, but then he felt exposed and uncomfortable. He itched all over. Was it his washing powder? Did he need to switch? Maybe he should put the light on and write it down or he'd forget. They said if you couldn't sleep you should get up, instead of lying in bed feeling increasingly crazy. But how did you know you weren't about to drop off, and getting up might derail that, wake you even further? The other problem with summer insomnia was that it began to get light around four, and you had a small window before the birds started singing and the planes started zooming and then it was basically morning and you may as well get up. God, he missed the dark nights of winter.

Tim had read that after three weeks of insomnia, you would go insane, and honestly, on these long hot nights he really could feel it shading the edges of his mind, warping and twisting him, and he was scared of what he might become. Often, in the months after it happened, he would find himself somewhere he had no memory of going. Usually just a room of the house, but once standing in the middle of the road, cars beeping and swerving around him. He hadn't blacked out, not exactly, it was more that his brain had simply stopped recording the world for a few minutes. And here he was, jerking back to himself. It was dark, the dazzle of the street lights harsh on the edge of his vision. He was in the park. Inside it, at night. Tim had a moment of the strangest dissociation – had he done something he'd forgotten about? How much time had he lost?

No. *Get a grip, Tim.* He'd simply come into the park at night, and not quite remembered the journey across the road. When he found he still couldn't sleep, he had risen from bed, pulled on a tracksuit, and stuck his feet into the Crocs he used to take the bins out. There was a strange excitement to being out so late, the remnants of his failed sleep clinging like cobwebs. Like an especially lucid dream. Outside was warm as day and almost as bright, with the glow of street lights and security lamps burning all night long. He'd got in over the gate, placing a foot on the bar of it and swinging a leg high over the iron spikes. The spike on the gate had dug into his thigh but nothing serious, the skin wasn't broken. He'd dressed in a black tracksuit and felt slightly stupid about that. There was nothing illegal about being in the park at night, was there?

He looked around him now, dizzied by the vastness of the space when empty. No children, no dogs, no mothers, no young hipster couples with lattes in their hands, matching their strides, confidently in love. Just him and the trees waving slightly in the breeze. It was deadly silent, given this was London. No trains running. No rustles of animals in the bushes – frozen with fear at the sight of him, perhaps. The swings moved very gently to and fro, giving out the faintest creak of the chain. He felt king-like, powerful. Like he might climb on to the picnic table and shout, or go down the slide, which he'd never be able to do in the daytime, a childless adult man. But he'd come here for a reason, which was to get another look at the house, and try to figure out what had caught his attention the night before. His brain was very slowly trying to knit something together, a pattern or idea, which in the past he knew it would have done in seconds. It was frustrating. Tim once again approached the side fence of the park, beyond which lay the big houses. There were doors, clearly, behind the bushes, opening into the park. Most were so overgrown they couldn't have been opened in years. But on one, the black-painted door had torn branches of ivy all around it. It had been opened recently. This was the right house, the one where he'd seen the disturbance. He was sure of it. The one that was being renovated.

He lumbered over to the fence, hopped it, crashed through the metre or so of bushes in between it and the wall, and tried the door, sure it would be locked, and it was. Too late, he worried about fingerprints. But nothing had happened – there'd been no crime. All he knew was that some deep sense in the base of his neck told him there was a story. And that was his job, to tell people what had happened and why. There was not always a why, of course. Things just took place, terrible things, bombs and shootings and gas attacks, and he'd always been there. His concern had been to tell it well, the best of anyone, so much so that he rarely let himself absorb the horror of what he was reporting on.

He looked up – the house was in darkness, windows boarded over from the inside. There was no obvious way into the garden, no plants growing over the wall to provide a convenient foothold, no trees with helpful branches. In any case, he thought he could make out a wire running along the back of the house, the baleful red eye of a security alarm blinking on a black box. He stepped back. As he stood and watched, a light suddenly winked on, on the top floor, what would have been the servants' rooms when the house was built. A thrill went through him. The house looked deserted, with its boarded-up windows and scaffolding, but it wasn't. Someone was there, and had seen him, perhaps. It occurred to Tim that if they could see him, this might seem sinister, a bearded man, dishevelled, staring at their house in the middle of the night. Perhaps there was a woman or child who would be scared, and at this thought he was overwhelmed with shame again for what he'd become, a figure of fear to the small and innocent. This was stupid. It was just a house, and maybe whoever lived there liked to dance around at night. Probably it was nothing.

'What are you doing?'

A voice cut through the static in his head. For a moment he thought he'd started hearing his own thoughts even louder, actual audible hallucinations, but then he realised someone was watching him through the bars of the fence. A woman was standing on the pavement outside the park. Her hair was sticking up, and she was wearing pyjama bottoms and a cardigan, her feet in flip-flops. He stared back at her for a moment, the woman and him, total strangers, in the strangest of situations, in the middle of the sleeping city.

Mary

She didn't know what had come over her. Somehow it was all too much, the stuffy flat with the damp creeping along the ceiling, the two children sharing the small room, even though the place was worth at least half a million pounds. Holding her breath as she rocked Leo for hours, in case Audrey woke up too. When she saw the man in the park, she had simply laid Leo in his crib, slipped her feet into her flip-flops, picked up the keys, and walked out of the flat. In the middle of the night, leaving her children asleep. Admittedly with their father in the next room, and surely even he would wake up if anything went wrong.

It felt dizzying to cross the road in the dark, everything so silent, the houses shuttered. A fox streaked past her, barely even afraid, its tail striped like a racoon. A hot breeze stirred the trees and made the swings creak eerily. With no idea what she was doing, she marched over to the fence, where the man was beyond the bushes, staring up at the backs of the houses.

'What are you doing?' she called, her voice sounding loud in the quiet.

He flinched. So violently it alarmed her, and she backed away. He said, 'Oh. God, I don't know. What are *you* doing?' His voice was deep and hoarse.

Good question. Some urge for escape maybe, or to find out more about the house, or maybe even say sorry for shouting at him in the street. 'I – I saw you out of my window and I wondered how you got in there.'

'Over,' he gestured vaguely. 'It's easy to climb.'

'But why?'

'I thought I saw something last night. In one of these houses.'

A shiver went through Mary. 'Oh. I saw that too, then.'

He glanced at her. 'It seemed odd. Some kind of movement? Like . . . a fight maybe.' Hearing him say it out loud made Mary more sure that was where her unease had come from. The motion she'd seen, there had been an edge of violence to it, even from a distance.

'Yeah. Something like that.'

'So . . .' He gestured again, as if to explain that the weirdness of it had sent him into the park at night. There were several explanatory steps missing there, she felt, but all the same she was here herself. Then he said, 'If you want to come in too, I think you could get through the fence there. There's a gap.'

Don't be ridiculous, she was going to say. *I am a mother with two children asleep in my house, of course I'm not going to break into the park in the middle of the night with a strange man.* Instead, she said, 'Really?' She wondered for a second why she wasn't afraid of him, this burly stranger.

'Yeah, you're only little.'

And so Mary found herself crouching down on the road, then squeezing through a gap in the fence. He was right, she did fit through.

She stood up. 'You're my neighbour, I think. I almost ran you over yesterday.'

'Oh! That was you?'

'Yes. Sorry for shouting.'

'It was my fault. I get distracted sometimes.'

She asked, 'What brings you out here in the middle of the night?'

'I don't sleep.'

'Me neither. I have a three-month-old and a two-year-old. I haven't slept since, oooh, 2017.'

'At least you have an excuse. Me, it's just – like I forgot how.'

'I'm sorry.'

'Thanks. It makes the days seem very long.'

'God, I know. Like the tenth circle of hell, where everything is a *Peppa Pig* episode.' He laughed, politely, and she wondered if he knew who Peppa Pig was. God, she wished she didn't. She said, 'So – what were you doing? You were staring at those houses.'

'Trying to work out which one it was with the movement. I think it's this one that's being renovated. The doors, you see.' He pointed and she could see one had been recently opened, the plants broken around it. 'It's alarmed.'

Mary pointed. 'Yeah. And look, there's a light.'

They stood side by side, looking up at the house. One room right at the top was now softly lit, as if by a lamp or night light. She was sure it had been boarded up earlier, but now it seemed covered by only a thin blind. As they watched, a shadow moved behind it. Mary was shocked at how her heart leapt. She exchanged a quick glance with the stranger and saw he was thinking the same. How odd, the connections you could make in seconds, and not even know someone's name.

'They saw us.'

'Yep.'

A second went by. All time seemed suspended, the faint night breeze washing over her bare feet and lifting her hair. She felt suddenly elated, young again, as if she'd snuck from her parents' home as a teenager. Then – an even sharper thrill – the blind at the window was pulled back, and a face appeared, three storeys up. An impression of a white oval and pale hair around it. Sharp chin. Then it disappeared just as quickly, as if the person had been yanked back. The light went out suddenly, as if a board had been put back in place. Mary made a small noise in her throat, her whole body tense. What had she just seen?

'Well! That was weird. A kid, maybe?' Trying to convince herself.

He was frowning, as if working something out. 'Did you recognise them?'

'No.' It was too far away to see. But did she? 'I don't know . . . a little bell maybe.'

'Yeah. I've seen her before – it was a girl, right? I saw her today somewhere. I'm sure of it.'

She wasn't sure what he was driving at. 'You mean just out and about?' That made sense; she had seen him earlier as well.

'No.' He was fumbling in his pocket and taking out a phone, thumbing at the screen. 'Look.' She saw it was a news story on the BBC. 'Do you think . . . God, am I mad to think that could have been Samantha Ellis up there?'

Samantha Ellis. Who was that? Mary was confused for a moment, as if she could feel the cogs of her mind grinding, catching. She had been smart, once. Maybe she never would be again, as if her brain had shrunk and turned to mush against her skull. Then she understood.

'Oh! The missing girl? You think she's inside this house?'

The man shrugged. 'Why not? She has to be somewhere, doesn't she?'

23rd July, 2013

Post by mrsdunne2be

Hi all, just bought a house on Cliveden Road – number 14 – but having terrible trouble with garden drainage – practically floods every time it rains. Have complained to the council but you know what they're like 😦. Have tried the house next door but it's empty, am thinking could be issue with groundwater building up on their property. Soil is clogged for some reason. Anyone know who owns it?

Tim

As soon as he said *Samantha Ellis*, felt the syllables of the name passing through his mouth, he was sure. There was something here, he didn't know what, but something, a link to the case. That electric pulse up and down his spine, that instinct for when a hunch was true, it had not gone.

'Do you know much about the story?'

The woman was frowning. 'No – not really. I mean, I didn't see her face. If it even was a her.'

'I know, but I just – I got something. A flash.'

She frowned deeper, as if realising for the first time that she was standing in a park at night with a strange man. 'Should we call the police then? If it's her – was she being hurt, do you think?'

That idea punctured his elation somewhat. What could he say? *I saw a face at a window for a second, in the dark, and I thought maybe it was this missing girl.* They'd think he was mad, and maybe they'd have a point. He was holding his phone still.

'Shall I do it then? Call?'

'We should. Shouldn't we?'

He didn't see any other option so he dialled 999, absurdly worried about what might happen. They'd laugh at him, or punish him in some way. The phone rang, and a woman with a tired voice picked up, asked him what his emergency was.

'Yes – yes, I need the police. Not urgent, well at least I don't think.' On TV when people rang the police they were always frantic, being chased by a murderer, spurting blood out on to their hands. In reality it was very calm, a number of options to go through. She asked for his name.

'Ummm – it's Tim. Do you really need it? Um. Darbandi.' An irrational fear that she'd remember him from the news, know what had happened to him. 'I'm calling because I think maybe I – we – that is, me and another person, we think we might have seen that missing girl. Samantha Ellis. The other person's name? It's, um, sorry I don't . . .' He held the phone out to the woman. 'Probably easier.'

She took it, and he thought of the strange intimacy of someone else using your phone. 'Hello?' He could hear the dispatcher's voice on the other end, tinny and distorted. 'Are you reporting a crime, ma'am?'

'Maybe. I don't know.'

'And your full name?' said the tinny voice.

'Mary Collins.' Mary. So close to Mariam it gave him a little jolt. 'Look, it might be nothing, but we think maybe we saw this missing girl in the window of a house near us. I don't know what number, but it's on Cliveden Road, kind of in the middle.' She gave her own address too. 'We thought there was something going on. Someone being hurt, maybe. No, it's hard to say exactly why. Just . . . an impression. The house is all locked up, with this insane security system. That seems suspicious if it's meant to be a building site. No, that's not – alright.'

The woman – Mary – rolled her eyes and passed the phone back to Tim, who gave a few more details, repeating what she'd said for a third time. The house, the face in the window, the vague sensation of violent movement two nights in a row. Each time he repeated it, it seemed less robust, until he felt quite silly. 'OK. Thank you.' He hung up.

'Well?' She looked at him expectantly.

Tim shrugged. 'She said they've had hundreds of sightings of Samantha. I suppose that's normal in a high-profile case.'

'But – aren't they going to check it out?'

'They said so, yeah. I didn't sense much urgency, to be honest.'

Mary made a noise of annoyance. 'And if it is Samantha? What, we just leave her there, with God knows what happening to her? She might get killed!' The word seemed to drop between them like a stone, knocking them both back to awareness of the bizarre situation. She blinked. 'I have to . . . Um, listen, I really didn't see much. The light was in my eyes. But I'll look the story up a bit more, see if it rings any bells, and then maybe we can . . . I don't know what. We can hardly break into the house.'

She'd said *we*, this stranger. It was a long time since Tim had been part of a we. Ever since Alice asked him to leave. 'No. Yeah. I'll do the same. I used to be – I'm a journalist.' He still was, wasn't he? He was technically still on staff. He saw that this had impressed her, reassured her slightly.

'Oh, right. Are you working on this story?'

'No, I'm – I've been off sick. I got injured. Overseas.'

'I'm sorry.'

Tim's heart was racing and for a second it was hard to gasp in air. He'd said it, told her his situation, and she'd accepted it as a sad fact, something he was recovering from. And maybe he was. Maybe it was just the kind of thing that happened as part of a life, not the pivot of everything, the hole it all drained away into. She said, 'Well, I have to get back. I'll – maybe I'll see you around?'

'I live at number six,' he said. 'The basement flat.'

'Oh right, we're seventeen B. One of the maisonettes.'

Another we. She was married, of course. A husband to go with the children she'd mentioned. 'I'm Mary – I don't think I even said. Well, you probably heard.'

'Tim.'

'Well, nice to meet you.' She smiled at the oddity of it, and he laughed a little, and it was a nice moment, a connection. A long time since he'd felt that.

'Bye then. Oh – let me help you.'

He held back a bush for her while she squeezed out through the gap in the fence. As she straightened up, he saw the shift of her breasts under her T-shirt. She wasn't wearing a bra – she'd come out here in her pyjamas, trusting and vulnerable. He felt a moment of fear for her, that he could not have expressed.

'Night then.'

'Night.' He said it although it must be close to 4 a.m. – the sky was already lightening, the birds twittering in the trees. Too late for sleep. But all the same, when he let himself back into the flat, he found that he went to his bed and lay down on it, thinking he would just close his eyes for an hour or so, rest. It was a lie he often told himself, that rest was almost as good as sleep. It wasn't, not at all. That was the last thought he remembered before he fell into sleep as if over a cliff, the way other people talked about it, *the moment my head hit the pillow*. When he woke up, thick-headed and exhausted still, it was almost nine. Five hours. That was the most sleep he'd had in a long time, and he even felt vaguely cheerful as he dragged himself to the shower. Today he would work. He would do what he did best: find things out.

Mary

The next day it was mid-morning before she got a chance to think about the night before. She'd been woken at seven – a lie-in for her – by Jack, puffy-eyed and frantic.

'I tried to get them up but . . . Jesus, I don't know how you do it. Help?'

Mary slowly came back to herself, from the treacle-thick sleep she'd fallen into. Jack had been snoring when she came back to bed, hadn't even noticed her absence. What if she'd vanished, like Samantha Ellis? Left her family wondering for ever?

Downstairs was a scene of devastation, Audrey coated in porridge as if the bowl had exploded, howling in rage at the world, and Leo in his bouncy chair emitting a noise like an air-raid siren. 'Oh dear.'

Jack was not dressed for work yet and smelled sour, his hair sticking up. He had the thick and springy hair of a younger man, and she felt a rare stab of affection for him. He was trying. He'd let her sleep, that was more precious than a mini-break to Paris. Her foray into the park, her strange conversation with her neighbour – Tim – felt like a return to her old self. Someone who kept secrets from her husband, not for bad reasons, but just because she was a human with her own life, parts of her body reserved to herself, bathroom doors that locked. 'You shower, I'll sort them.'

As he went, muttering to himself that it was a madhouse, she picked up the baby and settled him against her body. Immediately he calmed. He just needed her, her smell, the warmth of her skin. 'Alright, Miss Audrey, what's all this racket?'

Audrey too subsided, not being able to talk and howl at the same time. 'Daddy made the wrong porridge.'

'Oh dear, silly Daddy. Well, tomorrow we'll make the right one.'

Audrey looked wrong-footed by this breeziness. 'Hungry.'

'If you're hungry you can eat that, there's nothing wrong with it.' It was in fact the same porridge she always had, just not cooked for long enough, so it was slightly lumpy. Perhaps Mary's mother was right, she indulged the child's fussiness too much.

Soon, Jack came thundering down again in his suit, grumbling that he hadn't had time for breakfast. Mary, who rarely got time to even pee in the mornings, had little sympathy. 'Bye then.'

'Bye.' She didn't even look at him, let alone offer her face for a kiss. Her mind was already on Samantha Ellis, what she'd google once she got a minute.

He fiddled with the door. 'Oh! It's open.'

'Is it?'

'Yeah. I'm sure I put the chain on last night.'

Had she left it unlocked when she returned? She tried to think, found she had no memory of coming back through the door. Life was increasingly like this, her brain switching to autopilot from sheer exhaustion, like when you catch yourself an hour into a motorway journey with no recollection of it. 'Hmm, that's weird. I guess you just forgot.' Gaslighting. She was gaslighting her husband.

'Strange. God, I'm so tired I can hardly remember what I've done.'

Mary bit her lip, tried not to say how much more sleep he was getting than her. She'd left the door unlocked; she had no moral ground to stand on today.

Jack went off to work still grumbling, and she tidied the kitchen in between attending to various outbreaks of tears, anger, and bodily fluids. By eleven Leo was napping in a clean Babygro, and Audrey building blocks in front of *Peppa Pig*, absorbed in it with a cult-like intensity. Given that everything else bored her after two minutes, what was the strange power it held? Never mind, just be grateful for it. Feeling briefly like super-mum, Mary made coffee in the actual cafetière and sat down at the kitchen table with her laptop. She went to Google and put in Samantha Ellis. Immediately a flood of news stories, images of the slim young girl with fair hair, usually in a high, tight ponytail. In one she was wearing a crop-top and hoody jacket, as if she'd just left the gym, but Mary knew young people all dressed like this now, as she had in the nineties, sports gear and no sport.

It pulled at Mary, the mystery of it. Where could the girl have gone? There was always someone about on the streets of London, no matter the time of day. Even when she was ill-advisedly in the park the night before, several people had passed, looking in at them with contained curiosity. Perhaps someone had bundled Samantha into a car, unseen by any passers-by or the many cameras along the route home. Or had she slipped out of her life, decided that such a hard-working, low-paid future was not for her? It was impossible to tell from the pictures Mary found on her Instagram, holding her breath as she clicked on them, like holy artefacts. The last post was a picture of a hand, flashing a gel-art manicure. Three days before Samantha disappeared. Maybe, just maybe, taken to a house only steps away from Mary's own. She went to her post on the true-crime forum, was pleased to see several answers. Nothing helpful – someone saying women shouldn't walk alone at night, someone else lambasting them, a link to stats on missing persons in London.

Her peace was shattered as a howl came from upstairs.

'Audrey, be a good girl for a minute, OK?'

49

She raced up the stairs, finding Leo in his cot with an arched back and a filthy smell in the room.

'OK, OK, shhh.'

She took the chance to glance over at the park towards the house – perhaps the police had already been in and found the girl? Wouldn't they have let her know, if they'd rescued someone based on her tip-off? There was nothing on Twitter or the news sites. As she was changing Leo, she had an idea. Baby on shoulder, she rummaged about in the top of her and Jack's wardrobe, pushing aside tennis racquets and old shoes, until she found a small leather pouch. In the kids' room, she took the binoculars from the pouch and put them to her eyes. She'd never been sure how to use them; a gift from Jack's parents, keen birdwatchers. Mary would have preferred an offer to babysit.

She twiddled the knobs on the side until the houses came into focus. There was the one, easily identifiable by the high fortified wall and the alarmed door. She trained her sights on the top window, where they'd seen the girl's face. It was boarded up, seemingly from the inside, no sign of any life at all. She was just about to give up when the board twitched, along with her heart – someone was there! She held the binoculars as steady as she could. A face appeared again – oval, pale. Fair hair. Mary squinted – could it be? It was definitely a young blonde girl, yes. Wearing what looked like a black hoody. Behind her, Mary spotted a mattress on the floor, a lamp. For a second, the girl glanced right her way, though she couldn't possibly see Mary at this distance, and Mary's entire body convulsed with a shock that was almost sexual. It looked like her. Samantha. Was it? She tried to increase the focus, but the face was gone. Just a flash of it. Had it really been her?

An ominous crash from downstairs. God knows what havoc Audrey could get up to if left alone for five minutes. And sure enough, when she raced down, holding Leo tight, she caught her daughter dipping a paintbrush into the smashed cup of coffee, using it to daub a picture on the white wall. Streaks of brown liquid were pooling on the skirting board.

'Audrey!'

The child looked up, almost cross at the interruption. ''Mpainting, Mummy!'

'On the wall! Audrey, that's very naughty!'

She shrugged. Perhaps Audrey was some kind of budding Picasso and this would make a hilarious childhood anecdote one day. Mary shifted the baby on her shoulder, glad they'd gone for the wipe-clean paint, and made a decision.

'Right. Put your shoes on, we're going out.'

◆ ◆ ◆

'Too HOT, Mummy.'

'Yes, I know.' The streets of the neighbourhood were thick with pollen and traffic fumes. She thought of her various friends who'd left London, prefacing the announcement of their moving away from the city – *we just thought, it's so bad for them to breathe the air all day long*. Audrey coughed, as if to underline the point, dragging a stick along the gates of the house they were passing.

'Put that down, darling, it's dirty.' Her heart was not in it, and Audrey could clearly tell, because she shot Mary a look and kept doing it. They were on Cliveden Road, a street of large red-brick Victorians, most divided up into flats. Which was the house with the light in it, the girl's face in the window? Was it really Samantha in there? What if Mary, unimportant mother of two, could manage to find this missing girl, and bring her home?

She looked up and down the street, counting the houses. It had to be one of the three in the middle of the street. She paced away from Audrey and her stick-rattling, pushing the buggy with

Leo inside, sucking insistently on his two middle fingers. Number sixteen was a large, apparently undivided house – only one bell – with a high, secure-looking fence all along the front, complete with keypad. That alone made it stand out – most of the houses on the street just had rickety iron gates with no locks, swinging open, often rusting. Mary craned her five-foot-five height up, rising on to her tiptoes. A neat front garden, gravelled over, with a few regimented shrubs in pots. A black-painted door, with another keypad winking. The windows boarded up, which made sense if it was being renovated. Why all the security then? Where were the builders? She wondered what would happen if she rang the bell—

'MUMMY!'

She jumped. Audrey was standing crossly beside her, tugging on her skirt. 'What?'

'Why did you STOP.'

'Well, that's a bit rich, darling, seeing as you can hardly walk down a street without stopping to pick up a stone or stare at a dog or throw things down a drain.'

'MUMMY.'

'OK, sorry, let's go.'

'Looking for someone?' said a voice.

Mary didn't know why she jumped. Of course there was someone watching, this was London after all. A man of about sixty was watering plants at the house across the road. He wore a red polo shirt and cream slacks, and she knew instinctively he was the kind of man who'd have a whole set of screwdrivers about the place. The kind who knew things. Exactly who she needed, in other words.

'Oh, it's silly really. Do you know who owns this house?'

'Not sure, love. It's been sold for renovation, but I didn't see the buyers. Empty for donkey's before that, really falling into rack and ruin.' His own house was, of course, well maintained; the windows and door painted a smart navy, the paving stones in the little drive

52

weed-free, a ring of raised beds against the waist-high front wall, making use of all the space. 'Why did you want to know?'

She hesitated. 'I thought I saw something from my flat. In the top window – a person.'

'Oh?' He carried on watering, a steady trickle emerging from his silver can. 'No one living in there at the minute – it's a building site.'

'I know, but I really thought I saw – something. A woman. I thought – maybe she was being hurt.' It sounded so stupid when she said it out loud. There was also no sign the police had been round – clearly they hadn't taken the tip-off very seriously.

His expression hardly changed. 'Well, that's strange. Got one of those duplexes in the next street, have you?'

'That's right. We look out over the park.'

He thought about it for a moment, carefully directing a stream of water around a red flower. Was it a geranium? Mary wished she knew about things like that. How was she supposed to teach her children when she didn't know the names of things? 'You know, I've got one of them doorbell-cam things. Present from my oldest lad, he's almost thirty, all into the tech, I hardly know what to do with it. But I could check for you, see if there's any comings or goings? We've had a lot of trouble with that house. No one wants a new development, not on a quiet street like this. And all the noise and dirt of building work. I've lodged a complaint with the planning board.'

Of course, a door-cam. Why hadn't she thought of this? The modern mania for surveillance, trading privacy for the illusion of safety. 'That would be amazing, thanks.'

Nigel, as she learned was his name, went into the house to fetch a laptop – an old square one, not a Mac. He also brought Mary a cup of tea, which she blew on gratefully until it cooled, and a juice box for Audrey, who was poking sullenly in a flowerbed. Leo slept, with a peace he never achieved at night.

Nigel set the laptop on the flat front wall and squinted down at it. 'Let me see now. It records all the time, think our lad said. What day would you be looking at?'

'Two nights ago. Late, about four in the morning maybe. Then again last night. I'm up with my kids, you see.'

They talked about their children as he looked for the files. Nigel and his wife had four, all grown up, the youngest at Manchester University. He detoured into a photo folder and showed her pictures of them, plus his three grandchildren. She nodded along, polite but impatient for the security footage. Eventually he scrolled to the right part of the archive, a ten-minute clip of the night-time screen, in green and black hues. The twist of trees in the breeze. An urban fox limping across the road, its eyes shiny and opaque in the dark. And no one, no person at all, coming in or going out of the door of number sixteen. He fast forwarded through the night and the next one, but there was nothing bar the odd car driving down the street.

'Oh,' said Mary, obscurely disappointed. 'Nothing.'

'Looks that way.'

'Oh well, thank you very much. I'm sorry to have taken up your time. I suppose – well, maybe I was mistaken.' But she'd seen something. She knew she had.

'No trouble at all,' said Nigel, shutting the laptop.

'You've lived here long?' Mary drained her tea, which was in a faded mug with a picture of four children on the side, clearly the Nigel offspring.

'Grew up in that house. Very different then! None of these coffee shops or craft breweries.'

'Ha, yeah,' said Mary, reflecting on how she'd never have moved here if it wasn't for the coffee shops and craft breweries. And also on how much of a packet Nigel and The Missus must be sitting on with a house that size. When she gave him back the mug he shook her hand, oddly formal. His handshake was a little too firm, like men of his age's often were. She hid her wince.

He said, 'You see anything odd round the house again, you come to me. I run the Neighbourhood Watch in this area. We have to look out for each other, don't we?'

'Absolutely.'

How nice, Mary was thinking. A real sense of community, of putting down roots. They'd lose all that if they moved to some commuter town where they didn't know anyone. She'd say as much to Jack next time he broached the subject.

At this point Audrey cracked. 'MUMMY, I WANT TO GO HOME, I NEED A POO.'

Rolling her eyes, Mary shepherded the child away with a wave back at Nigel, but already she was thinking how she'd explain what she'd found out to Tim – this number sixteen must be the house, and for some reason it was locked up like Fort Knox, but no one had been seen going in or out. How could she get hold of Tim? She should have taken his phone number. It occurred to her briefly this might be dodgy – a married woman giving her number to a strange man – but she dismissed it. They were simply united in the momentum of a mystery. Of finding Samantha Ellis.

Tim

Tim had woken up that day with a pleasant sense of having things to do. Not too many, not so much that he'd become overwhelmed and unable to get out of bed, but some structure to the day, corners and edges. First, he had an online appointment with his therapist, who was miles away in Scotland. He wasn't sure why – the arrangement his company had with a private health provider. She was a soothing woman, Mhairi – kind of like Mariam too, although she pronounced it as if it had a 'v' – with a gentle burr of a voice and cropped grey hair, a lot of silver jewellery and draped scarves. The fact that he'd never met her in person gave him comfort somehow. Like it wasn't real.

'How are you this week, Tim,' she said in her calm voice. Her questions were like the slow paddling of ducks on water, never phrased as questions. No upward inflection.

'Um. Alright.'

'Are you sleeping.'

'Well. No.'

She had suggested many different things, like people always did when they heard you had insomnia. Lavender pillow sprays. Hot baths. Whisky, though alcohol made your sleep quality worse. Counting sheep. Any number of apps and meditations. Tim had tried these of course, the monotony of a voice urging him to relax his body limb by limb, the blue light of his phone stealing into the room like an anxious thought.

'Have you been out, met anyone.'

'Actually, I have.' He was proud of himself, like a child almost. 'I went to the park a few times. Met one of my neighbours. A lady with kids.' Mary. 'And I found a new work project. A story I want to write about.'

'That's great, Tim.' He'd known she wouldn't ask what the story was – there was some basic lack of curiosity about her. She saw him just as a collection of symptoms. Insomnia, anxiety, PTSD. 'Any more hallucinations or blackouts.'

'No.' That was a lie. He'd had both. But it was OK, he was getting better. Coping.

'So. Shall we do some processing.'

Even as he nodded, a terrible fear had risen up in his throat. Sometimes he would try to distract her at this point, talk about his life, ask her questions. Talking was so much easier than what she called *processing* – essentially, making him relive what had happened, so that it could be dealt with by his brain and stop rearing up at inconvenient moments, like a supposedly dead serial killer in a horror film. Cure him of him seeing snipers on roofs and hearing gunshots on quiet London streets. He knew how it worked, but he was still afraid. His brain would do anything to not think about that day, not be back there.

Her voice dropped to an even more soothing register. 'So, Tim. I want you to go back to the day of the accident. What do you see.'

It wasn't an accident. Stupid.

'Um . . . I'm walking along the street. It's very hot.'

Mariam was beside him, and he could hear the light tread of her sandals, the swish of her headscarf, some silky material. She had laughed at something he'd said. Then there was a second he would always remember, when his body knew it had happened before he

57

did. He was in the doorway of the hotel and she was a pace ahead, because he'd let her go in front, to be polite. The slice of sky outside was blue, so blue. The dusty street, the noise of horns and voices. The smell of petrol and slightly rotted food and something else, her perfume maybe. The feel of sweat on his lip and lower back. Then a noise so big he couldn't hear it, and a feeling of being thrown, as if by a huge hand, down to the ground.

'Who's there?'

'Mariam. Mariam is there.' He'd told this story so many times, relived it, the force of it, and then—

Tim found he was out of his seat and halfway across the room, shaking, sweating. He dragged himself back to his sofa, the therapist's face on the rectangle of his laptop. 'Um. I'm sorry.'

'That's alright, Tim. You're doing very well.'

It was so stupid. He was in his flat in South London, not the doorway of an unstable building in a Middle Eastern war zone. But his brain did not seem to know that. He was gasping, as if his throat were once again coated in dust, his chest weighed down with rubble. 'I can't. I'm sorry, I can't.'

'That's alright. We'll come back to it next week. You've done so well.' She was always saying that, but had he? A grown man who was unable to sit and remember a period of his life that had only lasted a few hours? Pathetic.

After his session, he could feel himself putting it away again, packing up the feelings like a tent into its bag. It was over for another week. There was often an elation, a relief that he had somehow got away with it. He sat down at his laptop again, once the place he'd felt most in tune with the world, and flexed his fingers. On Google he typed in *Samantha Ellis*. He was going to start tracking this story, and maybe even break it, find this girl. He wasn't sure he really believed she was in the house across the park, but all the same she had to be somewhere. And if he could do this, perhaps he could believe he had some value in the world.

He researched the story a little, watching a video of a press conference her stepdad had given, begging for information. 'Please, if you have her, let her go. And, Sam, we just want you to know, if you can hear, that we love you very much, and we're counting the days till you're back with us.' No sign of the mother or sister. Then Tim prepared to do something he now found extraordinarily difficult – make a phone call. He was a journalist, for God's sake, he'd once lived on the phone, especially in the days before the internet. He'd despaired of younger trainees who would send an email and wait, or trawl online for answers. But now the phone seemed fraught with anxiety. The person might not be there, they might not want to talk. They might be rude. He made himself punch in the numbers, throat closing up, heart hammering. As he listened to the dial tone – one, two, three times – he realised his deepest fear was not any of those things. It was that he might already be forgotten.

The phone was picked up, and the sounds of a newsroom – voices, typing, other phones ringing – gave him a Proustian jolt.

'Hello?' Slight note of impatience in the South London voice.

'Nick, mate! It's Tim.' Slight pause. 'Tim Darbandi.'

'Of course, of course. God, how are you, mate?'

'Good. Well, you know.'

He was remembered, and his old friend's voice was now filled with warmth. Tim exhaled, thinking of their days side by side as trainees on the news desk, the only two non-white faces there, though without his Iranian surname Tim knew he could pass, wouldn't face the micro-aggressions Nick did, always being mistaken for the cleaner or security guard.

'Mate, what a disaster. I'm so sorry.'

'Um. Yeah. Thank you.' He didn't know how to talk about it yet.

'You're doing alright?'

'Physically, all healed up. Bit of a limp is all. But the rest . . .'

'Yeah.'

A silence between men, the inability to put suffering into words. Tim felt the usual pressure to make it alright for the other person.

'And you? How's . . . Kara?' He grasped for the name of Nick's wife and gratefully found it. He'd been at their wedding, a marquee in Surrey, rain pattering on the roof, grass caught round Alice's heels.

'Brilliant – expecting a little extra in October.'

A child. People's lives moving on, continuing along the tracks his had lurched off. 'That's amazing. Congratulations.'

Nick did not ask after Alice, so Tim knew word had got out. No little extras for him. His woman was gone, jogging round parks in tight Lycra, running right out of his life, and it was all his own fault.

'So listen, I have a work question, believe it or not. This missing girl story, are you on it?'

'Oh, the Ellis case. Yeah, we've been covering it. No developments though.'

Tim had to tread very carefully here. His stock was low, especially after the incident, and he couldn't voice his suspicions just yet. *Oh hey it's me, your mentally broken ex-colleague, and I think I saw a missing girl in an abandoned house.*

'Anything that's not been in the news? What's your feel for it?'

Nick's voice grew cagey. 'Are you on it? I thought you weren't . . .'

'No, no, still on leave. I'm just interested. It's near me, you know.'

Ease returned to the voice, now Nick knew Tim wasn't trying to poach his scoop. 'Well. You know the basics? Left the nursing home, camera picks her up walking down the road, never gets home. Police are stumped – she's just walked into a CCTV black spot and disappeared. They're hoping someone might have driven by with a dash-cam, that sort of thing. Going through Uber and buses. Nothing so far.'

'Right. And any obvious suspect, a nasty boyfriend? The stepdad?'

He heard Nick shift, putting his feet up on the desk drawer perhaps, moving his tie out of the way. Constrained by space and clothes in a way that Tim suddenly viscerally missed. That office smell of coffee and photocopier ink, the creak of inadequate chairs, the dust in the keyboards.

'I thought that too, but he seems genuinely cut up. Knew her since she was three, she considered him her actual dad.'

'And the real one?'

'Deadbeat. Don't think she sees him – lives down south some-where, we're trying to find him. Got a feeling he'll talk, maybe for an incentive.'

'No boyfriend?'

'Family say no. But they wouldn't necessarily know, of course. I've got someone going through Facebook and that. Snapchat. Whatever they use now.'

A reminder that Samantha Ellis, technically an adult, was young enough to be Tim's daughter. An entirely different genera-tion, who'd never lived without the internet. He didn't know if that was a blessing or a curse.

'I could lend a hand,' said Tim in a rush. 'I'm not doing much right now.'

'Oh—'

'Freebie, mate. Technically I'm still on the payroll.' He wasn't allowed to work while on sick leave. But what harm could it do, running internet searches from home? He could hear Nick come to the same conclusion.

'I am a bit short-handed. This year's trainees, man, straight out of Oxbridge. No idea how to doorstep or even use a landline, seems like.'

'Brilliant. If you could fire me over what you've got so far, I can dig a bit. Discreetly.'

'Thanks, mate. If you could keep it under your hat . . .'

'Sure. Sure.'

'Will do. I won't lie, it'll be great to work with you again. I was so sorry . . .' The note of genuine emotion embarrassed them both. Nick cleared his throat. 'Well, it was just shit.'

'These things happen. Came out intact, anyway.' That was a lie, but a necessary one. 'Talk soon then. Love to Kara.'

Tim hung up, sweating and panting. He'd done it, rung up someone and maintained the facade of being a functioning human being who remembered names, pitched for work, understood the ins and outs of a job. Maybe this case would be the saving of him.

He was just waiting for Nick's email when something shocked him right out of his seat – a loud rapping at his door.

Mary

'Mummy, go home. Go *home*!' Audrey was not impressed with being dragged out of the house yet again, following a brief toilet stop, to a strange block of flats nearby. Leo, still in the buggy, was letting out small grunts and sighs with the sheer effort of living.

'In a minute.'

Maybe he wasn't home. She had the number right, didn't she – six? It was one of the shabby Edwardian houses, converted into four or five flats. The front door was open and the hall was dusty, leaves blown in, piled up with post from tenants who had long moved on. Then she heard shuffling footsteps and the door opened. Tim stared at her, wild-eyed.

'Hi! Sorry, it was open.'

'Oh.' She could see it was a violation, to come to his home like this. He was dressed in white sports socks, black tracksuit bottoms, and a very old holey T-shirt. Still unshaven, his hair too long. Briefly, she wondered what she was doing coming here.

'I saw something. The girl, in the window. I had my binoculars, I saw her from my top window.'

'Oh really? I've been researching it – a colleague from the paper, he's going to send me some details. Friends of hers, people to approach, that sort of thing.'

'MUMMY.' Audrey was glaring at her crossly. 'WHO IS THIS MAN.'

'Just . . . a friend of Mummy's.' Was he that? 'This is Audrey, and Leo.'

'Hi, Audrey, hi, Leo,' he said, with a formality that was oddly sweet. Audrey frowned heavily.

'Sorry,' Mary said to Tim. 'I just – I got overexcited, I suppose. I really thought it was her, as far as I could see from a distance. Samantha.' She lowered her voice, though Audrey could not possibly know what she was talking about. 'The hair, it's the same, the way she holds her shoulders.' Mary copied it, scrunching them up as if incredibly tense. Well, you would be tense, wouldn't you, if you were being held hostage in an attic? Was that really what she thought? She didn't know. 'I spoke to the guy across the street earlier too. He has a door-cam, he let me look – there was no sign of anyone going in either night, so she must be being kept in there.'

It sounded so crazy, she could hardly believe it herself.

Tim was nodding, scratching absent-mindedly at his beard. It must be very itchy in the heat. 'Yeah, I think so too.'

'So – do we call the police again? See if they've checked it out yet?'

She saw him hesitate, and realised what it was because she felt it too. The harsh bump of reality. Surely their suspicions couldn't actually be right. But if it really was true, Samantha had to be rescued right away.

'Yes. We should.'

'I found the front of the house – all locked up just like the back. I'm pretty sure it's number sixteen.'

'Right.' She looked behind him, where she could see a slice of messy flat; clothes on the floor and curtains still drawn. He was holding the door as if he didn't want her to see in. 'Have you got

64

your phone? I forgot mine.' She'd been in such a flurry to tell him her news.

'Hang on.' He ducked into the flat then came back with it, already dialling. 'Hello? Yes – yes, it's the police I want.' He waited. 'On hold.'

'I'd hate to be reporting an actual active crime, speed they move.'

'Yes,' said Tim, into the phone. 'Tim Darbandi. I called last night. About the missing girl, Samantha Ellis? Has anyone followed up the sighting yet?' He put his hand over the phone. 'She says they're swamped.'

'Well that just isn't good enough!' exclaimed Mary, hearing the 'Karen' in her own voice. 'We both thought we saw her, that has to count for something?'

Tim was talking into the phone again. 'Alright, but we've found out a few more things. No one went into the house that night – a neighbour has a door-cam – so someone must be holding her there, you see? Against her will.' He listened. 'So – will you actually come to check it out? I see. Isn't that what you're for? No? Alright.' He hung up with a deep sigh.

Mary glared. 'Let me guess, they aren't coming?'

'They said it's a matter of priorities in the investigation.'

'But – here's two credible witnesses saying we saw her!' Were they credible, though? She was a sleepless mother who couldn't remember if she'd locked the door at night. And Tim – well, something was clearly very wrong with Tim. Could she really swear she'd seen Samantha? Perhaps she'd got the wrong house, it was quite far away after all. And she was so very tired. Less sure of herself, she said, 'What are we going to do? Leave it with them?'

'We can't! She might be in there, terrified, getting hurt or abused or who knows what?'

She was surprised by his fierceness. 'So – what do we do? If the police won't look into it?'

He shrugged. 'See what else we can find out about the place. Previous owners, who bought it, that sort of thing.'

'And then? If the police don't believe us but we still think she's there?'

He straightened his shoulders, as if with some new resolve. 'Then we try to get into the house.'

Mary nodded. 'So . . . we're looking into this. Really?'

'I don't see why not.'

'But you're a journalist. I'm just . . . a mum.'

'You saw her too. Plus, you may be a bit more . . . believable than me.' He gestured to her, meaning presumably she was outwardly holding it together. She wasn't so sure about the inside.

So they were doing it. Two total amateurs, complete strangers before all this, were going to team up to find a missing girl.

17th April, 2011

Post by anikasouthlondon

Hello, all. Wondered if anyone knows what to do about overgrown tree roots? I live on a street in South Kenborough, Cliveden Road, and my neighbour has a big tree, oak I think, really overgrown, encroaching into my garden. Would like to get a tree surgeon in but can't find out who actually owns the property, any ideas please MSers?

Tim

Tim had always loved libraries. As a small boy in a Yorkshire village, with his foreign surname and dark looks, they'd been a sanctuary. His mother would take him on the bus and leave him there while she did the weekly shopping, and he could lose himself for hours among the books and encyclopaedias. He remembered there'd been a large map of the world pinned up in the kids' section, and he'd promised himself he would get out of Yorkshire and go to those places. And he had. He'd won a scholarship to a posh school, refined his accent, become Tim Darbandi, Senior Foreign Correspondent, flying around the world covering everything from US elections to coups in Africa. Until it happened. The incident. Now his only link to that life was the drawerful of airline masks he strapped over his eyes every night.

He pushed open the door of the high street library, realising he'd never been in here before. He barely had the concentration to read these days, and even before that had only scanned the news like the junkie Alice complained he was. He went up to the desk and approached the librarian, a middle-aged woman in a flowing cardigan and long silver earrings.

'Um, hi . . .' God, his voice was loud. He lowered it. 'Hi. Is there any way to check old property records here – maybe historical maps of the area?'

She directed him to a quiet back room with some bound records and a computer terminal. A teenage boy was doing his homework, a buzz coming from his large headphones. Tim gave him an awkward smile. He wondered when he would stop feeling so ill at ease in the world. That morning, he'd looked up the Land Registry from home, paying £3 to check for previous owners of 16 Cliveden Road. He learned it had been sold six months before, but not to a person, to a company. Ex Libris Inc. Before that, it was owned by someone named Jonathan Harvey, who lived in Australia. Then he was off, looking Ex Libris Inc up at Companies House. He discovered it was a shell company, encompassing several global property firms, but he couldn't work out who the actual owner was, hidden under a layer of smaller businesses. Almost deliberately obscured. A faint wave of pleasure went through him. This was interesting. This was a story, maybe. It was unusual, a company owning a house in the outskirts of London, a residential area for couples with one kid, who'd usually move on when they had their second. Though Mary hadn't, not yet.

How strange it was he knew so little about her, what she did or what her husband's name was, assuming she had a husband. Audrey, the little girl was called. It was an old-fashioned name; there was a trend for it. He'd forgotten the baby's name. Tim felt so utterly removed from that world, of babies and marriage, as if he was missing a vital component. Alice had wanted it, he knew, and he'd put her off with vague promises about building his career. He wondered if she'd met someone else, a man who could give her that, who'd be home at weekends to fix the gutters and make lasagne, instead of haring off to Heathrow, to wherever trouble was. How brave he'd thought himself. Instead, he had perhaps just been selfish, making it clear to her with decision after decision that she was not the most important thing in his life. Not even close.

The librarian was suddenly behind him, and he felt a craven impulse to shut down his screen, though there was nothing scandalous on it. He'd been like that at work, reluctant to share his leads or sources. Hence why Nick was his only friend left in the business.

'Just checking you found it all OK – the records are digitised on these terminals.'

'Thanks. I'll manage.'

He logged in and scrolled through the old maps of the area. Cliveden Road, along with the park, had been built in the late Victorian era, and through census and electoral data he was able to find out that number sixteen had initially been owned by one large family, with several servants, then in the thirties sold and divided into flats for rent. He then turned to old phone book records. In the seventies, more than twelve people were listed as living there, so probably it had been used as bedsits. One resident at that time was a Keith Harvey – perhaps he had owned it, left it to Jonathan Harvey, the last owner. A son? The news databases Tim subscribed to brought him the obituary for someone of that name, in a small Australian paper – so the absent owner had died, put it on the market earlier that year?

Tim suddenly realised he'd been there for a while, and that an older man in a cardigan was hovering to use the computer, so he gathered up his scraps of paper and leaking pen, amazed he could make a mess of the space so quickly. On his way out, he passed a bus stop, and saw the number 37 lumbering towards it. Immediately a terrible need rose in him. He shouldn't. Should he? But there was no harm in getting on a bus, was there? No one could say he was doing wrong by that. He slapped his bank card over the yellow reader and took a seat by the window. In twenty minutes he was in a slightly different area, greener, cleaner, the houses smartened up with fresh paint.

He got off almost by muscle memory and walked down a side street, passing familiar houses, the corner shop, the florist with bright bunches outside. Hung a left, then suddenly caught himself. He couldn't just walk down the street – he had no reason to be here, and if anyone saw him it would look very bad indeed. He half-hid behind the overgrown hedge of number twenty-one – Alice had always wanted him to deal with it, confront the owners, be the kind of man who cared about small home crises rather than global ones. And then there she was. As usual, she hadn't closed the expensive wooden shutters she'd insisted on, and so he could see her plainly in the glow of the TV. From the fluidity of her movements, he guessed she was following a yoga video. She wore an outfit he recognised, blue leggings and a grey top with a racer back. Her red hair was knotted on top of her head. She had no idea anyone was watching, and the unconscious grace of her gestures, her intense concentration, was like a knife in Tim's chest. That had once been his place, behind the expensive blinds, beside the woman, and he had thrown it away in favour of chasing disaster.

'. . . they didn't collect the cardboard last week, I told you, you'll need to take it in.'

The in-sync steps of a couple striding along the road with a spaniel on a lead. Both in dark-rimmed glasses and baggy, trendy clothes. Tim knew them – number eleven, he thought. They glanced back at him curiously, as if half-recognising him, but with his beard and overgrown hair, they probably hadn't made the connection between this loitering man and the confident journalist they'd once known in passing. In any case, before they could figure it out, Tim turned and walked quickly away. Behind her window, Alice stretched on, oblivious.

Mary

At the same time, Mary was bringing her own particular skill set to bear – being part of the local Mum Mafia. And Barney, of course, the sole dad doing paternity leave. She admired him – God knows, Jack would never have countenanced it – but he was quite annoying all the same. Convinced he knew more about child-rearing than anyone, just because he'd listened to a couple of parenting podcasts while jogging round the park. None of the mothers seemed to have time to jog. She met the little group at a coffee shop on the high street, an overpriced one that had recently opened up with chalk boards and bleached-wood furniture. Audrey's nursery had insisted she still attend one day a week or she'd lose her place, so Mary went in with Leo in his sling, waving at the small group. There was Francine, Barney of course, and Alana. Barney was holding court on something, and Mary definitely heard the word 'podcast'. She caught Francine's eye and gave her a small sympathetic smile. She paid for a coffee and pastry at the counter, calculating the calories that would further sit on her hips and thighs. It angered her, that she even thought about such things, instead of celebrating the miracle of her body in creating life. Alana was whippet-thin and at CrossFit three times a week, despite having given birth to Darcy just six months ago. Francine had Andrew, who was one, in a buggy, and Barney had his daughter Chloe strapped to his front, her eyes peeking out from a large hood. Poor kid must be boiling.

'Hi, guys.' Mary sat down, freeing Leo from the sling to wriggle about on her lap. 'What's up?'

Francine said, pointedly, 'Barney was just telling us about this sleep-training podcast.'

Alana, who was drinking a green tea, said, 'Mm, the thing is, doesn't it create a sort of dependency, if you go in so often? Better to leave them, maybe.'

Barney tutted. 'If you want to instil attachment issues right from the get-go.'

Francine, the peacemaker of the group, who was today sporting bright pink dungarees and a T-shirt with a badger on it, changed the subject. 'How are you, Mary?'

'Oh, not bad. Getting maybe ten minutes' sleep. If it's not one, it's the other.'

'They're in the same room, aren't they?' said Alana, dabbling her teabag into her cup. 'That's not good; they wake each up, you see.' As if Mary had a wide choice of sleeping areas for her children and had for some reason opted to put them in the same stifling box room.

'It's so hot at the moment. I don't think that helps. And of course it's bright by four.'

Barney sighed. 'I know. Poor Chloe, she's so terribly clever, she hears the birds and thinks it must be morning.' Chloe gurgled, as if joining in.

'How's the mat leave?' said Alana to Mary. 'I hear your cover is working wonders! You'll have to watch yourself!' Alana's husband Charles worked at a rival family law firm, so she usually knew everything about Mary's work before Mary did.

Mary gritted her teeth. 'So nice I won't be going back to a mess.' If she'd go back at all, when perfect Francesca seemed to be doing such an amazing job. 'What about your work?' she said to Alana, a little pointedly. 'They're OK with the three days a week?' Alana had barely taken any maternity leave, as if she'd simply had the baby then got on with her day.

Alana flicked her hair. 'Absolutely. Job share working marvels, and it means I can be here for the kiddos, take them to all their activities. Flora's really coming on at tennis.'

Mary settled back. 'I wanted to ask you all something. Anyone seen that big house that's being renovated on Cliveden Road?'

Barney was nodding. 'I noticed when I took Chlo on her nature walk earlier. It's a pretty intense security system for a building site.'

'Weird, right?' She bit into her cinnamon roll, feeling the rush of sugar along with the caffeine. Probably a bad idea – assuming she ever did get the chance to sleep that night, it might keep her awake.

'Did it sell recently?' said Alana. She lived four streets over, but they were always thinking of moving, so she kept a hawk-eye on house prices. 'I wonder how much.'

'We could look it up on Zoopla. It's massive, whole house I think, not a flat.'

Alana had her phone out. 'Cliveden Road? This it?' She held up a picture of the house, minus the head-height fence.

'Yeah. When was that posted?'

'Six months ago. We actually looked at this place,' said Alana, peering at it. 'Massive pile – we decided it was too big, needed too much work. It was turned into flats, years ago – bedsits, really. It was in a terrible state.' The archived pictures did show a shell of a house, dirty old curtains and smeared windows, piles of bricks in corners. A real fixer-upper. 'Anyway, it didn't stay on the market long, so someone must have snapped it up. Braver than me.'

'Why the interest, Mary?' said Francine, crumbling a scone. 'You're not thinking of moving?'

'God, no. Well, not to the next street. I just thought it was weird to have so much security in an area like this. It's all shuttered, like they're up to something dodge in there, you know?'

Such as hiding an abducted girl.

Alana frowned. 'I don't know, I saw on the local forums there was a burglary over by the station last week.'

Then they were off on their second-favourite topic, after sleep-training – local crime rates.

Mary let the conversation run, because it gave her the perfect opening for her next question. 'Anyone been following that story of the girl who's missing? Samantha someone?'

'Awful,' said Francine, shaking her head. 'Snatched after work, by the sounds of it. I've told Gary he's to pick me up from the station if I'm ever coming back late.'

'You think that's what happened?'

'Must have, if she set off walking and never got home.'

Alana said, rather crushingly, 'She's probably dead, the poor girl. They'll be looking for her body.'

Francine leaned in. 'You know my cleaner, Theresa – she's lived here for decades – she said this wasn't the first girl who's gone missing from the area. There were at least four over the years, all in South Kenborough.'

Alana sniffed. 'Hardly unusual in London – there's rather a lot of people here, Francine. Anyway, this girl lived a few miles away.'

Mary shot her friend a supportive look, mind whirring – other missing girls in the area? That could be a good lead. Hadn't someone replied to her forum post with a link about it? She hadn't read it properly at the time, fixated on Samantha.

Alana was the kind of person who palpably enjoyed imparting bad news. You could see it in the purse of her lips, the light in her eyes over the rim of her green tea. 'I shouldn't be telling you this . . .' *Then don't bloody tell us*, Mary wanted to shout. Instead she pasted on a tight smile and listened. '. . . But this council area has the highest rate of missing women of any borough in the country.'

Francine gasped obligingly. 'Oh my God, why?'

'Oh, lots of factors. It's terribly deprived in parts, you know.'

Mary was annoyed for some reason. This was *her* disappearance. She wasn't about to let Alana hijack it with a socio-economic narrative.

'Maybe there's a serial killer,' said Francine, dropping her voice.

Mary sat forward. 'Is there any evidence for that?'

'Look at the stats.' This was another classic Alana phrase. 'Crime rates simply spike in areas of high population growth. It's one of the reasons we're thinking of moving.' That annoyed Mary even more. She couldn't afford to move somewhere nicer in London, serial killer or no serial killer. Bloody Alana.

Francine and Barney were nodding along mournfully. Barney virtue-signalled with, 'So awful, the epidemic of violence against women. I've started crossing the road if I'm walking behind someone at night. It's really the least I can do.'

'When was the last case?' said Mary. She was aware of how intense she sounded, and how worryingly wrapped up in this she had become. She didn't even know for sure if she'd seen Samantha Ellis.

'About ten, fifteen years ago. A girl went missing, actually from Cliveden Road. Eighteen she was. Didn't come home from a night out.' Francine gave a theatrical shiver. 'You just never know.'

Mary hated that too, the idea that every bush rustled with rapists and killers. It seemed a way of keeping women at home, scared and compliant. But what if Francine was right, and someone was taking all these girls and women from their area? Serial killers did exist. Someone had to live near them. What if there was one on her street, and he'd taken Samantha too?

'Did anyone see PMQs today?' said Barney, who'd once worked in politics and didn't like you to forget it, and the conversation swung away from murder to the incompetence of the government, though Mary knew Alana's husband had gone to school with the business secretary. Francine then asked who'd seen the latest Scandi drama on BBC4, and the chat turned to fictional dead girls. Much cosier than a real one. But Mary was sure Samantha was not dead – she'd seen her at the window, hadn't she? Yes, she was almost sure. Next she had to dig a little into the girl's life, and find out what might have made her leave, or who could have taken her from it.

Tim

In the old days, pre-Leveson, when Tim had trained as a journalist, you'd do anything you could to get a story. Pose as a police officer, go round to the house and break the news of a death before the family had even been told, talk your way into the compound of a homicidal general in a country crumbling around you. These days, you had to be more careful. And the truth was, he wanted to be. Now that it was him who'd been cracked like an egg against a pan, he knew how hard it was to keep yourself together in a crisis. He imagined it would feel that way for Samantha Ellis's family. Blowing hard on hope to keep it alive.

Provided, of course, they'd had nothing to do with her disappearance. Tim had a natural cynicism, finely honed from years of reporting. If you imagined the worst a human could do, there was always someone who'd done it. Nick had, good as his word, sent over the Ellis family's address, and in any case Tim could have worked it out from seeing its exterior on the news, the family with bowed heads going in and out of the small detached house in the cul-de-sac, police officers coming and going, sometimes carrying mysterious objects in bags. Samantha shared a room with her half-sister Marlee, apparently, who was twelve – the child of Samantha's mother, Maggie, and her second husband, John. Stokes was his surname. On the scene since Samantha was a little girl, three years old.

Tim's radar was twitching at that, in a way that made him ashamed. This John Stokes could be a perfectly decent man, heartbroken at the loss of his stepdaughter. Either way, he hoped to find out.

Confidence was the key. There were no police cars evident on the cul-de-sac of detached houses. The front garden was well-kept, with gnomes solemnly arranged around a little pond, fishing rods out. The outside of a house said so much about what was going on inside, like a face ravaged by sadness. A Golf was parked in the drive, waxed to a blinding shine. The gutters were clear, the front door newly painted. The work of John Stokes, perhaps? However, Tim had covered enough stories to know that a neat facade didn't mean there weren't horrors behind the clean windows. That girl whose step-grandfather had begged for her return, knowing all the while she was dead in his attic. The mother who'd wept for her missing child, fully aware that she'd spirited the girl away herself. That was the rule. Trust no one. But at the same time, don't leap to conclusions. Run your hands over the surface of these people's lives, and feel for the cracks.

Trying to put on his old self, like the suit he'd dug out of his wardrobe, rumpled and musty, he marched up the front path – no weeds between the slabs – and rang the bell. It was answered after a few moments, and Tim's heart stuttered in his chest as he stared into the face of the girl who'd opened the door. It was her. Wasn't it? Samantha. Was she home already?

Then he righted himself and realised it could not be her, that it was a younger girl, though there was a strong resemblance. A teenager in an oversized hoody, with ratty blonde hair and red swollen eyes.

'Yeah?'

The sister, of course.

'Marlee, hi. I need to speak to your parents, please.'

He hadn't told any lies or made false pretences. Just said what he wanted, with great confidence. It was amazing how far this could get you.

She looked confused, but stood back, allowing him in.

'Dad's at work. You have to take your shoes off.'

Tim did so, ashamed of his ragged socks. He always felt a bit like a vampire at times like this, stepping over the threshold. *Well, you invited me, you should have known what you were getting into.* The house was also well-kept, if a little fussy, the hall table crowded with framed photos, the wallpaper reflecting a chintzy sheen that was dated, not middle class, but clean and neat. The mother, Maggie Stokes, was in the living room in front of the TV, rolling news playing with the sound off. She had a vacant stare and was worrying her hands together. Was it strange that John Stokes had gone to work on a Saturday – or at all when his daughter was missing? Tim had learned he ran his own business, a property guardianship firm, so maybe he couldn't afford to let it slide.

'Mrs Stokes, hello. I'm Tim Darbandi. Marlee kindly let me in.'

Marlee was hovering, as if unsure she'd done the right thing.

The mother's gaze was hazy. She'd probably spoken to dozens of police officers, and some, like him, would be sporting a nice suit, though his didn't fit so well. Realising how he looked, he'd also trimmed his beard and hair with the kitchen scissors. The result was choppy, but more respectable, and he was surprised at how these small rituals, the clothes and grooming, made him feel. Almost like the old Tim, who'd sit in broadcast studios around the world, mic on his lapel.

'I'm not with the police, I should say that right away. I used to work for the *Gazette*. Now I'm more . . . a solo outfit.' That was the first time he'd articulated the likely future of his career. 'I'm here because I've taken a great interest in Samantha's story. I know what it's like in these cases, the police don't always tell you what's going on, do they? And you hear things on the news or on TV and don't even know if it's true. You're just in the dark and it's awful.' Mrs Stokes barely reacted to this.

Marlee burst out, 'Someone had a newspaper at school. It said all these things about her, that she had all these boyfriends like, but I knew they weren't true.'

Tim nodded sympathetically. 'Right. That's the trouble, they're so desperate for detail they sometimes don't check the facts.' *They*, he said, as if he was no longer part of the press. Perhaps he wasn't. 'So what wasn't true?'

Marlee perched on the edge of the sofa, warming to her theme. Her hands were hidden in the sleeves of her jumper, like the heads of shy turtles. 'They said she went out partying all the time. She didn't. I shared a room with her, she was working most of the time.'

'Hmm. She only had that one boyfriend, didn't she?' A guess.

'Jackson,' said the mother, speaking for the first time. Her voice was dry and cracked. 'But that's been over months.'

'So what kind of things does Samantha do? Work, and what else?' He was careful to use the present tense.

The sister said, 'Not much these days. She was working loads, trying to save up. She'd go out with Shell the odd time, up town. Don't think she had a new boyfriend though. Bit sick of it, after Jackson, always ringing her on nights out and stalking her Insta and that.'

Insta was Instagram, Tim thought. If he was going to do this properly he'd have to learn social media, something he'd so far managed to avoid by always reporting from conflict zones. Perhaps Mary would help him, she was bound to know more than he did. 'Anything else?' So the ex-boyfriend was jealous maybe. That was a possible lead.

Marlee shrugged. 'Watching TV mostly. Doing make-up off YouTube, that sort of thing.'

'Right. That's all really useful. Listen, would you like me to look into this for you, see if I can tell you more than the police?'

They looked at each other, as if puzzled. They hadn't quite grasped who he was or where he stood in things, and that suited Tim.

'Alright,' said Maggie Stokes.

The effort of the one word seemed to cost her, and she sank back down into the chair, eyes drifting to the screen. It showed white-suited techs searching a riverbank, behind the big Sainsbury's in Bell Green, and Tim knew this was a story about Samantha, about looking for her body.

'Would you mind if I used your loo before I go?'

She jerked her head. 'Upstairs.'

'Thank you.' He nipped up before the sharp-eyed sister could follow him.

It was a small house. One room, with a double bed and the same chintzy decor, clearly belonged to the parents. There was a box room with a bulky computer. The door of each room had a key in its lock. The third room had two twin beds, one neatly made with a plain black cover, and one with a pink girly one, unmade. On a dressing table, one half had some hair straighteners and make-up, and the other a pair of swimming goggles, a plastic cap. He wondered how Samantha had felt, sharing a room with her much younger sister. The walls were entirely bare, no posters or pictures of any kind. A wardrobe ajar, clothes stuffed inside – to Tim's inexperienced eye, they looked on the plain and dowdy side. Was it good stuff, the products on the dressing table and the clothes? Alice would have known, perhaps Mary too, but Tim had no idea. No obvious clues – to get those he'd have to look in drawers and things and—

'What are you doing?'

Marlee, in the doorway.

He decided to come clean. 'I'm sorry. I just really want to find your sister, and I thought there'd be something in here that would help. I should have asked though.'

She came in and sat on her bed, cross-legged. She chewed on the sleeve of her jumper, and he suddenly realised it must belong to Samantha, it was so big for her. 'You really want to help?'

'I do. Can you tell me anything else, anything at all?'

Marlee hesitated. 'She had a new phone.'

'Oh?' Why was that suspicious – she had extra money? An older boyfriend had given it to her, maybe? 'What model? Had she lost hers recently?'

Her expression said he wasn't getting it. 'No, like an *extra* phone. She had two.'

Ahhh. A little ping of interest ran through Tim like electricity, here in this crowded suburban bedroom with its smell of body spray and face powder. A smell that reminded him of Alice, of something gone from his life. 'What kind?'

She shrugged. 'Like a cheap one. Sometimes at night she'd get texts on it, when she thought I was asleep. I saw the light. She kept it under her bed.'

'Is it there now?' That would be too easy. His heart was racing.

She shook her head. 'She took it to work that night. She always had it with her.'

'And what was the last thing you said to Samantha?'

Marlee thought hard, creasing up her young brow. She was so young it was almost painful, and it reminded Tim how young her sister was as well, even if technically an adult. 'She was heading out to work the night shift. But she put her make-up in her bag, I thought that was weird. Like it's well grungy at that home. People wee on you and stuff, she didn't wear her full face there, no point. And she put in nice clothes too – this little black minidress with sparkles. High heels. Stuff she'd been hiding behind the wardrobe.'

Tim tried to follow this. 'So, what, she was maybe going somewhere after her shift?' That put a different spin on things, if she hadn't been walking home after all when caught in that frame of CCTV. If she'd been going somewhere else. To meet someone, maybe.

Another one-shouldered shrug. 'Her make-up bag was, like, her favourite thing. She had some really nice stuff she'd bought recently.'

'Did you tell the police about this, Marlee?'

'Kind of. I said she had make-up with her, but I don't know if they, like, got what I meant by that. If they got the, eh, what's the word?'

'The significance?' He could just imagine a male police officer, barely out of his teens, writing that down – *victim took make-up with her* – not understanding. He wouldn't have understood himself without Marlee's explanation.

'Right. So then I didn't think they'd listen about the phone.' She stared up at him, her eyes clear and trusting. She looked so much like the pictures of her sister that it jolted him. Almost as if Samantha herself was begging for his help. 'Please – I really want her to come home safe. But I think something was going on, that phone and those messages, the new stuff she had, and she wouldn't tell me about it.'

'Were you worried about her?'

She sighed, with the weariness of a much older woman. 'I've been worried about her for months.'

Tim was about to press for more when he heard the door slam downstairs. A man's voice called, 'Where are you?'

Marlee tensed. 'It's Dad,' she whispered. 'He hates journalists – you should go. Quick, while he's in with Mum.'

Tim crept downstairs. In the living room, he could hear the man speaking in a low murmur, presumably to his wife. The door was shut, so Tim couldn't make out what was being said as he wrestled with his shoelaces, shoving his feet into the unfamiliar dress shoes. Then, just as he was easing the front door open, a shout: 'Marlee! Come here.'

The girl appeared at the top of the stairs, motioning Tim out. He opened it as quietly as he could and fled. For a moment he paused to look back, catching sight through the window of a middle-aged man in a checked shirt. John Stokes, the stepfather. Tim itched to talk to him too, but instinct told him to heed the girl's advice, and get out of there.

Mary

All week Mary looked forward to Saturday – time to herself, another adult who was legally responsible for the children – but somehow it never worked out. She was woken at five by Audrey standing over her and gently dropping Duplo on her face.

'Ow! Darling, wake up Daddy, it's Saturday.'

'Daddy won't wake up,' said Audrey. 'Mummy get up.'

Mary rolled over and saw that, sure enough, Jack's face was pressed down into the pillow, his eyes screwed shut. He was awake but refusing to admit it. She shook him with less than wifely affection.

'It's Saturday.'

'Mmm.'

'Your turn!' She added a small kick, trying to nudge him out of bed.

'Mary, give me a break. I'm not well.'

'What? You were fine yesterday.'

'My throat was scratchy. I hoped it would go away, but . . .' He gave a little ineffectual cough. Mary glared at him. A cold. A bloody cold. She didn't have time to get sick, so why did he? But she could hardly refuse to care. That wasn't what a nice wife would do.

'Fine. I'll get up.' She lumbered out of bed, and Audrey caught her hand.

'Build Lego, Mummy! Make pancakes!'

'Ummm . . . just a minute.'

Jack called, 'I'd love a coffee, babe.'

She turned to glare at him again, and he gave another cough and pulled the covers over his head. Mary stored up the resentment to take out on him in some small petty way. Burn his dinner just a bit. Iron his shirt so it stood up funny. She went to the children's room to get Leo, who was wet and sodden, sucking on his fingers and kicking his legs like a galvanised frog.

She rolled up the blind and looked across the park to 16 Cliveden Road.

Are you there, Samantha?

They had learned quite a lot, Mary and her strange shambling sidekick. Or rather, she was the sidekick. She needed to let Tim know what she'd found out from her friends, but still didn't have his number. Other girls missing in the area, a possible serial killer. It sounded ridiculous, the kind of thing a bored housewife would dream up after listening to too many podcasts. She was also still turning over in her head what Alana had said about her mat cover. It shouldn't matter – she should be glad a younger woman had a chance to progress. But fear ate away at her, that she'd stepped out of the ring for too long, and could never truly go back.

'MUMMY.' She jumped at Audrey's bellow.

'What?'

'I want PANCAKES.'

'Oh, I don't know, love, it's so messy . . .' How did you even make pancakes? She couldn't remember.

'Daddy makes pancakes.'

Bloody Jack, setting unrealistic standards. She'd looked forward to a lie-in, then him bringing coffee to her, some leisurely time on her phone to google the case and surf the true-crime forums. Now instead she'd have to bathe and change two children, feed them, entertain, and bring coffee to her malingering husband. For a moment she indulged in her favourite fantasy, where she'd broken up with Jack after their first date; the one where he'd turned up in his football kit with a giant bag of sweaty socks, and she'd never had kids, and instead moved to Paris or Barcelona and taken a string of interesting lovers. The smell of croissants drifting up to her window, the voices of the *quartier* . . .

'MUMMY! MAKE PANCAKES I'M HUNGRY!'

'Alright! For God's sake.'

She picked up Leo, realising too late he'd leaked out of his nappy and transferred the damp to her dressing gown. She took him to the bathroom and cleaned him off, changed his nappy and put him in fresh clothes. He gurgled up at her, absolutely delighted to be three months old and with her. 'There you go, sweetheart.' She booped his nose, making him laugh.

Audrey appeared in the doorway like a vengeful ghost. 'MU—'

'Yes, yes, pancakes now, come on.'

Washing Audrey could wait until later. She was at least partly potty-trained, and could be relied upon, most of the time anyway, to go by herself. In a few years Leo would be done as well, and then no more nappies. Just another two to three years of nappies! Oh God. She wanted it with a passion she could almost taste.

She led Audrey downstairs one by one, touched by the child's intense concentration on each step, Leo wriggling in her arms, playing with the buttons on her pyjamas. She found recipe books and whipped up a batter with Leo attached to her breast. She sizzled butter, poured in the first pancake. Audrey scowled.

'Not like *that*, Mummy. Fat ones.'

God, had Jack been making American pancakes all this time? How come he'd never left her any?

'Well, these ones are nice too. Sit down.'

Audrey looked suspicious, but luckily a full tantrum was diverted by being allowed to put her own chocolate sauce on the crêpes. Mary sat with Leo on her knee, drinking a cup of tea held carefully away from the baby's curious hands, watched the light fall into her daughter's hair, which really needing brushing.

'Nice?'

'Yes, Mummy.'

Audrey had chocolate everywhere, but who cared? Oh God. Jack's coffee. She sighed deeply. Even when you thought you were doing a good job juggling so many things, you realised there was yet another ball in the air, and it was about to fall down and hit you in the face. Oh well. Probably he was asleep and wouldn't remember.

Her mind turned to Samantha, as it did now in any quiet moment. There had to be a way to get into that house – Mary was a suburban mum, the least threatening person imaginable. Surely she could use that to talk her way in, and find out what was going on there. And now, with Jack out of the way, might be a very good time to try.

With a rush of energy, she stood up.

'OK, everyone – let's get dressed! We're going for a walk.'

Soon, Mary was loitering in Cliveden Road with both children. It was quiet on the Saturday morning, the occasional rising scale of a laugh or a child shouting. Few cars passed. She glanced over at Nigel's house, which was number thirteen and had the neatest garden on the street, but saw no signs of life.

Mary slowed right down, which was saying something given the crawl she usually progressed at. Leo was in the buggy, grizzling to himself from time to time, probably from the heat. Audrey was engrossed in a flower she'd plucked from a garden on the way. She'd managed to get soil across her pink dress already.

Mary approached the daunting gate of number sixteen and rang firmly on the intercom. It was hard to believe anyone was inside the fortress-like house, shuttered up as it was, building materials stacked outside, but a few moments later it clicked and a woman's voice said, 'Yes?'

Mary's heart raced. 'Oh hi, it's me, gosh sorry, I'm so late! Couldn't find the place!'

'I'm sorry, is it a delivery?' There was a slight accent, perhaps German or Scandinavian.

'It's me, Mary!' She should have used a fake name, perhaps, but Audrey was sure to ask questions if she did. She already had her head cocked to one side, wondering what on earth was going on.

'I don't understand what you want?'

'Cath, is that not you?'

'There is no Cath here.'

'Oh gosh, I must have the address wrong! Isn't this sixteen Martin Street?'

'No, this is Cliveden Road.' The voice was tinny, plainly annoyed at the intrusion.

'Oh my God. I must have written it down wrong. Look, can you see me?' She waved a hand – it was a video intercom, surely. 'I have two kids with me, we've had a long car journey.' Please let Audrey not comment on that lie. 'I'm trying to find my friend's new place, I must have it wrong – any chance I could come in for a second?'

A hesitation. 'I don't know . . .'

'Oh please! I won't be a moment. It's just – God, this is so embarrassing . . . I really need the loo, it was a long drive, and I'll need to message my friend and, God, I just don't know what to do, I really don't.' She even summoned some tears, fresh from the memory of being in exactly this situation once after a long drive to Surrey.

The woman sighed, but Mary had gambled it would look stranger not to let her in, and sure enough the gate clicked.

'Just for a moment. It's really not a good time.'

'Oh thank you! You are so kind!' She manoeuvred the buggy into the small front garden – gravel, plants in pots – and dragged Audrey by the hand.

'What is this place, Mummy?'

'It's OK, we're only going in for a second.' Hopefully that would be enough.

The door, painted shiny black, had been opened by a woman of about fifty, with fair hair in a bun, and a plain grey suit. A PA or something, maybe? Would someone like that be in the lair of an abductor? It made no sense.

'Oh thank you, gosh you are kind, is this your place? I'm Mary.'

'I work here.'

'I thought it was a building site, looked totally shut up, wondered if I had the wrong address!'

The woman did not unbend. 'It's being renovated. You were lucky to catch me, I'm only here to check on things.' No builders though, no sign of anyone else in the house. Mary itched to run upstairs, throwing open doors seeking Samantha. 'Please, the bathroom is there.' She indicated an unpainted door to the right, the floor also bare boards. No personal touches. Mary took her time parking the buggy in the hallway, unbuckling Leo and bringing both children into the bathroom with her. Her mind was racing – she hadn't considered anyone would actually answer the door to her, and now she was inside. Did she really believe someone was holding Samantha here, in this half-renovated suburban house, full of the unlived-in smells of new paint and wood dust? It seemed ridiculous now she was here.

'Where ARE we, Mummy?'

'Shhh.' She closed the door after her, waited a few moments then flushed the loo. The bathroom was much more finished than the rest of the house, spotlessly clean, neutral greys and wood. A stack of hand towels under the angular sink. Maybe that would look nice in their bathroom. No, that was ridiculous, Audrey would have them on the floor in seconds. Why would there be towels in an empty house – for the builders, perhaps?

'MUMMY!'

'OK, OK. Here, play with my handbag.'

That could occupy Audrey for hours, ferreting out lipsticks and tampons and taking all the coins from Mary's purse, transferring them to her pockets. While she had brief silence, Mary went through the cupboards in the room, Leo under one arm. Some more towels, a few expensive toiletries. Not enough for someone to be living here, more like an occasional pit-stop to freshen up. What did that mean? If Samantha was here, surely she didn't have access to a downstairs bathroom with a window that opened. Mary glanced overhead – no sound. Nothing. Maybe she'd got this very, very wrong. Either way she had to get out now – she'd taken a crazy risk coming in here with the kids, and the full weight of it suddenly hit her. What was she doing? Jack would go absolutely mad if he ever found out.

She ran the taps, washed her hands. Expensive squirty soap. Audrey was outraged. 'Mummy, you didn't wee!'

'Shh. Come on.'

She went out to find the woman hovering with a knitted brow. There was no other noise in the house – perhaps it was sound-proofed. Or perhaps no one was there at all.

'Oh thank you, what a relief! Turned out I had the address totally wrong, it's about five minutes away. What am I like?'

This would have been the perfect moment for Audrey to protest that they actually lived round the corner, but she didn't, perhaps cowed by the strange place. The woman gave a brief chilly smile.

'Well, if that's all . . .'

'Yes, yes, thank you.'

She hadn't found anything out. But just as she was unbraking the buggy, she spotted something else, thrown into a corner of the hall, half-hidden. A pair of strappy pink shoes, with high heels and complicated buckles. Cheap, the kind of thing you'd buy from a discount bin on the high street. Surely they didn't belong to this woman – they were exactly the kind of thing Samantha Ellis had worn in so many of her pictures.

Mary gulped suddenly, realising how exposed she was, in this fortress of a house with her two small children.

'Th-thank you again.'

She had to get out. The door was open, two, three steps away. She pushed the buggy straight at it, then out down the path and to the street, grasping Audrey's arm so tight the child began to howl.

'Sorry, sorry, darling.'

She didn't breathe normally until they were off Cliveden Road and round the corner, safe. She told herself she'd never do anything so reckless again – but even now she was already thinking about what she could find out next.

3rd February, 2017

Posted by annacrouch

Be careful out there ladies – my daughter (14) was just followed back from the school bus by a man. She said he was older, fifties maybe, but it was too dark to get a good description. I've rung the police but you know what they're like, totally useless. Stay vigilant and make sure you don't have headphones in.

Reply by Lucy74
So it's our responsibility not to get attacked? Nice.

Reply by peteinpenge
This wouldn't have happened if the (Labour!) council hadn't cut the budget for street lighting. I lost the hood ornament off my Merc last week too. It's not safe.

Tim

It was a long time since he'd worked with anyone. Not since Mariam, in fact, but he didn't want to think about her, or the fact that Mary and Mariam were essentially the same name. This was London, not Syria. All the same, he felt the need to say something to her as they sat in her car outside Sainsbury's the following Monday.

The kids were elsewhere today, and he was glad of that. It put him on edge, the way they might hurt themselves at any minute, wander into traffic or hit their heads. Perhaps that was why he'd never wanted children with Alice. Their awful vulnerability. He'd scanned her profile again deep in the night when he couldn't sleep, hating that there was such an easy way to tap into her life – stalk her, essentially. This morning she'd posted a shot of a smoothie, and he'd spied a second glass in the background, or thought he had. Was she living with someone else already? In their house? Perhaps she knew he was looking at her posts, somehow?

To Mary he now said, 'You know, if there is anything in this, Samantha having a second phone, it could be dangerous.'

Mary frowned. When the car's stereo came on it had been playing what he assumed was a CD of children's songs, but she hadn't seemed to notice, so it was still going. Something about a pig, that sang with a high child's voice.

'You mean drugs or something like that?'

'Who knows? Organised crime, perhaps.' The house being owned by a company had set off his sensors. 'It's just, you have the little ones, and I would hate for anything to happen.'

She turned to look at him, her face astonished. 'You don't really think we're getting close to something, do you? I mean, we're just nosing about. It could be nothing.'

'It's not dangerous yet, I don't think, but – it could be. So if you wanted out . . .'

A fierce expression came over her face, as she leaned on the steering wheel. 'You know, I might just seem like some suburban mum now, up to her ears in Pom-Bears, but I used to have a proper job. I was a lawyer – I *am* a lawyer. I'm not some fragile woman.'

'I don't see you like that,' he offered, unsure how he'd offended her but knowing he had. 'I just wanted to say – there's no obligation to carry on.'

She sighed. 'Well I know *that*.'

'OK.' After a while, he said: 'What are Pom-Bears?' and she laughed, but didn't answer. They'd updated each other on everything they'd found out – his visit to the Stokes house and the library, and her managing to get into the house itself, plus her friend who'd been inside the place before it was renovated, and the talk of other missing girls. Tim was actually impressed. If he was honest, he had, in fact, written her off as something of a suburban mother. But she'd talked her way into 16 Cliveden Road, reporting a building site as expected, but with one crucial incongruous detail of a pair of women's shoes. Tim didn't entirely grasp the significance of the shoes, but Mary seemed to find it conclusive.

Then he spotted a teenage girl coming out from the staff entrance of Sainsbury's along with several other employees, all in the maroon and orange uniform. As the others walked off, she stopped to light a cigarette, illuminating her thin pale face, dark hair scraped back in a bun, a spot on her chin. She looked dog-tired, and Tim suddenly felt guilty about being here. But not guilty enough to stop.

'That's her. Shell Baker.' Samantha Ellis's best friend, who they'd come here to doorstep.

Mary was suddenly nervous. 'How do we play this?'

'You should go. She might be frightened, a strange man coming up to her.'

It was the middle of the day, but all the same, he was hyper-aware of such things now. The effect that he had on people, the way they saw him. Mary undid her seat belt and got out, smoothing down her jeans and top. She turned back, panicked, and tapped on the window. He rolled it down.

'Who do I say I am?'

'Just the truth. We thought we saw Samantha in a house near us, but aren't sure. Keep it vague.'

She took a deep breath and approached the girl across the car park, and he could see this would work – she looked like a normal mum, probably asking where the trollies were or complaining someone was in the mother and child parking bays. With the window down he could just about hear.

'Excuse me – are you Shell?'

The girl tensed. 'Yeah?'

'Hi, sorry to just barge in on you like this. I'm Mary. Shell – I've been following Samantha's story, I'm so sorry about that by the way, and I think – well, the thing is I thought I saw her the other day. Near where I live.'

Shell scowled. 'You should tell the police then.'

'Oh I did, but the thing is, they get so many tip-offs, they aren't really inclined to follow them all up. Cuts, you know.'

Everyone knew about the cuts. He saw Shell nod.

'So? What d'you want me to do?'

'We just wanted to know anything else about Samantha, to check whether it was her or we're barking up the wrong tree altogether. Any pictures you might have. Anything you think hasn't come out in the news.'

'You from the press?'

'Oh no, no. Just a neighbour. Just a mum, really.' Technically it was true, for Mary at least. 'And that's my . . . that's Tim there.'

Mary glanced over at Tim, beckoning, and he got out of the car, approaching slowly, as if this girl was a wild animal he might startle with his presence. He was aware Shell would probably assume he and Mary were a couple, and perhaps that was good, would put her more at her ease.

She sighed and stubbed out her cigarette on the wall.

'Alright. Got loads of pics.'

She clicked into her phone, handing it over to Mary. Mary scrolled through the photos, holding it so Tim could see. Shot after shot of Samantha and Shell, getting ready for nights out, glammed up, pouting their lips and jutting out their hips. People seemed to take pictures differently now, to know how to arrange their bodies, instead of awkwardly beaming out, full-on, arms hanging lumpen by their sides, like all the pictures from Tim's youth. The clothes Samantha wore here looked different, didn't tally with what he'd seen in her room. Dresses with bits cut out of them, shoes spiked like weapons.

He cleared his throat. 'Did she mention anything to you – like was there anyone she was worried about, one of the relatives at her work, or a boyfriend?'

Shell shook her head, though her bun didn't move a millimetre. 'She didn't have a boyfriend. Not for a while.'

'That was the ex – Jackson?'

She seemed surprised that he knew this. 'Yeah, Jackson. They split a while ago.'

'Do you know why?'

'Jealous, wasn't he? And Sam's a free spirit, she didn't want to be tied down.'

What did that mean? She'd cheated on him?

'Do you know if they were still in touch?'

Shell shrugged. 'Saw him last time we were out. That new club in Beckenham. Had words.'

'What kind of words?'

'Dunno, too loud to hear. But he called her a whore, shouted it right across the club.' Shell seemed to slightly relish this story.

Mary and Tim exchanged a glance. She said, 'And work? Did anyone bother her there?'

Shell shrugged. 'Sometimes people's sons would ask her out – or the grandsons. No one she liked though.'

Mary handed the phone back – clearly there were no clues to be had among the parade of almost-identical pouting shots. 'Was she OK for money, do you know?'

'Who is? Pays fuck all, at the care home. Really hard work as well. Sam, she's smart you know – just hated school. She wanted to get out.'

'Out of the care home?' said Tim.

'Yeah. And that house. Have her own place, you know?'

Tim felt the little shiver over his skin again. 'She didn't like living with her mum and dad?'

'He's not her dad,' said Shell scornfully. She caught Mary's look. 'Nothing like that. He never touched her. But she's nineteen – too old to be in with her sister. She wants more out of life, like.'

Mary said, 'So – she needed money? Did she have extra work on the side?'

That could be an explanation for what happened, couldn't it? A pretty young girl, taking a job as an escort or dancer, or perhaps a one-off arrangement. One night only, a large fee, a man getting obsessed.

Shell was nodding. Her face took on a guarded look. 'You're really not from the police? Or the papers?'

Mary smoothed over the lie. 'We just thought we saw her near where we lived – both of us did – and we're sort of sleuthing, I suppose. It might be nothing, of course.'

'OK. Look, I don't know where she is, or if she's even in trouble, but if you say you saw her . . . I don't know. Maybe you're right. So, yeah, she took on an extra job recently. She tried that Only Fans, but she shares a room, doesn't she, even though they've got a spare, cos John needs it for his "office" appaz. So she found this other website where girls can earn money. She wouldn't say what it was though. Not sex. She told me it definitely wasn't that. She said it was like being an escort, only more . . . specialist.'

'But you didn't tell the police.'

'Nah, don't trust them. Maybe she'd come back and be mad I ratted her out.'

'So, Shell – you think, I'm sorry – you think Samantha is OK, she's just gone off with this job somewhere?'

Mary was tactful. Shell had spoken of her friend throughout in the present tense, and although jumpy, she didn't seem like a girl who suspected her best mate was dead.

'I mean, I hope so – she did say she might go off for a few days and I wasn't to worry. But like, it's been a while now and she hasn't texted. She said she wasn't allowed her phone always, on the job. So yeah, I am a bit worried but, you know.' Another shrug. 'I don't really know.'

'Shell . . . I do think you should tell the police this,' said Tim. She narrowed her eyes at him. 'Just in case. You've no idea what this job was, or the website?'

She shook her head again. Her face took on a sudden scowl. 'She wouldn't tell me – didn't want me on her turf, I reckon. But the money was good – she had a lot of new things the last while, and a new phone. Clothes and that, shoes. Guess she didn't want me muscling in on her brilliant new gig.' The sudden sarcasm was surprising.

Mary said, 'And you think it was – going with a man?'

'Honestly, I've no clue what it was. She wouldn't ever say. It was dead annoying.' The word *dead* seemed to clang to the ground beneath their feet.

Tim tried, 'Does Sam have any connection to South Kenborough, do you know – Cliveden Road, specifically?'

'Nah.' Shell blinked. 'Need to go back in now, break's over.'

As they turned to go, Tim tried one more thing. He decided to ask the same question he'd asked Marlee Stokes. 'Shell – are you worried about Samantha?' She had seemed unsure, like someone gradually realising their friend was not fine after all. But if so, wouldn't she have told the police everything she knew?

The girl's eyes narrowed again. 'Worried? Nah. If someone has her, it's them should be worried, you ask me.'

Mary

Mary was late picking up the kids from Francine, but she knew her friend wouldn't say anything, would probably not even be aware of it. She'd decided she could no longer bring them with her as they investigated – she still went cold and sweaty when she thought of the risk she'd taken, bringing them into that house – and Francine was always happy to have them. Sure enough, when she rapped on the door and heard the call of 'Come in, it's open,' she found both of hers and all three of Francine's in the kitchen, gathered around a table of crafting materials, all of them laughing like drains. Even Leo, who surely had no idea what was going on, was transfixed by some crinkly paper.

'Had fun, then?'

Francine jumped up. She had a smear of paint on her cheek and looked the picture of happy motherhood. 'Mary! Look, Audrey, Mummy's here.'

'Want to stay,' said Audrey, daubing glitter on an old egg box, without looking up. 'Stay here always.'

Mary forced a laugh. 'You can't stay here always, silly! We have to make dinner for Daddy. Francine, thanks so much, you're so good. I'll have yours back another day, yeah?'

Though the idea of five children at once made her physically sick. Francine's were ten, six and one, all obediently crafting away, the baby in a high chair, Leo in a matching one. Yes, Francine had two high chairs, just ready to go. Jasmine, the six-year-old, was drawing a picture of a rainbow, with a skill well above her age. Dexter, the oldest, was editing photographs on an iPad. Francine and Gary had bought him a pro camera for his birthday, and he took better pictures than she did, Mary thought, glancing over his shoulder. Mostly images of the park and surrounding areas.

'Hello, Mrs Collins,' he said, politely. Even after years of marriage, Mary always looked around for Jack's mother when she heard that.

'Hello, Dexter. Those are very good. That's the park, is it?'

'Yes. I'm documenting my local area, for school.'

Documenting. He was so advanced. But that was an idea, wasn't it – perhaps he'd captured something in his shots that might be useful. A picture of Cliveden Road, maybe. 'I would love to see these, Dexter, if your mum would send me them, maybe? You're very talented.'

Francine glanced over. 'Oh sure, I'll email you or something.'

'Thank you. Isn't your mum kind to have my two, Dex!'

Francine beamed. 'Not to worry, I love it! Such poppets.'

Audrey was rarely described as a poppet. How did other people do it, take care of so many kids in an atmosphere of calm and creativity? Even when she'd had one child Mary had never managed crafting without a full-on tantrum and glitter in her hair for weeks.

'Did your cleaner say anything more, by the way?' she asked, faux-casual, gathering up the children's things. They had more baggage than a nineteenth-century millionairess. 'About the missing girls, the Samantha Ellis case?'

Francine was rubbing glitter off Andrew's face. 'Hmm? Oh, maybe. She talks a lot, Theresa. I'm afraid I sort of tune it out some of the time.'

'And she's lived in this area all her life?'

'Oh yeah. Knows it like the back of her hand.'

'Any chance I could get her number?' Francine looked surprised. 'Thinking of getting some help once a week – our place is such a tip.'

'Oh, you should! She's a real lifesaver.' Not that Francine really needed help – her husband earned enough at his merchant bank that she'd never need to work again. Whereas Jack, having miraculously recovered from his cold by Sunday, had spent the day out 'for a walk', leaving a seething Mary alone with the kids for hours. As she hauled Leo from his chair, his face falling as he had to abandon his crinkly paper, Francine laid a hand on her arm. 'Seriously, Mary. Any time you need a break, just give me a shout.'

Mary's eyes filled with tears as she bent to put Leo in his buggy. 'Oh thank you, that's so sweet.' Was it so obvious she needed help? And yet here she was, abandoning her kids to play detective, interviewing strange girls in car parks.

They'd learned something valuable though – that Samantha's disappearance was perhaps not random. The girl had maybe been doing escort work on the side, and who could blame her with the terrible pay in those care homes? And what of Shell's comment, that whoever took her would have to watch out? Her best friend wasn't worried about Sam, thought she could take care of herself. So why was Mary, a total stranger, obsessing over her fate?

As she walked home, Leo wailing and Audrey loudly complaining that she hadn't finished 'my eggs', Mary turned it over in her head. What to do next? She could hardly start delving into sex trafficking or organised crime. And how could those things connect to a nondescript house in South London anyway? She needed to watch herself, not get carried away with this mad plan. Be more like Francine, an angel in the home. Urgh. Mary didn't feel very angelic.

'Daddy,' shouted Audrey, suddenly running ahead along the pavement towards their block of flats.

'What – no, Daddy won't be home yet.' But the child was right in a way – there was a man on the doorstep of their block. A stranger. As Mary grew closer, wheeling the buggy faster, she saw that he was wearing a police uniform.

◆ ◆ ◆

The policeman was very young and very handsome, that was the first annoying thing. PC Chris Oliver, he'd announced himself as. He had a smattering of stubble, olive skin, dark hair, tanned forearms, like an actor in a TV drama. The white of his uniform shirt gleamed against his throat, and Mary found herself staring at the pulse beating there.

'Mrs Collins?'

She shook herself and remembered where she was. She'd unlocked the door and invited him in, mind racing. Why was he here? Was she in trouble for going to Cliveden Road?

'Yes. Sorry. What was it you wanted?'

'You rang us a few times over the past week, is that correct?'

So they were finally following up her calls. She wished Tim was there. 'That's right. We thought – a friend and I thought – we'd seen something in one of the houses across the park.'

'The missing girl, Samantha Ellis?'

'Yes.' She forced herself not to comment that they'd better hope Sam hadn't been in immediate danger, given the slowness of this follow-up.

'And you went to the house yourself, Mrs Collins? Two days ago?'

Mary gaped. How did they know? She hadn't told the PA woman her full name or any other details.

He produced something from his pocket, in a little bag. Her driving licence. 'You left it in the bathroom there.'

Bloody Audrey, rooting around in Mary's bags. She loved to play with the cards. Stupid, stupid. What kind of sleuth left her

ID at the scene, for God's sake? 'Um, I just needed to use the loo as I was passing.' She realised what a terrible alibi that was, when she lived one street away.

'In the same house you rang us about?'

'Look. I've told you everything. I went in to use the loo, and I think something's up. Why so much security on a building site? And someone's been living in the house, there are towels and things so it can't be totally abandoned. It's weird.'

He wrote down what she was saying, laboriously, clearly thinking it was ridiculous. His hat was resting on her kitchen table, the glass of water she'd poured him sweating in the heat. 'Why do you say that?'

'Well, it's just obvious, isn't it. It looks like they're making an office or something, but why would they do that in this area? It makes no sense.'

'People are allowed to make houses into offices.'

She sighed. 'Of course. But why here? I mean, you move to zone three if you're going to have kids, right? Why would a company come here?'

He looked blank. 'So what exactly is it that concerns you, Mrs Collins?'

She hated that *Mrs*. It made her sound ancient, when she couldn't be that much older than him.

'Well, it's not a home, it's clearly being renovated, the woman obviously didn't want me in there, and I saw a girl that looked like Samantha in the attic room, as I already said – and there were things in the house.'

'Things?'

He was pretty, but she was going to get cross if he didn't step up the old brain processes. 'A woman's things. A pair of shoes.'

'You said a woman was there, though?'

'She wouldn't have worn that type of shoes. And anyway, it's a building site. Why would there be high heels?' This was why they needed more female officers. How could she explain to a twenty-something man the intricacies of female footwear? 'They were sort of cheap ones. Kind of . . .' She didn't want to say tarty. 'Tacky.' Same kind she'd seen Samantha wear in the pictures on her friend's phone. 'Look, I know you think I'm mad, I can see that. But my friend and I really think we saw someone on the upper floor of that house, who looked a lot like Samantha, and what with all the security around that house, isn't it at least worth checking it out? How would you live with yourself, if she was really in there?'

He laid down his pen. 'We can't follow up every lead. I'm sure you understand that.'

'Yes, but we *saw* her. Surely you could have searched there instead of harassing me?' Had she gone too far? Never mind, she had to lean in to her outrage now.

'From a long way away, at night.'

'I'm just asking you to search the house. Get a warrant, or whatever it takes.'

'We already spoke to the homeowner, who assured us no one is in the house. Not even builders at the moment.'

'And people never lie to you about having girls locked up in their attic. Anyway, if you mean that woman I saw, I'm sure she isn't the owner. She seemed like an employee, a PA or something. Who really owns it? That's what you should be finding out.' She had a thought. 'Look, you should talk to the man across the street from number sixteen – Nigel. He has a door-cam, you could check his footage to see who's going in and out of the house. That way we'll at least know for sure Samantha isn't there – could you live with yourself, otherwise?'

He sighed. Just a little, but audibly. 'I'll see what I can do. But I have to ask you to stay out of this investigation, and leave that house alone. It's private property and if you go back again, you'll be trespassing.'

Tim

Tim had talked his way into the nursing home with almost embarrassing ease. He just said his mother needed a bit more help and he was exploring his options, and, like a shot, a woman in a cheap suit had popped out from the office and nabbed him for a tour. That made him think of his actual mother, in a different nursing home up north. He should visit her. He hadn't told her what had happened to him, not sure if she would understand. He couldn't bear to make the journey, be trapped in a train for hours, or have her see what he had become. His father had been dead for almost seven years. Tim had been so excited to tell him he was going to the Middle East the first time, but his father had said nothing; just very quietly left the room. He would have said what happened was Tim's fault in some way, to put himself in a place most people were desperate to leave. Perhaps it was true.

The woman – Margaret was her name – had said something. 'Sorry?'

'I asked if your mother was a sociable lady.'

Not really. A quiet woman, who'd made a marriage seen as scandalous and never commented on it even once. 'Oh yes. Loves activities and chatting.'

'Wonderful. We do have a full schedule here.'

They were passing a lounge where people sat in chairs, the TV tuned to a home renovation show. Tim suppressed a shudder. There'd been a time after what happened when it looked like he might have to go into a place like this, a psychiatric hospital or rehab facility. He had to focus. Engage his bloodhound nose. Although he did want to help Samantha, he had to admit his mind had also wandered in certain directions. A front-page story if he cracked this. Being interviewed on TV again. A triumphant return to all he had lost.

He asked, 'What about the staff? A lot from Eastern Europe, I suppose?'

Margaret hesitated. 'We do have some wonderful caring staff from overseas. But quite a few locals as well. We're one big happy family here!'

Tim clicked his fingers, as if suddenly twigging. 'I've just realised why I recognise the building. Didn't that girl work here, the one who's missing?'

She turned boot-faced. 'Terribly sad. We all miss Samantha and we're so worried for her. But it was nothing to do with us, of course.'

'Didn't she get taken from outside?'

'Well, no, not from outside. On her way home. So sad. We do advise our staff not to walk alone at night.'

But he bet they didn't pay them enough to do otherwise.

'So it's not a dangerous area?' Tim feigned worry.

'Absolutely not.' She lowered her voice. 'There's been a suggestion she might have been . . . mixed up in something. Drugs, maybe.' Then she realised what she'd said. 'Though of course we vet all our staff very carefully. We really hope she's just gone off, a miscommunication maybe. Hopefully she'll turn up safe and sound.'

Margaret the manager clearly was not going to tell him anything further – he needed to speak to some of the other staff.

'Thank you. Would you mind if I had a little look about? Just want to get a sense of the place. Mum is so sensitive.'

She hesitated. 'Of course. We have some lovely grounds.'

'Thanks. I'll take a look.'

The 'grounds' were a patch of lawn with some sad geraniums. He imagined Samantha huddled out here, smoking perhaps, like her friend Shell, planning a new life. Everyone said she was smart, whip-smart. So why this underpaid job, why the lowered horizons? Why hadn't she gone to university? He needed to talk to the ex-boyfriend, Jackson, and also the stepdad.

He realised a woman in the pink staff uniform had come out the back door of the home, and was hovering near the bins, casting him glances. They locked gazes, and he dispensed with his cover story. 'Hi. I'm Tim.'

'You are asking about Samantha?' She was about forty, dyed blonde hair scraped back in a bun, tired eyes. Polish perhaps.

'Yeah. Did you know her?'

'Very smart girl. Unhappy here, but why would she not be?'

'Were you working that night?'

She nodded. 'We do night shifts together. Sam, she does not mind. Me, I prefer days, but . . .' She shrugged. He got it – sometimes she had no choice.

'So how was she that night?' He peered at her uniform badge – Lena, it read.

'Looking at her phone always. Distracted. Forgetting things.'

'Did you notice she had two phones?'

The woman nodded. 'This is strange, I think.'

'Which phone was she looking at that night?'

'Both. Then she asks can she leave early, because most people are asleep. Bit cheeky, but I say OK, maybe she'll do the same for me sometime. She went to brush her hair and do face.' She swept a hand over hers. So Sam had made herself up before leaving work

110

early. Had someone collected her by arrangement, further down the road?

He thought how to phrase his next question. 'Lena – do you think, was she alright, Sam? Was she mixed up in something?' Would she know that idiom?

She pursed her lips. 'Maybe. Don't know what. I found something. Wait.' She went back inside, banging the door, and Tim waited, shifting from foot to foot. Then she was back, lugging a pink holdall, the pleather peeling off the straps. 'This hers. Look.'

Tim took the bag, realising too late he was getting his prints on it, and unzipped it. He laid it on the ground and squatted to look into it, feeling the strain in his calves. He glanced up at Lena, who just shrugged again. Inside were the kind of things Tim had never seen close up, let alone touched. Alice had scorned such accoutrements, and he'd never been bothered. There were three costumes, he counted. A maid, a dominatrix – black rubber, surprisingly heavy – and a schoolgirl. He withdrew his hands, feeling grubby. 'Where did you find this?'

'Empty room. She get fired, Samantha. Same day she went.'

That certainly wasn't the official line. 'Why?'

Another shrug. 'She been doing something in empty room. With these. This bag, in the wardrobe. Hidden.'

He tried to put it together. Samantha had been doing something involving these outfits, and had been caught, and fired for it? The day she'd vanished had been her last day at work? The care home had, perhaps understandably, not wanted it known they'd just fired her, the bad publicity it would attract. He felt the frustration of the language gap, which sent him back in time to Mariam's gentle translations, so helpful. 'Well, OK – maybe you should hide it back there?'

She shook her head vehemently. 'You take. Me, I cannot say anything. I need this job. But Samantha – I think maybe she needs help. So you help her.'

'Well – alright.' What could he do with it? Show it to the police, if they ever called him back, maybe. 'Is there anything else you can tell me, Lena?'

She hesitated. 'There was another girl who work here. Not a good girl. Karolina – Latvian.' Her tone was deeply disapproving. 'She know Sam.'

'And is she still here?'

Lena shook her head. 'She do not stay long – money not enough. But I see her one time, in that same room. The empty one.'

'And you don't know what they were doing in there?'

'I don't ask questions.' She said it quite fiercely, and he wondered at the experiences it suggested.

Just then the door opened and it was Margaret, looking frazzled. Tim bundled the bag under his arm. Wouldn't she notice he had one he didn't arrive with, a pink bag at that? 'There you are, Mr Smith!'

He'd almost forgotten the fake name he'd given, embarrassingly obvious. 'Sorry, got lost, was just asking this lady where to go.'

Margaret gave a thin smile and escorted him inside and back to the front door, plying him with leaflets of smiling older people playing chess and clapping. She must have known he wasn't a genuine customer. But sometimes it was easier for people to believe your lies than to question them. He checked the time – it was early still. Time enough for a detour on the way home, because the pull had been getting stronger the last few days, and he knew he had to see her.

Mary

She gazed at the collection of items she'd pulled from the tatty hold-all Tim had turned up at her door with. Some horrible middle-class part of her didn't want them in her house, spread on the rug in front of the TV. A collection of cheap outfits; a schoolgirl, a maid, a rubber dress. Handcuffs, a leather paddle. The kind of thing you might buy in a high street sex shop to spice things up with your husband.

'We can't keep these,' she said abruptly.

Tim was on the opposite sofa, an untouched cup of tea by his feet. It was the first time he'd been in her house, turning up at her door with no warning, and he seemed highly restless, barely making contact with the seat, eyes darting about him. Leo was asleep in his bouncer and she could hear Audrey in the front hall, playing around the stairs. She liked to watch for the post coming through the letterbox.

'You mean take it to the police?'

'Of course.'

'But they didn't believe us. How do we know they wouldn't just throw it in an evidence locker, forget all about it? Anyway, it didn't sound like you were flavour of the month with them.'

She'd told him about her visit from the handsome cop the day before, the warning to stay away from the investigation.

'But we can prove it was hers! The woman who gave you this, why didn't she come forward?'

'I think she was afraid they'd sack her, like Samantha. Which I don't think the police know about either.'

Wasn't it a crime to hide evidence too? But how did they even know that's what it was? Mary looked at the bag again. There was something in there still, and, with distaste, she slid her hand inside.

'What's this?' She pulled out a small square object with a clip on it. 'It's a webcam, isn't it?'

'Looks like it.'

A collection of sexy clothes and a camera, and Samantha had been fired for doing something in one of the empty rooms of the care home. Coupled with what her friend had told them, there was only one conclusion to draw.

'I guess she was a webcam girl? Like she told Shell?'

Tim looked confused. 'What's that?'

'I read an article about it.' During the one chance she ever had to read anything these days, while getting her hair done. 'These girls get paid to go on camera naked, or record videos, do what punters ask them to – sort of like live interactive porn.'

Tim was frowning, and she wondered if she'd embarrassed him. 'That doesn't chime with what her family said. That she was working most nights, or watching TV with her sister.'

'They'd hardly know, would they?'

'I suppose not.'

Mary was thinking it through. 'So – could she have connected with someone while doing her webcam work, agreed to meet them in person for a bigger pay-out? If only we had that other phone of hers. That must have been what she used to arrange it.'

Suddenly the post clattered through the door, and Audrey let up an excited shout of 'MUUUUUUMEEEE', and Tim jumped so hard he kicked his cup and some tea slopped out of it onto the edge of the rug.

'Oh God, I'm sorry, I'm so sorry.'

'It's OK. Definitely not the worst stain that's ever been on this rug.'

She hunted for a cloth, rinsing it under the sink, while Tim hovered, agitated. Audrey came trotting in, the post mashed in her sticky hands, and looked at him curiously.

'He spill tea.'

'Yes, just an accident.'

'Naughty man.'

'No, not naughty.'

Mary went over to dab at it, thankful they hadn't bought a paler rug. The only way to fix most of the furniture in the flat would be to set fire to it in a giant heap. But Tim would not calm down, despite her reassurances.

'Look, I better go, leave you to it. I'm sorry. About the rug. Sorry.'

'It's really OK. Don't go – I wanted to do some research into the other missing girls.'

'I can't – I just can't be inside here. I'm sorry.'

'Wait – Tim, the bag!' But he'd already gone, leaving it all strewn out on her living room floor. Audrey was advancing on the rubber dress, sensing something new and forbidden. 'No, darling, don't touch that.'

Mary shoved the clothes in, zipping the bag shut, and carried it through to the hall closet, where she put it on the highest shelf. It troubled her. The possessions of a missing girl were now in her house – was Tim right that the police wouldn't take any notice if she went to them again? They certainly hadn't so far, and indeed she'd only earned herself a reprimand. Mary knew she had to leave it for now. But all through the evening she could feel the bag's presence in the cupboard, like something rotten that might spread its influence throughout her home.

2nd November, 2018

FOR SALE: CLIVEDEN ROAD, LONDON – four-storey Victorian house in desirable area. Has been converted into flats but is offered as a complete building. Would suit a buyer keen for a project, potential gem in need of renovation.

Tim

Jackson Ryan worked in a gym as a personal trainer. It was a very fancy gym – large car park, tennis courts, the dome of a swimming pool at the back. Mary wouldn't stop going on about it. 'It's so nice, isn't it?' She'd picked up a brochure as they sat in reception, having asked to speak to Jackson. The harassed young woman behind the desk, juggling two computer screens and three ringing phones, had said vaguely she'd look for him. It was mid-morning, but a steady stream of guests came through the gates, blipping in with their cards. They all wore stretchy clothes and looked alert and energetic, off to yoga or Boxercise or for a game of squash. The pool was behind a pane of glass, and he could see swimmers stroking up and down, and the roof above was also glass, which Tim was trying hard not to think about; how it could shatter and fall on them. It had been another difficult night – he'd finally dropped off just before his alarm trilled at eight.

Mary had left her little girl at nursery today, she said, but had the baby with her in a sling, and Tim couldn't help but feel uncomfortable about this, bringing something so innocent to the increasingly seedy hunt for Samantha. The child's huge round eyes seemed to see right into Tim. He was embarrassed about the way he'd run out of Mary's house the day before, feeling the irresistible tug to be somewhere else. He had to be careful. Behaviour like that could reveal himself. And he'd once again gone to see *her* – it had to stop, but he wasn't sure how.

Tim had never been one for exercise – he'd considered it for people who didn't live a rich life of the mind. Anyway, he'd always been rushing from airport to hotel, no time to get into a consistent fitness routine. Alice had joined a gym after Christmas the last year, on learning she'd put on eight pounds in a week. That had been the beginning of the end for them, a new life for her, one of the body, of discipline, not giving in to every urge for a glass of wine or slice of cake. So Tim couldn't help some residual bitterness against gyms, but he still envied these people. They seemed so purposeful, so full of pep. Maybe it would help him sleep, if he joined one. Not this place though, it looked expensive, as Mary was now speculating.

'Look, there's a spa and everything. I'd kill for a spa. And a kids' club! God, I could get an hour to myself. I bet it costs a fortune though – Jack would never allow me.'

How strange to hear a grown woman, professionally qualified, talk about what her husband would allow her to do. Not so far from Mariam as Western women would like to imagine. But he wasn't thinking about her.

Luckily, at that point, a muscly young man came towards them, and the receptionist pointed at Tim and Mary, without taking the phone away from her ear.

Jackson Ryan. A backwards name, surely. He ambled over, with the wide-legged, arm-swinging stance of those with too much chest muscle. His arms were tattooed, and he wore the grey T-shirt of the gym staff, stretched over his pecs, and tracksuit bottoms. His head was half-shaved in a complicated pattern. Tim took an instant dislike to him – there was a slightly manic look in his eyes that might have been caused by carb-starved hunger or endorphins or drugs, or all three.

'Yeah?'

'Hi, Jackson. I'm Tim, this is Mary. We're looking into the disappearance of Samantha, and we'd love to chat to you about it if you have a minute.'

He frowned. 'Police?'

'No.'

'Press?'

'Well – sort of. But really we're just hoping to find her.'

He folded his meaty arms. 'I've already been offered thirty k for my story. So I can't talk to anyone else until that's sorted.'

This didn't surprise Tim at all, but from the corner of his eye he saw Mary frown. 'We're not writing a story about it. We just think we might have some information about her, and the police won't listen unless we have more evidence, so maybe you can tell us whatever you know? I'm sure you want to help find her.'

The slight note of judgement in his voice did the trick, and Jackson lowered himself into the faux-leather chair opposite their sofa, flicking a glance at the baby but saying nothing.

'You're not recording? Cos that's illegal, like.'

It wasn't, actually, but Tim held up his hands to show he had nothing, and Jackson nodded. 'Look. I hadn't seen Sam for weeks, OK? We broke up. But it was, like, amicable.'

'Why did you break up?' said Mary.

He shrugged, causing a ripple effect in his chest muscles. 'Guess we just wanted different things. She had – ambitions, you know. Wasn't happy watching box sets and cooking every night. I don't drink much, need to keep my macros down.'

Tim had no idea what that meant, but Mary was nodding. 'She wanted to go out more?'

'All the time. And she wanted more money, more travel, a flat in town maybe, just . . . more. Tried to get her a job here, in the café and that, but it wasn't good enough for her, was it?' A note of bitterness. 'I didn't need that negativity, so we split. That was it. No hard feelings.'

'Do you know if she had any extra money recently?' he said. 'We've heard she suddenly had cash to splash around. A second phone and that.'

Jackson looked cagey. 'Who told you that?'

'A few different people.'

'Like I said, we broke up, so I wouldn't know.'

Mary leaned forward on her knees. 'We heard you had a bit of a row, last time you saw her out in town. A few weeks ago?'

He sneered. 'Oh yeah? Says who? Bloody Shell, that's who. Well, maybe you should ask Shell why *she* fell out with Sam.'

'She did?'

'Oh yeah. Big bust-up.'

'Why?' said Tim, again sensing the story, the edges of it buried in soil.

'How'm I meant to know? Jealous, I guess. Look at this.' He extracted his phone from the pocket of his tracksuit bottoms and scrolled through it. 'Here. She deleted it but I screenshot it. Thought Sam should know what her "BFF" was saying about her.'

He was showing them a screenshot of an Instagram post. It was a picture Sam had taken of a new outfit, posing in what looked like the loos of a fancy bar or restaurant. Various encouraging messages beneath, flame emojis and moving pictures that Mary had previously told him were called GIFs. Then Michelle Baker had posted, *We could all get that if we took our kecks off for money, babe.*

'What does that mean?' Tim handed the phone back to Jackson.

'Dunno. Don't care. But things weren't right between them either, so don't listen to what she says about me, OK?' He glanced at the clock above reception. 'Anyway, I have a client now. Don't come to my work again, OK? I'd nothing to do with wherever Sam is.'

'Wait!' Mary put a hand on his arm. 'Are you worried about her? Or do you think she's gone off?'

'Sam can take care of herself.'

Same thing Shell had said.

'Please, Jackson, is there anything you can tell us – a man she might have mentioned? Someone with money?'

He hesitated. 'There was someone who kept texting her. Did my head in, to be honest. Part of why we split, I don't need that.'

'The name?'

'Eric. I think, anyway. Look, I have to go.' He smiled at a middle-aged woman coming in the door, ponytail bouncing, neon-pink top zipped up to her neck. 'Susan! Ready for some epic burpees?' His demeanour had totally shifted, and he walked the woman into the gym without a backward glance at them.

'What do you think?' said Tim to Mary, as they headed back to the car, the baby carried in front of her.

Mary looked reflective. 'That I should get a trainer myself. His arm was like a steel girder. I can hardly lift the hoover these days.'

'About what he said, I meant!'

'Oh yeah. Not a nice guy, I don't think. I'm wondering if anyone saw that post while it was up – Shell must have deleted it pretty sharp, but not before Jackson screenshot it, so maybe other people did too. Maybe it caused some issues for Sam, her secret life – her work finding out about it, that sort of thing. Seems like Sam had fallen out with quite a few people in her life recently, doesn't it? Her boss, her best friend, her boyfriend . . .'

Mary was right. Maybe like someone who was planning to run from their life, and burning it to the ground first, tossing a match behind them as they walked away.

'Anyway,' she said. 'Let's go somewhere and make a list of what we know.'

◆ ◆ ◆

Tim was getting a headache. They were now at the café in the park, and Mary had her phone out, in a battered case with various children's stickers on the outside, and was taking him through Samantha Ellis's social media accounts. It was dizzying – so many pictures, colours and those little picture faces; a language he didn't understand, like when he used to travel to different countries.

Mary said, 'There's no sign of any Erics in her followers. I'll keep looking.' The baby was fast asleep beside her in his buggy, seemingly exhausted. Tim could hardly imagine such peace.

'I just – there's so much on here. Anyone could stalk her, if they wanted.'

He was a little breathless with the risk of it. Sam had posted a picture outside her work, and moaned on Facebook about her shift times, so someone could know exactly what time she left in the dark. She had multiple images taken from her bedroom window, and even one with her ex-boyfriend's car, showing its number plate. Her birthday, her date of birth, her middle name, her likes and dislikes, this was all so simple to find out that Tim wondered if there was any need now for the investigative skills he'd honed over years. If people just shared everything, who needed to find things out? No wonder the younger journalists were horrified at the idea of picking up a phone and calling someone.

Mary was nodding sadly. 'It's what they do. Young people.'

'Are you on this?' He gestured to the screen. There were so many different sites and apps, how did anyone find the time to update them all? She was leaning over him, her arm brushing his, and the heat of her skin made him realise how long it had been since someone touched him voluntarily.

'No. Well, Instagram. And Facebook sometimes. I post on mum forums the odd time, I suppose. And I did one on a forum for true crime. But that's it.' It sounded a lot to Tim.

'You know people can find things out about you from these. Like this picture here of her house, the car. Someone could locate you in seconds if you ever post things like that.'

Mary looked a little alarmed, then cross. 'Well, I don't.'

'Your kids, do you post their names up online?'

'Of course not.' But he saw her eyes flicker. 'I mean, I wouldn't put where they go to nursery or anything. That's mad when people do that. Pictures of them in their school uniform on the first day, their names, all that.'

Tim could not imagine why anyone would put themselves through this, being in the public eye, reading messages from total strangers. He'd looked at Twitter a few times after he came out of hospital, and been appalled by the things people were saying about him on there. They felt he shouldn't have been there in the first place, a Western man in a foreign country, that he'd put Mariam in danger. All the worst things his own brain whispered to him late at night when he couldn't sleep. He thought of Alice, her carefully coordinated online presence, all hashtags, run times, and smoothies. Did she know that if she posted her times online, someone could also see her usual routes? Wait for her, maybe? On the darkening autumn nights? Maybe he should get in touch and tell her to be careful. But no, she wouldn't welcome that.

'I'm going to look into these other missing girls.' He opened his laptop, a gesture that evoked strong muscle memory, and logged on to the café's Wi-Fi.

'I texted my friend's cleaner,' said Mary. 'Not much use – just wanted to talk about her sciatica. But she said at the time of the last disappearance people were really worried, kept their daughters in, picked them up from the bus stop, that sort of thing.'

'They thought there was a killer in the area?'

'Seemed to have.'

Could it really be true, an unknown murderer living here all this time? If so, the story would be the rebirth of Tim's career.

After a while hunting through local news stories from the last three decades, he had a list. A grim list. Four girls or women had gone missing from the local area in that time – and all of them had lived within half a mile of Cliveden Road. He ran his eyes over the names and pictures, trying to commit them to memory. He felt he owed them that, at least. Susan Granger. Harriet Keeley. Emma Baker-Smith. Laura Colebrook. All aged between sixteen and twenty-five.

Mary stared at the pictures on his screen. 'What's the gap between the disappearances?'

Tim quickly calculated it. 'Doesn't seem to follow a pattern. Two in the eighties, one nineties, one in 2007, that was Laura Colebrook. Nothing until now.' Could they be connected – was it simply the fact of London's large population, high crime rate?

'So . . . they can't all be runaways, can they?'

In the eighties and nineties, this area had been run-down, working class. Accordingly there was hardly any coverage of the first three disappearances, in 1983, 1988, and 1994. Small items in the local press – LOCAL GIRL MISSING. Renewed appeals as anniversaries stacked up, one year, two years. Ten years. Twenty. It seemed clear police had dismissed them as girls running off, perhaps falling in with 'a bad crowd'.

Tim pulled a napkin towards him and began to scribble on it, a rough map of the area. 'Look, this is where each of them was last seen. Susan walking home from her job in the bakery, spotted by a neighbour on the next street from her house, but never got back.

124

That bakery's closed down now, it's a craft brewery. Harriet, she got off a bus on the high street after her shift at a factory in Croydon. Emma, she was at home in her flat, she rang her mother and said she was settling in for the night, then never seen again. And Laura – that was later, the area was more middle class. Plus there was rolling news and the internet. People noticed, in other words.'

Mary had been typing as he spoke, and found video footage of the Laura Colebrook case, which she now played, tinny sound coming out of her phone and causing several people nearby to tut. The slightly grainy look of old-ish film stock, the haircuts and suit shapes of twelve years before. A press conference with a creased-face detective in a cheap suit, and two shell-shocked parents trying hard not to cry. The endless flash of cameras as the detective read a statement.

'We're appealing for anyone with information to come forward. Laura hasn't been seen in three days and her parents are extremely worried.'

The mother spoke then, and her face was carved in terror.

'Please, if you're holding Laura somewhere, let her go. She's our only daughter and we love her very much. Please, I'm begging you as a mother. Let her go.'

But perhaps she had already been dead by then, the desperate pleas pointless. Could you even appeal to someone like that, who'd take a girl right from the street? Did they feel any empathy?

The clip then showed a bit of extremely blurry CCTV, a girl walking down a street in the middle of the day, jerky-stepped from the old technology. Laura Colebrook, just finished her GCSEs and gone out to get some traveller's cheques for an upcoming holiday to Greece, an end-of-summer blowout with her friends.

'That's the high street!' Mary exclaimed. 'Look, Boots is still there. And that's a flower shop now.' She fell silent. Somehow, on a bright weekday afternoon, Laura had set off from the travel agent to her home, just four streets away, and never made it back. 'She lived on Mountbatten Street. My friend Alana lives there. Close to home.' He nodded. It must be more visceral, for a woman to see this. 'So . . . do you think the same person took all of these girls?' she asked.

'Maybe. It's not unknown, is it? Serial killer at work for years, and no one ever joined the dots. The police might not have paid much attention, if those earlier girls were seen as rough or lower class. Like they'd just run off, you know.' Absent-mindedly, Tim was now drawing a line between his own dots, making a lopsided circle. Samantha had disappeared a little further away, a mile and a half as the crow flew. But Cliveden Road, if that really was where Samantha had been taken, was bang in the middle of the circle he'd drawn, and now they had seen her there too – or thought they had. Question was, where was she now? Still in the house he could actually see from their table, a helpless prisoner? The idea made him shudder.

Mary exclaimed suddenly, looking up from her phone. 'The post I did, on the crime forum! There's been a new response.'

'Oh?'

'Oh my God – it's from a police officer. Retired.' Mary held her phone out in triumph and Tim peered at the small screen. 'She says she worked on the older cases, and she'd be happy to speak to me!'

Mary

Angela Robinson had moved out of London when she retired ten years before, but luckily only to Wallington; a quiet street with a pond and village green at the end. 'Helping with the grandchildren, you know,' she said. Mary did not know, seeing as Jack's parents spent all their time in France and her own mother, widowed for five years, was living her best life at yoga retreats and book groups. She had politely refused to offer the between-one-and-five-days-a-week childcare some of her friends provided for their children: 'The thing is, love, I've done my time. The system is really broken if a working family can only manage by grandparents giving up their retirement, don't you think?'

Mary agreed: seeing as nursery fees for two children would be two grand a month, this was largely the reason she'd taken her full maternity leave and perhaps wouldn't have a job to go back to. She knew she should be grateful for this time with her children, but the months seemed to stretch ahead, featureless. Maybe she'd email Geoffrey, her boss, see about going back early. Jack would go mad – he'd have to actually start picking up some of the slack. Today she was once again trespassing on Francine's generosity with baby-sitting. She knew she shouldn't, but she was so tired it seemed to have eroded parts of her. Like guilt, and shame, and even concern for her children's development. They'd be better off crafting with Francine than trailed around by her in the heat.

Angela Robinson was more than a helpful grandmother, however – she had been the lead detective on the Laura Colebrook case, back in 2007. And she'd agreed to see them.

'Come on, come in.'

She was a brisk woman, dressed in loose grey trousers and a white shirt, her hair in a greying bob. Her house was comfortable, a little tatty round the edges. When she led them into her conservatory, a similarly aged man was visible in the back garden, doing something with tomato plants. She had made tea without asking; the strong, bitter kind with skimmed milk, and no biscuits.

'So. What can I help you with?'

Mary and Tim sat down opposite on a small sofa made of wicker. It creaked under their weight.

'We're looking into the Samantha Ellis case.'

'Yes, you're a journalist I know, or you used to be.' She was shrewd, this woman. That was probably why she'd risen to the rank of DI, even in sexist times. She turned to Mary. 'Are you a journalist too?'

'Oh no. I'm a lawyer. Well, I'm on maternity leave. Tim and I, we thought we saw her, Samantha. In a house in South Kenborough, where we both live. But the police don't seem to take us seriously.'

Angela had her arms hooked around her crossed legs. 'Obviously I know no more about the case than you do.'

'Right. That's not why we're here. We're here about . . .'

'The other girls?' She nodded at Tim's look of surprise. 'Oh come on, you didn't think you were the only people to spot that link? It's the worst, really, when retirement approaches and you're thinking of your cucumber frames and painting holidays in Devon, but there's these cases that just won't leave you alone. Where you know you were the only one that cared, that saw the patterns, and you just couldn't solve it, no matter how hard you tried.'

Mary set down her mug – the tea was undrinkable – and leaned forward. 'So you thought they were connected all along, the disappearances?'

'Not at first. The first one, that was before I joined the job, but the second, Harriet, I was the first officer on the scene. WPCs, they called us then. We had to wear skirts and little hats. Her parents were in bits – I was naive then. I believed the older officers who said she'd turn up, she'd gone off with a boy maybe. But she didn't. And her mum just kept saying, no, she wouldn't do that, she'd never had boyfriends, she was shy and young for her age, and eventually I realised the male officers just weren't hearing it. They'd moved the case from one pile to another in their heads. It was actually Harriet's mum who told me about the first girl – she'd remembered it happening and warned her daughter. But years had gone by. They forgot to be scared.'

Tim said, 'Who do you think it was? Did you have a profile?'

She shook her head. 'It wasn't really a thing in those days. But we knew all the same. It's a man, probably in his twenties or thirties back then, so now in his sixties maybe. My age. Someone who lives in the area.'

'How big an area?'

'The streets around that park, probably. He must have been very familiar with it. And able to disappear fast, since no one saw any of the girls being taken, in such a built-up area too.'

'We live in those streets,' said Mary uneasily. She had a daughter. Why did no one tell you these things when you moved in? *Good school catchment area, but it's also in a murder catchment, hope that's cool!*

'So did I. I moved my own family after the third one.'

129

'Why wasn't it in the press?' said Mary. 'If there was . . . you know, a serial killer.' It sounded over-dramatic, but that was what they were talking about, wasn't it? Three murders made a serial. This was four, maybe five if you included Sam.

Angela Robinson shrugged. 'Girls go missing all the time. Even now, there's probably fifty cases of missing women on the books of the local police. It's only the odd one, like this Samantha case, that breaks through. If the girl is white, and pretty, if the family are savvy enough to get the media interested.'

That was even more unsettling. Then Angela fixed them with her shrewd gaze and said: 'You know about the murder, yes?'

Tim and Mary exchanged a blank look.

'Colette Johnson, in the seventies? I wasn't sure that was linked for a long time. The others had just disappeared. But she was killed in South Kenborough – a house on Cliveden Road.'

Mary's nerves were jangling. 'You don't remember which house?'

'Not off the top of my head. But it was a nasty one – she was strangled, then stabbed. Place was a bloodbath.'

'They never caught anyone?'

'No. But he got interrupted – her son was coming home from school, passed the man in the hallway. Unfortunately he didn't see enough to do a sketch – just the man's back as he ran away. Plus, he was only small. Seven, I believe.'

Mary shivered to think of it – the young boy rounding the hallway, the sound of a scuffle upstairs, the footsteps down the stairs behind him as he found his mother gasping, choking, hands to her collapsed throat. Blood everywhere.

'The man just disappeared?'

Angela was nodding. 'Right. So he must have lived nearby. Nowadays I think it was the same man who took the other girls, and he must have not had time to hide the body in that first murder.

But there was no DNA back then, and it's too late to get any now. I think the police decided she'd deserved it, Colette, because she'd taken the odd paying client. Just to make ends meet.' She moved her sharp brown eyes between them. 'So we've established someone was killing women in that area and getting away with it. You think the same person has Samantha?'

'We thought we'd seen her in a house on Cliveden Road.'

That made Angela raise her eyebrows – finally they'd told her something she didn't know already. 'Who owns it now?'

'We don't know,' said Tim. 'Some shell company. Were there any suspects, in that murder?'

'Well, there was the landlord,' she said. 'He lived in the building, he'd been coming round to check up on Colette at all hours – he didn't like that she was on the game. Felt it lowered the tone of the house, but couldn't prove it, so he wanted to catch her in the act.'

Tim said, 'Was his name Keith Harvey?'

She nodded. 'Yes, I think that's right.'

'So it was number sixteen then. The same house.' Tim sounded excited, and Mary felt the same rising in her, and was ashamed. A woman had died, probably several of them.

Angela was saying, 'That sounds right. But he moved to Australia in the early nineties, then he died. I tried to find him when Laura Colebrook went missing. It can't have been him, if the cases are linked. And I suppose Colette's son would have recognised him.'

Tim was nodding. 'The previous owner was someone in Australia. A relative of this Keith, I imagine. Inherited it when he died, left it to rack and ruin, then it was sold earlier this year when he also died.'

Angela said, 'Most likely it was one of her clients who did it, and no way to trace any of them. Very sad case. I do hope this

Samantha isn't another one – perhaps she's just gone off and she'll turn up soon.'

Feeling deflated, Mary thanked Angela for the tea, not that she'd drunk much of hers.

She nodded. 'I'll admit it would be quite satisfying to finally close that case. But do leave it to the police, won't you, if you find anything? Amateurs rushing in would be exactly the thing to derail the case, prevent a prosecution.'

'Of course,' said Mary, though she wasn't at all sure she would.

As they went to her car, Tim impatiently wrenching open the door, Mary saw Angela's husband standing in the side return holding three large courgettes, soil clinging to them. He raised his hand to wave them off. How nice, she found herself thinking. A garden. Roots both literal and metaphorical. Maybe it wouldn't be such a hideous thing after all, to move a little further out of London.

Mary had barely started the engine before Tim was typing away on his phone. 'I can look up a birth certificate for Colette Johnson's son, find out what his name is.'

She pulled out from the pavement. 'How awful, losing his mother so young. Seeing her dead like that, and knowing he could almost have caught the guy.' Seven wasn't so many years older than Audrey. Her mind was racing ahead. Would that warp a person, finding your mother murdered? Make him likely to abduct young women? Maybe act the same thing out on them?

Tim made a sudden grunt of excitement. 'Guess the son's name.'

'What?' He held the phone so she could see a copy of a birth record. Eric James Johnson, born in a hospital in Croydon, not too far from where they were. 'I can't look, I'm driving. Her son was called Eric?'

'Mother Colette Johnson. No father listed.'

'So . . . the Eric Samantha knew, it might have been the same one whose mother was murdered in a house on Cliveden Road?'

He was typing still. 'Definitely it might.'

'Oh wow. So we just need to find an Eric Johnson who might have bought the house recently?'

'Well, I've found this guy. Owns a couple of development firms.' He flashed her his screen again. There were press shots of a tall dark-haired man with the mayor, announcements that his company, EJJ Homes, were renovating part of the Nine Elms development. Mary wondered what it was like to be the kind of person who'd think nothing of naming their business after themself.

She tried to keep her eyes on the road, though mounting excitement was making her hands shake. 'Click on his Wikipedia there.' Tim read out bits of information – Eric Johnson had humble beginnings, a London state school and no university, went into the building trade before buying and flipping his first house in the nineties. The kind of success story that was pointed to as evidence that anyone could make it, no one needed to struggle if they would only change their attitudes. He was married, but Tim found an article saying they had recently separated. Balding but trim, in expensive suits. The sort of man who secretly ran the city, the country. 'Does it say where he lives?'

'We can find out via Companies House, maybe. If he's registered as a company director.' His fingers flew. 'OK, here's another report on the murder, with photos.' Another quick glance at his phone. The picture was too blurry to make out, a black and white shot of what looked like a thin, careworn young woman.

Something caught her eye on the screen and Mary drew a sharp intake of breath, swerving suddenly to the pavement and stopping the car. 'Did you see that? Oh my God! Scroll back.' Tim looked where she pointed. Her veins were pounding with excitement, the sheer thrill of discovery. It was a colour picture of Colette Johnson, blonde, skinny, tired. 'Call up one of Samantha?'

Tim typed with a heavy thumb, and there was Samantha – her face was engraved on Mary's mind, the blonde hair in the ponytail, the sharp chin and nose. 'They look the same, right? Her, and Sam?'

Tim looked them over carefully. 'There's a similarity, yes.'

Her eyes met Tim's over the phone, and she could see the same triumph in his. They had really found something. A motive, a secret, and above all a reason for this rich man to have bought a house on such a nondescript street. 'We have to find him,' she heard herself say, like a character in a film. 'This Eric Johnson, we have to get to him.'

Tim nodded. 'I know how.'

Tim

Mary seemed very nervous. She kept asking if it would be OK, and that was making him second-guess himself, when he'd done this kind of thing a hundred times before. It was like riding a bike – if you didn't do it for a while, you'd start to ask yourself, can I really?

'It'll be fine,' he said again.

He'd no idea what Mary had done with her children, but it was the next day and they were on the Tube heading towards Bond Street, standing up in the busy carriage, and he was doing his best to not panic. Underground. Buried, effectively.

He hadn't slept again, and had eventually given up and spent the night scrolling the internet for any more scraps of information about the case. It was so hot, it felt like there was hardly a breath of air to suck in, clogged with other people's perfume and hair spray and body odour from arms hanging on to poles. He looked about him at the people staring into space or at phones. None of them seemed aware that above their heads were tons and tons of soil, tunnels built in Victorian times. What if today was the day when enough stress had built up over the years, and it all collapsed?

Mary had said something. Distracted, he asked, 'What?'

She repeated, 'Is it not against the law, you know, to just walk in there?'

'Of course not. It's an office building.'

'I know but . . . we don't have an appointment. He might be annoyed.' They hadn't been able to find any evidence online that Eric Johnson, the probable owner of the house, and Samantha had known each other, but Tim was confident he could brazen it out.

'People being annoyed at you isn't the worst thing that can happen, you know.'

All the same, Mary still looked uneasy. Sometimes he thought she spent too much time around humans whose brains were still unformed. She had dressed differently today, in a grey shift dress and low heels, and she smelled of something that reminded him of his mother, some dusky floral scent. He sensed it was a big deal for her, to go into town, saw how she hesitated while changing trains, baulking at the tides of people that surged down the underground corridors. They all seemed to know exactly where they were going, tapping along sure-footed in heels or smart shoes.

When they reached their stop and rode the escalator up into the noisy shopping centre that topped the station, he could feel his breath easing with each glimpse of sunlight. He would have walked or taken the bus if he'd been alone, but Mary had headed for the Tube and it was too hard to explain what was wrong with him, that he now struggled to be inside things, or under things.

Soon they'd reached the office block with its glass front and revolving door. The memory it recalled, a woman walking ahead of him into a building, windows gleaming in the sun, brought such a surge of emotion he had to swallow it down, and Mary saw him stumble a little.

He brushed it off. 'Um . . . it's OK. A bit hot.'

Politeness dictated he should let her go ahead, as he had done that day, his hand hovering near the small of Mariam's back. Thinking how, in a different country, a Western one, he might have let it touch her, feel the cloth of her loose top. Her hair looped up and hidden, to be spread out only for him, its shining coils sliding down her shoulders. How he'd loved that.

He found himself holding his breath slightly as Mary walked in, taking the first turn of the revolving door. They would not have both fitted, and for a second he watched her on the other side of the glass, sealed in, and then he took a deep gulp, like a diver, and pushed in too.

Inside was cool and hushed. A man with a headset, young and handsome, sat behind a large desk. Tim straightened his spine, tried to appear more professional, not like someone on the edge of a nervous breakdown.

'Hi. I'm Tim Darbandi from the *Gazette* – I'm here to interview Mr Johnson?'

Sometimes that would work, a confident statement of intention couched as something arranged. But the young man was wise to that.

'Do you have an appointment?'

'He'll want to talk to me, I promise.'

'Mr Johnson is the CEO, I'm afraid he has many demands on his time.'

This was the moment. Aware of Mary hovering, the cloud of her anxiety, and his wish for her to see him as a good man, he laid his hands on the cool marble of the desk, noticing how his fingers left sweaty trails.

'I'd like to speak to Mr Johnson about his mother. I've uncovered information about her death. Her murder. Believe me, he will want to take this meeting.'

He was surprised at himself, and could feel Mary's surprise too. Somewhere inside this broken shell, the old Tim was alive. The young man hesitated, then got on the phone and murmured into it. Tim stood back a few steps, enjoying the cool of the lobby, the gentle sound of a water feature that gurgled along one wall. Eric

Johnson had done well for himself. Had he also taken a girl and held her prisoner in an abandoned house in South London? Tim hadn't even been able to prove it was him who owned the place, thanks to the network of confusing shell companies.

'Will this work?' whispered Mary.

'Nine times out of ten.'

And sure enough, the young man was beckoning them over, an air of irritation on his good-looking face. Tim felt a petty surge of satisfaction as they were given ID badges and told to take the lift to the tenth floor. His blood began to sing in his veins, and he even smiled at Mary as they approached the lifts. A small enclosed space, a metal box suspended metres above the ground, was not his usual comfort zone, but he pushed it down, only a whitening of his knuckles betraying his fear.

The tenth floor had the hush of deep carpets and soundproofed meeting rooms. They were met by a woman in high heels and a suit, with a neat crown of fair hair and glasses. She was anxious, he could tell, under her professional calm, but what was more surprising was how Mary reacted. Her body jerked, and she fell back a step, fumbling with her handbag.

'Come with me. Mr Johnson is very busy, but he has a small window now if you hurry.'

Her heels made no sound on the carpet, but left sharp indentations with every step. As Tim looked behind at Mary, he saw the footprints slowly erased, forgotten by the material.

Mary beckoned him, and he lagged a few paces behind the woman's quick steps.

'It's the same woman,' she hissed. 'From the house, that day I snuck in.'

'It is? Did she recognise you?'

'I don't think so.' Mary looked quite different today – perhaps the PA woman, or whoever she was, would not expect to see the harassed mother of two small children in a central London office. So that was good – they were perhaps on the right track here, and Eric Johnson really was involved.

The woman stopped outside a heavy wooden door with a keypad on it. She hadn't offered them tea, or even water, on such a hot day. Eric Johnson was rattled. That was good too.

'He really can only spare you five minutes. You're lucky to even get that.'

She swiped a card from the lanyard round her neck, and the door opened silently. Mary was still hanging her head, and shuffled after the woman and Tim, into another even quieter corridor, with panelled wood walls and a deep-blue carpet. The woman led them to the end, another door. She knocked, and a buzzer sounded, and this door opened too. She stood back, indicating they should go through.

Sunlight came from the doorway as Tim stepped into a large, lovely office, the kind he would have liked for himself. Art and books on the wall. A floor-to-ceiling window looking over London. A man was standing at the shelf, glancing at the titles there, in a way that felt staged. Middle-aged but trim – older than Tim, but he didn't look it, because he shaved and had his hair cut well and wore a nice suit. He was mixed race, perhaps. Also like Tim. But that was no good, feeling kinship with this man, who might have taken Samantha.

'Tim and Mary, is it?'

The door shut and the efficient PA, or whatever she was, disappeared. Mary glanced around at the sound of it shutting, slightly wild-eyed. For a moment Tim wondered what he'd gotten her into.

'Yes, I'm Tim Darbandi.'

'Of the *Gazette*, I gather – they sent you here?'

He'd googled that in the time it took them to come up in the lift. He'd likely already know what had happened to Tim, his entire backstory.

'I work at the *Gazette*, yes.' He ignored the second part of the question, as a politician would. 'This is Mary, my . . . associate. We're here because we live near Cliveden Road, in South London. Do you know it?'

No flicker of tension. 'A little.'

'You bought a house on that road recently, did you?'

He laughed. 'I buy a lot of houses, Tim! Or rather, my firm does.'

'One single house, though?' Tim wasn't going to mention the man's mother yet. He'd play the game a little first.

'If it's worth it. Can I ask why you want to know about this one?'

Tim glanced back at Mary, who was looking terrified. 'We think we saw something in that house. A missing girl. Samantha Ellis, have you been following the story?'

'Of course. Poor girl. You think you saw her in the house?'

'We both saw it. A blonde girl, and it looked like something was being done to her. Violence.'

He frowned. 'When was this?'

'Last week, two separate times.'

'Did you call the police? The house is empty, as you probably know, being renovated, if I'm thinking of the right one.'

Mary spoke then, her voice sounding shaky. 'We did but they have so many tip-offs, they didn't believe us.'

'That's a shame. I have a lot of properties, as I'm sure you understand, I can't be personally involved in all of them. Perhaps someone broke in, was squatting there?'

'That woman was there. Your secretary.' Mary's voice had grown stronger.

He was wrong-footed by that. 'She's my executive assistant, and it wouldn't be unusual for her to visit my development sites from time to time, check the work is progressing.'

Tim tried, 'If Samantha was being held at one of your houses, surely you'd want the police to investigate?'

'Of course. I'd be more than happy to allow entry to the police, but if they don't believe it's a good lead—'

'The same house your mother was murdered in?' Tim blurted out. 'Isn't that just a bit suspicious?'

He froze, then quickly recovered. Eric Johnson was a clever man – he'd had to be, to get where he was. 'That's true, as it happens, although not widely known. Sixteen Cliveden Road was the house I grew up in – or at least in a bedsit there. I suppose, sentimentally, I wanted it off the market.'

'You found her,' Mary said, and he glanced at her. She blanched.

'It's not something I like to talk about. I'm sure you understand.'

Tim pulled the conversation back. 'A missing girl spotted in the place your mother was murdered? How do you explain that coincidence?'

'Do I have to explain it? This is London, people have died in most old houses. I own a lot of buildings, so it's hardly a surprise I'd want to buy my childhood home. What you don't seem to have is any evidence this poor girl was in the house.'

'We saw her,' said Mary, but there was a quaver in her voice. She'd be easily talked out of this, Tim knew. She'd lost confidence in herself since becoming a stay-at-home mother. 'We both saw her, more than once.'

Eric Johnson reached for his desk phone, the picture of helpfulness. 'Well, there's an easy way to sort this out. I have some friends in the force – I'm more than happy to ask them to look round the house, right now if possible, and clear this up once and for all.'

◆ ◆ ◆

Things moved fast after that. Eric Johnson got on the phone to someone he called 'Phil', who seemed to be a fairly senior police officer, and minutes after that they were being ushered downstairs to a town car that had drawn up outside the building, and were travelling through the lunchtime traffic back to where they'd come from. Mary looked shell-shocked.

'The police are really going to look in the house now?'

Tim shrugged. 'That's what he said.'

He felt obscurely annoyed at this turn of events, the way the property developer had taken control of what was supposed to be an ambush. Eric Johnson was going in a different car, and they were to be met there by detectives from their local station, the same ones who had dismissed them before. Johnson had said they were most welcome to look round as well once the search was completed, to 'set their minds at ease'.

It was dizzying, and disappointing, the way one phone call from a powerful man had led to this. One word from him could do more than months of Tim's digging. But they were going to check the house out – that was something. However, he had a hollow feeling in his stomach. If Johnson indeed had been holding the girl there, the drive would give him plenty of time to have her moved. Surely they were not going to turn up at the door like in *The Sweeney* and find poor Samantha tied to a radiator, grateful and weeping. No, he had a bad feeling about all this. It was too easy.

The journey took an hour, stop-start at a hundred red lights, and Tim found he couldn't say much, his hands sweaty against the black leather seats. The car had a chemical smell that made him feel nauseated, reminding him of a hundred airport pick-ups, tropical heat giving way to chilly air freshener, a bottle of water provided. Nosing through crowded streets, the people outside staring in at him like an animal at the zoo. How had he ever thought he'd seen these countries? He'd been cosseted through them, with hotels and Jeeps and air conditioning. It wasn't the same as living on that dusty, blood-soaked earth.

Soon, he began to recognise landmarks, and they were almost home. They swung into Cliveden Road, and sure enough the house was surrounded by police officers, several vans parked up outside. Outside the house opposite number sixteen, a sixty-something man stood, holding a watering can and watching the proceedings avidly. When he spotted Mary, he waved at her frantically.

'Well done! You sort him out, girl!'

Mary gave a cringing wave back.

On the opposite side of the road, Eric Johnson was talking to a woman in a trouser suit, with shiny dark hair in a plait over one shoulder. She wore blue gloves and an annoyed expression.

'This them?' she said to Johnson, as Mary and Tim got out of the car. Mary had barely spoken a word the whole journey. Johnson nodded. 'This is the house where you saw Samantha Ellis being attacked?' the woman said, to Tim and Mary.

'Well, we thought so,' said Mary, who'd rowed back considerably from her position in the face of all these uniforms.

The woman – a DS, he guessed – sighed. 'I can tell you there's no one here. No sign anyone has been living at the property – it's a building site, as Mr Johnson told you.'

Tim didn't believe it. 'She could have been moved. Did you do forensics?'

The detective, who was perhaps in her early thirties, raised her eyebrows at him. 'A full forensics sweep is not necessary in this situation, sir. Do you know how many tip-offs we've had about this case? We had one just an hour ago saying Samantha was at the Poundsaver in Bromley.'

Tim opened his mouth to say it wasn't a vague sighting, then shut it again. He had a horrible feeling in his gut, the place where stories nudged him – this wasn't right. Had he been wrong about it – looking at it all upside down?

'What about the shoes?' Mary blurted. 'I saw women's shoes in there – in a corner.'

'There's nothing.' The woman beckoned them past the open gate of the house, the few steps down the front path – gravel, neat plants in tubs – then opened the front door, which was ajar. She pointed inside, and the place was empty, just a small bathroom to the right, dusty wooden floors throughout. 'See? Nothing.'

Mary stared. 'But – there was more! When I came there were towels in the bathroom, and toiletries.' But plainly it was all empty now – Tim could see the sink and loo even still had stickers on them, as if never used.

The detective turned to the property millionaire, who looked cool and unruffled, standing in the front garden scrolling on his phone. 'Mr Johnson, you've been very helpful to come here personally. I hope we haven't disturbed anything on the property.'

'Not at all, DS Mendes. I do hope we can put this to bed now. I've never met the poor girl – but of course I'll do everything I can to help, though I can't think what.'

'Thank you.' She snapped off her gloves and eyed Tim and Mary. 'You both live round here, I gather? Perhaps you can see yourselves home.'

Tim looked up at the house again. Something propelled him forward, and he pushed through the shiny door and into the house. He breathed in a smell of new paint and plaster. The lower rooms were finished, varnished floors, no furniture. The stairs untreated wood. He pounded up them, dimly aware of someone shouting after him, 'Mr Darbandi! Mr Darbandi!'

Second floor, several more rooms, unfinished, holes in the walls and floors. Third floor, the same. There were no doors yet, so he could quickly see into each room. One more set of stairs, the attic room. He burst into it – it was dirty and dark, the walls splashed with stains. He looked out the window and saw the park where he'd stood that night, and further away, picked out Mary's window among so many others, then his own. There was nothing else in the room, no furniture at all, clearly untouched so far by the renovations.

'Mr Darbandi.' Breathing hard, the detective was behind him. 'I have to ask you to leave – this is private property.'

He'd just had to see. 'She was here,' he said, aware of how pathetic he sounded. 'There was a mattress, furniture. It's all been moved.'

She sighed, and he could see she didn't believe him, that no one would, that it was all over. 'Right. Well, we've no evidence Samantha was ever here, and it's hardly a crime to move furniture around, so you have to come with me now.'

He followed her out. There was nothing else to do.

Mary

They withdrew to the park, by mutual silent agreement, and took up their usual table. The teenage waitress came over, the one with the pink hair, but Mary was too despondent to even order a complicated coffee. She knew she should get the kids from Francine's – she was really pushing her luck dropping them off so many times, and Leo would need a feed – but could not face it yet.

'Um . . . tea please. Tim?'

He shook his head. He was frowning fiercely, and looked like an angry bear. 'I don't understand it.'

'I know. I was so sure.'

But had she been? Or in her exhausted, sleepless state, had she simply gone along with what he believed? She tried to call up the memory of the binoculars, heavy in her hands, the leather smell of them, the glimpse of a pale blonde girl at the window, blinds whisking shut. Had it been a different house? She'd miscounted the windows?

'Look, it's not over.'

'What?' Mary was shocked at how happy it made her when he said that. She wasn't ready to give this up yet, she realised. 'How?'

'So she's not in there right now this second. Doesn't mean she never was, does it? And his mother *died* in that house – it can't be a coincidence!'

She was nodding, a surge of energy rushing through her. 'So what can we do?'

'I think we need to find Samantha's secret online stuff – if she was doing, like you said, webcam work.' He said it squeamishly, as if holding the words at arm's length. 'Talk to that Karolina she worked with, her dad if we can track him down. I'll ask my mate at the paper what he knows.'

What could Mary do to help? She thought of her meagre investigative skills.

'Oh! He's in the middle of a divorce, this Eric Johnson, right? I bet I can find out who represents him. That's what I do, I'm a family lawyer.' The act of saying it, *I'm a lawyer,* made her feel better. She still was, wasn't she? Not just a mum. 'Maybe there's something we can find out from the wife too.'

'Great. OK. So we're not giving up?'

'Sam's still missing, isn't she?' Mary took her phone out. 'The main site I know for webcam work is called Little Secrets. I read an article about it.' In the hairdressers', of course. The article had been couched in concern, pretending not to be salacious. 'Apparently girls can earn a ton of money on there, and it's safer, because they don't actually meet the men. They just sort of act things out for them. Say what they want to hear. People can pay for them to take off their clothes, that sort of thing. It's kind of like YouTube.'

'Jesus,' muttered Tim, scandalised.

She found the website – all totally legal – and clicked on the interface, confused by it. It looked a bit like Twitter. 'So the idea is you get subscribers, they each pay a bit of money every month, and you post videos and photos for them. You can also do live sessions and those cost more. But we don't know what name she went under, so how can we find her?'

She tried searching for *Samantha*, but a bewildering array of accounts came up, avatars of pouting women, feathers and leather and lace. She felt a bit grubby from it, though told herself it was a legitimate way to make money, if the girls felt comfortable with it.

Tim was clicking away on his phone too, the same frown deepening on his forehead. 'She'd have to have promoted herself somehow. Let's look at the accounts of all her friends, see if anyone liked something from that site.'

So they trawled through Samantha's Facebook and Instagram again – the sadness of seeing the same post at the top, knowing there might never be any more – and those of everyone she was friends with or followed, and their friends too. It took ages, and felt agonisingly slow.

'Anything?' she asked Tim, rubbing her wrist. Her hand hurt from scrolling.

'She's friends with a Karolina on Facebook. Eastern European surname. That must be the colleague Lena mentioned.'

'So we find her next?'

He nodded. 'Tomorrow?'

The next day was Saturday. Mary had no idea how she'd explain it all to Jack. But she knew she would, somehow, whatever it took, because she couldn't give up now.

17th June, 2007

Reposting to try and boost. Laura Colebrook has been missing from South Kenborough for four days now. She's described as five six, sixteen years old, slim build with blonde hair. She went missing on her way home from the bus stop on the high street and her parents are frantic. If anyone has any information, please contact the police immediately.

Tim

Tim had been in some desolate spots in his life. Raqqa, Syria, under heavy bombardment. Rwanda after the genocide, one of his first reporting jobs as a young rookie. On the scene of the Omagh bomb in Northern Ireland, the utter disbelief and horror all around him. But this place – a bedsit in Croydon – somehow made him feel more hopeless than any of them. They had come to find Karolina Berzins, Sam's former colleague at the care home, before she'd left or been fired in mysterious circumstances. He was already writing the copy in his head, the long-form piece he might publish about the investigation. *As we arrived, I felt we had stepped over the line, into a different world. The nerves were written all over my companion's face as she saw the graffiti in the stairwell.*

Tim was jangling with caffeine and adrenaline, no sleep for what felt like a week or more. He didn't care, because he actually had something to do with his time – he'd cancelled his therapy, even, telling Mhairi he'd lost his voice. He should update Nick on what he'd learned, the possible link between Sam and the other missing girls, the webcam work, which he knew would play well with the paper's moral-majority readers. After years in the business, he could think in front pages – *Sex Shame of Sad Sam*. It would make people feel better, if they could tell themselves there was a reason she had been taken. That she wasn't a good, pure princess snatched from the street by an ogre. She'd done something to bring this on herself. It was horrible, but it was just human nature.

If Tim could get a story in the paper, it would also be proof he hadn't lost his touch. He'd been so sure Eric Johnson was involved in Sam's disappearance – he was still sure – but the house was empty and they'd need even more evidence to get the police to believe them.

Now, he rang the doorbell on the tenth floor of a tower block, the stench of urine overwhelming all the way up in the lift, which had smashed mirrors and was scrawled with graffiti. But the studio flat, when Karolina opened the door, was nicely kept, the walls painted in fresh magnolia and an anonymous but clean grey carpet on the floor. A glimpse of a shoebox kitchen, everything washed up and tidy. She'd hung the place with paper lanterns and fairy lights, framing the large double bed that filled the space. Her laptop was propped on a stand at the end of the bed, a webcam pinned on top and angled to the bed. Aside from a rack of clothes out of shot, there was no other furniture. Karolina let them in and sat on the bed, cross-legged, while Tim and Mary hovered awkwardly by the wall. 'What do you want?' She was direct. She wore a grey and pink tracksuit, dyed hair pinned up, long nails that looked fake, though Tim didn't know much about that.

'Hi, Karolina. I'm a journalist and—'

'Yeah I know who you are. I have call in ten, so be fast.'

A webcam session, he presumed she meant. He'd been researching it, and even joined the site to learn more – as Mary said, girls were paid extra to perform private sessions, acting out what the client asked for, wearing outfits they liked, or sometimes even just making conversation. He wondered how much it paid – the place was small, but Karolina seemed to be doing OK. 'Samantha Ellis. You worked with her?'

'Yes. Nursing home.'

'You didn't like it?'

'No money. But rooms are bigger than here, so I used an empty one.'

'They didn't like it?'

She shrugged. 'I don't care.'

Mary spoke. She looked terribly nervous, and was holding herself as if trying not to touch anything in the room. 'Did you get Samantha into it – the online work?'

'She saw me one night, doing session. Asked questions, I told her. Anyone can do it – just make profile, start posting, get money.'

'And – do you know if she met anyone in person?'

Karolina frowned. 'I would have tell her not to. Not safe. They do ask, offer cash, but always say no. Not worth it. And it's different – this way, no one touch me.'

Would Samantha have been desperate enough for money that she'd have agreed to meet someone in person? But why – she had a nice home with her family, she wasn't destitute? Though she'd been fired from her job, of course.

'Did she ever mention a man called Eric – or have you come across someone of that name, a punter?' Tim didn't know the correct lingo for this modern world, the boundaries of sex work and dating so blurred.

'Many Erics. Many of all names.'

'No one in particular?'

'She would not share her clients. If he is rich.' Karolina inspected her long acrylic nails, picked some dirt out from behind one.

'So she didn't tell you anything?' he said. This was something of a dead end.

A shrug. 'We are not friends. I just show her the website.'

'Do you know her profile details, maybe?' Mary tried. Then she froze, and Tim saw she was looking at some items on the bed, peeking from under a pillow. A purple vibrator, a riding crop.

Karolina followed their gaze and rolled her eyes. She scrolled through her phone then held it out to them. They were looking at a profile on the site, publicly available. The name was SexySchoolgirl99, but the picture was of Samantha Ellis. Not one they'd ever seen before – she was wearing a leather-look corset and pouting. But it was her alright.

Tim made a note of the name – the police would have to look at this now, surely? And maybe, just maybe, Eric Johnson would be among her followers.

Mary

It was strange to do what had once been a daily journey for her, so finely tuned that she knew exactly where to stand on the train platform, what tunnels to walk down at London Bridge, which coffee stand was the fastest at making a latte. Now she felt like a newborn calf on unaccustomed heels, sweating into her suit and forgetting how to work the ticket barriers like a tourist. Her office was just off Lincoln's Inn Fields, the green of the square almost covered in workers soaking up lunchtime sun, shirtsleeves rolled and faces held to the sky. Did she really miss it, living her life under artificial lights and breathing recycled air, always anxious in case the nursery rang or the trains went down? Both kids were in today, Leo for the first time, and she was right on the edge wondering how he'd cope taking a bottle.

Keying in the code for the door set off a muscle memory. Same as she'd always done, but she was not the same. Like two beloved weights around her ankles, she could never forget about her children even for a second.

'Mary! Hi!'

The receptionist, Jemima, had cut her hair, added blue streaks. Mary wondered what Geoffrey, her extremely old-fashioned boss, thought about that. Soon her face hurt from adopting a rictus smile, waving at people, explaining over and over what her baby was called and how old Audrey was now. Yes, loving the time with them. Missing the office. Yes, great to be allowed this 'keeping in touch' day, so nice to see everyone. Not getting a lot of sleep.

'But of course you wouldn't change a moment,' said Louise, a colleague with three teenagers, a slight edge in her voice.

'Of course not,' said Mary, thinking of the night both kids had been sick with norovirus and Jack was in Manchester for work in a five-star hotel. She'd had to run the washing machine five times and the flat had reeked of vomit for days.

Automatically, she had made her way to her old desk by the window, ready to drop her bag and pull out her chair, before remembering her status had changed. Someone was in her seat, a younger woman with thick dark hair piled on top of her head, glossy lips and a chic wrap dress. She smiled. 'Hi, Mary!'

Of course. The new her.

'Mary, Mary, welcome back, lovely to see you. I see you've found Francesca.' Geoffrey had come over, the sleeves of his pink-striped shirt rolled up. He smelled of strong coffee and halitosis. Mary put back on her smile.

'I hear she's been doing a great job.'

'Oh yes, we couldn't be happier. You'll have to watch yourself, ha ha ha!'

Mary did not laugh. Even squeezing out a smile was hurting her face. She was relieved soon after to escape into the morning meeting, pulling up a chair along the beautiful mahogany table, and nod along, carefully blank. The idea of a keeping in touch day was to remain up to date with the firm's business. But in reality, after several months, she had no hope of knowing which cases were what. So many relationships ending – would she and Jack become a statistic? She was pretty pissed off with him all the time at the moment. Every night he slept through and she sat up with the kids, it added to the debt in their relationship. And they never talked. He was rarely home before eight and by that stage she'd be wrestling both children into bed. They might watch an hour of a Netflix series before bed, but Mary often fell asleep before the end. He hadn't even noticed she was conducting an amateur investigation right under his nose. She'd told him on Saturday she was going to a yoga class with Francine, and he'd just accepted it, though he'd complained about having to watch the kids. Hadn't seemed to realise she set off in a summer dress and with no yoga mat.

This led her mind to the encounter with Karolina, in her tiny flat. She'd seemed happy enough – maybe that kind of work could be rewarding, compared to a low-wage slog? Mary hadn't heard from Tim today, and she wondered if he'd found any links between Sam and Eric Johnson – it turned out followers were hidden on Little Secrets, but maybe there was another way—

'Mary?' Geoffrey was looking at her expectantly. She'd missed something.

'Sorry – can you run through that again for me? I'm not totally up to speed.' She rifled through the meeting notes, as if she understood them.

'I was asking if you took a view on the Newman divorce.'

Newman? She'd no idea who that was. Everyone was staring at her.

'I – your recommendations sound fine to me, Geoffrey. Spot on, I'd say.'

She'd no clue what he said, and he knew it, because he shot her a brief look before turning to Francesca, who of course had all the facts at her gel-manicured fingertips.

After the meeting, Mary got what she'd really come her for – a chance to chat over lunch with her work BFF, Melia. Tall and beautiful, she navigated the white upper-class world of London law with aplomb. She had two teenage boys and was refreshingly open about how difficult they were, how much food they ate, the mess they left. She complained as they ate their lunch in Lincoln Inn's Fields, under the blazing sun that showed no signs of abating. 'Their shoes, Mary! The size of barges, all over my house.'

'And here was me thinking zero to three was the hard stage.'

'It's hard all the time. No nappies for me now at least.'

'That's something.' Mary pushed aside the remains of her sourdough sandwich, which had cost six pounds. 'Listen, I wanted to pick your brains a bit. You've heard of Eric Johnson?'

Melia took a bite of cucumber. 'Oh yeah. Owns half the City.'

'Who's doing his divorce, do you know?' A high-profile split like that would have all the big family law firms sniffing about.

'Freeman and Turner for him, Southey's for the wife. My friend Katherine works at Southey's, from Pilates.' Of course Melia did Pilates, and book club, and sang in a choir. Mary followed her life like a prisoner eyeing their release date – someday, somehow, she would have time for herself again.

'Any chance you could put me in touch? Off the record, like.'

Melia's eyebrow went up as she speared a bit of rocket on a wooden fork. Eight pounds for a takeaway salad. Mary feared she was losing her grip on London. 'You're going to have to explain.'

'I just – he's bought a house near me, in the next street over. It's causing some disruption in the neighbourhood.'

Melia nodded. 'Noise, that sort of thing? Big trucks full of double-glazing reversing down the street?'

'Yeah, that type of thing.' In fact there had been no noise or traffic at all, which was strange in itself. The building work, if there had been any outside of the security installation, seemed to have ceased. Mary kept thinking of the towels she'd seen, gone without trace on her next visit. She hadn't imagined it, had she? Someone had been there, at least part of the time.

'Well, I can certainly loop you in with Katherine. She won't be able to tell you much, of course.'

'Of course.' No lawyer, especially for the kind of clientele they handled, would risk breaking confidentiality. But perhaps she could give Mary a flavour of the man. 'You've not heard anything?' Gossip was different to confidentiality.

'Well, strictly between us, I did hear around that Annabella, that's the wife, got tired of his internet habits.' Melia raised her eyebrows, which she clearly found time to get threaded.

Mary blanked. Shopping? Twitter? 'Oh, you mean . . .'

'Yeah. He graduated from porn to webcam sites, is what I heard.'

'Really?' Mary's spine began to tingle.

'Oh yeah. He spent a fortune on the girls, apparently. Can you imagine? Our fellas might be totally useless, but at least we don't have to worry about that.'

'Mm.' But did she? Jack could be up to anything for all she knew. She probably wouldn't care, was the sad part. As long as she could get some sleep. 'You think he met any of the girls in person? That would be the next step, right?'

'God, probably. I always assume that whatever the wife knows is just the tip of the iceberg.'

'Hmm. Depressing.'

So he might have met Samantha. But how were they going to prove a link?

'Keeps us in business anyway.' Melia looked at her watch. 'I suppose I'd better get back to the grindstone. You're off?'

'Have to. Nursery pick-up's at three.' How she was going to manage when back full-time, she had no idea. They hugged. 'Say hi to Jason and the boys.'

'You too. Love to Jack.'

She probably wouldn't mention it to Jack, Mary thought. He likely wouldn't even remember she'd come to work today.

◆　◆　◆

Mary picked the kids up from nursery, both of them with sodden nappies and exhausted and fractious – and wrangled them into their car seats. They smelled different, not hers, of cheap perfume and boiled food. God, this was so hard. She wanted to keep them at home and care for them herself. But she also wanted, needed, her job, her identity outside the home. On the way back, the traffic had built up from the after-school rush, and Leo began to screech, bucking and writhing in his car seat. Not to be outdone, Audrey started shouting. 'Mummy. Mummy. MUMMY!'

'WHAT?' snapped Mary, her nerves fraying as a woman in a Jeep cut her up.

'I saw a bus.'

'Right, yes, very good.'

There were approximately two hundred buses on this road every day. But she continued her commentary anyway. Mummy, a bike. Mummy, a dog. Mummy, a truck. And then, as they neared home and Mary began searching for a parking spot – 'Mummy, a p'lice car.'

'What?'

'A P'LICE car.'

Police? Audrey was right. There was indeed a police car parked outside the flat.

Tim

Tim waited anxiously at an outside table in an area of London that never used to exist – Coal Drops Yard. As the name suggested, it had once been an actual yard that held the fuel to drive trains north, dirty and rat-infested. That was all swept away now, and replaced by expensive shops that sold candles and identical piles of plain black T-shirts which somehow cost a hundred pounds.

He needed to calm down. His foot was jiggling under the table, and he could hardly contain what he had to tell Nick, what had happened earlier. He had to be careful, make sure he wasn't written out of the story he'd tracked down so carefully. And what a story it had turned out to be. He hadn't even told Mary yet, which he felt a little bad about. But he'd promised. And she would know soon enough – the whole country would.

God, he was tired. There'd been no sleep at all last night, but for once there was a reason. He'd lost a bit of time on the Tube, coming to himself somewhere near Angel, but it was alright, everything was going to be fine now.

Nick was late. Tim swept the crowd, ever vigilant for something he couldn't name. Muscles taut and ready to run. Eyes scanning every rooftop for non-existent snipers. Catching on any rapid movement, children running through fountains, their screams shrill. Students in the same clothes he'd worn in the eighties.

Mothers with babies, talking on their phones. Businesspeople in suits. He wasn't sure where he fitted, now he wasn't really a journalist. It had defined him for so much of his life, he didn't know who he'd be or what he'd do without it. Could he write anything where the pages would not be imprinted with what had happened? Crowded places like this were hard. Every time a woman walked towards him, with shiny dark hair, he thought it was her, and his heart leapt into his throat. His pulse was tripping like a snare drum.

He stiffened as a plane roared into view in the grey oyster sky. It was just a passenger jet, not a bombing raid.

Come on, Tim, get a grip.

No sign of Nick, but he recognised someone coming towards him, one of the business types in a trench coat, stabbing at a phone. Oh no. It was his old boss, Janine, head of news. Still his boss, technically. She was coming right towards him. He wasn't really supposed to be working, so for a moment he thought about bolting, leaving his five-pound coffee. But she was almost at his table.

'Tim.'

'Oh, er, hi, Janine, I was just—'

She forestalled him. 'I know you were expecting Nick. I'm afraid that's not going to happen, Tim. A condition of your medical leave was that you didn't undertake any paid work for our paper.'

'It's not paid,' he said. Stupid.

She rolled her eyes. Janine was a good ten years younger than him, steely and polished, with skin that showed not a line or blemish, shiny blonde hair tied back from her stern face. She kept her hand on her phone the whole time, as if dealing with him was just a brief inconvenience in her day. Which probably it was.

'Irregardless.' Not a word, he wanted to tell her. 'We can't have you working for the paper in any capacity, after what happened. And you've upset a very important investor with your poking about, on top of that.'

He didn't know what she meant, and then he did.

'Johnson? Don't tell me he owns part of the paper?'

'Five per cent. So the board would appreciate it if you didn't go around accusing him of kidnap, under the paper's name. You've left us open to a defamation suit.'

He opened his mouth to tell her what he knew, the story he was sitting on – that would show her alright, teach her some respect. But no, he didn't want to just give it away. It all seemed to crowd in on him, the unfairness of it. Didn't she know who he was, how many awards he'd been up for, how much money her precious paper had offered to tempt him over from his last job? He'd been reporting from the field while she was still at school. He'd been shot at and bombed and almost gone down in three plane crashes. And now he couldn't even work on a piddling local crime story?

'So what am I supposed to do, Janine? Just give up my entire career, the thing I've worked for since I was a kid? I'm forty-seven – this is all I've ever done.'

Her glossy lips tightened. 'Most people would try to save their dignity, Tim, and move on to something else. Since you haven't had a story in print for over a year.'

So that was it. They couldn't fire him as he hadn't technically done anything wrong, but they were trying to get him to fire himself. Take himself away in disgrace, like a bad smell. An absurd part of him wanted to stay on the payroll forever, out of spite. But it meant he couldn't write for anyone else either. If he couldn't report, there was no point to him – especially with the story he was about to break. The words were in his mouth before he knew it.

'Fine. You'll have my resignation letter tomorrow.'

She relaxed a fraction. 'That's the right choice. There's plenty of things you can do with your life, Tim. It doesn't have to be this. We're all supposed to have multiple careers now, aren't we?'

'What as? A coffee barista?' He looked over bitterly to the young and handsome man behind the counter of the café. An aspiring actor or one of the fashion students, maybe, judging by the three earrings in his ear. Well, it was her loss. She'd know that later on today, and he had some satisfaction thinking how much she'd kick herself.

'I don't know, Tim. But please don't ask for assignments again. I've had to give Nick a written warning.'

Poor Nick. Someone else dragged down by Tim, and a baby on the way as well. He stared down at his coffee until Janine clacked away, phone out and chatting already. He watched her go into one of the expensive candle shops as he glugged the last bitter dregs of his drink. He needed a new plan – how best to break this story in order to redeem his career, and his entire life.

Mary

Oh God. How had this happened? She was in a police station – she had never even seen inside one before. How sheltered her life had been, how boring. How stupid she'd been to think she could solve a case like this. Mary sat in the little interview room, wringing her hands together, feeling how sweaty they were. What would Jack say? She'd had to call and leave a message with his work, say the kids were at Francine's again – her friend's eyes had been popping when Mary rolled up with both kids, Audrey clinging and confused and Leo howling.

'I don't understand. You're going to the *police* station?'

'Yes, they – I don't know, they want to ask me questions.'

'But why, Mary?' *What have you done*, was the implicit query.

'I don't know. They think I might have seen Samantha. The missing girl, you know.'

Francine had looked baffled. 'And did you?'

'Maybe – look, I'm sorry, they're waiting for me.' The police car had followed her to Francine's, cruising like a shark behind her little Fiat. There hadn't been time to call Tim, even, let him know what was going on. 'Will you keep them? Leo'll need a bottle, there's some in the bag. I've rung Jack but he's in a meeting.' He was always in a bloody meeting. And how was she going to explain it to him, what she'd been up to all this time?

'Of course!'

And Mary had wrenched herself from her children, her guilt like a physical wound, and got into the police car. People coming out of their houses to look. It was so shameful. All because she had meddled, like a foolish middle-class mum.

The interview room had no windows, no way to know what time it was or how long she'd been here. Did she need a lawyer? She wasn't being arrested, they'd said. Just questions. So why could that not be done at home? It must be serious, to take her away from her two small children.

She jumped as the door opened, and two detectives came in. The same woman from the day they'd searched 16 Cliveden Road, in her early thirties, a well-made-up face and her hair neatly back in a bun, serious grey trouser suit. Powerful energy. Also with her was a younger man, chewing gum, handsome in a slightly shambolic bearded way, sleeves rolled up and tie loose.

'Mrs Collins.'

'Um – Mary is fine.'

The woman nodded, drawing up a chair with a scrape on the bare floor. 'I'm DS Diana Mendes, as I'm sure you recall, and this is DC Nick Andrews, from our cyber-crime department.'

Cyber-crime? What? 'Um, hi. I'm not sure why I'm here.'

The DS flipped open a notebook. 'Mary. You rang the station several times over the past two weeks, reporting that you'd seen Samantha Ellis in a nearby house. However, when we searched it the other day, there was no sign of her. Correct?'

'Eh – yes.'

'How well do you know Tim Darbandi, Mary?'

'We met about two weeks ago, I suppose. We're neighbours, but you know how it is, never saw him before.' That was a bit mad, now she thought of it, that she'd trusted him so readily when she knew so little about him.

'And you've been trying to solve this case together?' Her voice had barely an inflection, but Mary knew what she was saying all the same, and blushed.

'We just thought it was her we saw. Samantha. And at first we couldn't get, ah, you didn't send anyone to check the house. I know you're busy. But we were worried.'

'But as you're aware, there was no sign of anyone there. The house is being renovated. Yet your interest in the case didn't stop, did it?'

Mary sighed. 'We saw someone. We really did.' But even as she said it, doubt crept in. It was a long way away, the road that overlooked the park, and her eyesight wasn't what it had been since having Leo. No one told you pregnancy could actually make you go blind. 'I mean, we weren't completely sure it was her. We just thought it was worth checking out.'

Oh God, had Eric Johnson made a complaint perhaps, because they'd basically accused him of abducting Samantha? She and Jack would lose the flat if she had to go to court. Not to mention her job, if she ended up with a criminal conviction. How would she explain all this to Jack, that she'd been gallivanting about playing Nancy Drew with a strange man?

'Are you aware of Tim Darbandi's history, Mary?'

The male detective still hadn't said a word. He had a laptop in front of him, and was staring slightly above Mary's ear, as if thinking about what he might have for dinner.

'He's a journalist, he said. On sick leave after he got injured abroad.' And hadn't she thought that was cool? So dangerous, so important, unlike what she and Jack did for a living.

'He didn't tell you what actually happened?'

'No . . .' She looked between them again, embarrassed, with a growing sense of fear in her stomach. What was this?

'Well, that's not important right now. Can you look at this for us, Mrs Collins?' Mrs again. Not Mary. The other detective suddenly sprang into action, flipped up the laptop – a cheap square one – and spun it for her to look at. 'We retrieved this footage from a doorbell-cam on Cliveden Road. Is that Tim Darbandi?'

Clearly they'd followed Mary's suggestion of getting Nigel's footage. So why was she here? On the screen she was looking, from across the street, at number sixteen, its shuttered windows and forbidding fence. As she watched the greyscale footage, sharp as a pin, a car drove past, slow enough that she could see the driver's face – Tim! It was Tim!

'When was this?' Did Tim even have a car? They'd always taken hers when they went out investigating.

They paused the footage and exchanged a look that made her heart beat faster. 'The date is on it, Mrs Collins.'

She looked – earlier that day, just after three in the morning. 'That's him, yes. But . . .' Her words trailed off. She could now see there was someone in the car with Tim, a young woman, a swinging ponytail. The resolution on the camera was really amazing, maybe she should get one, if they ever had a house. But also— 'That's her! Samantha. Isn't it? Where is she now? Is she safe?'

What was this? Had Tim got into the house somehow, found Sam was there after all, and rescued her? If so, why hadn't he told Mary?

The woman detective folded her hands. 'We were hoping you might tell us, Mary. Since this video was taken earlier today, Samantha Ellis has not turned up.'

Mary was in total bewilderment. 'What?'

'She didn't arrive home. She didn't appear at a police station or any other public building. As far as we're concerned, she's still missing. What does that look like to you?'

They pressed Play again, and on screen Tim drove the young woman away, down Cliveden Road and off into the night.

'Um – he's taking her somewhere?'

But where? It didn't make any sense. If he'd found her, wouldn't he have gone straight to the police?

'It looks to us as if he's moving her somewhere more secure. Against her will.'

'No, no, you've got it wrong. He wouldn't do that – probably he was just taking her home.' But then why hadn't she arrived? And why hadn't he told Mary – she hadn't heard from him all day. 'Look, I'm sure this is just a misunderstanding. Ask him, he'll tell you.'

'We'd like to. Do you know where he is?' asked Diana Mendes.

'Well, no.' When had she last spoken to him? 'I saw him on Saturday.' They'd made a vague plan to meet at the usual place and time tomorrow, and compare notes on their digging. It seemed ridiculous now she looked at it in the cold light of the interview room. Like she'd made him up in her head. 'I don't know where he is today.'

'Apparently he had a plan to meet a colleague near King's Cross earlier today. However, he hasn't arrived back home since. We've had officers waiting outside his flat, and if he doesn't return soon we'll have to gain access without him.'

Mary stared between them, disbelieving. Tim had been with Samantha. He'd put her into his car and driven her away. Now he was the subject of some kind of manhunt. And she, Mary, suburban mum of two, had been his unwitting accomplice.

Samantha

She'd worked out that she was now outside of London. Kent, maybe, or Surrey – somewhere in the Home Counties. She'd been in the boot of the car for about an hour, she thought. It smelled like petrol and there was a pair of muddy trainers in there with her, that kept bouncing and hitting her in the face. She couldn't push them away, since her hands had been tied behind her, attached to her ankles with a length of nylon rope. Hog-tied, wasn't that the word for it? She was furious about that, or she would be when she stopped being so scared. They were in the country, since she could hear the wind in the trees and the sound of birds outside, but not too deeply in, as she could also hear the rush of cars in the distance. That meant people were nearby. If she could get out of here, she had a chance.

'Here' was what seemed to be a small holiday chalet or hut, the windows boarded up from the outside. There was a bathroom – a toilet, cracked sink, and shower hose – but the toilet stank of chemicals, so she thought maybe it wasn't on the grid. If she'd had her phone she could have googled, although more likely she'd have looked at the map to see where the hell she was, or even more likely called for help, but of course she didn't have it, and it felt like her arm had been chopped off. She was just . . . stuck here. It was hard to accept.

For a long time she had shouted and pounded on the walls, wearing herself out, leaving her hands sore and red. No one had come – there must be no one nearby. People would come if they heard her, wouldn't they? She didn't like to think about the alternative, that they'd heard but decided it was none of their business. Or that someone had passed near, maybe walking a dog, and it had been in the brief moments she'd stopped screaming to draw breath or cry.

She was smarter now. She was still alive, so maybe he wasn't planning to kill her. She just had to figure this out. There was food, long-life stuff and noodles she was supposed to heat up on the camping stove, tins of beans and supermarket bread. It was unhealthy, but she wouldn't starve. There were big bottles of water, and since it was warm outside she didn't need heating. There didn't seem to be any electricity – she'd flicked a few light switches but nothing happened. But it stayed bright until ten at least. She didn't want to think what might happen if she was still here when the days got shorter. That seemed ridiculous. This was clearly a temporary place. But what was his plan for her?

Although the walls seemed flimsy, she hadn't managed to kick a hole in one yet – he'd taken her shoes also – and the door was locked with several padlocks, as well as the windows, which in any case were too high and small to get out of. This must be a bloody depressing place to have a holiday, if that's what it even was. It was summer – would people not be staying here if it was a holiday place? She didn't know. She had tried to stack up furniture and see out of the one window where the board had slipped, but there was only a rickety stool and she'd fallen off, bruising her wrist. She had cried then, hurting and angry and, yes, a bit scared. She was doing her best not to let the fear in. That stopped you thinking straight. So, she couldn't get out the door, she couldn't break the window – it was too high and she had nothing to swing against it – and no one seemed to be coming when she shouted. So what was she going to do? She imagined her picture on the news, posters up on telegraph poles. The kind of thing you looked at and thought, oh she must be dead, poor girl. But she wasn't. That had to count for something. She wasn't going to be a girl on a poster, someone as good as dead, you were just waiting to find their body. She was breathing and shouting and furious and she was going to live. She just had to figure out what to do.

It hadn't escaped Sam that she was only here because she'd wanted more. Because she'd not been satisfied. Wanted a better job, a place of her own, just . . . more. Away. A whole other life.

She'd sort of drifted into working at the care home. The teachers at school were always saying she could do better, go to university, but she didn't see much point. There were university graduates working at Costa, after all. There was always work, if you were willing to do the hard and dirty jobs. She didn't mind. The old folk couldn't help it, and she liked looking after them, the small things that made them happy. She'd never been a good sleeper, and many of them didn't sleep either, so there was always someone to talk to, a TV or radio going. Never the long, lonely silence of the dark. She usually walked about to check on them, keep herself occupied. The other night staff rarely bothered, watching TV in the small office, or dozing off themselves in a spare room.

One night, she'd been going down the corridor, checking on the old people asleep in their rooms. The doors all had a little glass panel in them, like prison, so the staff could make sure no one had died. Some of them slept so soundly it was hard to tell. That night, she noticed one room – 57 – had the glass bit covered up, some sort of thin black scarf draped over it, trapped between the door and frame. All the same, a sharp light was leaking under the door. Not like a lamp. Something harsher than that – and Sam, child of the internet that she was, knew what it was. A ring light. Was someone filming something in that room? How weird. She put her ear to it, and sure enough she could hear a low murmuring voice. She knocked.

'Hello? Is someone in here?'

This room was empty, she remembered now. No one should have been in there at all. She knocked again.

That was how it all started. Funny to think, if she hadn't gone in the room that night, she might not have got to know Karolina, and then she definitely wouldn't be in this other room with the door locked and no idea when or if she was getting out. But it started before that, really. If she'd been a good sleeper she wouldn't have done the night shift, or taken that job in the first place. If she hadn't wanted out of her life she wouldn't have done any of it, but it was impossible to think of that because then she'd be a totally different person. So you could say in a sense there was no way to avoid what had happened to her. No way out of this small, dusty room, where no one seemed to be able to hear her no matter how loud she shouted. No way to prise open the old door with its rusty lock, or break through the half-rotted windows. No, there was no point in thinking that way, since it was inevitable she'd ended up here. What she had to do now was find a way to barter herself out.

Tim

'. . . So then he said there was scope to convert it into a bedroom. I said how are we going to get a bed in there? You'd hardly fit a cot.'

'Mm, mm, I remember when we bought . . .'

The voices of the women rose and fell as they trundled past him with their giant buggies. One looked back, quizzical, probably wondering why he was hiding in the bushes, and Tim frowned at his phone, as if he'd just stopped behind the tree to do something important. Maybe he was a banker, a lawyer, out for a lunchtime jog. They didn't know he couldn't manage a long walk these days, let alone a run.

He checked the time. It was 3.57 p.m. If he'd worked this out correctly, if she was still the creature of habit she used to be, she should be coming soon. And yes, look, there she was, in her bright pink windcheater. It was new. He didn't recognise a thing she wore on these runs, from her orange-blazoned trainers to the headband that kept her red hair tucked off her face. Her face was red as well, but she'd never looked more beautiful. Had she always been this lovely? Had he even noticed, on the brief nights he came home to sleep, before racing back to the airport, a conference, a press event?

He held his breath as Alice jogged past, so close he could almost reach out and touch the sleeve of her top. Would she glance up and see him? The idea was both a thrill and a terror. No, she always had headphones in, oblivious. That was dangerous. Anyone could be following her, tracking her route online, noting the time she went out at, almost to the minute every day, the exact same path about the park. Really it was her own fault Tim had begun to wait for her here, unseen. Just to watch her. Make sure she was alright. She ran with ease, hardly panting, and he could see she was fitter since they'd split, slimmer. Better all round. Whereas he was so much worse in so many ways.

This was the fourth time Tim had been here and he was aware it was becoming an obsession, something he could not tell other people about. Something that would make them, especially women, wrinkle up their faces and draw away in fear and disgust. He shouldn't be here. There were things to do, people to talk to, Mary first of all. He couldn't explain it. Any time something went well – and God knows nothing had for a long time – he wanted Alice to know.

He should have called the police right away, he knew, admitted what had happened in the early hours of that morning. But he'd been asked for time, so he'd agreed. Anyway, he had to play his hand carefully, use what he had to claw his way back to the top. Now enough hours had gone by, and he could work out his angle. He'd tell Mary and the police and then he'd hit up his old contacts, sell the story to the highest bidder with the offer of a nice staff job on the side. This could be his ticket back. No more grovelling for grunt work from people he'd trained up himself. The return of Tim Darbandi, Special Correspondent.

With a head full of the future, Tim made for home, taking the bus for ten minutes and walking the rest of the way, quickly growing sweaty in the dull heat. If this was all over, if he got his career back, what to do with his life? Start rebuilding it, brick by brick, although it was as shattered as the buildings on the street that day? Was there any chance, however slim, that Alice would forgive him?

Tim rounded into his street, eyes drawn automatically to the top floor of the house on Cliveden Road, though he knew there'd be nothing to see. Vaguely, he noted the police cars drawn up on the pavement, but it took him a few beats to realise why they were there. Outside his flat.

He stopped short in the middle of the road, aware he was a shambolic, sweaty figure, unshaven, just back from spying on his ex-wife from behind a tree. Too late, he saw what must have happened. Of course. How could he have been so stupid? He knew there was no point in running. He just stood there frozen as they came towards him, two police officers, a man and a woman both in grey trouser suits. The woman was older, not the one who'd led the search at Cliveden Road. Maybe this wasn't connected? The futile hope died. Of course it was. He could not seem to think of anything to say.

'Mr Darbandi.'

He couldn't speak so he just nodded.

The woman officer said, 'I'd like you to come with me, Tim. You're under arrest for the kidnap of Samantha Ellis.'

Mary

Time seemed to have lost all meaning. There was no clock in the room, and she'd been asked to leave her bag in reception, so she had no idea how long she'd been in there.

'Am I under arrest?' she asked, exhausted. She could smell how sweaty she was, feel the grease on her forehead. She had never been so tired, as if the weeks of no sleep in the hot flat, the stress of the investigation, and the terror of where she found herself had all crashed together.

'No,' said Diana Mendes. 'You're just helping us with our enquiries. Aren't you?'

'I'm trying.'

'Are you, though? If I were in your shoes – a mother, a lawyer – I'd be doing what I could to avoid arrest.' So it was on the cards, if she didn't tell them everything she knew. But she didn't know anything!

'I am.'

Diana Mendes appeared totally unruffled after the hours of questioning, her white shirt still pristine. 'So, let's go through it again, Mary.'

Why did they do this? Were they hoping she'd slip up, that she was lying? But she wasn't. She was trying her best to be truthful. But she was so tired, it was hard to remember. 'I met Tim in the park one night – we both thought we'd seen something in the house. Like – violent movement. That's the best way I can describe it.'

The detective tapped her pen against the chipboard table. The room was dingy, with no windows, a dirty blue carpet and cream walls marked by people's chairs. Mary couldn't help but feel they'd have taken her to a nicer one if she wasn't in trouble.

'Here's what I don't understand. You have a lot on your plate – two small children, a husband? How did you find the time to investigate this case so deeply? You'd tracked down Samantha's work colleagues, her ex-boyfriend, her best friend . . . it's actually impressive.'

By neglecting my family, that's how. 'I just – it seemed important.'

'You thought you could solve the case better than us?'

'Well, no, but you didn't believe we'd seen her.'

'We checked it out, Mary – she wasn't there.'

Mary opened her mouth, then shut it again. 'So what do you think? Tim had her the whole time? All these days he's been working with me to try and find her? In his tiny flat?' She shut down the memory of Tim not letting her in, not wanting her to see the inside. That didn't mean anything.

'You tell us. Has he ever mentioned having access to another building – a house, a garage, even a shed?'

'I've told you everything. He seemed like he was really trying to look for her – like he knew nothing.'

'But he's been odd – jumpy, secretive?'

She thought of the other day, when Tim had spilled the tea and fled from her house in distress. 'He hasn't been well.'

'Maybe he didn't know what he'd done. If he never sleeps.'

Mary shook her head. 'It just seems – unbelievable.'

'Or he's a very good liar. You'd be surprised how well some people can lie, Mary, even to themselves. To the point where they almost believe they're innocent.'

Her mind had been picking at the question for hours. Was it possible? That Tim had abducted Samantha, then kept her somewhere for weeks? How else to explain the camera footage, Tim driving with Samantha in his car? The car she hadn't known he owned?

'Where did he keep her then?' she said, feebly. 'All this time? His flat's too small, someone would have heard.'

'Any number of places. Maybe he even had access to the house where you say you saw her. We're looking into it.'

Tim had rushed into 16 Cliveden Road that day, past the police, up the stairs. What if he'd left his DNA during that visit? Or worse, gone in on purpose, to cover for the fact that the police would find it there anyway?

Suddenly Diana Mendes stopped and looked at her phone. A tight smile came to her face. 'We'll have to leave it there for now, Mary. I'll be back – I'd appreciate it if you stayed a while.' And she left, shutting the door behind her.

Mary knew what this meant.

They had found Tim.

Tim

.

Tim didn't understand what was happening. He was trying to do what his soothing-voiced therapist said, and take note of his sensations, process what his body could feel and see, ask himself what was real and what wasn't. But this was definitely real, no matter how crazy it seemed.

He was in a police cell, small and stuffy with no windows, a bare blue mattress beneath him. He was wearing a grey sweatshirt, fraying at the cuffs but clean, since his clothes had been taken for forensics. His nails had been scraped and his hair combed. A plastic cup of water sat in front of him, and he was afraid to pick it up in case his hands shook so much it spilled. They'd promised him a meal in a few hours, and told him he could have legal advice if he wanted. He could choose his own lawyer, or have the duty solicitor. The only one he could think of was the woman who'd done his divorce, and he knew that was the wrong kind – same kind as Mary, and he wondered how she was, if she knew what was happening. When the duty one arrived, the interview would start. He knew he'd been arrested, picked up outside his flat by the flank of police cars. For the kidnap of Samantha Ellis, they'd said. He had started to babble, explain that no, it wasn't what they thought, but they'd stopped him, reminded him he had the right to remain silent, so he had exercised that right. Until the lawyer came and it could all be cleared up.

He was trying to work out what must have happened. At first he'd thought it was Alice, that someone had called the police about him spying on her. But no, the police had been there waiting, and anyway, they'd said it was about Samantha. So someone must have seen him with her in the car, and got the wrong idea. If he could just explain – but why would anyone believe him? He'd known for months how he looked, the way mothers would gather their children to them as he passed. Dangerous. Off the rails of normal society. Stalking his ex-wife. Unemployed and obsessed with a missing girl. Of course they would suspect him. But where had she gone? It didn't make any sense. Was he being set up? Was Mary in on it?

Tim's head hurt, and he would have liked to lay it down and sleep. Nothing made sense any more. He didn't know what was up and what was down.

The door opened suddenly, and the detective from the house search was there. She looked fresh and young, the opposite of how he felt.

'Hello, Tim. We're ready for you.'

Her manner was not unpleasant – could she really think he'd kidnapped a girl, then lied about it for weeks? Or maybe she was just professional. Either way, Tim got up and shambled towards her, painfully aware of how pathetic his defence would seem.

Mary

Mary was let go after four hours of questioning, and called an Uber to get back from the police station, still in the same sweaty work-clothes she'd worn all day. Her mind was turning in circles. Tim couldn't have done this. He just couldn't – and yet there he was on the screen, clear as day, and there was no one to prove he'd not been keeping Samantha prisoner, no one to say he'd been blame-lessly at home each night instead of visiting his captive girl. She'd never been inside his flat, so for all she knew Samantha had been there all along.

As she unlocked the door of her own flat, thinking about how full of people her own life was, how she'd always have an alibi, she saw Jack was sitting on the edge of the sofa. No sign of either child, and the place was unnaturally quiet and tidy. He didn't have the TV on, which was weird.

'Hi.'

Jack sighed, standing up and pushing his hands over his face, so the flesh around his eyes lifted up like dough. 'What the hell's going on, Mary? You were at the *police* station?'

'It was just – a misunderstanding.'

He glared at her. He must have seen she'd been acting strangely, dashing off at all hours, on her phone non-stop, preoccupied. Behavioural standards had worsened for both kids, and Leo's sleep-training had gone out the window. How much did he know? Enough, it seemed. Because next he said, 'Mary. We need to talk.'

It was never a good thing when your spouse said *we need to talk*. Her stomach turned over itself and she busied herself taking off her jacket and heeled sandals, revealing her dirty feet. She didn't know why she was trying to buy time. To make her excuses maybe, not that she really could.

'Look, I know I've been distracted . . .'

Jack stood up and followed her into the kitchen. 'Will you just look at me?'

'Oh God, Jack, I'm so tired, and sweaty, I just . . .' Mary yelped as a loud noise interrupted her, and turned to find Jack shaking his hand, shards of plaster on the ground by his feet. 'Did you just . . . punch the wall?'

'Ow. Christ!'

Since when did Jack punch things? 'Are you alright?'

'Mary, for God's sake, stop stalling. I want to know what the hell's going on. Is there someone else?' he demanded. His face was ashen. He was still wearing his suit, his tie loose and top button undone.

'What?' It was so far from the truth that Mary just stared at him. 'Have *I* got someone else? You're the one who's out all the time, working late, making bloody protein shakes. I mean since when do you drink protein shakes?'

'Since I put on a stone eating Creme Eggs in front of the telly,' he snapped. 'And I've been out at the gym, if you must know, trying to shake it. Answer the question.'

'How could you even think that, you moron? I'm a suburban mum with two small kids. I'm on *maternity leave*. People don't have affairs on maternity leave!' She didn't know if that was true, but it hardly seemed the sexiest time. 'I had ten stitches in my vagina, you absolute tool.' Audrey. Where was Audrey? Hopefully in bed, but no, she was sitting on the stairs regarding her mother curiously, the ear of her stuffed rabbit clenched between her little white teeth. 'Hello, darling,' said Mary weakly.

'What's *vagina*?' mumbled Audrey.

'Nothing, nothing. Go back upstairs.' Jack hadn't shut the top stair-gate. He didn't think about these things. And he had the cheek to ask if she was having an affair! When would she get the time? When Audrey disappeared, Mary rubbed her face. She had to shower and take off her make-up. 'Of course there's no one else. God.'

He was still cradling his reddening hand. 'What's going on, then? I saw you with a man, in the park. Laughing, having coffee. Not even with the kids – and now I hear you've been leaving them with Francine all the time! So who is he if you're not having an affair with him?'

'Tim?' The idea she would have an affair with poor, broken Tim was both ludicrous and vaguely offensive. If she had an affair, it would be with the hot young barista with the man bun. 'Of course I'm not.'

'Who's Tim?'

'Our neighbour. He's . . . well, we've been . . . God, it's really hard to explain.'

'Try, Mary.'

Mary was surprised at this hitherto unsuspected core of steel in her husband. Seeing him there, clothed in the armour of his work self, his jaw set and eyes cold, he was almost – well, he was almost the man she'd fancied so much when she'd seen him across a crowded pub ten years ago.

'It's not as easy as—'

'Mary. As far as I'm concerned, you've been sneaking about, you aren't telling me things, you're neglecting our children, and now you've been at the police station for hours. I need you to explain it to me, and now.'

Mary felt her nose ache, and tears filled her eyes. 'I know, OK? I just – I can't cope any more.'

'With what?' His voice softened slightly. 'Well don't *cry* about it, come on.'

She stepped into the kitchen, fumbled for some kitchen roll. 'You don't know what it's like. I can't sleep. I literally haven't slept more than four hours a night since Audrey was born. And don't say you're awake too, because I hear you snoring when *I'm* awake, all night long sometimes.'

'I know it's been tough. But that doesn't explain your behaviour!'

'I needed something for me. I'm being pushed out at work, they have this young hotshot with no kids, of course, and my brain feels like an old holey sock, and I just thought I could help, that maybe I could actually do something here, OK?'

'What do you mean?'

'We – Tim and I – we were trying to – find someone. Solve a case.'

He leaned back against the counter. 'But, Mary, that sounds completely mad – you mean you've been running round like some kind of suburban Miss Marple? Did you take the kids with you?'

She hesitated. 'At first. Sometimes.'

'For Christ's sake, Mary! You put our kids in danger! Our babies!'

The tears were coming fast now, because he was right – she'd taken them both into that house, and she would never forgive herself for that. 'I was just trying to help someone. And you never notice me any more, Jack. I'm like an unpaid nanny and cleaner.'

He looked stung. 'That's not fair.'

'It's how I feel.' She dabbed at her face, the cheap kitchen roll quickly bunching and falling apart. 'I know I'm doing a terrible job at anything right now. I just . . . can't seem to stop.'

Jack was silent for a moment. When he spoke again, it was quieter. 'I didn't know you'd been struggling so much.'

'You can't see I never get a second to myself? While you're off doing spin classes or whatever?'

'Honestly, I don't feel I do either. Work's been crazy – they fired twenty per cent of the staff in the last six months, so I can't afford to put a foot wrong. My life is just Tube, office, sleep. It's why I joined the gym, for something that's mine. Sometimes I'm jealous of all the time you get with the kids.'

Mary grunted. 'Ha. You're welcome to them, believe me.'

Jack took a few steps towards her. 'We'll try to figure this out. But can you at least try to tell me what on earth you've been doing? Who were you trying to find?'

'Alright, alright, I will. But you have to let me finish before you say anything. It's going to sound mad.'

'Can't be madder than what I've been thinking.' So steely. If she was honest, she didn't hate it. Not at all.

Sometime later, Mary realised there hadn't been a peep from either child in a while. That was probably a bad sign, but, on the other hand, they couldn't be mortally injured or she would have heard their howls.

'So, that's it. We were trying to find this girl Sam, and we thought she was in the house. The police wouldn't do anything so we . . . investigated a bit.'

Jack looked shell-shocked. 'And Tim's been arrested?'

'Yes, but he didn't do it. He couldn't have! It's mad.'

'Why are you so sure?'

'Because he's, well – he just couldn't. You don't know him. He's too broken. And he really wanted to solve it, like a dog with a bone. That doesn't make any sense if he took her in the first place.'

Did it? There was an uncomfortable lump of doubt, lodged in her mind like a pebble in a shoe. He could have forgotten.

They were saying Tim wasn't right, that his lack of sleep meant he couldn't tell dreams from reality. That he was even more broken than she'd realised.

'So where is she?' Jack was clearly struggling with this, his wife turning Jessica Fletcher on him, but without the sense of style.

'I don't know. She's still missing.'

'This is insane. You could have been hurt – disappeared yourself, even! Mary, you're a mother. You have responsibilities.'

'I know. I know, OK?' She hadn't told him about taking the kids into the house, too ashamed. 'Believe me, I've said all this to myself.'

'And you really believe Tim's not the one who kidnapped her?'

'I think I do. I mean, I hope he's been telling me the truth. I can't be entirely sure.'

And there was the problem. How much further would she go for this man, a virtual stranger?

'Well then. I guess you better find some proof he didn't do it,' said Jack, and Mary realised he was right. But how?

Tim

Diana Mendes faced Tim across the chipped wooden table of the interview room. On her left was an older male officer with a notebook in front of him. On Tim's left was the duty solicitor, whose name he had already forgotten, a woman in her late twenties with bright blue nail polish.

'Interview with Tim Darbandi, DS Diana Mendes leading, DC Rohan Singh assisting. Also present is Carlene Harris, solicitor.'

Carlene. He had to try and remember that. But first he had to make them understand.

'I didn't do it.' His voice sounded croaky and unused. 'It's true that I, I see things sometimes, I don't sleep and I have these dreams, but I'd know if I did something like that, wouldn't I?'

'I don't know, Tim. You tell us.'

'Can I tell you what I think happened? What I remember?'

'That's why we're here.'

Tim ran his hand through his already sticking-up hair, leaned forward in the seat, and in a low voice began to tell her what had happened the previous night.

◆ ◆ ◆

Someone ringing on his doorbell was a rare occurrence these days. It was always a delivery, sometimes ones he'd forgotten ordering in the middle of the night, sleep masks and fake melatonin and various herbal supplements, evidence of his increasing desperation. Nothing worked, of course. Not the expensive white noise box, to block out the traffic and squeal of foxes, not the potions he rubbed on his temples and sprayed on his pillows. Nothing. The last person to knock on his door without a delivery had been Mary. So he thought somehow it might be her when he wrenched his door open at 2 a.m. Of course he wasn't in bed. The earlier he went, the longer he just had to lie there awake.

He buzzed whoever it was into the hallway of the flats, then went to open his door. The person standing there was a young woman with fair hair bundled up under a baseball cap, wearing a black hoody and leggings. He waited for her to hand him a package, but instead she looked him in the eye, and a deep current of recognition ran over him. *It couldn't be.*

'Are you Tim?'

'Um – yeah, but . . .'

'You've been looking for me, I hear. I'm Samantha.'

Diana Mendes stared at him across the table. 'Say that again, please?'

'She just came to my door. Two in the morning. I buzzed her in, and – well. There she was.'

'So what did you do?'

'I let her in, of course.'

He couldn't think what else to do. Here was this girl, who he'd been picturing chained up in an abandoned house, or moved somewhere even worse, and she was in his kitchen, fit and well. He didn't know what to say to her.

'Can I have a glass of water?' she said.

'Of course.' He fumbled one from the cupboard, ran the tap till it was cold. Where had she come from? Where had she been? He wasn't even sure he was awake, that this wasn't some twisted insomnia dream.

'I guessed this was your flat, watching you come in and out.'

She had been watching *him*? But she was missing. Abducted. His head hurt. 'Oh.'

'Thought it was time to come out and say I'm fine.'

'You're fine?' he repeated, stupidly.

'Well, yeah. I was never actually missing. This whole misunderstanding is so dumb.'

The detective's mouth was hanging open, and the bushy eyebrows of the other officer were almost at his hairline.

'A *misunderstanding*?'

'That's what she said. She wasn't missing at all – she wasn't in any danger.'

'I just wanted to lie low for a while,' Samantha said. 'I had this job offer, loads of money for a few days' work, but I didn't exactly want people to know about it. I told Mum I was staying with Shell, and told Shell I was at home. How was I to know they'd check up with each other, and go to the police? Like, bloody hell, I'm nineteen, am I not allowed to do my own thing for a few days? And then you, sniffing about. I thought it was all getting out of hand, the police

189

and that involved, so I'm here to tell you I'm alright, OK? You can see I'm alright. You can back off now.'

He was struggling to get his head round it. 'So – you weren't in any danger?'

She rolled her eyes. Her skin was very clear and pale, with the bloom of youth his own had long lost. 'I was fine. Till you thought you spotted me and made trouble. What were you even doing in the park at night, man?'

'I – I don't sleep.'

She made a 'huh' noise. 'Anyway. Like I said, I was just away. Doing some work.'

'Like you do on the website? The webcam stuff?'

She hesitated, her eyes growing warier. 'You know about that? Well, it's nothing to be ashamed of. I just didn't want everyone knowing my business. I'm paid well, I didn't get hurt, I knew exactly what I was getting into. Can't say that about everyone that wants to see you naked.'

'Was it Eric Johnson?' Tim said baldly. 'Is that who paid you for the work?'

'Who?'

No reaction at all. Was she just a very good liar, or did he have this wrong all along?

'So she said she was away doing sex work?' Diana Mendes's tone was so sceptical her words practically dripped on to the table. 'Did she say who with?'

'She wouldn't tell me. Just that it was work.'

Samantha drained her water and sat the glass down. 'Ta. So, anyway, when you got the police involved I had to reappear.'

'Where were you then? All this time?'

Was she saying she'd never been in the house at all? Who had they seen in the window, then?

She shrugged one shoulder. 'It doesn't matter.'

'Why didn't you come forward when you saw people were looking for you?'

'I didn't know to start with. Couldn't take my phone with me. Like a few days off grid, that was all. Then it all blew up, and I had to think how best to do it. To come back without getting anyone in trouble. Can't have scandal. There's an NDA.'

So she wasn't going to tell him who'd paid her. Tim tried to assimilate this. It was as if all his mental architecture had collapsed. He wasn't going to find her, because she wasn't lost. She was absolutely fine, and had only stayed away this long because of his actions in the first place.

'What will you do now?'

'I'll go home to my mum, if you'll drive me. You got a car?'

'Yeah, but – we should call the police, shouldn't we?'

She shook her head. 'I have to tell my mum first. I hate the thought of her worrying. And I need to make sure it don't come back on my client. Else I'll have to pay it all back, the cash, and no way am I doing that, after all this. So you can drive me, and you can keep your mouth shut till tomorrow afternoon at least. You owe me, yeah?'

It made a terrible sort of sense. He had tried to help her, and in doing so had caused her trouble. Not the first time he'd done that to a woman. At least this one was alive and well.

'You promise you'll call the police once you're home? They're out looking for you even now.'

'Yeah, yeah. You can do it yourself, if you want. Give me twelve hours though, deal?'

Tim was bewildered. 'Where will you say you were all this time?'

'Staying with a mate. Didn't take my phone, blah blah.'

'But why? I mean, they won't believe that.'

'I was getting fired from the nursing home – you figured that out, I know. Bloody Lena. Just trying to help, I suppose. I'll say I went to look for a job, people got their wires crossed, all a misunderstanding and I'm fine. Happens all the time that people go missing and they turn up after a week or two. Everyone'll forget about it soon enough.'

'So you just drove her home? Without telling anyone?'

It sounded so stupid when the detective put it like that. This supposedly missing girl, and he'd let her into his flat, leaving prints everywhere, and taken her in his car, the car he'd never even told Mary he had, because he'd been too scared to drive for months in case he blacked out at the wheel.

'Yeah.'

The detective was staring at him. 'Alright, Tim, but if you drove Samantha back to her home in Bexleyheath, wouldn't you go the other way? Not down Cliveden Road, where the camera picked you up?'

This was true. 'Um – she said she wanted to see the house she was supposed to be in.'

It sounded so stupid. But how could he refuse Samantha's request to take her home, when he finally had her in his sights? In his own car too. No wonder they'd been spotted. Really, he only had himself to blame.

'I dropped her off in the cul-de-sac where she lives. She said not to come to the door – but it was only a few houses away. What could have happened to her in that time?'

Nothing, surely. She must have got home OK. But then where was she? Or had it all been an elaborate set-up – had Samantha, or someone controlling her, *meant* for all this to happen to Tim? She'd come to his door on purpose, used a glass to leave her prints – and it was only a matter of time before the police found her DNA in his flat, they were searching it even now – and made him drive her in his own car, down the very street that had a door-cam always recording. How could they know about that though? It felt like a set-up. But why? That was what he couldn't figure out. He was even starting to doubt himself now, so crazy did it sound.

Diana Mendes sat back. 'Well, Tim – some of what you've said is corroborated. We have you on ANPR driving towards Bexleyheath. But we don't have any sign of Samantha, and her family say she never came home. So as far as I'm concerned, you're still the last person to see her alive.'

Mary

There was no police presence round the house on Cliveden Road. No sign that a girl might have been held there against her will for over a week. The police had clearly decided Samantha was never near the place, that Eric Johnson was merely a nice property developer who'd bought his childhood home to do up, understandable, made a lot of sense. Tim didn't sleep, he sometimes wandered about at night to get out of his hot, cramped flat. He'd seen Samantha walking home from the care home that night, he'd taken her. He was a man with a troubled past, shambolic, injured. The picture fitted. But Mary didn't believe it. He was broken, yes, but she'd seen the instinct was still in him, to track and find the story. He couldn't have deceived himself to the extent that he'd forgotten it was him who'd taken the girl in the first place. Could he? So she was helping him. She was going to try and prove they'd been right, that Samantha had indeed been in the house, but not held by Tim.

The trouble was she didn't entirely believe it herself. How did Sam get into his car, in that case, and why was he driving her late at night? None of it made sense. Could Tim really have dreamed it all up, to that level of detail?

The park was full of families enjoying the sun, eating ice creams, screaming on the swings, wrangling dogs. Childless, Mary felt self-conscious as she approached the back railings – Jack had agreed to go in late to work, given everything that was happening, and she'd persuaded him she needed to go for a walk by herself. She should have borrowed a dog – that gave you a watertight excuse to be crawling around in the bushes. Ignoring a few querying glances, she crouched down and pushed her way into the space between the bushes and the garden walls of the houses, an unloved and overgrown space with a strong smell of urine and sweet rotting alcohol. A number of cans and bottles were scattered about, along with a drift of rubbish from the café, paper cups and bags.

It wasn't much of a plan – she had the vague idea that if Sam really had been in the house, it must have been cleared out in a hurry before she and Tim turned up with the police. It had taken an hour to drive to Cliveden Road from Eric Johnson's office, plenty of time to get rid of any furniture, but maybe not to carry it far away. Samantha must have had some possessions, if she'd been there all that time. A mattress, some clothes, at least.

She trawled through bits of rubbish, chewed-up tennis balls, litter, a plastic bag with the handles tied and what looked like dog poo inside. Had anything else belonged to Sam? Had she drunk from that bottle of Oasis? What was that over there? Mary crawled even deeper in, realising she'd have to put all her clothes in the wash when she got home. What looked like a piece of sacking or something. A mattress. It was a mattress! Had they perhaps dragged it here before the police came, in this area of scrubland between the houses and the park? Mary snapped a few pictures with her phone, though there wasn't much light, then crawled out again, almost ending up at the feet of a hot neighbourhood dad and his two be-scootered children and small yapping terrier.

'Found it!' she said cheerfully, holding her phone aloft. The man blinked, and there was a small pause as she stood up, shaking leaf litter and soil from her clothes.

As she made her way out from the bushes, her mind was fermenting over what to do. Tell the police? Maybe they could do a DNA test on that mattress. But would it even prove anything, if they could be sure Samantha had used it? Maybe they'd say Tim had left those things there. If only he had an alibi for the night Samantha had gone missing. Those weren't easy to come by when you lived alone, sadly, and there was no way to prove he'd stayed in his flat that night, trying and failing to sleep, instead of roaming the roads, in the car he hadn't even told her he owned.

Mary was just brushing dead leaves from her T-shirt, when she spotted someone she knew. It was Nigel, the man from 13 Cliveden Road, standing on the park path with a small shivering dog on a lead.

'Oh, hello.'

He stared at her. He was wearing a blue polo shirt and oversized dad jeans. 'It's you.'

'Mary, yes. You gave the police your door-cam footage?' She could hardly blame him, when she'd suggested it in the first place.

He gave her a dubious look. 'Don't think I should discuss that with you.'

Maybe not. She was certainly not cleared of suspicion herself. 'Alright. Have you seen any more activity around number sixteen?'

'I'm keeping a close eye on it. Anything untoward happens, I'll be sure to see, don't you worry.'

'Good.'

He frowned. 'But you shouldn't be poking about, should you? Best to leave well alone, now the police are involved.'

'I know.'

'Not grubbing about in the bushes or whatever you were doing.'

'Alright, yes, I'm going.'

He was reminding Mary unpleasantly of her father. She hoped he wouldn't tell the police she was still sniffing about, or she might find herself arrested after all.

Tim

The lawyer they'd sent for Tim, the twenty-something woman with trainers in a tote bag, said the police could hold him for up to five days before charging him, if they got all the extensions they could apply for: 'And in the circumstances, they probably will.'

'What does that mean?' he'd asked her, feeling her judgement. She wasn't much older than Samantha.

'Well, she's still missing. They'll want any information you have on her whereabouts.'

'I don't have any.'

He didn't think she believed him. In the meantime, he was moved back and forward between the cell, with its blue plastic mattress, and the windowless interview room. He was fed and allowed sleep, not mistreated. The questions were insistent. Had he taken Sam from the road outside the care home? Had he been stalking her? Where had he held her? How had he encountered her in the first place? He'd gone to the nursing home, they knew about that – was that the first time or had he been there before? He'd been following Samantha on Little Secrets – could he prove he'd only joined the site the previous week? They knew all his history, exactly what had happened to him. Was he unstable since his injury? He'd been fired, hadn't he? He'd done his best to insert himself into the investigation, something the police were trained to look out for.

Was that because he'd taken her himself? And, most of all, they wanted to know where she was now.

Where's Sam, Tim?

Where have you put her?

Is she hurt?

If she's alive you can still help yourself. Only a few years for kidnapping, not life for murder.

But he couldn't help them, or indeed himself, because he really didn't know where she was. He told them the same thing over and over – Samantha had come to his door, asked him to drive her home and not call the police until the next day.

And why did you agree to that, Tim?

Because she said I owed her. And – the truth, the base truth of it – *I wanted the story. If no one else knew about it, the story was mine to break.*

He could tell they didn't believe him, and he wasn't surprised, since it sounded ridiculous. So it was back to the cell for another eight hours of 'rest'. As if he could rest.

Sometimes he would drift off in a thick doze and even dream, vivid dreams he'd wake from confused. He'd been sitting with Mariam in a café in a more tolerant neighbourhood of the city, sharing a coffee, her headscarf slipping to show her glossy black hair. Her hands with their painted nails on the table, a breath away from his. He had wanted to touch her, no matter who was watching, but couldn't. His body was rigid, his arms glued to the shiny zinc surface of the table. Or else he would dream of that day, the terrible one when he'd taken a taxi from the airport to her flat in the gated compound, and been stopped by the armed guard.

Sir, you must wait.

I'm here to see Mariam, he'd said, and seen the guard's expression change, and he backed away to murmur into a radio.

That was the first time Tim had been arrested, and in his dream he recalled the smell of the small room at the station – tobacco and stale sweat, the brush of the fan over his face, stirring the hot air. The endless questions.

When did you last see her?

Do you have a key to her apartment?

Tim all the while asking what had happened to her, not even knowing.

Please. Is she OK? Is she OK?

Catching snatches of Arabic from the corridor. A growing dread in his throat, like he was going to be sick. Eventually, someone told him what had happened, a small man with a luxuriant black moustache and a sand-coloured uniform, and nothing had ever been the same since.

Outside, the slam of a door made him jump. The officers passed by every so often to look at him, make sure he wasn't killing himself. A flash of eyes through the glass insert in his door. Tim lay on the bunk, raised a half-hearted salute. He wasn't killing himself, not that he hadn't thought about it before. He had to figure out what was going on, and that alone was giving him strength.

Mary

'Please be careful. That's really valuable.'

The white-suited figure – impossible to tell if it was a man or a woman – turned its head to her, then set down the blue glass vase Mary had bought in Venice once. It wasn't actually that valuable, she was just trying to retain some control over what her life had become. The fact that, at 2 p.m. on a weekday, her flat was being searched by CSI techs, under the supervision of Diana Mendes, who now came through the front door.

'Is there a problem, Mary?'

'Um, it's just – I hope you won't break anything.'

She shot Mary a look. The search was entirely voluntary, to see whether Tim might possibly have stashed anything in their flat, but Mary got the distinct impression her servile cooperation was the only reason she hadn't been arrested yet. She'd shown them her mattress pictures, but they clearly had no interest in Cliveden Road, its possible secrets.

'Perhaps you should wait outside, as we suggested. Or go to the park?'

She was never out of that bloody park.

'Alright. I'll get the kids.'

They were upstairs, supposedly napping, but fat chance of that with a forensics team pulling the house apart. She climbed the stairs wearily, to find Leo hot and wet, and Audrey hot and grouchy. Cleaned them up in the bathroom, led them downstairs, Audrey asking over and over who these people were, Mummy?

'They're just . . . looking for something. Like a game.'

Some game. And would they find anything – was it possible Tim actually had hidden evidence in her house? No, that was insane.

She was just strapping on Audrey's shoes outside, with great protest, and manoeuvring Leo into the buggy, when she heard a commotion from inside the flat. Oh God. What had they found? A few moments later, Diana Mendes opened the door. Mary was aware of how vulnerable she was, standing outside her own home, one child clinging to her neck and one glued to her leg.

'Mary. Can you identify something for us?' Wearing gloves, the detective then held up something Mary recognised, but which it took her a few moments to place. A bag, pink peeling pleather. 'This was in your hall closet.'

Samantha's bag. She couldn't believe it. Tim really had brought it round, and Mary had taken his word that he'd found it at the nursing home, and he really had left it at her flat. She'd shoved it in the hall cupboard, failed to give it to the police when she should have, and a thrill of fear went through her at the realisation that she had hidden evidence about the case, evidence that would surely have Samantha's DNA all over it. And the worst part was she had known full well it was there, and forgotten all about it.

◆ ◆ ◆

Jack came home many hours later, as she was forcing baked beans into the children, both coated in tomato sauce. She heard his weary tread, the way he cleared his throat as he took off his shoes. Things had been strained between them since the other day, and no wonder – his wife had been questioned by police after helping a virtual stranger, now suspected of kidnap and maybe murder. What was she doing? She'd lost her wits entirely perhaps, after two years of no sleep.

'What's wrong?' he said, coming in and putting down his man satchel. 'The pictures are all askew.'

'Um . . . the police were here. They asked if they could search the place. Voluntarily. I thought I'd better say yes.'

'Alright.' He looked around him at the disarray she hadn't had time to tidy, trying to assimilate. 'But . . . it was OK? They wouldn't have found anything.'

'Eh . . . they did, actually.' She couldn't meet his eyes, focusing instead on the red ring around Leo's mouth.

Jack was beside her in a moment, taking the spoon from her. 'Your hand's shaking, you're going to hurt him. Tell me what happened.'

So she told him how Tim had brought the bag over, and left it with her, and she'd put it into the hall cupboard.

'In our home.'

Mary nodded miserably. 'Well, yes. I didn't think anything of it.'

'You knew it belonged to a missing girl, and you didn't think anything bad would come of it?'

'I'm sorry,' said Mary, close to tears. 'I've made a real mess of this.'

'What was in it – did you look?'

'Outfits,' she mumbled.

'Outfits?' This was her husband, the man she'd made two kids with. Why did it feel so hard to talk about sex with him?

'Yeah, like . . . sexy ones. Dressing-up.'

'Christ.'

Audrey was already looking up from her beans, red-faced and avid with curiosity.

202

Why had she ever got involved in this? In the documentaries she watched, the crimes were always solved by plucky civilians on the right track, spotting the clues the police had missed. No one ever mentioned that when you let yourself brush up against dark things, they left indelible marks.

'Mary.'

'What?'

'Look at me.' She turned, reluctantly. 'This is serious. You know that, don't you? Your friend's facing big charges – kidnap, maybe murder even. And you've helped him – that's a crime too. Also, this man you basically accused of taking her, Eric Johnson? His firm's a client of ours. The reason I know this is because my boss called me in earlier and told me I should warn you to back off. You could be accused of defamation, and a man like that doesn't hesitate to sue. Did you even think about the impact of what you're doing? For God's sake, you'll be fired if you get convicted – maybe even if you're arrested. We'll lose the flat, maybe. This is bad, very bad.'

Tears were once again slipping down her face. 'What can I do? I know I made a mistake.'

'For God's sake just – stop! Tell the police everything you know. Stop trying to protect this Tim – he isn't worth it, and now it's your own family on the line.'

Tim

He was woken by the key in the door of his cell – so he had slept, at least, though he didn't know how long for. The custody sergeant was a friendly, overweight man who'd been kind to Tim throughout. In the olden days Tim would have tried to get him onside with a chat about football – he'd guess Crystal Palace, or West Ham, in this area – but he was too dispirited, out of the loop of normal life.

'On you come, fella.'

He followed, bleary-eyed and aware he smelled. He'd been able to take just one shower in all this time, with the kind of cheap soap he remembered from childhood. The glamorous detective, not a hair out of place, was waiting for him in the same stale interview room.

'Hi, Tim.'

'Hi.' He was too exhausted to be hostile.

She slid a picture across the table to him. 'Recognise this?'

Tim peered at the shot, marked with an evidence number. It was a pink holdall, shabby round the edges. Samantha's bag, the one he'd left at Mary's house when he'd panicked and run that day.

'Um . . .'

'It's Samantha's bag, isn't? Her prints are on the webcam, and she's wearing these outfits in her pictures on Little Secrets.'

'Yes. But . . .' How to explain why he had this?

'It's got your fingerprints all over it too, Tim.'

He raised his head, feeling weighed down with hopelessness. Of course they would charge him now. They had more than enough evidence.

'Did you get this from Mary?' he mumbled.

'She says you left it at her flat, yes.'

Tim stared at the grain of the table. Mary had betrayed him. She'd given them the piece of evidence that would now convict him, instead of leading them to Samantha, as he had hoped.

'I . . .'

His voice sounded hoarse, used up. How to even explain he'd been given this by Lena at the home? Would she want to give a statement? Somehow, the weight of knowing Mary had given up on him made him unable to say a word in his defence.

Diana Mendes moved the picture aside. 'Here's what's going to happen now, Tim. We're going to get your solicitor back in, and I'm going to formally interview you about this bag, how you came to have it in your possession. And you better hope that your answers make sense to me, because so far nothing else does.'

Tim continued to stare at the table. It was over. The interview was just a formality. He'd definitely be charged, then taken to remand. He wouldn't be back out in the air again, or in his little flat. There was no hope for him – no matter what, he would be punished, but not for the things he'd actually done. In a way, it was almost like he'd expected it.

Mary

Tim had been charged. Kidnap, which was the official name of the crime. His lawyer called early the next morning, as a courtesy, and Mary thanked her, standing in the kitchen unable to feel her legs. She'd known this would likely happen when they took the bag away the day before, but it was still a shock.

'Um – is there a chance I could face charges too?'

She'd helped him, if he was guilty. Harboured evidence. They might say she was an accomplice.

'It hasn't been mentioned.' The young woman, who probably had a dozen cases to juggle, sounded harassed. 'I really have to go.'

'Wait! Can I just ask, did Tim ever give any explanation for what happened – her being in the car?' She had to know if there was some answer, some excuse.

A sigh. 'He says Samantha turned up at his door and asked him to drive her home.'

'Oh! Well, that kind of makes sense?'

Did it? Mary couldn't tell any more.

'But she never arrived home. So, you know.'

'Yeah. Right, thank you.' Mary hung up and stood in the kitchen for a moment. Was this it, the moment she gave up on Tim? Left him to his fate? It would be so easy to stop all this, win back Jack's trust, take care of her neglected children. But no, even as she ran through it in her mind, she knew she wasn't done yet, and was already going into her WhatsApp to once again find someone to take her kids.

◆ ◆ ◆

The house – and it was a proper house, with lavender paint on the door and window frames, a paved front garden with plants in pots and neat recycling bins – was on a road Mary knew was in the highest council tax band in the area, having fantasy-searched for properties there on many a boring afternoon. So Tim had not always been the resident of a dingy basement flat, he'd once lived here.

Mary girded herself to go and ring the bell. It was most unlike her, all this forcing her way into places. She'd have been outraged if someone came to her door with no warning, and yet here she was, doing it to others. She so desperately wished she could talk to Tim, and find out his full explanation for having Samantha in his car. But since that wasn't possible, she was going to talk to someone she had not previously known existed – his estranged wife, Alice.

Alice would give him a character witness, maybe. Tell the police he could not possibly abduct a girl and hold her hostage. Mary hadn't even known Tim was divorced until she googled him the night before – she'd really known embarrassingly little about him, and had not even thought to look him up. Yet here she was, still running around trying to help him. She'd even left her kids with Alana, pretending she had a dentist appointment, and had to endure a lecture about flossing. She hoped Jack didn't find out. He'd gone back to work today, things still difficult between them. Maybe they would never get past this.

The paint around the door was very clean, recently redone, and even the bell shone. Someone who lived here stayed on top of things. Like Mary once had. She rang it. A few moments passed, then she heard the swell of approaching footsteps, and a woman answered it, wearing yoga leggings and a vest top, her red hair knotted on top of her head. She looked down at Mary's hands, as if expecting her to drop off a package.

'Hi,' said Mary. She swallowed. 'Are you Alice?'

'Yes?'

Alice Martin. She'd either never taken Tim's name, or gone back to her own. But either way, this was his wife, ex-wife.

'I'm Mary. I – I'm a friend of your husband's – Tim.'

Alice stood poised for a moment, her hand on the door, not shutting it in Mary's face, but not letting her in either. 'Oh?'

'Yes, well, more of a neighbour really. He's in trouble, Alice – he's been arrested. Charged with something, actually. Can I come in?'

Again, Alice thought about it. Then she sighed and stood back. 'Alright.'

Mary was ushered into the front room of someone who clearly did not have children. It was so clean, no dust along the picture frames or smudged fingerprints on the shiny bases of the lamps. Lots of draped throws and cushions in a stiff, shiny fabric that looked uncomfortable. Alice went out, then came back with a glass of water, which she placed on a small table, on a coaster, by Mary's knees. She hadn't offered anything else, or indeed asked if this was wanted.

'Thank you,' said Mary.

Alice perched on the arm of the opposite sofa. Mary wasn't sure if she'd just come back from exercise – she didn't look sweaty – or if she dressed like this all the time, ready at the drop of a hat to break into a Zumba routine or downward-facing dog.

'So what's he done?'

'Um, well, nothing, I don't think. There's been a bit of a . . . misunderstanding.'

As best she could, Mary explained the story so far. How they thought they'd seen Samantha in the house, and started investigating it, but now this strange bit of door-cam footage, Tim apparently driving the girl somewhere. Alice did not react throughout.

'I thought he'd given up work,' was all she said when Mary had finished.

'He's off sick, I think. But – it seemed to energise him. He was working on the story.'

'Oh yes. He always did like to play the rescuer.' Alice was fiddling with her nails, pushing down the cuticles. They were buffed and shiny, shaped in perfect ovals. Mary fought the urge to hide her own raggedy ones. 'So what do you think I can do about it?'

'Well, I know he's had some troubles in the past. He didn't tell me all of it, but I know he doesn't sleep. And the police think, I don't know, he might have done this and convinced himself he didn't? Hallucinated taking her home and dropping her off? Or he's just lying, I guess.'

The woman met her gaze square on. 'You believe he's innocent?'

'Yes.' Mary quailed. 'I think so, but . . .'

'But?'

'It's just so strange. It makes no sense. So maybe he is, you know . . .'

'Hallucinating?'

'Yeah.'

Alice nodded. 'He has before. When he came back from Syria. He told you about that?'

'Not really. I know something happened to him, he was caught in a bomb attack?' She'd seen it online – Tim even had his own Wikipedia page, a fact that had impressed Mary despite the situation he was now in.

'A drone strike, took out the hotel he was staying at. He was lucky enough, missed the worst of it. Seven people died. There was a woman with him, his translator. A local woman – Mariam. Tim had been having an affair with her, and she died because of it.'

Mariam. Almost like her own name. In a rush, she saw it all. This woman Mariam was killed in the attack, and Tim had survivor's guilt as well as PTSD, so he didn't sleep, and sometimes he imagined things. Oh, poor Tim.

'How awful for him. He must feel so guilty, if she died and he lived.'

Alice sighed deeply. 'I could have done without dredging all that up again, but you see, Mary, Tim's very damaged. And he's capable of lying. Mariam was by no means the first – just the first he was serious about. When you came to the door, it reminded me. More than once I had a woman on the phone or ringing my bell, asking me to give him up.'

'Oh.'

That explained why she seemed so unsympathetic to his plight. And was that a bad sign, if his ex-wife felt nothing for him, no care or concern? The Tim she knew, kind and gentle and broken, this was not him at all. He was a total stranger to her, she saw that now.

'I'm sorry he's in trouble. But I can't get involved.'

'You could tell them—'

'What, that Tim doesn't lie? He does. That he wouldn't hurt a woman? I don't know that for sure. Let me show you something.' She took her phone from the pocket of her leggings and scrolled through it. 'There.'

Mary looked at the screen. It was Alice, in too-bright lighting, her pretty face a mess of bruises, purple and yellow, her eye swollen shut. The date mark was a year before. She'd taken it for proof, maybe, for evidence. Mary didn't want to think about what that meant. Her stomach flipped over.

'He—'

'He didn't mean to. He was dreaming, a nightmare about the attack, and I went to wake him up. We had tried again, after the Mariam thing – well, he was so broken I could hardly kick him out. But you see, I can't rule out that he would hurt someone. In his right mind, he wouldn't. But he hasn't been in his right mind for a long time.'

'Oh my God.' Mary wanted to lean forward and put her head between her knees. 'I'm so sorry, Alice. I had no idea. I just – I wanted to help him. We got each other involved in this, this, wild goose chase.'

Her mind was spinning. What if it had all been a lie? What if Tim was convinced Samantha was in that house because *he'd* been keeping her there? It was empty, after all. Perhaps he'd found a way in. And once the police knew about the house, he'd moved her somewhere else. She felt sick.

'My suggestion is, you help the police. If you have some kind of rapport with Tim, and you think this girl might be alive, try to talk to him. Maybe he'll tell you where she is.'

She still couldn't believe it. 'You honestly think he would do this, kidnap a girl and lie about it, trick me and the police and even himself? Your husband?'

Alice stood up, as if drawing a line under the conversation. 'Ex-husband. Do we really know what anyone's capable of, even ourselves? You know, a friend told me she saw him in my local park last week. Sort of loitering in the bushes. That seemed weird, since last I heard he was living a few miles away, so when I went for my run the other day, I kept an eye out, and it was him. Hiding behind some trees, watching me. And he was outside the house one day last week as well. I pretended I didn't see him, but it's weird, right? I don't want to say stalking, as such, but . . . that's who he is now. He's broken. Neither you nor I can fix him.'

Mary realised she had no choice but to leave then, slinging her bag over her shoulder. On the way out, she saw a man had come downstairs and was hovering in the kitchen, doing something with a blender. He looked younger than Alice, broad about the chest and arms. A gym guy, like Jackson Ryan. His hair was wet.

'Alright?'

'Fine,' said Alice crisply. 'I'm going to the gym in ten, if you want to come.'

This was her life now, exercise classes and smoothies and handsome younger men. She had moved on from Tim, and Mary could not blame her.

'I'm sorry,' she said, not really knowing what she was apologising for.

Alice held the door for a second before she shut it. 'I'm glad you're helping him,' she said. 'I'm glad he still has a friend. But really, Mary, some people can't be helped. All they do is drag you down with them.'

She closed the door, leaving Mary face to face with the shiny knocker and fresh paint.

Tim

The first sensation was a mouth full of dust. The skeleton of the building, the inner workings that should never have seen the light of day, coating his tongue and teeth with grit. He felt it cover his face, clinging to him. His immediate panic was that he couldn't breathe, something was weighing on his chest and he couldn't force air in – but then he shifted and something eased and he could. The air he sucked in was full of dirt, making him cough, but he could breathe at least and so would not die in the next few minutes.

The building had collapsed. A bomb, his brain told him. Happened all the time. Aerial strike, most likely. Mariam had been a pace ahead of him as they passed through the door. The lintel had perhaps protected him a little. He'd been letting her go first, chivalrous. But where was she? He tried to call out, but his voice seemed stuck in his throat.

'Mariam?'

He realised his ears had blown, and all he could hear was a dull ringing inside his own head. He tried to move a hand and felt a cascade of masonry. How much was on top of him? He could see nothing but black, the sensation of stone almost pressed to his face, a few small pockets of air allowing him to draw in breath. The random fall of debris, the scatter of atoms, a burst of pressure here or there, this was all that had saved him. A strange euphoria spread from his chest, despite the pain and weight there. He couldn't feel his legs at all. All the same, he had survived. He would take this as a sign, a badge of honour, a fallen soldier in the field. He would change his life. Tell Alice they couldn't go on like this. Choose one life – out here, doing the work, with Mariam – or another, back home in safe London, with coffees in the park and the occasional trip to see West End musicals and eat mediocre Chinese food. Not carry on this double existence, where no one was really happy with him, not his wife or his lover.

But he had to find her first.

'Mariam?' A small voice escaped him. 'Mariam?'

Nothing but the ringing, and in the distance, voices shouting. Men. Not her. The sound of scrabbling, and soon a chink of light opened up. They were digging him out. Oh, thank God.

Tim had once reported on an earthquake in Peru where people were dragged from the rubble after three days, four. A frantic search, knowing the minutes were ticking away, that there would come a point when they'd look at each other and realise now they were just searching for corpses. He'd been lucky. He was alive and they were already digging for him.

Perhaps it was just this building that had fallen, not the whole street. It made sense to target a hotel. Strange flotsam from what had been the lobby lay around him, polished marble and the soil of a pot plant and a bit of brass rail. Had there been other people? He couldn't remember what he'd seen in that instant of entering before the world collapsed – the reception staff, of course. A few guests. He tried not to think what had happened to them.

The chink of light widened. A glitter on everything, broken glass from the windows. Thankfully they'd been replaced the year before with shatterproof, so disintegrated into harmless diamonds instead of chunks that flew through the air and impaled into skin, eyes, throats. He felt something brush his face – the robes of the man digging. A glimpse of his eyes and a dark beard. Tim lay helpless, unable to move his arms, his face gradually exposed to the light. The relief was almost crippling. He was alright. He would be alright. Other men were working at his body, scooping his limbs free, and he could see now he was whole, one foot twisted in an unnatural angle. That was OK. Feet could be fixed.

They had him out now, a small cascade of rubble falling from his body, his trousers and jacket white with dust. They lifted him to a stretcher, and he was impressed they'd got there so fast, in a country like this that was barely held together. Perhaps they worked harder for the Westerners.

On another stretcher, something lay crumpled. He saw that it was her. Mariam. She was whole too, her eyes closed and face as pale as the broken walls around them. Was she breathing? She looked in pain, which must mean she was alive. They placed him beside her on the pocked ground of the street – somewhere near his ear, he could hear rushing water – and he willed his hand to move towards her. Was she alive? If she was alive that was his choice made. He promised it in the moment, lying on the street with the sky white and hot above him, his eyes shut, his body flaring into painful life. He promised it to her and to the universe, though she could not know. His arm crept away from his body, groped along the concrete then found the rough fabric of her stretcher. The robe she put on when they went out, though underneath she wore jeans and T-shirts, hugging her body, her hair long and shiny. His fingers found hers, ice-cold and dusty. He squeezed as much as he could. *Please be alive, please.*

'Mr Darbandi. Mr Darbandi!'

Tim started awake, from where he'd dozed off on the bed, plastic mattress and no blanket. Strange, but the shock of arrest had somehow reset his brain, and he found he was sleeping all the time in the police station. But here was the custody sergeant again at his door. Tim's heart juddered in his chest. He could tell things were bad for him. It was something in the way the man, previously friendly, wouldn't meet his eyes. They were here now, to take him away to prison, hold him until his trial. For kidnap. He hadn't done it, but he'd been charged all the same, and this was all going wrong, but Tim was powerless to stop it. He simply had to accept his fate.

'They're ready for you. Come on.'

Tim tried to wrench himself back to the here and now. He was not in Syria, buried under rubble. Instead he was here and Mariam was dead and he was in more trouble than he'd ever been before.

Samantha

Sleep. That was all there was to do in this place, and Sam had never been good at that. She didn't understand how people could just drift off. Like it was so easy, like falling off something and then you woke up and you felt good. It had never been that way for her. She had a memory of being really little, two or three, and standing up in her cot howling for her mum, just because she was bored. Her mum coming in, frazzled, smelling of smoke and vodka. *Jesus Christ, Samantha. What is it now?* Then when John arrived on the scene, and later Marlee came along, it was all about what a good sleeper she was, *not like this one*, with a head-jerk at Samantha. As if Marlee would have dared do anything else, being John's daughter. Things changed when he moved in. Yes, it had been a bit chaotic before that, dinner sometimes a cupcake in front of the TV, staying up till midnight watching Disney films, wearing party dresses to school. Her real dad flitting in and out of her life, sometimes sparkling and fun, sometimes broken and shaking in rehab, making Mum cry. But sometimes Mum was fun too, and dreamy, and if she cried at night, she was usually smiling over breakfast. With John it was all rules and regulations, no sweets during the week, bedtime at six – six!

Samantha had been sharing a room with Marlee since she was seven, and her sister was the most silent, still sleeper in the world, to the point where Sam sometimes crept across the room to shake her, listen for her breath. But she wasn't dead, she was just peaceful. Samantha had no idea what that was like. Even if she did sleep, she'd wake up with the sheets twisted about her like a snake, hot and then cold and hot again. *We're not like other people*, her dad had said, when she last saw him, which was almost ten years ago now. *We're night people, you and me.* Not the clear-eyed, up-at-seven-and-on-with-the-day type. But she was forced into that life, living at home, having to work in the care home at all hours. Nineteen and sleeping in a single bed – nowhere to go even if she did want to lose her virginity. She'd never told anyone she was still a virgin, even Shell; it was just too embarrassing. But Jackson lived with his mum too, and she was always banging on the door asking did they want tea, and neither of them had a car, and they couldn't afford a hotel, and she wasn't doing it behind the bushes in the park like so many of their friends, so eventually they'd split up. No, she had to get her own place. So she'd made the choices she'd made, and here she was. Trapped.

So far, in her time here, she had tried and exhausted several escape routes. She'd tried smashing the window by throwing things – nothing to break it with, no sharp or heavy small items in the place. The pot he'd left for heating water was too flimsy, and the cutlery was all plastic. She supposed he had thought of that. Then she'd tried the one door, which looked flimsy, but he'd closed it from the outside with padlocks. That made her even angrier – what if there was a fire, would he just let her burn to death? So she couldn't get it open either. Next, she'd turned her attention to the old wooden-slatted walls – surely they couldn't be that strong? She had the idea she might be able to dig a hole, wiggle some of the boards out. But the only implements were the plastic cutlery he left for her to eat the cold, pre-packaged food he'd brought, and the fork had splintered and broken within seconds. It seemed crazy that she could be trapped in what appeared to be such a run-down little hut, but apparently she was.

The next plan had just been the random shouting and screaming, but if no one was nearby, who would hear? She had no idea where she was. It could be miles from anywhere. She'd been racking her brains to think if he'd said anything that could give a clue. She'd found a few old leaflets in a corner, and that, combined with the sinister murals of children splashing in a pool, made her think she was in some kind of holiday park. That was bad news, because it could be miles from anywhere – it explained the noise of the sea late at night, also. Who would stumble into a place like this? Teenage kids, dog walkers. But she knew enough to guess it was probably an abandoned site, locked up, with threatening signs about CCTV and dog patrols. There probably weren't any actual cameras or patrols, unfortunately for her.

So what was left? She had the idea to paste up a sign on the high window, saying HELP or GET ME OUT, but of course she lacked large bits of paper, or anything to write with, or Sellotape to put it up. Some of the food had come in a paper bag, so she'd saved that, and scribbled on it with the ketchup he'd brought in a little packet. It went everywhere, leaving her hands red and smelly, as if she'd killed someone. The writing was so smudgy no one would be able to read it unless they came right up close. She'd stuck it with some mashed potato made with boiling water on the stove, and the smell of red sauce and starch filled the place. The water was an idea though – she could perhaps throw it in his face as he came in. But it would take time to boil. He'd hardly wait patiently in the doorway as she put it on. Maybe she could pretend to make him a cup of tea, like she was cooperating, like she was being a nice and good girl, then throw it at him, duck out the door while he was howling in pain. Or stab him in the face with the plastic cutlery? Hit him with the saucepan, swing it hard? It would still hurt, enough to stop him in his tracks for a second, and that was all she'd need. Yes, that was an idea. A new plan. How many plans was that now? Six? She'd need the car keys – that would probably mean putting her hand into his pocket, an idea that gave her the creeps. Otherwise he'd come to and chase her and she had the disadvantage of not having a fucking clue where she was. She was fitter and younger, but she didn't much like the idea of running over waste ground or through a forest, especially as he'd taken her shoes.

She didn't really like to dwell on the fact that nothing had worked so far. She just had to keep going, forge ahead, try one thing and then another. Leave failure behind her, kick the dust of it from her heels. Everything that didn't work out was a road you didn't walk down, leading you to the one that was right for you. Above all she had to get out of this hut, and seeing as she had exhausted all her avenues for breaking out, she had only one thing left to her – talk her way out. After all, hadn't a teacher at school, Mrs Oliphant, a great big woman they all called Elephant, of course, once said *You could talk your way out of anything, Samantha Ellis*? She just had to hope old Elephant had been right.

Mary

Mary lurked outside the high-end boutique, sweating under her cotton T-shirt. God, she really wasn't cut out for this amateur detective lark. A middle-class mother was even more invisible than a little old lady like Miss Marple, and yet she still kept getting into scrapes. Still trying to help a virtual stranger, who she clearly knew next to nothing about. And why had she not given up? Done her best to protect herself and her family, left Tim to his fate? She didn't know. Maybe because she still felt Eric Johnson had a hand in this after all – why else would he be putting such pressure on Jack's boss? Or else she just wasn't ready to give up, admit she'd been wrong about Johnson, about Tim, about everything.

Instead of going home to rescue her kids from Alana, she had driven to Barnes, an area she didn't know well, and parked in a very expensive car park. There was nothing on the radio news about Tim being charged, but she knew it would likely be announced soon, and he could be named at this stage. Then everyone would know, and his disgrace would be complete, and so she was here, in a last-ditch attempt to save him. Distracted as she was, she was still impressed by how nice it was; cute shops and cafés with pastel-striped awnings, brightly painted houses, neat flowerbeds. She found a boutique called Pretty Little Things and stopped outside. It was fine. It was just a shop. She was allowed to be there.

Inside was filled with beautiful things – candles, draped scarves, those expensive matches in little bottles, cardigans and print dresses and adorable kids' shoes . . . Mary suddenly remembered she wasn't here to shop.

'Can I help you?'

Behind the counter, a woman was tying handwritten price tags on to a tray of gold earrings. She was tall and dark, wavy shiny hair, in a dress from her own collection. Annabella Johnson, owner of the boutique. Wife, soon to be divorced, of Eric Johnson. Mary recognised her from her Instagram account, which she'd been discreetly directed to by Melia.

'I'm OK. You have so many nice things.'

'Thank you. Feel free to browse.'

The place even smelled nice, a sweet woody scent emanating from the diffuser on the side, sold for £49.99. Mary would have liked to live in this shop, far away from her own home which usually smelled of porridge and bodily fluids. She'd better buy something to maintain her cover. Those dinosaur dungarees would be so cute on Leo, and Audrey would love the sparkly shoes. She put them on the counter and, with a smile, Annabella began to wrap them in tissue.

'So cute, these.'

'I know. Do you have children?' Mary asked.

'No.'

That was something. She couldn't bear to think of that man, so suave and powerful, who'd maybe abducted Samantha, also being a father. God, she had to say something, otherwise she'd come all this way for an expensive shopping trip.

'Listen, I – my name is Mary. I met your husband last week.'

Instantly, the woman stiffened. 'We're in the middle of a divorce.'

'I know. I live near the house he's just bought – in South Kenborough?'

Annabella seemed angry, stabbing at the till. 'He owns a lot of houses, he's a property developer.'

'Please – I know this must seem very strange and rude, but I'm so worried. I've got a little girl, and a baby boy, and I saw something in that house that made me so afraid. There's a girl missing near me – you probably saw it on the news – and I think maybe she was there. I know he's your husband, but I think he might have *done* something. I really need your help.'

That got her attention. 'He won't be my husband much longer. I haven't seen him in months.'

'So you must know what I'm talking about then. He's capable of it, isn't he?' It was a gamble, since she didn't know the reasons for their divorce. They could be on perfectly amicable terms, but having met the man, Mary didn't think so.

Annabella thought about it for a moment, hand resting on the tiny dungarees. So innocent, so sweet. 'I could get into trouble if I talk to you . . . the divorce . . .'

'Oh, I know, I totally understand. But you'd do the same as me I'm sure, if you saw something that wasn't right. I'm just a normal person, a mother.' Mary wouldn't usually play the mother card, but she was getting desperate. 'You seem like a good person – I'm sure you would want to help.'

The woman closed her eyes for a second, then sighed. 'What do you think he's done?' And Mary knew her gamble had paid off.

A while later, Annabella had put up a 'Closed' sign on the door, and she and Mary were drinking from hand-thrown mugs, perched on stools. Annabella stocked a gin sampler in a pretty box, and she had torn one open and poured the tiny bottles out. Mary had never drunk neat gin before and was mostly pretending.

'It's been so hard. As soon as I said I wasn't happy, it was like he turned his whole weight against me, all his money, his influence. Why shouldn't I leave with some cash, for God's sake? He can afford it and God knows I put up with a lot over the years.'

'These powerful men, they think they can get away with anything,' Mary prompted. The reek of booze filled her nose, but Annabella was gulping hers down. A drink problem, maybe? Driven to it by her husband?

'Oh, you don't have to tell me that.'

'Did Eric – was he the kind of man who might use sex workers?' she faltered. 'I'm sorry to ask. It's just I thought I saw this girl in the house, you see. And she was doing . . . that kind of work.'

'All the time,' his wife said bitterly. 'Pay-per-view. Webcams. Strip clubs. And I'm sure a lot, lot more than that. I turned a blind eye as long as he didn't actually sleep with them. But it all got too much. Now he's desperate to hide the evidence, in case I take him to the cleaners in the divorce. I just want enough to be free of him.'

'Of course. You're entitled.' Mary was wondering how she could present this evidence to Diana Mendes – was there a way to prove Eric had spoken to Samantha online? Then arranged to meet her in person? 'Was there anything in particular he liked?'

The woman hesitated. 'He'd kill me if I told anyone.'

Kill me. Interesting choice of words.

'I know when he paid the girls, it wasn't for sex. Or at least not always.'

'Oh?'

She clammed up. 'Look, I don't really know. But if he paid her, it may not have been what you think, that's all.'

What else could it have been? Mary didn't understand.

'You mean . . .'

'I really can't say any more.' She set down the mug of gin and wiped her eyes. 'I'm just glad we never had children.'

'You didn't want them?'

'He didn't. Said his childhood had been too terrible.' Her shoulders heaved a little.

'You still could,' said Mary tentatively.

'I'm forty-one.'

'Well. It's not all it's cracked up to be, believe me. I haven't slept in years, and this morning my son peed on me.'

Annabella rubbed at her eyes, make-up still immaculate. 'Well, I've told you what I can. I don't know if that helps you at all.'

It did and it didn't. It proved what Mary suspected about Eric Johnson, but didn't do anything towards getting Tim out. 'Thank you. I'm so sorry to intrude on you.'

'I just hope she's safe, that poor girl. You've told the police you saw her there?'

'Oh yes. They're looking into it.' It was technically true.

'I suppose I could talk to them, if you think it would help – but I don't really *know* anything.' That was the problem. Mary had to somehow prove a link between Eric and Samantha, and since the girl still had not turned up, how was she going to do that?

Tim

When they'd said he was being charged, Tim's mind had seized up. Prison. The worst possible thing that could happen now, utter disgrace and ruin. His tentative bridge back to work landmined, blown up. Crazy Tim, and now he'd kidnapped a girl, and hadn't he basically killed a woman in Syria? What was the story there? No one would quite remember, but they'd know he'd done something bad. And he had, hadn't he? He didn't kill Mariam. But he'd caused her death all the same. And he'd hurt Alice, broken things between them in a way that could not be fixed.

He'd been terrified when they brought him here, in a metal pod in the back of the van, stinking of sweat and fear. As he was brought in, he'd seen the eyes of the other men flick to him, and been sure that they knew. He was the supposed abductor of a young woman – he'd have a bad time in prison, wouldn't he? It was only a matter of time before the press got his name. Once, it would have been him reporting it, hanging around the station badgering the press officer for a name, some information. Now he was the story. Now he was in a cell, with a proper bed this time, though narrow and hard, a high window of bubbled glass letting in some faint light. Four blank blue walls, a bare floor, a toilet and sink. This was it. This was his world now, maybe forever. How long did you get for kidnap – life? Maybe they could make a murder charge stick too, even without a body. The least he could hope for was ten years. He'd be almost sixty, assuming he could survive in here. People died all the time in prison, knifed in stairwells, hanging themselves from sheer despair. And what would be the point of going on if he were convicted of kidnapping a girl – he could never come back from that, never work again, never make things right with Alice. His life was as good as over.

Tim sat in the cell for hours, staring at the breakfast he'd been handed to eat in the morning. A brown banana, a stale pastry wrapped in plastic. Was this it now – he'd never enjoy a meal again? There must be a library in this place, classes of some kind. If he got convicted, maybe he could teach the other guys to read and write, find some purpose to life again. He would catch himself thinking these thoughts and try to stop. *He hadn't done it.* He was sure of it. Almost entirely sure. Yes, the insomnia muddled things. He'd seen things that weren't there. But the opposite wasn't true, was it – he hadn't forgotten things he really had done?

Aside from the blackouts, the lost time where he'd found himself in places he didn't remember going. But wouldn't he have remembered abducting a girl? And why would he then have tried so hard to find her? Tim probed his own motivations, recalling how much he'd wanted to get inside that house and save Samantha. Was that his guilty conscience, knowing he'd taken her? Had he somehow got into the house and put her there? No. No, he had to believe it wasn't true. He'd dropped her off at her family's home, or at least very near, round the bend of the cul-de-sac. Where had she gone after that?

A shout went up somewhere in the building, and Tim tensed, listening to the sound of running feet, jangling keys. He'd always thought he was tough, travelling to war zones, roughing it. But the truth was he'd been soft. He could not survive in here long, and he knew it. He lay back on the uncomfortable bed and waited for a sleep that once again didn't come.

Mary

When Jack came home from work that night, he found her sitting at the kitchen table, head in her hands. She'd been there for hours, surfing the internet, turning the facts over and over in her head, adding up the evidence against Eric Johnson and finding him neither entirely innocent nor entirely guilty. There was a vigil planned for Samantha on Wimbledon Common; various celebrities had appealed for information on the case. The mood increasingly sombre, as people concluded she must be dead.

'There's no dinner, before you ask,' Mary said.

'OK. Anything to cook with?'

'Nope.'

'I see.'

'Tim's been charged,' she mumbled. 'It was the stupid bag. They used it, his prints on her stuff, to trap him.' It had been on the six o'clock news, his name and his picture, an old still of him reporting from some war zone, sand and guns in the background. Jack would see it soon, so she had to tell him.

Jack gaped, putting down his satchel. 'What about you, will you be charged?'

She'd likely lose her job if so.

'I don't know. They think I'm some idiot who's been duped by him. Better that than his accomplice, I guess.' He said nothing for a moment. 'What?'

'Mary . . . if they've charged him, that means they're sure he did it.'

'I know, but . . .'

'No, listen. You have to stop this. Stop leaving the kids, stop running about, stop helping this guy. He probably took this girl. And you've been helping him! You'll be lucky if you don't get done for it yourself. And our kids, your job, our life . . . is it really worth risking all that, for some weirdo you met in the park?'

No. It wasn't. Mary put her head in her hands. 'I know. You're right. I'll stop now.'

Jack picked his bag up again, his burst of anger abated. 'I'll take the kids to the supermarket. You need a bit of time, obviously. But when I come back I don't want to hear another word about this bloody man.'

After he went, Audrey loudly protesting it wasn't time for the shops, it was time for Peppa, and Leo's bewildered eyes peeking out from a sling – probably wondering who this strange man was taking him away from his mother – she found she couldn't get up from the table. Jack would be at least an hour with the kids at the supermarket – he'd no idea of the absolute obstacle course he'd volunteered for, Audrey no doubt screaming on the ground until she got a ride in the Thomas train, Leo perhaps being sick inside his sleep suit. She felt a surge of gratitude that he was trying. He was really trying, and she had to try too, claw herself back to being a competent wife and mother. There was laundry to do, dishes to clear, and the house was filthy. But Tim had been charged. He would be in prison now, on remand. And it was all her fault. And still they were no closer to finding Sam – assuming she still believed Tim – which meant the girl was being held by someone else. Maybe the same person who'd taken four other girls from the area, over the years. But maybe, just maybe, it was more likely that the person charged with her kidnap was the one who'd abducted her. That the police were right and Mary was very wrong. Had she, by trying to help, actually made things worse?

She was so despondent she sat there until the doorbell rang. Distracted, expecting yet another Amazon delivery of exercise gear for Jack, she went to answer, and on her doorstep was Eric Johnson.

Mary froze, wishing she'd thought to use the chain on the door. He was a strong man, he'd easily be able to push it in.

'What do you—'

'I need to talk to you.'

Why had he come – did he know she'd seen his wife earlier? Was he trying to shut her up? God, why had she sent Jack away? Why hadn't she bolted the door? Why was she such an idiot?

'I'm not going to hurt you,' he said impatiently. 'But this is getting out of hand. I want to tell you the truth.'

'The truth?'

'About Sam. About where she was all this time.'

Mary let him in, of course. He had a force of personality she wasn't equal to, and after all of this, she couldn't resist finding out what he really knew.

'How did you know where I live?' she said to the man she suspected of abduction and maybe murder. Her eyes flicked around the room, wondering what she could do if he lunged at her. Would he really try that, in her own home? There were knives in the kitchen, a heavy and ugly vase, also from Jack's mother, by the fireplace.

Eric Johnson stood awkwardly in her living room, twirling his keys. He drove a Jaguar, she noticed.

'We do some work with your husband's firm. I said it was an emergency.'

She could have been cross with the violation, but then she'd turned up at his office and buttonholed him, and probed his wife for information. She folded her arms, not asking him to sit down, trying to seem strong.

'You've been talking to my wife,' he said.

She was very aware of the space between them, no more than ten paces. What could she even do if he came at her? She edged away, towards the kitchen and the knives.

'I couldn't think what else to try. My friend's facing prison, and I know he didn't do it.' Did she? She was almost sure. A treacherous snake of doubt slunk about in her brain. 'I know you pay for girls to . . . do things. And Sam was doing that kind of work. She was there in your house. I know she was, I saw her.'

'Yes. She was there.' For a moment, Mary didn't believe he'd said it. 'She stayed for two weeks nearly. But you had it all wrong. She *wanted* to be there! She needed a place. The money from her webcam stuff was good, but she'd nowhere to film it. Obviously she couldn't do it at home, with her family there, and she got caught at work, and they fired her.' That explained the bag of clothes Tim had found, and fitted with what Lena had told him.

'It looked like she was being strangled – I saw it! I knew I saw it!' But somehow she'd almost convinced herself she was crazy, seeing things. But that didn't mean she was wrong.

Eric sighed. 'My mother was killed in that room. I was seven. I came back from school to find her gasping for breath, clutching her throat, I . . . it was too late to save her, but she was still alive. She was . . . thrashing. She'd fought him as hard as she could. There was blood everywhere, all up the walls, the floor . . . I couldn't save her. And the worst thing is, I saw the man leave – he brushed past me in the hallway – and I didn't remember a thing about him. He's still out there, for all I know.'

Mary was wrong-footed by his honesty. 'Well . . . I'm sorry, but . . .'

'So I bought the house where it happened, as you know. I want to solve this, and catch the guy, if he's still alive. Put him behind bars at last.' He caught her confused look. 'I don't expect you to understand, but I hoped there might be some clue in the house. Or a way to jog my memory, let me see the man's face. When I got talking to Sam online, she said she needed a place to stay, and I saw a chance. I let her stay there in return for acting out the scene a few times.' Mary was still gaping. 'I didn't hurt her. She just . . . she looks a bit like my mother. So we set the scene up like it happened then, the gasping, a knife left behind, me in the corridor . . . I just hoped maybe I'd remember. I'd been trying to buy the house for years, but the owner was a bit cracked, lived in Australia, didn't care the place was falling down. When he died it came on the market and I saw my chance to solve this thing. I've been pulling the place apart, looking for some kind of evidence. And then you came along, shouting about how you'd seen her in the house getting attacked. I didn't want it coming out in the press. It's perfectly legal, but you know how people are. They judge. And I'm going through a very expensive divorce – I can't afford to have it come out now.'

Mary felt like she was losing her mind. Sam had been there voluntarily, and what she'd seen was just the re-enactment of an old murder? To try and solve it?

'But – I watched the door-cam footage for that week and there was no sign of her going in and out – how did you do it?'

His gaze shifted. 'I have a key to the back door, into the park. And we only did it at night – I didn't want people seeing and talking. Well, you've proved what a risk that was.'

'And why are you here now – did Samantha get in touch?' That would be such a relief, Samantha turning up safe and sound, Tim cleared of all charges, life back to normal. Even though it would never be quite the same, after all this.

He shook his head. 'That's why I came. I haven't been able to get hold of her for days, and I'm worried. She really is missing this time, I'm sure of it. But I don't know why.'

'Tim didn't do it,' said Mary fiercely. 'He's been in a cell most of the week.'

'I know, I know. I never thought he did. I was just protecting myself, you understand that, don't you?'

'So what – you set him up?'

He nodded reluctantly. 'That guy across the street. With the camera.'

'Nigel?'

'Yeah. He's been making trouble since I bought the place – lodging complaint after complaint, I don't know what his problem is. I knew he had his camera on all the time, filming everything I got up to. So if your friend drove down that street with Samantha in the car, Nigel would pick it up, and probably send it to the police. Classic busybody.'

Fury boiled in Mary's blood, so much that she caught her breath. 'So . . . you made the police think Tim was some kidnapping crackpot. And me, a crazy sleepless mother who was seeing things. I might have been charged too – I've got little kids! You threatened my husband's job, even! You came to my house! And, worst of all, it's delayed finding out Sam is missing for real now.'

He sighed again, and Mary could see he was genuinely worried, dark circles under his piercing eyes, stubble on his chin.

'Look, I'm sorry about what happened. I felt threatened, and I took action. She agreed to it – she was supposed to ask your friend to drive her somewhere, then we'd have him on camera, and her prints in his car and flat, her DNA.'

She couldn't follow. 'But . . . *why?*'

'I know who he is, your friend. He's brought down several friends of mine over the years, with his stories. Ministers, CEOs – powerful people. I didn't want the same to happen to me. I hoped that being arrested would stop him digging into me, distract the police for a few days – I never thought he'd be *charged*, for God's sake. I didn't know they had other evidence.'

The bag. Mary's fault, that one.

'So where was Sam supposed to be?'

'She was meant to lie low for a few days in a hotel – I gave her money – then pop up and say she was fine, all a misunderstanding, just let Tim sweat for a while in custody. But she never did, and I don't know why.'

'She asked him to drive her home, he said. To her family's house.'

He ran his hands over his face. 'Look, I don't know what to tell you. Obviously that wasn't the plan. I don't know why she went there, or where she is now. So that's why I'm here. I want to help. I'm going to tell the police the truth. That yes, she was staying at my house last week, but consensually. I can show them the texts where we arranged it.'

She gaped at him. 'You'd really do that?'

Eric rubbed his hands over his face again. She saw suddenly that he was attractive as well as rich. He could have everything, if only he could get past what had happened to him as a child.

'You might not believe this, but I don't want your friend rotting in jail for something he didn't do. And I care about Sam. Someone really has taken her now, I think. And someone killed my mother. And you said there were other girls who'd gone missing

234

round here. So – what if it's the same person? Taking girls, and now he's taken Sam?'

Mary blinked. His mother's death seemed so long ago, but if it was only forty years, the killer could easily be living in the area. It could be anyone she passed on the street, sat beside in the park café, stood behind in the queue at the Co-op. A murderer hiding in plain sight for decades. Was that who had Samantha? But how did that fit with Tim driving her home – where had she gone after that?

'So – what do we do?'

'I'm going to let the police search the house. A proper forensic search this time. And they can dig up the garden if they want, I didn't get around to that yet.' At this, Mary shivered. What if those missing girls were waiting beneath the grass of number sixteen? And Sam – she had actually been missing for three days now. What could have happened to her in that time?

'Won't you get in trouble?' He'd certainly misled the police, if not outright lied to them. Surely that was a crime?

'Probably. But it doesn't matter.'

'Alright,' she said. 'It might go some way to make up for what you did.'

Maybe if he confessed, the police would formally clear Tim. She worried it wouldn't be in time, though. He'd had so little to lose, and now even that had been taken from him. He might not survive in prison, even on remand. And then there'd be a trial, and his entire past would surely come out, and that might break him.

'I'm sorry. I really am – I never meant for this to happen. It just . . . spiralled.'

'You should be sorry. You've done more damage than you know. You—'

Just then, the key turned in the front door, and with a babble of voices, Jack came in trailing both children. Leo had been sick down the back of Jack's Hugo Boss coat and Audrey's face was coated in chocolate.

'Daddy, Thomas wasn't finished, he wasn't *finished*!' From her agitated tone, a war-crimes level injustice had been done.

'Yes, well, we couldn't stay all night, Audrey, could we, it's past your bedtime.' He finally looked up and saw Mary and Eric Johnson poised in the living room. 'Oh.'

'WHO THAT MAN?' said Audrey loudly, dashing in. Mary caught her arm and steered her to the wet wipes before she could touch anything. She met Jack's eyes, saw the same question there. She shrugged. Really, she had no idea what to say, or how to start explaining any of this.

Tim

Time seemed to lose all meaning in prison, under the constant glare of the lights, the sounds of banging and shouting all night long. His run of sleep in the police station had gone, and he was resigned that he might never feel rested again. For whatever remained of his life – but whenever he thought of that a jolt of fear sent him to his feet, pacing around the small cell. What could he do? Nothing from in here. He just had to hope someone on the outside was trying to find the truth. That the police would eventually believe him and let him go. He had the tiniest shred of hope that Mary might be working on his behalf – but why would she? She had too much to lose and, after all, she'd given them the bag that sealed his fate. Thinking about it, he didn't even blame her. He'd dragged her into this and she had to save herself, at least for those kids; their round, wondering eyes and tiny fingers. They needed their mother, and no one needed Tim.

Sometime later – he had no idea if it was morning or afternoon or evening, even – a guard unlocked his cell. A young man, muscled and strong.

'On you come.'

'Where am I going?'

Was he being released? He hardly dared to hope.

'Rec time.' Of course – he wouldn't be kept in his cell round the clock, that wasn't allowed, though he'd read that some prisons were so short-staffed you could be in there twenty-three hours a day. Breathing your own stale air, never seeing the sky. Tim followed the man down an echoing corridor to a large tatty room, with a pool table and some board games. Several men in grey tracksuits sat about at the chipped tables, many smoking. Tim could have worn his own clothes, being on remand, but he'd had no one to bring them.

He wasn't sure what he was supposed to do, so he wandered over to a shelf of torn paperbacks and pretended to look at them. As he crossed the room, he felt eyes on him, raising the hairs on his neck. Then he realised why – there on the table was one of today's papers, one that Tim had briefly written for in the late nineties, and his own face was on the cover. MAN CHARGED OVER MISSING SAM. So his name was out. He looked different now – it was an old shot, where he was clean-shaven and confident, but they must still know it was him.

Tim turned to the books, heart pounding in his ears. Every day he was in here things got worse and worse, and if he didn't get out soon, and clear his name, there would be nothing worth going back to.

Mary

Diana Mendes looked at the kids, her expression a mixture of distaste and grudging affection.

'You must have your hands full, with these two.'

Mary had dragged them with her to the police station first thing the next morning, and they were now in some kind of depressing family room with sticky toys and books. Eric Johnson was being interviewed in another room, hopefully confessing to everything. Jack had unbent somewhat now it was clear Tim had been set up, and hadn't even complained about her taking the kids with her today. He was 'working from home', though she suspected he wasn't getting much done, and that was her fault too. But it would all be OK if only the police let Tim go.

'You worked in law before this?' The judgement felt implicit.

'Yeah. Family law.' She still did work there, but didn't feel contradicting the police officer was wise just now.

Mendes said nothing, but the brief raise of her perfectly groomed eyebrows spoke volumes.

'You don't have kids,' said Mary. It wasn't really a question; the answer was obvious.

'Not planning to, no. I mean – it's everyone's choice. But it's hard to do both well, right?'

In the short silence afterwards, Mary felt the weight of that truth. She was trying to live two lives in the time given to one woman, and she was doing both badly. Not the perfect mother like Francine, who'd given herself over to it, and not the perfect career woman like this detective, or Alana who seemed to do both with aplomb. She was failing and her life had become untenable. She had only involved herself in this case, a wild goose chase for a girl who wasn't even missing, because she wanted to feel useful.

She stood and wiped a trail of drool from Leo's chin as he gnawed on a plastic block – she wondered when they were last cleaned. What poor kids would end up having to play with the toys in a police station? Well, her own just now.

'You're right,' she said. 'I'm in over my head. But Tim – I really don't think he did this. Eric told you the truth, didn't he?'

'He told us Samantha was safe in his house until four days ago. What I don't currently know is where she is now. Tim Darbandi was the last person seen with her.'

'Other girls have gone missing in the area though – four of them! Could it not be connected? Tim's only lived here a few months.'

'We're aware of those cases, Mary. But they were a long time ago, and we've never proven any link between them. A lot of people do go missing in London, unfortunately. Several every day, in fact.'

Mary pleaded. 'He's a good man, Tim. He's broken, yes, but he's not bad.'

Diana's expression said what Mary knew to be true – there wasn't such a thing as bad men and good men. Any man could turn on you, in the right circumstances. She thought of Jack punching the wall. The shadow over Alice's face when talking of Tim, waking with his fist in her face.

'You really believe that?'

240

Did she? Would she put her life, her safe suburban life, maybe not the easiest right now but still running along the tracks of the normal, would she put all that at risk for a man she barely knew? He was clearly unstable, his mind full of holes, his nerves and memory shot. He didn't sleep. He had cheated on his wife, and injured her, though perhaps without meaning to.

'Yes. I really do. He didn't take Samantha. Neither did Eric, or so he says. So it must be – someone else.'

Diana nodded. 'Then you better hope we find her, and soon.'

Tim

Tim was in his cell, eating a cardboard bowl of cereal that came in a little box, like in a cheap hotel, when his door was unlocked and he was beckoned out.

'Darbandi. Come on.'

'What's going on?'

'Take your things.'

He didn't have many things yet – there'd been no time. His phone and keys were being held somewhere, like when he was in hospital after the blast, and it was strange how quickly that made you feel helpless. He followed the guard down the cream-painted corridors.

'What's happening?'

'You're getting out.'

'What? But – I was charged.'

'Bail application in your favour.'

The guard didn't seem to care either. One less person to look after. But Tim couldn't trust this development – what if something worse was waiting for him? A different prison, less orderly? The kind you saw on TV where they'd pour boiling water over your hands, filthy and violent? Or a cat and mouse game, the police hoping he'd lead them to Samantha, wherever she was, if she might still be alive? But he wouldn't be able to help them. He had thought and thought about it since his arrest, but he had no memory of taking her at all. Just that backwards glance as she walked towards her family home.

He signed forms, took back a plastic bag with his watch, phone, and keys. The phone was dead, of course. He was read out a list of conditions of release – no contacting witnesses or family members, a 10 p.m. curfew, regular check-ins at his local police station. Then he was led to another gate, and another, until he began to glimpse the bright daylight. He began to panic.

'Is this real?'

The guard sighed. Other things to do. 'You're still charged, mate. Just out on bail, like? Happens on remand, yeah? Not always inside? Just need to watch yourself, don't break the conditions, check in with the police when they say.'

Tim had known these things on paper, as a journalist, but it seemed so surreal to be living it. Really, he'd known so little about many things.

Then he was through the glass and walls and gates in the car park, into the real world again. It was a very little change, as small as walking from one room to another, but he began to gasp. Two people were waiting by a car, and one turned and he saw it was Mary. Mary, come to get him. And behind her a handsome stubbled man in a suit, with his tie loosened. Her husband?

'Tim!' She ran towards him as if to hug, then stopped short. They'd never touched before, and this would perhaps be a strange moment to start. 'Are you OK?'

'I think so . . . what's going on? Why are you here?'

'We got you out! I went to the police, they went to a judge! It was kind of exciting. Anyway, you're still on remand officially, but you can come and go, you don't have to be in here, isn't that great? It means we can find Sam now. Prove you're innocent.'

She believed him. He didn't even entirely believe himself, but she did.

'Why?' he said, baffled. He met the eye of the scruffily handsome man, whose eyes were ringed in black, the working father of young children. They exchanged a brief mistrusting glance. 'Why am I out?'

Mary was bubbling over. 'Eric Johnson confessed! It was him who set you up, got you on camera, all of it. Samantha really was there in the house, but he says he paid her! She wasn't in danger at all, wasn't even missing, but now she is! Jack helped me with it.' She turned proudly to the man. 'Oh, this is Jack. Husband. Jack, Tim.'

They shook hands, Tim shamefully aware of how rough his were after almost a week of prison soap.

Jack said, 'So you're the reason she's been running about all over town.'

Clear message – *back off, man.*

'Believe me, I tried to stop her.'

Mary scowled. 'Will you two quit? I'm an independent adult and I saw what Tim saw. I wanted to help. Use my brain before it atrophied.' The husband muttered something and Mary grimaced. 'Yes, I know I made some mistakes. I'm trying to fix them. Come on, Tim, we'll take you home.'

'But . . . what now?'

He trotted behind them, holding his meagre things in a pile before him. He knew that a trial could take months, so what was he supposed to do in that time? Hang about waiting to be put inside again, and then convicted? Sent to prison for life? What if they did find Samantha's body somewhere, and he still had no alibi, no other suspect to save him, the last person to see her?

Mary glanced back at him as her husband unlocked the car. She looked almost comically determined, given that she had a cuddly toy pig sticking out of her handbag.

'Now we find out who really did it. Because Sam's still missing, Tim. Eric doesn't know where she is, she's not been in touch. I think she wasn't in danger before, when we thought she was – but she is now.'

Mary

Of course Mary and Tim weren't allowed anywhere near the police search of 16 Cliveden Road. In fact, Diana Mendes specifically came to Mary's door to tell them, 'I don't want to see either of you anywhere near the search.'

'Is Johnson allowed?' said Tim. He hadn't wanted to go home to his own lonely flat just yet, so he was at their kitchen table, drinking tea. Audrey had climbed on to his feet to play with her Lego and he seemed too afraid to move.

'It's Mr Johnson's house. He's entitled to be present, as he's not suspected of anything himself.' Mendes said that with a slight stress. Mary ignored it.

'Isn't he in some kind of trouble? Lying to the police?'

'That's not actually an offence, you know, more's the pity. Anyway I can't discuss Mr Johnson's situation with you.'

Fine. For the following hour, she and Tim positioned themselves in the children's bedroom, cramped up against the window taking turns with the Christmas-present binoculars, which were coming in surprisingly handy.

Tim had them at that moment, so Mary was squinting through the dirty glass, trying to make out what activity was going on in the back garden of the house. Blurred white-suited figures could just about be seen.

Tim exclaimed, 'They're digging! I bet they've brought in GPR.'

'You know I won't know what that is.' He was as bad as *Line of Duty* for the incomprehensible acronyms.

'Ground-penetrating radar. It shows if the soil's been disturbed. Or if things are buried there.'

Things. People, presumably.

She shivered and reached for the binoculars. 'Let me see.'

Mary had never quite understood how to use binoculars. The blurry image wavered around for a while until she found the right spot. The big oak tree at the back of the house. The back door was open, which she'd never seen before, and there were three white-suited people. She could clearly see the flash of a spade, and a horrible thrill went through her. What if they were digging up bodies right now? What if the missing women were under the soil?

And Sam. But no, it would be obvious if she was buried there, the grass would have been newly disturbed. She had to believe Sam was still alive somewhere.

Eventually she tired of watching a blur of white in the distance, and went to make dinner, but Tim stayed up there, fascinated. It was probably what had made him such a good journalist. Patience, and focus. Obsession, almost. But it got results. Jack and the kids were in the living room watching Peppa and playing with blocks, so Mary left them to it. She was still tiptoeing around him, aware that she had a lot to apologise for.

As she put things in the oven, she set the news to play on her phone, and inevitably it switched to a report about Tim.

John Stokes, Samantha's stepdad, standing outside their house again. 'My wife and I are extremely dismayed that the police have chosen to release on bail the man they charged with taking our daughter. What if he does it again now he's free to come and go as he pleases? It seems a shocking dereliction of duty.'

Mary heard a creak, turned to see Tim on the stairs. She hit pause. 'Ignore it, it's not true.'

'But it's what everyone will think. Unless we can find her.'

'We'll do our best.' But really, if the police couldn't manage it, what hope did they have?

They were just picking over the remnants of the meal – fish fingers, oven chips, and beans, which Tim ate with every sign of enjoyment and asked for seconds – when the bell went. On the doorstep, an ashen-faced Eric Johnson. Mary let him in without a word, and he sank on to the sofa. Jack put his head in from the kitchen, wearing yellow washing-up gloves, muttered something that was no doubt to do with the stream of strange men coming through his house.

'They found something,' said Eric, quietly.

Mary motioned to Jack. 'Keep the kids out. And send Tim in.'

He withdrew, scowling slightly, and shortly afterwards Tim emerged, standing quietly behind her. 'You've got some nerve coming here,' said Tim, seemingly invigorated by his release from prison.

Johnson couldn't look at him. 'I know. I'm aware of what I did to you, and I regret that. But we have to think about Sam now. And . . . the others.'

'Well?' said Mary. 'What did they find?'

Eric drew in a long breath. 'Bones. They think – there seems to be several bodies, buried in the garden of number sixteen.'

'Oh! But that's . . .' It was horrific, if it meant what she feared it meant. 'That's . . . my God.'

'Yes. It looks like someone had access to the house, or at least the back garden – the same person who killed my mother must have done it to these women, only he didn't have time to bury Mum. I guess because I came back.' Suddenly he gripped Mary's hand. Startled, she noticed how soft his was, the nails neatly manicured.

'Mary, I want to thank you. I know I was angry at first, that you got involved, but – I wouldn't have thought to search the garden, if you hadn't told me about these other missing girls. The idea that we can maybe catch this guy, the man who killed my mother – well, it's everything. It's been my whole life, wondering. If I'd come back a minute sooner. If I'd taken note of his face, or been able to remember. If I could have saved her, or at least sent him to prison, stopped him doing it again. You know.'

She took her hand away, rattled. He smelled very nice. Expensive. She had to remember he'd framed Tim, paid Samantha to do something very dubious in the first place, driven his wife to despair. Not a good man, even if he was now on their side.

'Well, that's something at least. It will take a while though, won't it? Testing, finding clues, looking for suspects. It was years ago. And Samantha's missing right now.'

It might be too late, was what she meant.

'Yes. So I want to offer help. Outside of the police – they're too slow. Whatever you need. Resources, a private detective, a bodyguard – you've got it. Obviously I can't be involved myself, I have to keep my name out of the press. But I'll do what I can.'

That was big of him.

Mary said, 'I just don't get what's happened to her. Tim's so sure he dropped her near her home. How could she go missing between there and the front door?'

Casually, from the next room, Jack called, 'Maybe she didn't.'

'What do you mean?' said Mary.

Jack slammed the fridge, making all the jars rattle in the door. Shouted, 'Maybe she did get home after all – most logical explanation. Which means her family might know where she is.'

It was so simple. Mary wondered why she hadn't told him before, why she hadn't shared any of this with her husband, her life partner. Jack had a clear, analytical mind, uncomplicated by nuance; he had legal training, he would be perfect.

Then he said, 'Assuming you believe Tim that he *did* drop her off.'

Tim frowned. 'Um . . . I did. I remember pulling up right by the road sign, as soon as you turn into the street. She asked me to stop there, and not go in.'

Jack popped his head around the door. 'Mary. Can one of your mum mates mind the kids for an hour or two tomorrow?'

Mary frowned at that phrase 'mum mates'. 'I don't know – why?'

'I think we should go and see this girl's family. I assume you know where they live. Tim can't come, it's a breach of his bail, and I'm not letting you go alone.'

He ignored Eric Johnson, who presumably was not coming with them either.

'But – what will I say to them?' asked Mary, bewildered.

Jack was already moving back to the kitchen. 'Oh, you'll think of something. You've kept me in the dark all this time, after all.'

Who was this man? It was not really surprising that Tim had turned out to be different than she thought, when she hardly knew him at all. She'd known Jack for years and here he was, still revealing hidden depths.

'What about me?' said Tim. 'I have to do something.'

Jack gazed back at him. 'I thought it was against your bail conditions to go near the girl's family.'

'Yes, but—'

'If I were you, mate, I'd try to stay out of trouble, and be grateful you're not still in prison.' He cast a baleful glance at Eric Johnson. 'I mean, Mary and I are just lucky we didn't lose our jobs.'

Johnson sighed. 'I can only say I'm sorry. I responded to what I saw as a threat.'

'By *framing* me,' said Tim, fiercer than Mary had seen him. 'I was in prison, for God's sake.'

'I know. I'm trying to make amends.'

Jack said, 'Look, there's nothing you can do, and I don't think either Tim or my wife wants you around. So I suggest you stay out of it – you've done enough. And, Tim, you can't be running around like you were. This is serious – one wrong step and you're back in prison. You haven't been cleared yet.' Mary marvelled at him, so firm and strong. And that *my wife* had given her a strange throwback thrill.

Eric Johnson stood up. 'Fine. My offer stands though. Whatever you need. I want Sam found.'

When he was gone, shutting the door behind him, Mary found she could breathe more easily. She hoped she would never see the man again. 'He's right, Tim – we have to keep you out of harm's way. Why don't you go home and rest? You must be tired.'

Tim stood up. 'You know, for once, I'm actually not. But let me know what you find out. Jack's right – her family is the best place to start.'

Samantha

She'd been keeping track of the days by making little marks on the wall in the dirt – four so far. He'd not come at all in that time, so that meant he would perhaps come in three more days – once a week. She could dimly remember her maths teacher at school, saying *two data points is not enough to establish a pattern, you need three at least.*

It made her sad to think of Miss Crowley, young and hippyish and a bit posh, with a swinging ponytail of shiny brown hair and a smell of expensive perfume. She hadn't lasted long in their disaster-area school, of course, but during that year she'd nagged Samantha constantly. *You should be doing another A level. You should apply to university.* It was impossible to explain why that wasn't going to happen, why she needed enough money of her own to get up and out. The house had felt like a prison to her, which was laughable now she was in an actual prison, except that would be better because she would have people to talk to and regular meals and stuff.

If the scratches she'd made on the wall were right, today was Friday. He'd left her mostly cold food, packaged and processed, maybe in case he couldn't get to her often. She'd been outraged at first – she didn't eat carbs at all if she could help it, let alone the kind of minging long-life bread and cakes you got in corner shops, sealed in plastic and lasting for weeks. But after the first few days, when he didn't come and hunger started to churn her stomach in loops, she found herself cramming in the sweet, stodgy food, until it filled up the hole inside her. It cleared her head, made her less jittery. At least she had the camping stove, to heat up water and noodles, a really old one that smelled of gas and you had to light it with a match. She'd briefly considered setting fire to the place, but there was no guarantee anyone would see the flames in time, and she wasn't burning to death out here. There might be another use, however.

It was hard to tell what time it was. All she could see was the lightening and darkening of the high, dirty window. Another thing she was totally dependent on her phone for. When the sun began to lengthen and turn orange, she finally heard it – tyres on gravel. He was here. He'd come back, he wasn't leaving her here. She hated how relieved she was – to be grateful to him for anything at all. She moved in front of the stove where she had a pot of water waiting, heart hammering. He'd see the steam if she put it on to boil, wouldn't he? Maybe she'd offer him tea. Yes, that would work. Play nice. It was all he'd ever wanted from her. To be nice.

The sound of jangling keys, and the various locks shifting, and he opened the door.

'Stand back,' he called.

He was wise to her. He knew she might try to hurt him. As he came in, she held her hands up to show she was harmless.

'Well, I'm here.'

He was wearing shorts, the idiot. Men over thirty should never do that. It meant it was sunny outside still. She should be in a park, or maybe on a day trip to the seaside, or at a lido. Not stuck here.

'Are you alright?' he said roughly. Like he cared. 'It's been longer than I intended.'

'I was just making tea. Do you want one?'

252

She'd surprised him. His arms were full of shopping bags, another huge bottle of water. 'Well. Alright then. It was a long drive.'

She stored away that little clue – what counted as long from London? It couldn't be too far, she hadn't been in the boot for more than an hour or two, though that was certainly bad enough.

'OK.'

She turned to the stove and raised the flame, trying to keep her face neutral. There was only one cup – she put a teabag into it from the bag he'd brought, and listened for the rising noise of the boil. He was turned away, setting down food for her. A lot of food. That meant he wasn't planning to let her go any time soon. But she could escape. She could see the car keys in his pocket – she'd have to grab those, and that meant touching him, but she'd just have to do it. There was no other way. The water was at a rolling boil now, turning over and over like she felt inside. She picked up the saucepan carefully. Oh God. Was she really going to do this? What if he went all burnt and horrible, his skin puckering? She had no choice. He turned back, about to say something.

'What—'

Samantha flung the water. Right towards his face. But he ducked. It splashed over the wall, making the old paint bubble, and some got on to his shoulder. He made a noise of shock, pulling the hot material away from him.

'What the hell?'

'I . . .' Oh God. Could she say she tripped? No. He knew. He wasn't stupid. 'I . . .'

He looked at her for a long time, the odd stray drip running down his face. God, she hated that. Why didn't he say something? Shout, hit her? Anything but just stare, leaving her to wonder what her punishment would be.

'This is your problem, Samantha. You don't know when some-one's trying to help you.'

Somehow, this was worse than anger.

He picked the stove up, turning the flame off, gathering it in his arms. Then he came back and picked up the bags of groceries he'd brought, and went out, slamming the door, and she heard the locks click into place. The slice of light that had come in was cut off, leaving her in the gloom again, the shadows lengthening. Her one chance, and she'd fucked it up. He wouldn't trust her again now, and she'd lost her food now too. Samantha slumped against the wall, not even caring that it got grime all over her. What was she going to do now?

Tim

Colin Ellis, Samantha's biological father, was not what Tim expected at all. He'd pictured a wastrel, the opposite of John Stokes's rigid suburban respectability, dabbling in drugs or perhaps with a drink problem. Instead, Tim found the man at work in his studio on one of the back streets of Hastings, close enough to the shore for the swishing sound of shingle to penetrate everything. He'd taken the train, since his car was still impounded, and was sure he'd noticed a car parked outside his flat as he left very early in the morning, once again unable to sleep. He wasn't breaking any rules by leaving the area, but he certainly wasn't supposed to approach Sam's father. He had the feeling that he was under surveillance, that the police hoped he might lead them to her. But they would find nothing by following him, and he hoped he'd lost them by getting on the train. The news this morning was full of the bodies the police had found, eclipsing Samantha a little – '16 Cliveden Road' would soon be a byword for horror, for death. Tim was less interested – those poor girls were gone, and too late to save them. Sam could maybe still be found.

'I'm Tim – we spoke on the phone?'

Colin Ellis been easy to track down, with his own website for the driftwood sculptures he made. Tim had got his name from Nick before his arrest, then not had time to look into it before he was locked up. It felt good to be back investigating, even if he was on bail and technically banned from approaching any member of Sam's family. He didn't imagine the police would be watching the deadbeat father, so while Mary went to investigate the Stokes house, he'd come here. She would understand that he couldn't sit at home and wait. Or perhaps he just wouldn't tell her.

The workshop was full of statues, and although Tim knew nothing about art, he had to admit there was a strange beauty to them, wrought into twisted shapes as if some intelligence had worked on them instead of the blind churn of the sea. Alice would have liked them. At Tim's question, Colin had stopped work and pushed up his visor. He was one of those men who refuse to become less trendy as they age, grizzled beard, weather-beaten skin, leather thong round his neck. All the same he looked old, the marks of hard living on his face, the tremble of the hands that held his tools, the stoop of his back. He had Sam's eyes, and Tim faltered as he shook the man's hand.

'I'm so sorry about Samantha,' he said, taking his cue from Mary, who always knew the correct social response.

Colin Ellis nodded briefly. 'I don't see her much. Her mum wouldn't let me, not once she'd re-married. But the last few years we'd sent messages. She said she'd come down and see me maybe, this summer.' A short pause where they both wondered if that would happen, or if Sam would never do anything again. 'You're that journalist? The one they arrested then let go?'

Tim had been surprised Sam's father agreed to see him – like everyone else, he must know what had happened. He hadn't dared switch on his phone or look at his emails – Alice would have seen the news too, he was sure, and he couldn't bear to think of that. Did that mean Colin Ellis believed Tim wasn't guilty? It must do.

'I – yes. My neighbour and I, we thought we saw Sam, you see, a few weeks ago. Near where we live. And it all kind of spiralled from there.'

He explained the situation as best he could, leaving out the reason Sam was in the house in the first place.

Colin Ellis took it all in. He was a quiet man, with a suggestion of great depths.

Tim said, 'Can I ask, Colin – why did you and Sam's mother split up? We got the impression there was bad blood.'

He screwed up his face. 'You thought I'd taken her, is that it? Police were down asking. I know people do kidnap their kids, but not when they're nineteen, surely.' He picked up a lethal-looking saw, regarded it for a moment, then set it down again.

'No, no,' said Tim hastily, although they had of course thought this formerly. 'I just hoped you might know something about her. If there's anyone in her life she might have clashed with . . .'

'John.' A dark look flashed over his face. 'Her stepdad. You've met him?'

'Not really.' Tim had watched many videos of Stokes, giving interviews from the front of the house, begging for Sam's return, but had only seen him that one time, bringing a breath of something into the house. Some kind of strain, or even fear.

'Real pillar of the community, isn't he? Neighbourhood Watch, chair of the parish council, parent-bloody-governor. He's the reason Mags stopped letting me see Sam. Her and me, we weren't too good together. Took too many drugs, partied too much, in and out of rehab. Well, it's just a typical story. We weren't ready to have a kid, and poor Sam, she suffered from that. I was actually glad when he came along, John – he'd his own business, enough money, proper grown-up. I thought that's what they needed, while I sorted myself out a bit. But then he wouldn't let me see her. Told her I was a waste of space, basically. And I was, I'll admit, but I'm still her dad.' The bitterness coloured his voice like coffee stains.

Tim couldn't relate – he had no children, and likely never would. If he did, he imagined Alice would not have let them see him either, so low had he sunk. He shook himself out of self-pity.

'So you think there's something off about him?' Usually, the stepdad was the first person you'd look at – but Sam had disappeared on the way home from work. Or so they thought at first. Now, that picture was totally wrong.

Colin made a shrug, a gesture of helplessness. 'Thought I was imagining it at first, blaming the bloke for taking my family, all that shit. But Maggie – she's not what she used to be, you know? I've only seen her once or twice since we split, but I follow her on Facebook, or more like I don't because she doesn't say a word these days. She's bombed out of her head most of the time. And Sam . . . well, she never got on with him. Right from the start he was trying to make her this perfect little girl, hair in plaits, doing her home-work. That's not my Sam – she's like me. Wild.'

A shudder went through him and Tim realised the man was about to cry. He stepped back, alarmed.

'Um – it must be really hard, I'm sorry. Do you mean to say he . . . hurt them?'

'Don't know for sure. But Maggie, she's been in and out of hos-pital more times than a woman should. That's how she got on the painkillers, and now she's out of it most of the time. And Sam . . . well, she broke her arm when she was twelve. Said she fell off a swing. But I never believed it. Bruises, that sort of thing. And she changed. She stopped telling me things, then she stopped seeing me altogether.'

How had Tim missed all this? The catatonic mother and jumpy younger sister, all the references to Sam wanting out, away from her home. 'You think John Stokes has something to do with it, then?'

How did that fit with the missing girls from the area though, the bodies? John Stokes had no connection to South Kenborough, as far as Tim knew.

Colin shrugged again, dashing clumsily at his eyes. 'God, I don't know. But I wouldn't be surprised if she'd tried to get as far away as she could from that house.'

Tim stood, listening to the faint faraway sound of the sea on shingle. Could this be the answer, or was this a paranoid ex-husband speaking? A difficult home life would certainly explain why Sam needed money, why she'd be tempted by extra, well-paying work, however strange and seedy.

'So you think, what, she went home and he did something to her, Stokes? Or she didn't go home after all?'

Perhaps it had been another ruse of hers, a double-cross, pretending to walk to her house, then waiting till Tim drove off to escape again. Eric Johnson had said the original plan was for Sam to disappear again, not return home.

'Mate, I have no idea. If I did, you better believe I'd be trying to find her myself. Keep hoping she'll turn up here, so I don't want to leave and go looking.'

He glanced out on to the quiet street, as if she might appear, this phantom of a girl they were all hunting.

Tim sighed in frustration, dislodging some curls of sawdust. There was so much to this case that seemed impossible to figure out. Like they were going round in circles.

Mary

She could see, now she was here, how unbelievable it was that Samantha had not made it home. Tim said he'd parked at the end of the cul-de-sac, a small curl of detached houses in beige brick, and let the girl out. By the sign, he said. Acacia Close. There would have been nowhere for her to go but in, past the three houses on the left to her family home at the end. It had been the middle of the night, no one should have been around. The odd fox, perhaps. This wasn't the kind of place where people had security cameras. Lower middle class. Respectable, and quiet, but not rich. Mary had grown up in a place like this, and spent her teens gasping to leave. Had Samantha been the same?

They'd dropped Tim home the night before, along with a carrier bag of groceries, and the confused look of gratitude on his face had almost made her cry, as he lifted out the milk and bread and bananas. She'd made him promise to stay away from the Stokes family. It was too much of a risk.

'Go on then,' nudged Jack.

He had pulled up in the same spot where Tim must have parked. The kids were in the back, Audrey grouchily doing her best to keep herself from her lunchtime nap, Leo fast asleep, arms and legs starfishing in his chair. They'd brought them along in the end, feeling safer with them in sight. Mary looked at Jack hesitantly, then undid her belt and got out.

There were nine houses in the close, she counted. At one, bikes lay out abandoned, and from an open upstairs window she could hear the blur of cross childish voices. Another had neat beds full of stiff plants, and a collection of gnomes arranged around a stone bird bath. Another still was shabby, the paint peeling, no car outside, lace curtains in the window. The next belonged to Samantha's family. Her mother, stepfather, and half-sister, Tim had said. She tried to dredge up the girl's name. Old Mary would have had this at her fingertips, could present a case to court after five minutes' prep. Marlee. That was it. *Thank you, brain.*

As she hovered by the neat raked path, she realised she had no idea what she was going to say. *I've been looking into your daughter's disappearance. No, I'm not police or press or anything official. Just a busybody, basically.*

She glanced back to the car, her entire life inside the idling vehicle. She could hear a faint tinny sound that indicated Jack had already caved and given Audrey his phone.

She lifted her hand to ring the bell, hesitated. What on earth would she open with? *My friend was charged with kidnapping your daughter, but he didn't do it, I swear. How do I know – well, I don't, really.* Urgh.

She was about to turn and go, make up some lie to Jack about the family being out, when a head appeared at the side of the house. A girl, with long straight hair hanging unkempt round her face. She beckoned to Mary, who followed her, very unsure. She was now in a sort of side return between the house and the next one. It was neatly kept, the fringe of grass trimmed and the hedge shaped.

'Hi,' she whispered.

'I didn't want him to see,' said the girl.

Who was 'him' – Stokes? Was he home, during a weekday? Mary didn't want to think what might happen if he saw her. 'Are you Marlee?'

'Yeah. Who are you?'

'Mary. Kind of the same, ha ha.' The girl did not laugh.

'You didn't look like police or those reporters, so I thought you might know *him*.'

'Who?' Another him. There wasn't much space, and Mary was half-pressed into the hedge, deeply paranoid about how she'd explain herself should a parent appear.

'Tim.'

'Oh. Yes, I do. How do you—'

'He came here,' said Marlee impatiently. 'He was trying to find her. Sam. But now they're saying he might have taken her! I know he didn't.'

'Right, well, that's what I'm trying to prove. How do you know?'

'Because he wanted to find her. He was the only one who listened when I talked. The police, they just thought she'd gone off, I could tell.'

'Did you tell them Tim was here, the police?'

She shook her head, making her fine hair fly. She was dressed in an oversized grey hoody, with the name of Samantha's sixth-form college on it. Perhaps she was at the same one, or she was wearing her sister's jumper. She now lifted a cuff of it to her mouth and chewed; Mary resisted the urge to bat her hand away. The mothering was strong in her.

'I didn't want to get him in trouble. Is he in prison now?'

'He's just got out, but the police still think he maybe took her. So I'm trying to find out what did happen. He said he brought Sam back here, in the middle of the night last weekend. Dropped her off on this street after she turned up at his flat – that's why they had him on film, because he'd driven her. But she asked him to, he says.'

Marlee nodded, as if she'd suspected this. She was keeping her voice low, but Mary wondered where her parents were, why they hadn't noticed her slipping from the house. Maybe when they got to that age you couldn't be bothered, just luxuriated in not having to check every single second that they weren't drinking bleach or playing with knives.

'What night was it?'

'Let me see – last Sunday.'

Marlee counted under her breath, and suddenly she inhaled sharply and grabbed Mary's wrist. Her nails were sharp and ragged.

'There was shouting one night. I got sent to bed – Dad said it was another journalist come poking round.'

'So you're saying Sam did come back?'

A cool ocean of relief – maybe Tim really didn't do this after all. She hadn't been friends with a man who'd kidnap a girl.

Marlee shook her head. 'I don't know – she wasn't there when I woke up, and Dad's still frantic trying to find her, talking to the police and all. I don't know why they'd pretend she didn't come back, if she did.'

Mary didn't get it either. But where else could Sam have gone, in this quiet cul-de-sac?

Marlee froze again then. A man's voice, the slam of a door at the back.

'Marlee! It's time for lunch. Where are you?'

It must be the stepdad. Mary felt a rush of fear that surprised her, picking it up from the girl perhaps.

Marlee hissed, 'I have to go. Don't let him see you, whatever you do.'

'Wait – but, Marlee, what can I . . . what should I . . . ?'

Marlee's breathing had grown shallow, and there was sweat on her forehead. 'Please don't tell him I talked to you. Say you're a salesperson, I don't know, something like that.'

Her voice was a harsh, urgent whisper. Then a man appeared round the side of the house – fiftyish, in slacks and a polo shirt, with powerful forearms and close-cropped hair. Mary recognised him from TV – John Stokes.

He gave Marlee a look, that was all, not even a word. But the girl crumpled in on herself and began to sob.

'I'm sorry, Daddy! She just came – I don't know who she is!'

Mary didn't even blame her for the lie.

'Go inside.' He didn't raise his voice. He was softly spoken in fact, but somehow Mary began to sweat with fear herself. He turned to her. 'What are you doing here?'

'I – um – my name's Mary.'

'I know who you are. You're friends with that man.' He spat the word. 'The one who took our girl.'

'Yes, but he didn't take her. I'm sorry, this must be so hard for you all.'

Her head was reeling. Either this was a grieving father, and she was intruding in the worst way, or he knew where Sam was. Could it really be true? What about the other girls, in that case?

'You have no idea. My daughter's gone, and your friend had her in his car!'

'I know, but he said he dropped her off safely. I think some-one else is behind this. I . . .' How to explain without accusing him outright? 'Look, I know it sounds mad, but I really think the police have got the wrong end of the stick. Tim doesn't have her, so someone else must, and she might be in danger. If I could just explain . . . What are you doing?'

He'd taken his phone out and was pressing numbers on it.

'I'm calling the police. Reporting you for harassment.'

'No, don't do that, I'm honestly trying to help . . .' Mary raised her hands. 'Look, I'm going. I'm sorry for interfering, really I am.'

He watched her scuttle away, phone in his hand, and all Mary could do was creep around the front of the house, with the pulled blinds like shut eyes. Was there a chance Sam was there, inside the house, unable to shout or scream? Mary wanted to yell her name, but was too afraid. Had someone in her home done something to her, as happened to most murder victims? Standing in the deserted cul-de-sac, hearing a distant squawk that meant Leo was waking up, Mary felt the limits of her position. There was nothing more she could do.

Despite her run-in with Sam's stepfather, Mary was still somewhat buoyed up by her success getting Tim out of jail, like some kind of Erin Brockovich figure. She'd been right about Eric Johnson, and surely her actions had helped force him to admit his lies. And Jack had helped too, so he must think she was right. She didn't have to hide her investigations from him any more, and that was more of a relief than she'd realised. But now she had to figure out how to find a missing girl that so far two police forces had not been able to locate. And do it without childcare, while breastfeeding.

Tim came round while she was doing Leo's afternoon feed, Jack having taken Audrey up for her nap, and she saw his look of panic as she opened the door with the baby clamped to her chest. Oh well, if he had a problem that was his issue.

'Did you sleep in?' She hadn't heard from him all day.

'Um, yeah.'

'Good, you must need the rest.'

She made coffee for him while the baby sucked, pleased with her own multitasking. She could feed while being fed from. That was something, wasn't it? Even if she wasn't quite her old self, even if she couldn't complete the negotiations in the Domato divorce. Tim looked everywhere except at her – the ceiling, the table, the floor, which certainly didn't bear too much scrutiny.

'So what next?' she said, to distract him, once she'd filled him in on her morning's activity.

Tim was making a list on a pad. 'We know there's been a killer in the area for decades, never caught. With a connection or some means of access to number sixteen.'

'I think we need to investigate the stepdad more, don't you? Such a cliché. Did you see him when you went?'

Tim addressed the cabinet. 'Just a glimpse. Mum's totally out of it, tranks or something.'

'Afraid of him, maybe. So's the little sister.'

'Marlee?' said Tim.

'Yeah. She said she never thought you did it, if that helps.'

'It does, actually. What does she think happened? Did she say?'

Mary shook her head, wincing slightly as Leo grabbed her breast. 'No, she wouldn't say more. But she's scared, that's obvious.'

'We need to find out if there's any connection between John Stokes and Cliveden Road – maybe his company was hired to protect the empty building, that kind of thing. Otherwise I can't make sense of how it all links up.'

Mary nodded. 'Let me just detach my boob.'

They were like characters in a mismatched buddy comedy, she thought, as he raised his eyebrows in shock. Not much good apart, but together they might just solve this thing.

Tim

They set up a kind of ad hoc research desk at Mary's kitchen table, once it had been wiped clear of jam, and it took Tim back; the urgency and camaraderie. The in-jokes and gallows humour of reporting from a war zone, the frisson of knowing that, shielded as they were, all it took was one stray rocket or bullet and they'd be part of the disaster.

Tim's to-do list was growing. He hadn't told Mary about his trip to see Samantha's father, knowing she would disapprove, but she also seemed to think the stepdad was dodgy. She said, 'I'll research John Stokes online, see if he has any profiles. Marlee too.'

'According to Companies House, Stokes is the director of a security firm. Dog patrols and so on, and they also set up guardianship of empty buildings, you know, where people live in them to keep them from vandals. They do a lot of work for Kent County Council.'

Mary's eyes were bright. At some point she had changed her clothes and brushed her hair. 'That must be it then! Lots of places he could be keeping her. Can we get a list of the sites he manages?'

'Trickier, it's all confidential. We'd need to get into the offices somehow.'

'I could pull my "baby desperately needs a nappy change" routine.'

'I'd rather you didn't take the children with you,' called the husband crossly from the next room. Tim had forgotten Jack was there, playing with the baby in the living room in what seemed a passive-aggressive manner. 'Not exactly safe, is it, dragging them on your murder hunt?'

'Who's going to watch them, then?' Mary stared through the open door at Jack, and Tim recognised an unspoken couple conversation, such as he used to have with Alice when they were at her mother's and he was itching to leave. He wondered if he'd ever have that again, an intimacy that went beyond words.

Jack sighed. 'I'm not calling in sick again, Mary.'

'Tomorrow's Saturday, you idiot.'

'Yeah, well, tell that to my boss. I've hardly done a thing all week.'

'Your boss who gave our address out to a possible murderer.'

Jack went quiet at that, and Mary turned back to the laptop with a small smile of triumph on her lips. 'The offices are in Croydon, so I'd guess the sites they work on are all fairly local. It's a small company, only three staff – can't be looking after that many places.'

Jack cut in again, coming to stand in the doorway. He was wrestling with a piece of Lego, trying to separate it. 'Guys, I have to ask this. What makes you so sure she's still alive, Samantha? I mean, God, I hope she is, but she's been missing for a long time now.'

Mary and Tim looked at each other. Slowly, Mary said, 'We never considered that she might be dead. I don't really know why. I guess we just hoped.'

That wasn't the real reason, Tim knew. It was because their lives had become the story. It was because they needed her to be alive, or they wouldn't know what to do with themselves, they were so far in.

Mary

In the end, Mary turned to Francine yet again to mind the kids. Her friend wore a striped Breton top and cropped jeans, dusted with flour from baking, like a mother in a glossy magazine.

'I'm so sorry to ask again. It's just – the whole police thing . . .'

'It's really no trouble. I do hope they find the poor girl.'

'Yes. It's so worrying, her poor family.' Mary mouthed the platitudes, all the while very aware that Sam's family were now the top suspects as far as she and Tim were concerned.

Francine took Leo from Mary's arms, and he went with such placidity it made Mary realise just how much time he was spending here. Audrey had already raced ahead to find her hero Jasmine. The house smelled of cakes and expensive candles. How did Francine do it? How?

'I'm glad you came round – I wanted to give you something, actually.'

'Oh?' said Mary, her mind elsewhere.

'Come in a second and I'll find it.'

Mary stepped into the hallway with its original wooden floor-boards and Persian runner. Of course the place was tidy, shoes lined up by the door, no coats or toys or bits of half-eaten toast scattered around the place. Francine came back, still holding Leo, with her own baby toddling at her legs. Earth mother.

'Here.' It was a small USB stick. 'You wanted to see Dexter's pictures of the area, didn't you?'

Of course – she'd forgotten all about that. It seemed a long shot that a ten-year-old could have captured something important, but she took it anyway.

'Thanks, I'll take a look. I won't be long.'

Mary had turned to go when she ran into Alana coming up the street, leading five-year-old Flora, a mini-me in designer dungarees, by the hand.

'Mary!'

Alana was wearing her Burberry trench, which Mary knew was not even second-hand, her hair artfully arranged in a messy bun that Mary couldn't have achieved if she'd spent three hours trying.

'Hi! Dropping yours off at Francine's crèche too?' she joked.

Alana's lips tightened. 'Well, no, it's just that Jasmine really loves playing with Flora, so she insisted on a playdate. Personally, I'd much rather have the kids with me all the time.'

Mary didn't have time for this one-upwomanship. 'Right. Well, I have to run.'

'Wait, Mary. Did I really hear that you got arrested?'

'Not arrested. I was helping the police out – they think I might have seen something relevant to that missing girl, you know, Samantha Ellis? I can't really talk about it actually.' She aimed for a tone of lofty mystery.

'Spending a lot of time on this, aren't you? The kids are here all the time.'

Annoyed, Mary tried not to rise to it.

'Yeah, well. It's important, if I can help, and it gives me something to do. Back to work before I know it. God knows how I'll cope then, with two in nursery.'

Alana gave her a kindly, exasperated look, as Flora ran into the house.

'You know, Mary, there's no shame in not working. If you find it just isn't coming together.'

Mary paused. 'Meaning?' She wouldn't even have responded to the dig a few weeks ago. 'My kids aren't happy?'

Alana blinked but rallied. 'Of course they're happy, Mary! But you're not. Are you? Remember how it was before you went off with Leo? Always running between childcare and the office and cadging pick-up favours . . .' She laid a manicured hand on Mary's chapped one. 'I'm trying to help. I'm just saying, it isn't always possible, to do the mother thing and the corporate thing. There aren't enough hours in the day.'

To Mary's annoyance, hot tears came to her eyes. The spies in the films never cried during their assignations. 'You manage it!'

'Oh.' Alana dismissed this. 'I have Kevin, you know he's hardly worked since his company downsized. "Consulting" he calls it, more of a hobby than a job based on what he brings in. So I have no choice. And you know, I have the most wonderful nanny.' Of course Alana had snagged the best nanny in the area, a fresh-faced Colombian girl named Florita, who had seven brothers and sisters back in Bogotá and absolutely loved children. 'I couldn't do it with a full-time working husband like Jack. He earns enough for you both, doesn't he?'

'Not if we ever want the kids to have their own rooms.' She felt the impossibility of the London property market weigh her down like an anchor.

Alana shrugged. 'So, you move. It's what people do.'

But Mary didn't want to move! She wanted to be a chic London mum with a four-bed house, running about clutching three-pound lattes. Like Alana. Yet suddenly she realised, in a flash of under-standing so clear it almost dazzled her – there was no other solu-tion. This was the reality of it. Either she and Jack both worked full-time, or they had to leave the city. The acceptance of this truth was like falling down, then realising you were quite happy there on the ground, you'd actually needed a rest. She burst out, 'I just don't see why it has to be me. I never wanted to be a non-working mother, like my own!'

Alana brushed this off too. 'It's not for ever, what are you, forty?'

'Thirty-seven,' said Mary, a little stung.

'Exactly. You'll go back when they don't need you so much. Four, five years tops, they'll both be at school.'

It sounded like a long time, put like that. Mary sighed. 'Thank you. I do appreciate it.'

Alana suddenly grew sombre. 'I hope you catch the bastard and find that poor girl. I was assaulted when I was sixteen, you know, walking home from school. Police did absolutely nothing about it. I really thought this shit would be OVER by now.' And with that bombshell, and a clink of her diamond tennis bracelet, she was gone into the house.

Tim

Tim had never driven to Croydon before, and was surprised to find it something of a nightmare of one-way streets, bus lanes, and complicated roundabouts, that Mary nonetheless navigated with ease, chatting the entire time about the case, her kids, and some revelation she seemed to have come to that maybe they should move out of London after all. Finally she found the entrance to a multistorey car park, reeking of tyre rubber and wee like they all seemed to.

'We'll have to walk the next bit, I'm afraid.'

Tim's car was still being processed for evidence, even though he'd admitted Samantha was in it. Probably they were still looking for her blood – they hadn't dropped the charges on him yet, and he'd had to sign in at the police station that morning. He knew they must be watching him. Which made what he and Mary were doing today all the more stupid.

So far, they'd found no connection between John Stokes and 16 Cliveden Road. Perhaps his company had once protected it, given it had stood empty for years. The offices of Stokes's security firm were in a faceless glass-fronted building near the cinema – according to the internet they opened for a half day on Saturdays, so here they were, him and Mary, still trying to solve a case that had already almost broken them both.

Mary rang the bell on the intercom, and, without anyone speaking, it opened. She panicked again.

'What are we going to say? What if John's here?'

'He's not here.' Tim held the door open for her.

'How do you know?'

'He's just done another press conference.' He took out his phone to show her, sound off. John Stokes was standing outside his house again, in a sweatshirt and jeans, a grim, worried expression on his face. '*Find Sam' pleads family*, read the chyron.

'He's always on the news. Does that mean . . .' Mary still looked worried. 'I mean, would he do that if he had her?'

'Sure he would. Happens all the time that families give interviews, press conferences even, and they know fine well where the missing person is because they've killed them. In fact it's something the police are trained to look for.'

God, he hoped that wasn't the case. It would be unbearable to rake over all they'd done and wonder if a different decision or a quicker action could have saved Sam. If they were right, she had in fact been safe most of the time she was supposedly missing, and Tim had instead delivered her to her fate. The irony was too painful.

Mary said, 'He wouldn't have hurt her, would he, her stepdad? If he's got her, maybe he's just trying to teach her a lesson?'

Tim shrugged – he had no idea. The whole situation was not what they'd thought, like picking up an object and turning it on its end. When Sam had seemed to be in danger she was safe. When she seemed to be home, free and found, she was perhaps in danger.

'So what's our cover story?'

'You have a property and you're looking for guardians. Then you distract the receptionist, Zoe, and I'll see what I can find in the office.' It made it a bit too easy when they had staff pictures on the website. Nine times out of ten, if you pretended to know someone, they'd be too polite not to respond.

'Alright. God, I'm a hopeless actress too. What kind of property do I have?'

'You inherited a house with a shop underneath it. I don't know, improvise.'

Even more nervous now, Mary got into the lift behind him, and they ascended to the third floor, catching glimpses of Croydon's towers out of the grubby windows.

She was muttering to herself: 'Hi, I have a property and I'm looking for guardians. You do that, don't you?'

It was like every office he'd ever been to, wilting ferns in pots, chrome and leather chairs, wall art so inoffensive it was practically blank. He recognised the girl behind reception with a little lurch, having seen her picture on the staff list and knowing from LinkedIn that she'd previously worked at an alarm response company. Really, there was too much online nowadays, it made it frighteningly easy to get to people.

'Zoe, hi!' Tim strode towards the reception desk, channelling the kind of bluff businessman he'd spent his early career trying to call out. Behind it was a sullen girl with bleached hair, filing her nails. She looked up, puzzled. 'Lovely to see you again. Brought you a client!' He ushered Mary forward, and she gave the girl a fixed smile. Really, Mary was no good at all this cloak and dagger stuff. She was pathologically honest. 'Lady here's inherited a large commercial property in Purley, needs someone to take care of it prior to sale. Might be a while in this market, but I don't have to tell you that! I said you'd sort her out.'

Zoe frowned. 'Eh – yeah. You'll have to fill in some forms.'

'John here?' Tim jerked his thumb towards the back office. 'Thought I'd just say hello.'

'Eh, no, he's not in today. Family trouble.'

'Oh well, sorry to hear that.' Tim had decided it would be suspicious if he appeared too familiar with Samantha being missing.

Mary tapped the form Zoe had given her, on a battered pleather clipboard. 'Could you talk me through this? I've never done it before. The place belonged to my late uncle, you see. He didn't get on with my father, so I was really surprised to be left it, to be honest.'

Tim shot her a look – she was overdoing the improv – as a reluctant Zoe stood up and leaned over the reception desk. While she was distracted, Tim muttered something about using the loo, and sidled away. The rest of the office had that stultifying torpor he remembered from temp jobs before he'd broken into journalism, as if everyone's brains had slowed down from the recycled air and overhead lights. There were at least windows, with a view over grey Croydon. No one seemed to be about, maybe because it was Saturday, but one computer had, as he'd hoped, been left unlocked, the chair pushed back as if the occupant had just popped out. A few metres away was a door marked with the unisex loo symbol, and behind it he could hear a fan whirring. He didn't have much time.

He seized the mouse and found the email inbox – the person who sat here was apparently called Julie Okonowo. He searched for *John Stokes*, and sure enough hundreds of emails came back. He scrolled to the latest. Admin – parking reminders – meeting alerts – and then, one with the subject header DISTURBANCE AT GOLDEN SANDS SITE. *I'll handle this myself, Julie*, he'd said. *Probably just local kids but it's a big client and I want them to have my full attention. Tell the usual team to stand down.*

Golden Sands. What was that, a holiday camp? The ideal place to keep someone – isolated, abandoned probably, with lots of buildings to lock a girl up in.

He jumped as the door to the bathroom opened. A woman in a pink blazer stared at him. *Brazen it out*, said his journalist brain, back to full strength.

'Hiya, Julie – sorry to interrupt, just had to look for a file. Got it though.'

He walked quickly off before she could register the violation. They didn't have long.

Mary was still puzzling over the form with Zoe in reception. 'I see, so those fees are monthly, is that right?'

He cleared his throat. 'Just remembered the parking.'

It took Mary a moment to twig. 'Oh yes. God, don't want a ticket. Can I take some info with me to think about it?'

Zoe was confused. 'But—'

'Sorry, really don't want to rush such a big decision. I'll grab this leaflet. Thanks.'

They were almost at the door and free, when, with very unhelpful timing, the lift dinged, the doors slid open, and a man stepped out. Tim recognised him from the news report, and his living room that time – it was John Stokes. Stocky, powerfully built, angry expression on his face.

Mary froze, but he'd seen her.

'You?' His enraged gaze turned to Tim. 'You came here? And you brought *him* – the man who took my daughter?'

'I didn't take her and you know it.'

'Where is she? Tell me what you did with her!' He raised his voice, and Zoe poked her head out from the reception, eyes like saucers.

'You know I don't have her. Don't you?'

'It's disgusting the police let you go. I know what you are. Your past.'

'I've only ever tried to help Sam. Can you say the same? Her broken arm – what about that, Stokes?' For a moment, Tim locked eyes with the man. Then Stokes fished his phone from the pocket of his slacks and dialled.

'Hello, police please. I'd like to report a bail breach.'

Mary reacted faster than Tim. She grabbed his arm, hustled him out and down the stairs, running all the way to the street, feet clattering on lino. Outside, she stopped to catch her breath. 'Oh God. This is bad. You weren't supposed to go near the family, right?'

How close had he been to Stokes – less than fifty metres, surely? That meant he'd broken his bail conditions. That meant they could send him back to prison.

They were at Mary's car before she stopped panting. Stokes had not chased after them, but looking back Tim had seen him standing on the top floor, watching them with a strange expression on his face. Mary sank into the car seat, her hand trembling on the ignition key. 'Christ, Tim, you shouldn't have let him see you.'

Tim put his head in his hands. 'I didn't think he'd be there. Why's he in the office, when his stepdaughter's missing?'

'What did you even mean – you said something about her arm? How did you know that?'

He couldn't tell her he'd talked to Colin Ellis. 'I just – it was something I heard, that maybe he'd broken it one time.'

She pulled the car away, still shaking. 'We have to find her. Samantha. They'll come for you otherwise, take you back to prison. We have to find her before then.'

She drove them home, both on edge the entire journey for the swelling sound of sirens in their wake.

Mary

Their trip to the office had seemed like at best a waste of time, and at worst something borderline illegal that might derail the investigation, so Mary was shocked but not entirely surprised to be woken up by the police the next morning. It was so early even Leo hadn't stirred, and so the whole household was startled awake at the same time, before five, by the relentless ringing of the bell.

'Jesus Christ!' Jack was pressed along her, his legs twined in hers, which might have pleased Mary had she not been sitting bolt upright, heart hammering. 'What is that?'

'I don't know!'

'You didn't book the early Sainsbury's slot again, did you?'

'Not even they come this early.' She stumbled out, her feet groping around the floor for her slippers. The kids' room door was ajar, both wide-eyed in their cots, cross and shocked. Well, see how they liked a rude awakening.

'Mummy?' called Audrey.

'It's OK, darling, Daddy will get you up.' She shouted the last bit so Jack could hear he wasn't allowed to slip back into sleep.

Downstairs it was so early the sun wasn't even up, everything bathed in a stark pale light. She yanked the door open, ready to yell at whatever early-morning deliveryman this was, only to find herself confronted, in her T-shirt and pants, by the two model-good-looking police officers, Diana Mendes and the uniformed male one who'd come that first time.

'Oh,' she said weakly.

'Is this a bad time?' said DS Mendes. She looked perfect in a trouser suit and grey shirt ironed flat. Did she do her own, or use a service, or perhaps have an adoring man or woman at home to do it for her? Jack's shirts never looked that good when Mary did them.

'It's five in the morning,' she croaked grouchily.

'Yes, sorry for the intrusion. I'm afraid it's urgent. Can we come in?'

Mary hesitated. The place was such a tip after the late pizza dinner they'd had the night before. She hadn't even bothered stacking the dishwasher.

'Or we can do this down at the station?' Diana raised a groomed eyebrow.

'No, no, come in, sorry about the mess.' She ushered them in to the living room, wondering if she should excuse herself to put on trousers. Instead, she pulled her T-shirt over her knees as she sat down opposite them. 'Is everything OK?'

Clearly not. What had she done? Had John Stokes reported them?

'I'm afraid Marlee Stokes has gone missing.'

For a moment she didn't understand. 'Samantha's sister?'

'Yes. Her parents are extremely concerned. It seems she took some clothes and money, so it doesn't look like kidnap.' Diana Mendes fixed her with a stare. 'You saw her when you went to the house.' It wasn't a question.

'I – yeah. I just needed to . . . ask her some questions.'

For a mad moment Mary wondered if she'd fallen into the same trap as Tim, if someone had recorded her talking to the girl and put two and two together.

'You really shouldn't have done that – her father has complained. Did Marlee indicate she was planning to go?'

'She seemed very scared. Her father called her and she went running into the house. She doesn't believe Tim did it either.'

'She didn't say that to us,' said the hot male cop, whose name Mary had forgotten.

'I don't think she trusts you.' It came out more tartly than she intended. 'Look, I have to ask, have you looked at the dad? John Stokes?'

No flicker of reaction. 'Why do you say that?'

'Well, she was clearly afraid of him. And she said she'd heard shouting the night Tim dropped Sam off. So she must have made it back, you see? Maybe it's him who did it all – buried those poor girls at number sixteen, even.'

Just then, Jack came down the stairs, bare-chested and in pyjama bottoms, holding Leo to his pecs. He really had lost some weight. Mary caught the DS sweep her dark eyes over him and felt something she hadn't experienced in a long time – pride? Possessiveness?

'Oh hi,' said Jack, his voice tight with fear. 'What's – is everything OK?'

'Samantha's sister has gone missing.' Mary filled him in, as Audrey clattered down behind her father, unwashed in her vest and pants.

'MUMMY, WHO THESE PEOPLE?'

'It's . . .' God, she couldn't explain it was the police. Not to a toddler. 'Never mind, darling, maybe Daddy will take you upstairs for now.' Jack caught her look and reversed direction.

'Come on, let's do baths and teeth first.'

'But I'm hungry, I'M HUNGRY!' The wails dropped as the bathroom door shut, and Diana Mendes visibly winced.

'Mrs Collins, the situation is very serious. I can't have you sneaking around carrying out your own investigation, or I'm going to have to arrest you for obstruction.'

Mary swallowed hard. She was so stupid, letting herself forget the fear of Tim's arrest and charge.

'I'm sorry. I just – I wanted to help my friend.'

'You better tell me everything you know. Right now, you and your friend Tim are the last two people to see a couple of missing sisters, and let me tell you that doesn't look good.'

Mary sighed, and pulled her T-shirt further over her knees, knowing full well the handsome policeman could probably see her M&S pants. 'Alright. I'll tell you everything.'

When she'd finished with the long and breathless tale of the goings-on in Acacia Close, their visit to the office in Croydon, she looked between them for reactions. Diana wrote it all down in a neat blocky hand.

'You'd sign a statement of what Marlee told you about the shouting, that maybe Samantha had come home after all?'

'Absolutely.'

A glare over the notebook. 'You understand it's a criminal offence if your statement is false.'

'It isn't! I swear.'

'Alright.' A nod between them, and they stood up. 'We'd also like to talk to Tim Darbandi about your visit to the office in Croydon.'

Mary's pulse leapt – he'd breached his bail, so maybe they were going to arrest him again. 'Oh?'

'He doesn't seem to be at home. Any idea where he is?'

'Sorry. No.'

She'd dropped Tim back at his flat yesterday, and couldn't think where else he would be. She thought of his earplugs, the drugs he sometimes took to knock himself out.

'Do let us know if you find him. We'll be in touch.'

And they were gone, just in time for Mary to realise the hot officer had been sitting on a pair of her pants, which for some reason were half-stuffed down the side of the sofa. At least they were clean.

Tim

Since he'd been home, Tim had been desperate to recapture the bone-deep sleep he'd experienced in the police station, that dark oblivion. But back here, in his too-hot too-bright flat, his old friend insomnia waited for him. Lying awake thinking about them all. Sam, Mariam. Alice. John Stokes. Around four, he'd given up and taken an over-the-counter sleep remedy, swallowing twice the recommended dose, until his brain switched off.

He surfaced from it, heavy and dry-mouthed, to hear both his phone and doorbell ringing. Six a.m. He already knew it was going to be Mary as he lumbered from bed, pulling on tracksuit bottoms over his boxers. Mary – for it was indeed her – seemed to have done the same with some athletic shorts, the kind with perforated material round the bottom. She was hugging her arms to herself, and her hair was in disarray. From the way she held her phone, he realised she'd rung him too. His was always silenced at night. For a moment they just stared at each other, two sleepless people wrenched from even the meagre amount they did get.

'It's Marlee,' she said. 'She's gone.'

Somehow it seemed inevitable. His first thought, and he was ashamed of it, was – *at least I have an alibi for this one.* 'Taken?'

'Run away. I think she's trying to find her sister. Come on. I don't see any police cars on the street, but be careful.'

He didn't question her, just ducked back in for his phone and keys, and to shove his feet into his ugly Crocs, then he was trotting after her back to her house, alert every step for sirens.

'The police woke me up,' she said, fiercely. 'The police! I mean, what has my life become? Before all this I don't think I'd even spoken to a police officer. I know that makes me privileged, so don't say it.'

'Wasn't going to. So they're looking for Marlee?'

'They don't think she's been abducted. She took things with her. But Tim, I blame myself – she must have had an idea where Sam was, and I think I tipped her over the edge of going there to look.'

'Did she say where?'

'Obviously not or the police would be there right now.' Mary stopped, fished her key from the cardigan she wore over her nightclothes. She sighed. 'Sorry. It was just a stressful morning. And hardly even six yet. They're looking for you, by the way. They rang your bell, but I guess you were passed out.'

The bail. No doubt John Stokes had tipped them off. His heart began to race.

'I can't go back to jail, Mary.'

The thought of the small airless room seemed to suffocate him. He'd be useless then, unable to find Sam or Marlee. And this was his fault. By trying to help Sam, he'd somehow caused her disappearance, and now that of her sister too. That sweet girl in her oversized hoody. He had to help her.

In their kitchen, Mary's husband was making the little girl pancakes, as she prattled on about syrup (he thought anyway, he wasn't great at making out her speech). Jack nodded to Tim warily. The baby was in a mesh-sided crib chewing on the head of a toy dog. It was hard to imagine it, this many people orbiting around you all the time.

'So what's the plan?'

Mary was clearing plates off the table and motioning for him to sit down. He kept his hands off the table; it was quite sticky.

'Well, you can't stay at home. You have to make yourself scarce or you'll be back in jail. Then we need to find out where she could have gone. Where did I put my phone?' She looked around distractedly, then rummaged in the pocket of her coat, hanging over the kitchen door. She pulled out a USB stick, which she frowned at. 'Oh, I forgot about this.'

'What is it?'

'Photos, my friend's kid took them. He's always snapping away in the local area. I thought he might have seen something useful, so I asked for copies.'

'Well, let's take a look, can't hurt. We need to work through things methodically.'

His mind was running ahead. Where could he go – a hotel? Would the police find him there? He just needed time. They were so close to finding Samantha, he could sense it. And the holiday camp, Golden Sands, he felt in his gut that was the place. He hadn't told Mary about it. Another thing to keep to himself, and for good reason.

Mary plugged the USB into the side of her laptop, booted it up and scrolled through. Tim peered over her shoulder, aware of her smell of shampoo and maple syrup. There were a lot of pictures, mostly of small children and a smiling, dishevelled woman he thought must be Mary's friend. Football in the park, various blurred ones of squirrels and dogs. He was just about to say this was a waste of time when Mary paused.

'Look. Isn't that the garden of number sixteen?'

The picture had been taken out of a window – presumably the child's room. It showed the park, and in the distance the garden of what did indeed look like 16 Cliveden Road.

'Where do they live?'

'Harris Street, other side of the park. So you can see the back gardens of Cliveden Road from there, I'd guess.' She pointed at the screen. 'Look. Who's that?'

There was a figure visible in the garden, which was supposed to be sealed off, and looking at it, Tim could see the garden door was open. The one into the park, which he'd suspected someone had been going in and out of. He'd assumed it was Eric Johnson – but what if someone else had a key too?

'I don't know. One of the police officers?'

'It was taken before the search, look at the date. It's almost a month ago.'

Mary zoomed in, making it blurrier and blurrier. A man in a short-sleeved shirt, stooping down under the big oak tree, as if examining the ground. Suddenly she exclaimed.

'Oh my God, Tim – it's *Nigel*.'

Mary

The wait in the police station seemed to take years. She was acutely aware that she'd spent the morning with Tim, who the police were looking for, and that he was waiting with her car a few streets away from the station. Would they know somehow? Perhaps they'd been tracking her? The drive over had shredded her nerves, alert for any sign they were being followed. The plan was that she would talk to Mendes, and, hopefully with this new evidence, Tim could finally be cleared. She'd handed the USB in to the desk sergeant, a woman with dyed red hair and bleeding lipstick, who could not have been less interested. Mary tried again. 'You'll make sure it gets to DS Mendes? It's really important.'

The sergeant didn't look up from her computer screen. 'She has it.'

So why hadn't she come out? Mary had just handed over proof, or near-enough proof, that Nigel from number thirteen was the killer. He'd lived in the area for decades, during the time when all the girls had gone missing. He was a gardener and handyman, someone with the tools to bury bodies. And he appeared to have a key for the back door of number sixteen. She wondered why — maybe in the way that neighbours used to give each other keys when they went on holiday, to water plants or in case they locked themselves out. Did people still do that? Her own downstairs neighbours were a young couple in their thirties, who she'd never spoken to even once, but sometimes heard their music on a week-end night, far too late, and she'd nag at Jack to go and have a word but he always pretended to be asleep. But she couldn't think badly of Jack any more – he had the kids again today. She couldn't do this without him.

Finally, after what seemed like forever, the door into the station opened and Diana Mendes came out. Her hair was loose and shiny today. It was Sunday, and Mary wondered if she ever took time off.

'Mary. Do come with me.'

It was Mary again today, not Mrs Collins. Was that a good sign?

Mary followed her down a long carpeted corridor, irrationally worried that she'd never be allowed out again. They reached a small interview room, and Mary was ushered inside without a word, the door closing after them, muffling sound. Diana sat down opposite and waved Mary to the chair. The USB stick was on the table in a plastic bag.

'Where did you get this, Mary?'

'A friend's little boy took the pictures. He's ten – always snap-ping all kinds of random things. I looked through them and rec-ognised the man.'

'You're referring to the image from June twenty-fourth, I believe.'

'Right. It's Nigel, the man from number thirteen. I don't know his surname.'

'It's quite blurry, Mary.'

'Yeah, but I'm sure it's him. He must have a key to the garden of number sixteen. He's lived there years, he could have got it at any point. To water the plants or something.'

Diana looked confused. 'Have you any other reason to suspect this man?'

'He lives right across the street, and he's been there for years like I said. And he didn't want Eric to buy the house – had a petition against the renovation. Maybe he was worried they'd dig up the garden and find something there. It was his door-cam that recorded Tim, right? Don't you think it's a bit weird he has a camera trained on the house all the time? Like he's keeping an eye on it?'

She didn't seem convinced. 'We'll look into this. But I have to tell you, Mary, we're still searching for your friend Tim as a matter of urgency. I'll ask you again, have you any idea where he is?'

Outside in my car.

'Um, no.' She couldn't risk it. If they arrested Nigel, searched his house maybe, they might find something that proved he was behind the murders. 'Doesn't this sort of exonerate Tim though?'

'Hardly. And I don't see the connection to Samantha. Or Marlee.'

'Is there no sign of them?'

'We're looking. So if you have any information, I suggest you give it to me now.'

'Um – I don't.'

That was also a lie, but what could she say? *It's probably their dad, and we think he's hiding Sam at one of the sites he manages?* She tried, 'I really think she made it home that night, when Tim dropped her off.'

'Her family say she didn't.'

'But they might be lying!'

Diana sighed. 'Mary, I know you believe your friend is innocent, and certainly the evidence against him is shaky. But equally there's no evidence anyone else is involved in Samantha's disappearance. Tim is the only person we have on camera in her company. Him breaching his bail and now absconding is also not a favourable sign. Nor is the fact that he's been stalking his ex-wife for some time now.'

'Come on. Stalking's a bit much.'

'Following her and peering in her windows and obsessively reading her social media? Sounds like stalking to me.'

Mary bit her lip. 'Alright. Can I go? My kids need me.'

'You're free to go. But please do come to me straight away if you hear from Tim, or learn any new information.'

Mary wanted to mutter that there was no point, since every time she went to the police they didn't seem to believe her. Instead she thanked the woman and let herself be led back to reception.

Out on the grimy streets of Lewisham, she breathed fresh air with relief. She began the short walk back to the car, thoughts churning frantically. All they could do now, without risking Tim going back to prison, was go and check out the sites John Stokes managed. And there were dozens. Where would they even start?

She turned into the street where she'd parked the car. Looked up and down for her familiar red Fiat.

Nothing. There was nothing there.

Tim, and the car, had vanished.

Tim

He barely drew breath until he was out of Lewisham and heading south, through Bexleyheath and down towards Kent. He was juggling his phone on his lap to try and find the route, and trying not to think about the fact that he'd just stolen Mary's car. It rang several times, her name flashing up. She must be furious, but she'd be OK. She could easily get the bus home, or call an Uber. It was better for her if she didn't come, because he'd already put her in too much danger, dragged her into police stations and rancid bedsits and murder investigations. Mary was a nice woman, a lawyer, a mother of two. She deserved to live her safe middle-class life, and so Tim had left her behind while he went to try and save a missing girl. Two missing girls, maybe.

Golden Sands, an abandoned holiday camp that had closed in the seventies, was in Kent, between the Isle of Sheppey and Whitstable. The weather had turned, an uneasy grey wind whipping the trees as he sped the car to the coast. There would perhaps be a storm to break the run of hot, oppressive days. He slowed down to under seventy – the last thing he needed was to be pulled over and sent back to prison. He couldn't think about what might happen if he didn't find Samantha. A trial, which he'd probably lose. Then prison for him, maybe for a very long time. The loss of everything he had left, which had seemed so little, but all the same he could not bear to let go.

After an hour, the suburbs of London had given way to motorways and McDonald's drive-throughs. He saw a turn-off for Rawlston Beach, where the holiday camp had once attracted thousands of holidaymakers, who now likely flew to Majorca or Tenerife instead. He almost missed the turning, which took him on to a narrowing dirt road to the gates of the camp, a rusty chain fence across the drive. He parked Mary's car by the side of the track, and got out.

A restless wind whistled past his ears, blowing sand and dust. The only sound was the distant roar of the M2, and the wind blowing an old metal sign, faded away with age and missing letters – GOLDEN SANDS. In the distance, down an overgrown tarmac path, Tim could see low buildings, chalets and a restaurant, all abandoned. If Samantha was here, she would be in one of those. He began to walk towards it, feet crunching on the sandy ground.

Samantha

He wasn't coming. It had been three days now. She'd even checked and re-checked the smudges she'd made in the dirt on the wall, and it was definitely three days. Yet no sign of him. All she had left to eat was one packet of instant noodles, and after she'd tried to throw boiling water at him he'd taken the stove away, so she'd have to eat them dry, crumbling them with her fingers. What happened when that was gone? Her large water bottle was almost empty too. At the beginning she'd struggled to even lift it, pouring some on to the floor instead of the flimsy cup he'd left her. Now it was just a trickle and she could easily bring the huge container to her mouth.

You need to sort this out, Sam.

He wouldn't just leave her here, would he? He was just punishing her. Showing her who was in charge. Surely his plan was not to actually hurt her, let her slowly starve? Or not so slowly die of thirst? They said you had three days without water, didn't they? She had visions of being found when this place was finally knocked down and redeveloped, perhaps years in the future, a shrivelled corpse pressed up against the door she couldn't get through.

No. This was an old shack, there had to be a way to escape. She was young, she was strong, if a bit weak from hunger. And she was angry, with the strength that gave. She would find a way.

First, she scoured the dirty building from top to bottom. She was already so filthy it made no difference. Stupid, to have wasted so much precious water washing her hands and face. To think she'd been worried about skipping her usual skincare regime! Even at Eric's, although the place was half-built and the attic gross, there was a proper bathroom, brand new, so she'd been able to shower. He'd insisted on it, in fact. He was fastidious. Showers before and after. Even though he wasn't touching her in that way. She had to leave no trace of herself, bring nothing with her, even her phones. But this place was coated in the dust and grease of decades and she hadn't felt clean since she'd been here, her nails that she'd once been so fussy about ringed in black, and her clothes stained and sweaty. She had no mirror but knew her face would also be grimy and her hair dark with oil. She could smell herself, a rank sweet stink. What if she never got out of here, and just kept getting dirtier and smellier until she died? At first she'd dreamed of hot showers and posh gels. Now she dreamed of water, a tall and overflowing glass of it, beads of condensation on the side. A plate of roast dinner like her mum used to make, while she still could. Swimming in gravy and crunchy potatoes, fatty meat. God, she was hungry. And soon she would be thirsty. She'd been sipping the lukewarm plasticky water slowly but it was almost all gone. If only she hadn't gone home that night, instead of hiding out in a hotel like Eric wanted – stupid, to worry about her mother, to want her to know she was alright. Her mother had been too out of it to care for years now. If only Shell hadn't posted that bitchy comment on Facebook, deleted quickly, but not before he'd seen it. If only she hadn't underestimated him, believed she could explain it all away. If only, if only. Pointless to think that way.

So, what resources did she have in her grimy prison? Shards of plaster and masonry – potentially able to cut something. Her sleeping bag, which could maybe be ripped up to make a rope – but she was on the ground floor, so what use would that be? The plastic from her bottles and cups and cutlery, which could also be ripped into sharp pieces. But if he wasn't coming back, she couldn't attack him again. Anyway, he'd be wary of her now. He wouldn't let her.

Where was he, though? If he hadn't just left her here without food or water to teach her a lesson, then there was an even worse scenario. What if something had happened to him? He'd had an accident in his stupid car, despite his anal driving, and he couldn't tell anyone where she was, or there'd been an emergency and he couldn't get away. Or even more likely, he'd been arrested. Perhaps they knew what he'd done and had taken him in, but he wouldn't tell them where he was holding her. Either way, only one person knew where she was and if he didn't come, she was screwed. Samantha lay down on the dirty floorboards, her face pressed right against all the gritty grime. She had no idea what to do.

Mary

She should have gone home. That would have been the logical move when she realised Tim had stolen her car – go home to her children, take care of them, give up her amateur sleuthing. But instead she'd ordered an Uber to Alice's house, formerly Tim's house. He wasn't answering his phone, of course, and it just rang out.

Once again Alice was in gym clothes, slim and toned, her red hair in a bun, her make-up-less skin glowing. She sighed when she saw Mary at her door.

'Look, I really can't help you.'

'You told the police he'd been following you?'

'I had to. I've no idea what he's capable of, Mary. Neither do you.'

'He's taken my car.'

She digested this. Mary was still on the doorstep, and Alice had not stood back to let her in. 'That just proves my point.'

'Do you know where he might have gone?'

'How would I?'

'I think he's trying to find her. Samantha – her sister's run away now as well. I think Tim's in danger, Alice.'

Her face was crossed by a complicated look. Anger, and a hint of guilt. 'He's been putting himself in danger since I've known him. Probably he's missed it, the thrill of running from bombs and bullets.'

Was that what this was about – had Tim actually *wanted* to throw himself into harm's way? And dragged her with him.

'Please – I just need some idea where to find him. Is there anywhere he'd go, a place he has connections to?'

'I don't know. I try not to think about Tim if I can help it.'

She went to close the door and Mary blocked it, shocked by her own daring.

'I think it's because of what happened. The woman who died in the bombing. He's trying to, I don't know, redeem himself or something. He blames himself, maybe.'

Alice stared at her. 'Oh, no, you've misunderstood. Mariam didn't die in the attack.'

Mary was confused. 'She didn't?'

'She was injured, they both were, but they survived. And Tim came back a week later, with his leg in a cast. I picked him up from Heathrow. Are you married?'

'Yes.'

'You can imagine, I'm sure, the kind of welcome you'd give your husband if he almost died. Even if he annoys you a lot of the time. Maybe a selfish bit of me thought, this is it now, he won't be able to travel as much. He can stay here, and I can finally have a family.'

Mary was nodding hard. She understood this exactly. 'So what—'

'As soon as we get home, I'm putting his clothes in the washing machine when he breaks it to me. He's in love with this Mariam, they've been having an affair, and he's going back to Syria for her. They'll start the visa process and then get married, as soon as he's divorced me, of course.'

A short silence. 'Oh.'

298

'Yeah. So, well – that was that. We fought, I cried, but he'd made his mind up. He went to Syria. Then, I don't know what happened exactly, but he came back. She was dead. It had come out about their affair, and her family – well, they were quite conservative. Didn't mind her working or going to university, but the shame of this, an affair with a married Westerner, I suppose it was too much, how public it was, the two of them injured on the way into his hotel.'

'They *killed* her?' Mary was horrified.

'Officially it was an accident. But Tim believed he'd got her killed. We tried again but, well, he was just too damaged. So you see, he doesn't know what he's doing. He's unstable, he doesn't think clearly. If you go after him, you'll be putting yourself in danger too.'

Tim

Tim felt he'd been walking forever, and yet he didn't seem to be getting any closer to Samantha. The sun burned high through the clouds, crushing down like on that day, death coming out of the white sky. He was sweating and panting, less fit than he'd been then. Just . . . less. A shadow of himself in all ways.

The site was enormous, half-derelict chalets here and there, the paths cracked with weeds and the paint peeling, as if the wood had some scrofulous disease. How could he ever find someone here? He tried shouting 'Hello?' His voice croaked – he had forgotten to take any water with him and he'd been walking for almost an hour already, seeming to make no progress. Alice would have thought of that. How stupid he'd been, to hurt her like he had. Even though he'd loved Mariam, he had loved Alice too, and could have been happy with her. Instead he'd been selfish, and stupid, and it had resulted in disaster. Both women lost to him.

Mariam came to his mind, the way she often did, a smiling ghost, her heavy dark hair only he was allowed to see, her soft lips. The reserve between them if they ever went out in public, the forbidden touch that Tim found so very erotic. The way he'd last seen her, at the hospital that time, lying in bed with her eyes closed but awake, her hand resting in his. His own leg broken and serious lung issues. Dust turning her dark hair white, so he could see how she'd look when she was old, and it was that which made up his mind. He could not lose her again. His paper had demanded he come home right away, as their insurance would no longer cover him, so Tim flew out with his leg in plaster. And then, riding the wave of survival euphoria, he'd told Alice he loved someone else and had gone back, as soon as he could manage the flight, still limping, his paper furious. Ready to offer himself to Mariam, though who knew how they'd work it out. She'd have to come to the UK with him – they couldn't be together in Syria, not with her family – and immigration might be an issue, but he would sort it. He would be with her. She had been quiet for a few days, but communications were always patchy in a war zone. Anyway, it was romantic, wasn't it, just to turn up and declare himself.

The details of the drive from the airport were etched in his memory. The driver's BO in the chill air of the car, the smell of his cigarettes. Tim's own sweaty body from the plane – belatedly wondering if he should go to a hotel and shower first, but he couldn't wait. Surely she wouldn't mind him travel-stained, when they were both alive, a miracle. The cracked and dusty road around her apartment block, the buzz of the security guard's radio. Asking for her, seeing the man's face change. Then his arrest, the police station with the chain-smoking cops, and asking over and over what had happened to her, where was she, why could he not see her. Eventually the answer, after hours of questions. She'd fallen down the stairs in the apartment block, they said. Her neck was broken, she was dead. Just a sad accident – she had tripped, still unsteady on her feet – or perhaps she'd been unhappy, perhaps the bomb had broken something in her and she couldn't recover. Perhaps it was because he left, they implied. The CCTV had stopped working, apparently, so no one could tell what had really happened. But Tim knew. That brother she'd been so afraid of, with his expensive sunglasses and snapping gum. Her family had done this. Because of him. Because he was married, their affair exposed by the bombing they had survived, and she had not survived this. He'd got her killed. He, who had prided himself on helping women, reporting on their stories, insisting on female translators and camera operators, had directly caused a woman to come to harm, through his own selfish blindness. He had never been able to forgive himself. So he had to do his best for Marlee, and for Sam, and to keep Mary away from the place, because he'd done enough damage already.

Mary

Once again back at the same cul-de-sac, the bland neat houses of Acacia Close, that might have concealed so much. She'd taken another Uber there from Alice's, though every part of her knew she should be going home. Picking up the threads of her life, which was a good life, even if she didn't get much sleep. She still loved her husband, or at least fancied him, which was maybe even better at this stage. She had two beautiful children and her job was waiting for her, even if Francesca was stealing all her thunder. She had no need to run about after a virtual stranger, one with a dodgy past he hadn't told her about.

But all the same, she couldn't stop now. He'd helped her when she was lost, shown her a way back to herself, and she could not leave Tim to be sent back to prison. Let alone what might happen if he faced John Stokes.

The drive to the house had taken half an hour. Then Mary had lurked about the entrance of the street, hiding behind some wheelie bins, until John Stokes drove off in his black Audi. He was going too fast – far too fast for the street – to see her, but all the same she felt sick. If he caught her, what would he do? Maybe she should go after him, see if he led her to Samantha. But there'd never be time since she didn't have her own car – bloody Tim, leaving her in the lurch.

She flip-flopped up the curving street, wishing she'd worn quieter shoes. It was hot, the air greasy and restless. A storm coming, maybe. A snatch of pop music drifting from one of the houses. She didn't know why she felt so worried. Maggie Stokes was a frail, confused woman, she could surely pose no danger. She tried to think how she'd feel if both Leo and Audrey were missing, and the sudden lurch into her throat almost made her gasp. But what if Maggie knew where her girls were? What if John was holding them somewhere, and she knew all about it? It seemed unthinkable, but it did happen. There was no such thing as unthinkable.

Despite the quiet, Mary had the impression of eyes watching her from behind the slatted blinds and curtains. It was suburbia. People had time to peer out of the window. She decided it wasn't worth ringing the bell, and instead slipped around the side of the house, hoping no one would call the police about a burglar. The back gate was unlocked, letting her into the garden. It was neatly kept – the grass had even been cut recently. If her kids were missing she'd be crawling the streets, pulling up manhole covers and digging under bushes, not doing the garden. The house looked deserted, but the patio doors were ajar, to let in some air presumably on such a stifling day. Heart racing at her own daring, Mary stepped inside, her flip-flops echoing on the floor tiles. He was gone, wasn't he? Nothing to be scared of. Was there any chance Sam was here, as she'd thought before, silenced in an upstairs room? The kitchen was spotless, not a plate or glass left out. The tea towel folded on the draining rack. The place mats square on the table, as if put in position by a ruler. And now Mary noticed that some of the cupboards had padlocks on them, shutting them tight. What did it mean? She didn't want to think about it. Through into the living room, crackly carpet under her feet, a feeling of airlessness. The faint sound of a TV – someone was here.

'Hello?' she called, hearing her voice waver in the silence. 'Maggie, are you here?'

Oh God, this was mad. What if Maggie Stokes called the police, and both Mary and Tim went to prison, him for breaching bail, her for trespass, or harassment? Mary stepped further into the house. Maggie Stokes was exactly where she'd been last time, in the armchair in front of the TV, which played rolling news with the volume down so low it was barely audible. It was in a cabinet, which Mary saw also had a padlock, hanging loose. Maggie was staring into space at a point just above the TV. A sweating glass of water sat at her feet.

'Maggie.'

The woman jumped, splashing some of the water, and Mary braced herself for screaming, but she didn't react. Her eyes travelled over Mary.

'You're in your shoes. He doesn't like that.'

'Who – John?'

'He doesn't like it.' A vague recognition came to her eyes. 'You're that woman who was here before.'

'Yes, I'm – I've been trying to find Sam.' And why hadn't her own mother done everything to look for her? 'Is your husband here?' Mary knew he wasn't, but maybe he'd be back soon.

'At work.'

That could be anywhere, with his vast network of properties. Perhaps he'd gone to Sam, if he was holding her somewhere. Or perhaps Sam was long dead and this was all for nothing.

'And Marlee, she's – she's missing too?'

The woman's face was empty, fully made-up, her clothes and hair and face as neat and clean as the house. But her eyes were not. They wandered, a wildness trapped in there.

'She ran off.'

'I'm sorry. You must be so worried.' Mary sat down on the nearby sofa without being asked, close enough to touch the woman's arm, which she did, tentatively. No reaction. 'I have two little ones; I can't imagine how you must be feeling.'

'She'll be alright. She's just gone off somewhere, she'll come back.' An odd thing to say about a twelve-year-old.

'And Sam? Do you – what do you think happened to her?'

No answer. The eyes moved again, and she groped for her glass of water. It was empty, but she drank from it anyway, though nothing remained. 'She was always a handful. He only wanted to help her. Marlee, she was a good girl, but she's been led astray.'

'Maggie, I know this must be hard. But you know where Sam is, don't you? Does he have her – your husband? I know Sam came home a week ago.'

Did she know that? She was ninety per cent sure she could trust Tim, but doubt remained.

'He only wanted to help her. She was so wild.'

'John, you mean? Was he harsh on Sam?'

'Only for her own good.' Her voice was buttoned up, as if she was swallowing it down. Mary thought hard. How was she going to break this woman, who seemed to have shrunk from fear into a small, compact version of herself? There must be some love for her children in there. 'She had to learn. What life's really like – not these dreams of money and glamour. She needed to knuckle down and get a real job, earn some money.'

It sounded like she was parroting someone else's words.

Mary took out her phone. 'Can I show you this?' A video of Audrey dancing round Leo's bouncy chair, making him laugh, following his big sister with his eyes. A trill of joyful laughter. Reluctantly, Maggie Stokes's eyes turned to it. 'This is my daughter, and her brother. Sam was like that once, wasn't she? I know she's grown up now, and she fights you on a lot of things I'm sure – my daughter fights me on everything and she's two, for goodness' sake – but she's still your little girl.' The woman's mouth moved slightly. 'Please, Maggie. I know he's your husband and you need him, but Sam needs you more now. And Marlee. She's gone to find Sam, hasn't she? She might be in danger. So please – tell me what you know.'

A few seconds of silence ticked by, and Mary thought Maggie wasn't going to break, that she'd retreated so far into a chemical fug, or perhaps one of fear and coercion, that she didn't care what happened to her daughters. Then she said, eyes back towards the TV: 'I don't know for sure.'

Mary grabbed at it. 'But he's got her somewhere?'

'She came home. About a week ago. Wasn't missing at all before that – she'd left a note, you know. Saying not to worry, she'd be back. He was just trying to find her, that's what it was all about. Going on TV and that. He was ever so angry she'd gone.'

So they had never been really worried. The emotion she'd witnessed wracking John Stokes during his TV interviews and press conferences, it wasn't fear at all. It was rage. That Samantha had gone off, dared to live her own life.

'He wanted to track her down?'

It was something she'd heard of at work, women's husbands reporting them missing when they finally got the courage to flee domestic violence. So well-meaning people might report sightings of them, and the police would get involved to bring them back. Alana had once lectured her on this point, that you weren't actually supposed to repost missing person appeals, yet another risk in the minefield that was social media.

'He was angry.' Maggie's voice was flat, unaffected. 'Then Sam turned up at the door, safe and sound. He went ballistic. He'd found her outfits, her shoes and things – he knew what she'd been up to. Getting paid for it. Dirty. He was so angry.'

'So . . . he punished her? He took her somewhere?'

'Just to sort her out, that's what he said. Just for a little while.' Her eyes shifted to Mary, and some real feeling seemed to burn through. 'She will be OK, won't she? I don't want her hurt. She just needs to learn.'

'Yes, yes, I'm sure she will, if we find her soon – where is she, Maggie? Have you any idea? Has he gone to see her since?' He must have been bringing her food, surely, wherever she was.

She hesitated, as if slow wheels were turning in her brain. 'I think it's not far. Kent, maybe. Within an hour. It's like . . . some big old abandoned place. Near the beach. A holiday park.'

'Brilliant. That's brilliant, Maggie.' Not that many sites near the coast in Kent, surely. She'd be able to narrow it down fast. She stood up. 'Thank you. You've been very brave.' Then she remembered this woman had sat beside her husband and asked the country to help find a daughter she knew very well had left of her own free will. Still, fear could override love sometimes. 'You know . . . there are people who can help. I can give you some information, if you want? You don't have to live like this.' The eyes shifted to Mary again, slightly baffled, then back to the TV. That was it, the interview was clearly over.

Mary hustled to the door, phone out to search for old holiday parks. Too late, she realised she should have taped the confession. Would it stand up in court? Would the police even believe her after all their dealings? She didn't know. But at least she might be able to find Sam.

Samantha

She was having trouble staying awake. That was a bad sign, she knew, because she was someone who rarely fell asleep. It was always a big effort, as if fighting to trick her brain into looking the other way so the back part of it would blank out. She wished there was a button you could hold down to force quit your brain, like on a computer. But the last day or so – she wasn't even sure any more what was day and what was night – things had been hazy. The growling in her stomach had dulled somehow, and all she could think about was water. She dreamed of it, of gulping down salt seas and still being thirsty. Her skin was dry and flaky, the tips of her fingers wrinkled as if she'd been in water, ironically. She had a trickle of warm plastic liquid in the bottom of her big jug and nothing else. He hadn't come. He was leaving her here to die, or else something had happened to him. Maybe it wasn't true that he wouldn't hurt her. He'd broken her arm that time, hadn't he, furious that she'd touched his computer, but after that he'd been more careful. Nothing that showed. Usually nothing physical, but you didn't need that if you had your family terrified into doing everything you wanted. He'd had a tracker on her phone, Eric said – a Find My Family app. He'd taken the phones away while she was at his, even the cheap one he'd given her, so she couldn't be found, but she'd been found out anyway. She'd had the phone back for only a few hours before it was taken away again. Maybe she'd just pushed him too far this time.

Either way, she didn't have much time left. A day, maybe less. Her brain was shutting down non-essential systems. She hadn't needed to pee in the horrible back room for ages now. Just didn't feel the urge. Her vision was going round the edges, flashing lights and everything greying. She found herself thinking of her family. Dad, her real dad, that she'd only just got to know, and she understood it now, how sometimes it all just got too much, life, how you'd do almost anything, reach for a pill or a bottle of whisky, if that could make you feel better. He'd changed, he was different now. And sweet Marlee, a good little sister, even if Sam hadn't always protected her. Her mother, weak but broken, not her fault. Shell, her good friend once, could be again. Jackson even – he was a twat but they'd had some good times. She'd do anything right now to listen to him drone on about how he made his protein shakes. But that was liquid, and thinking about liquid drove her a little more crazy each time.

OK, Sam, so what are you going to do? Just lie down and die here?

She'd tried it all – prying open the shutters till her nails bled. Smashing at the padlock with a wooden slat she'd pried from the wall, until she'd bashed her own thumb and cried at the pain. Her hands, once always manicured, were a mess now, bleeding and torn. Shell would be horrified. But she might never see Shell again, dumb cow that she was, so bitchy the last few times they'd seen each other. Her snipey little Facebook comments giving Sam away. Of course *he* was friends with her on there. He'd insisted. He saw everything. *What did that mean, Samantha? I just wonder why someone would say that as a joke. I think I better have a look in your room.*

She'd tried throwing things to break the high windows, and standing on a pile of junk to climb up to them, but it wouldn't hold her weight and she'd fallen, twisting her ankle, which was purple now and pulpy in a really gross way, like over-ripe fruit. She'd shouted until her voice gave out, in case someone was nearby walking. She'd even tried throwing boiling water at him and grabbing the keys! That must have been it. She'd pissed him off, like she always did, and he wasn't coming back.

She did, however, have one match left, which she'd thought to hide in her bra before she threw the water. Just in case. He'd taken the matchbook, of course, but you could strike them against anything rough. Couldn't you?

As the hours ticked down, Sam found she was waiting. For what? For the last moment there was hope. She had to strike this match – and she would get only one chance to do it right, firm and hard against the floor – while she had enough strength in her hands, and her vision was clear enough to do it. But when was that? Because it was risky. If she was going to burn down the hut, there was every chance no one would see the flames in time, and she would suffocate to death out here, choking on dirty black smoke, gasping for a gulp of air to save her. She put the match down carefully – she was too sweaty to keep it close to her body. She wasn't ready yet. But she didn't have much longer.

Tim

He started to himself. He had lost time – blacked out again. No wonder, since he'd been awake since six. And before that, hardly slept for months. Hardly eaten, hardly drunk water. He was running on fumes, and the huge area of the holiday site was straining his injured leg, which was dragging behind him like a tired child. How long had he lost? He looked at his phone, which had no reception, and saw he'd been here for well over two hours. His skin was starting to tingle in the salty, sand-gritted air, blasted by wind, still hot as hell and no rain in sight.

He was near the beach now, a strip of shingle boiled by grey water. Dead fish scattered here and there along the shoreline. He tried calling out: 'Samantha. Are you here?' but his voice was swallowed by the elements. Could she really be here? Or Marlee – what if he was totally wrong, and neither girl was at the site? Or what if he was too late?

Tim stood on the desolate beach, and on the wind he thought he caught a snatch of something. Crying – a woman's voice. Was it real, or another hallucination? He began to stumble over the shingle towards the noise, getting it into his shoes, sinking up to his ankles.

Mary

Mary had taken a third Uber all the way to rural Kent, and was horrified at the expense and wastefulness. How would she ever explain this to Jack, that she'd gone off on a whim to an abandoned holiday park she'd found on an urban explorers' forum, not even sure if Tim was here or she had the right place? She couldn't face telling Jack that Tim had taken their car. *I told you so,* he'd say. She'd been helping a man who'd lied to her, making excuses every step of the way for his behaviour and her own. A sunk-cost fallacy, they called it. As if she had waded into the sea for a paddle and not noticed it seeping up to her waist. She couldn't go back – she had to keep going forward.

The driver had been very dubious, explaining to her that no one was here, the place was long shut down. That was OK, Mary insisted. Yes, she was sure he could leave her. And here she was, somewhere several miles out of Whitstable, a desolate strand of the Kent beach, crunching over stones and dirt. The heat somehow made it all worse, listless and baking, the occasional angry swirl of wind. She was so stupid. She'd no idea if she would even find anything here. The driver's tyres crunched on the dirt road, and he was gone. She was alone.

Mary had just reached the dilapidated entrance, the G of Golden Sands missing, when she heard a noise above the swish of the waves and the wind in distant trees. A car. Someone else was driving up the narrow, cracked road to the camp. As it got closer, she could see it was a black Audi. One that she recognised.

Tim

He'd lost more time. When Tim next came to himself, he was standing in front of a run-down chalet, its roof fallen in, and there was masonry round his ankles.

Oh yes, he thought. *I'm back. There's been another bomb.*

What had happened? He tried to think. He'd been trudging through the holiday camp, every step weighed down by heat and weariness. There'd been a noise, he'd run towards it. He'd been confronted with this – the caved-in roof, the rubble settling from a recent collapse. And he'd frozen, gone back in time as if through a sinkhole to the past. But it was now. He wasn't buried under rocks, waiting to run out of air. He had survived. Mariam had too, but he'd lost her all the same. Her neck, the pale neck he'd loved to kiss, had snapped as she fell from the top of the stairs. Was pushed.

There was another noise, one he also remembered from that day. Whimpering. Someone was in pain, buried under the fallen wood and plaster of the chalet. Someone was in there. A woman. Could it be?

'Sam?' he tried, his own voice dry and rusty.

Another groan – the voice of a young girl. Without thinking about it, Tim fell to his knees and for the second time in his life began digging through debris with his bare hands, hardly feeling the scrapes and cuts. He had to get to her. This couldn't happen again.

Samantha

She had been dreaming. She was back in Eric's house, a place where she'd somehow felt safe, despite its horrors. She'd loved to listen to him talk during their time together, often wishing she had a little notebook to write it all down. Sometimes she tried to remember everything he'd said, but she always forgot bits of it. He was someone who'd had nothing, and he'd built himself up to have everything. That could be her too. She would live in a penthouse apartment on the river, like his, and bring Marlee with her, have Shell over to stay. It would all be fine. And it still could be. She had to believe it.

It was strange how she'd been happy in Eric's house, despite having nothing to do and none of her stuff. It was her who'd pushed it more extreme, saying he should choke her a bit, carefully, for accuracy. Wanting to earn her place, to help him out, because he'd helped her. Maybe being happy was just about being free. No one knocking on the door if she stayed in the bathroom too long, rattling the handle. *Samantha? Can you come out of there please, other people want to use it. It's very selfish of you.* There was nowhere to hide things at home. Even right under her bed up against the wall, it would be found during the rigorous weekly cleaning sessions he insisted on. She and Marlee had to empty out their drawers in front of him every week too, in case of drugs, he said. She'd taken to carrying her extra phone tucked into the waistband of her jeans, under big baggy jumpers, but one time it fell out in the kitchen, right under her mother's nose. She'd picked it up and hid it before he came in, said she'd dropped a tin, which she got in trouble for. She watched her mother to see if she'd give her away, but Mum didn't say a word. That glassiness was a useful cover, sometimes.

Sam jerked awake. She wasn't in the cool quiet of Eric's house, the trees outside her window. She was in the boiling, filthy hut, and her tongue felt coated in dust, so dry she could barely swallow. The match. Where was it? She reached around the floor, frantic for a second, before her fingers nudged it. It was time. She knew it.

She was drifting between sleep and reality. She was seriously dehydrated, and she'd stopped even being hungry. She could barely summon the energy to stand up – any longer and she might not be able to escape even if the fire cleared her an escape route. It was now.

She was so scared. To deliberately set fire to the box you were locked inside, that was mad. But it was the only way. She picked up the match and drew it hard over the rough floor. But her hand wavered, and it didn't light. The top blackened slightly.

Come on, come on.

Another go. Nothing. Jesus!

Come on, Sam! This is your only chance!

Holding on to her own wrist, she struck hard and firm, and the match flared, a small golden light, a smell that took her back to bonfire night. Quick – light something! She held the match to her sleeping bag, dirty and ragged as it was. A tongue of flame licked along it, and Sam jumped back, shocked at the sudden heat in her face. It had worked. Now she just had to get out before the place burned down.

Mary

She didn't understand what had happened. As the black Audi approached, dust kicked up under its wheels, she'd started to run. Where to, she had no idea, and there was no point because he'd reached her in seconds and was out of the car, and then he had her by the arms. She didn't black out, the way people always seemed to on TV or in books. Instead, it was more like her body and mind had frozen the minute he laid hands on her.

Mary had not been touched by a man with violence, not ever. She knew she was lucky – at work she sometimes heard stories of horrific abuse in marriages, saw the clinical time-stamped images of black eyes and bloodied noses, arms in slings, bruises in the shape of a hand. But when it happened to her, when John Stokes got out of his car and punched her hard in the face, then tightened his arm across her throat so she couldn't breathe, dragged her into the passenger seat, she was so shocked and frightened she wasn't able to do a thing. Then he had sped off over the rough paths of the holiday park, with her bumping around beside him. She could not speak – there was no air in her lungs – and she heard herself making little animal noises of pain and fear. Her nose felt blocked, crunching on her face.

'Shut up,' he'd said, and he punched her again, this time on the side of her jaw. Mary had gasped. Shooting stars in front of her eyes, teeth rattling, her mouth filled with blood. Had he knocked one out? Oh God, she'd be toothless. For some reason her thoughts were all of vanity as he had stopped again, in front of an abandoned building, this time with stone pebble-dashed walls. He dragged her out, and she was as limp as a doll in his grasp, and she didn't understand why she couldn't fight back. He was pressing on her windpipe, and as panic rose, she thought of those women who'd been strangled during 'rough sex', their killers serving only a few years or no time at all. This was how they must have felt. The rising terror.

Oh God, I can't breathe. This isn't happening. It can't be.

But it was.

Now she was lying on the ground of a small room in that building – it looked as if it had once been a kitchen and dining room, and she was in what she thought was a kind of freezer, a sort of walk-in meat locker thing. The walls were metal and there was no light, and a faint smell of meat lingered. The floor was filthy with dirt and debris, but she couldn't seem to pick herself up off it. She had done her best to kick and rattle the door, but it was locked fast. She was imprisoned, and she wished Tim were here so she could tell him he was right – John Stokes was the villain in this story after all.

Tim

He had her. He had her. Hands bleeding and sore, he pulled Marlee Stokes from the ruins of the small building, choking and crying, her clothes and face white. She was OK, he could see. The place was built of wood and plaster, not heavy stone. Flimsy. She was alright, but she was terrified, crying and moaning. He laid her on the overgrown, parched grass nearby and tried to clear her face of hair and dirt.

'Marlee? It's me, Tim. Do you remember?'

Tears cleared streaks down her face. 'What happened?'

'I don't know. Did it fall on you?'

'I was looking for her. I tried to check every hut, but there's so many. There's like hundreds. It just came down on me.'

The old hut must have tumbled on her head when she pushed the door open – there were signs everywhere on site warning that the buildings were unstable, but Marlee was twelve; she must not have noticed or cared.

'You were looking for Sam?'

'He has her here, I know it. That lady came and said you drove Sam home. And I heard shouting and it wasn't a journalist, he was lying, I know it. I looked at his car satnav and saw he's been coming here.'

Tim tried to follow this half-choked-out speech. 'You mean Sam did come home after all?'

'Well yeah, you brought her, didn't you?'

To be believed was such a simple pleasure that Tim's heart leapt, despite the dire situation they were in. He squeezed the girl's hand in gratitude. He had not entirely trusted himself, he realised. But the proof was emerging – he wasn't crazy, he hadn't hurt Sam.

'Your dad has her?'

'He took her here, I know he did. But it's so big. I got the train and it took all my money and I had to walk so far over the beach. I'm so tired. And I can't find her.'

Tim helped her sit up, wishing he had water. He patted her back ineffectually – she was wearing a large hoody and jeans, both filthy. Her hair was matted. Poor kid.

'Come on, let's get you somewhere safe. I have a car.'

'But we can't go without her!'

'We'll call the police. You can explain your dad took her, and it will all be OK. He wasn't going to hurt her, was he? Just . . . scare her a bit?'

She bit her lip. 'I don't know. He gets so cross sometimes. It's like – we can hardly breathe, in case we do something to annoy him. Mostly Sam. She would take the blame for me, so he didn't shout at me. But he hated her, he was always so mad at her. One time, I think he broke her arm. Everyone said she fell off a swing but she was too big for swings. I think he did it.'

'Does he hit you?'

She nodded reluctantly. 'Sometimes. If I'm bad. But he doesn't like it when people see the marks.'

'I'm sorry, Marlee. It's going to be OK now.' Tim was helping her to her feet when she tensed.

'What is it?'

She pointed behind him. A column of black smoke coming from a distant chalet, roughly in the middle of the development. And as he watched, the first orange tongues of flame. Something was on fire. So Tim began to run towards the danger, as he always had.

Mary

She had drifted off for a second, a respite from the pain, but now it all came rushing back. The dirty floor beneath her cheek. Her nose, her chin, her entire face and throat radiating with pain. If she was passing out, that was a very bad sign. She had to try and stay awake. How long had she been in here? He'd taken her bag with her phone, and it was so dark, only a thin line of light under the door. *Come on, Mary, think.* No one knew she was here except the Uber driver. That had been very stupid of her; she would agree with Jack when he inevitably told her so, because she would see him again, wouldn't she, Jack and Audrey and Leo, in just a few hours when she got out of here? Even though John Stokes had attacked her and locked her in here, which must mean he had Sam prisoner. Marlee too maybe, punishing both daughters for stepping out of line. A controlling man, who'd kept his wife and daughters in a state of frozen fear. And now he had Mary. But she would get out – wouldn't she? Someone would come. Maybe Tim was here.

She was trying to sit up, gingerly touching her face, which felt like squashed fruit, when she smelled it. Smoke. There was smoke drifting under the small crack in the door.

The building was on fire, and she was locked in.

Tim

There was a fire. He couldn't get his head round it. Had Stokes set this – to kill Samantha? He was running towards it, gasping for breath now, dimly aware of Marlee at his heels. He tried to shout to her to stay away, but no words seemed to come out.

There was a black Audi parked outside the central building of the holiday park, which had once been a dining room with some rooms attached, presumably for staff, and Tim was sure the car hadn't been there beforehand. John Stokes was at its wheel, seemingly frozen, staring at the fire that was engulfing the place. Already the air was filled with black smoke, and Tim heard Marlee choke, and he could feel the heat as orange flames tore up the side of the building. Tinder-dry and built of old wood, it would go up in seconds. It seemed to be coming from inside the building.

'I think it's her!' Marlee shouted, gesturing with her bleeding hands. 'In there! She set it on fire, to try and get out!' She was running towards the flames.

Stokes snapped out of his trance, and got out of his car, began to lurch after his daughter. She veered from him.

'No, Daddy! I have to get Sam!'

Tim didn't think about it. He launched himself at the man, trying to remember his rugby days. Slammed him to the ground, jarring his own bones. But John Stokes was strong – he'd have to be, to kidnap his tall, fit stepdaughter and bring her here. He soon had Tim in a headlock, one arm over his throat.

'Get away – from my – family!' Gritted teeth. Red, enraged face.

Tim couldn't breathe. Sips of air, in in in. Just like that day. Pressure on his chest. A feeling of weakness in his limbs. Couldn't breathe. A strange fatalism took over. He had tried, and got close, but the man was furious, his eyes popping, and he was strangling Tim. There was nothing he could do. He wished he could have said sorry to Alice.

Then it stopped suddenly, and he could breathe again. His vision cleared and he saw Stokes was on his back, scrabbling like an overturned beetle. A girl was standing over him, holding a long piece of wood, and as Stokes tried to get up, she hit him again with it, hard and vicious, and his eyes rolled back in his head. Knocked out. The girl was dirty and smoke-stained, her fair hair almost black with soot. Then Marlee was hugging her, and sobbing, and Tim realised it was Samantha. Samantha had saved him.

'What . . . how . . .'

She was strangely calm. 'I set it on fire. I burned the wall down and climbed out.'

She'd set fire to a building with herself in it? Tim gaped at such bravery, clawing his way to sit up, still gasping in air, his throat raw and compressed. He had a brief moment of thinking it was all OK – he had found the girls, both safe, they were all fine – when he heard the screaming. A woman's voice, from inside the burning building.

'Help me! God, please help – I'm locked in here!'

It was Marlee who recognised the voice before Tim. 'It's her – the woman who came to the house! It's Mary!'

Mary

Every breath hurt, burning her lungs from the inside out. She had crawled to the door and put her mouth to the gap at the bottom, trying to suck in air, but the smoke was coming in that way too. The door rattled in its frame but didn't budge an inch. There was no way out, and the building was on fire. She didn't understand how this had all happened so quickly, how so short a while ago, barely half an hour surely, she'd been standing by the side of the road, safe, free, not dying of smoke inhalation. It took so little to end a life, snuff it out. All of her. Her colleagues, her friends. Audrey, Leo. Jack, and how she now regretted the time wasted with him, being annoyed or resentful. Maybe they'd never find her body, and he'd think she just vanished, left her kids and him. Or they'd find her blackened corpse and he'd always wonder why she'd come here, why she hadn't told him where she was going. Chasing after Tim, and who knew where he was? Perhaps Stokes had got him too, perhaps he was dead and Samantha also. All gone, and she'd wasted her life coming here to this desolate place. Leo would not remember her at all. Audrey might for a short while, but she would fade, and they'd always know their mother had given her life for a ridiculous chase, to find a girl who wasn't missing, with a man she shouldn't have trusted. That their mother had not been content to simply love them and care for them, to stay at home safe with them. This was all her fault. And now her chest was too heavy, and the smoke too thick, and it was over. There was a moment of fear, then a slackening. There was nothing she could do – she was lost.

31st August, 2019

FOR SALE – spacious two-bed maisonette flat in lively community area, close to Ofsted-rated outstanding schools, two minutes from park. One bath, good-sized master bed and second bedroom, recently refurbed to a high standard. 600k ONO.

Tim

Three Months Later

Tim peered from the bushes. His target was jogging slowly along the path, attired in a stretchy orange top and black leggings, panting and sweating. He waited, counting, his heart racing. What if he got spotted? Or the police were nearby? One, two, three . . . then he stepped out on to the path.

'Minister? Tim Darbandi from the *Guardian*. Do you have any comments on the revelations this morning, about your department's failure to implement the Trafficking Act?'

The immigration minister, a portly middle-aged man, looked alarmed at Tim's sudden appearance and, instead of stopping, veered around him.

'No comment.'

'Are you aware that, since the bill was passed, an estimated four thousand women have been trafficked into the country for the purposes of sexual slavery?'

'Um, I don't know if those figures are, um . . . No comment.'

Tim jogged along beside him. He was fitter than the other man, he realised. Since everything that had happened at the holiday camp, remembering how his lungs had burned and his legs ached as he'd run, the way John Stokes had thrown him to the ground with such ease, he had decided to finally get fit. He'd taken up running and even joined a gym – Alice would have been proud, though they weren't in contact, and probably never would be again. He wished her well and hoped she knew how sorry he was for all that he'd done.

He had a new job now, off the back of the blockbuster story he had to tell, and he was even sleeping a little better, with the strict routine and early starts. Sometimes he had nightmares about that day, digging Marlee from the rubble, the moment when he'd thought Mary was dead and it was all his fault. He'd tried to get into the building for her, into the flames, but she was behind a locked metal door, her knocks growing feeble, and he couldn't get it open and the whole place was coming down. Plaster and wood hitting his head, singeing him. Smoke so thick he could chew it. But just when he'd given up, choking and gasping, the wail of sirens had sounded. The police were there, and they had a bolt-cutter and got Mary out, pale and curled into herself in a heap, and he'd thought she was dead then too, her hair and skin black with smoke, but she had coughed and spluttered and an ambulance had arrived to save her.

Tim, Mary, Marlee, and Sam had all been rushed to hospital, treated for smoke inhalation and shock and severe dehydration in Sam's case, but they'd recovered. John Stokes had also been treated for the concussion Sam gave him, then when he woke up charged with the kidnap and imprisonment of his stepdaughter, perverting the course of justice, and assaulting Mary – he'd broken her nose and knocked out several of her teeth, and Tim shivered to think of the violence unleashed on her. But she was alright.

So was he. He was back doing what he did best, chasing down politicians, holding them to account.

'Minister?' he prompted. 'Just a quick quote and I'll leave you to your jog.'

The minister was running out of puff. 'I'm not sure of those figures, but we're certainly committed to ending trafficking, whatever it takes.'

Bingo. The quote he needed for the evening edition. 'You'll take steps to implement the act then?'

'Of course.'

There it was. Tim stopped, and the man panted off. He checked his Dictaphone had been recording, and headed back to the office to transcribe it, and make the front page.

Mary

Three Months Later

'Audrey, please put down the stick. Audrey – Audrey!'

Mary sighed as her daughter hared off over the open green space that was their new lawn. It was hard to believe all this land was theirs, after the postage-stamp-sized bit of London they had once laid claim to. The new house, in a village a few miles from Guildford, had four bedrooms and two bathrooms, a garage, a huge garden, a studio office. She was already wondering how they'd fill it all with their meagre furniture.

Jack was pretending to direct the removals men, who clearly had their own system and just ignored him, while Mary undid Leo from his car seat and followed Audrey into the garden. She didn't rush, as the lawn was totally safe and there was no traffic nearby that the toddler could dash into. It was so quiet, the only sound the cheep of birds.

She'd done it. She'd moved to the country, and although part of her was sad to have left London, given up, withdrawn, another part of her had relaxed so much she felt she could finally draw breath. The kids could have their own rooms, and stop keeping each other awake, so maybe Mary could get some sleep too. Work had given her some extra time off, to get over the trauma of her near-death experience, but she'd go back in a few months, taking the train as a commuter and putting both kids into the new nursery they'd found with ease, it not being as cut-throat here as the London scene.

It hadn't been an easy time – she'd needed extensive dental work on the teeth John Stokes had knocked out, and a small operation to reset her broken nose. Leo had cried when he saw her, all black eyes and bruised, pulpy face. But it could have been worse. There'd been a time, locked in that old kitchen, smoke pouring in and feeling the heat of the floor sear her skin, when Mary had truly thought she was dying. That her children would grow up motherless, through her own stupidity and recklessness. But then there'd been a loud cracking noise cutting through her fog, and someone was pounding on her chest. A vague impression of uniforms and lights and chattering radios, speeding inside a rocking ambulance, trying hard not to be sick, sucking oxygen into her scorched lungs.

When she came round in hospital, she was told Jack had become worried when he got three trip notifications in a row from their shared Uber account – she hadn't even remembered it was shared, it was so long since she'd gone anywhere – and called the police. They'd arrived just in time, because Mary hadn't had long left. She still got coughing fits now, and wouldn't be joining a gym any time soon, but she could at least run about after Audrey – and Leo, who'd started to crawl the week before. His face was round and swollen now too, a first tooth poking through. Growing up in front of her eyes.

'This is our new house,' she said, as he gazed at her with saucer eyes. 'We're going to live here, all of us.'

It was a fresh start. She knew Tim was doing well, had a new job, and that Samantha and Marlee were back home with their mother, who was being weaned off her medications and would have to learn how to be a parent again.

Mary had also been told in hospital, struggling for each breath through her shattered nose, with her damaged lungs, that Nigel Harper had been charged with the murders of five women between 1977 and 2007, including Eric Johnson's mother Colette, who'd given him a set of her house keys, thinking him simply a kindly neighbour who'd offered to cut the grass. Possessions from the missing women had been discovered in Nigel's shed, and his neighbours and wife of thirty years and four children were all shocked that such a pillar of the community was in fact a serial murderer. The families of the four missing girls now had their bodies back, their bones to be reburied, and whatever small comfort that might bring.

Eric Johnson had received a suspended sentence for obstructing an investigation, and perhaps unsurprisingly nothing had come out in the press. He had been in touch, again promising Mary anything she wanted, a new job, a promotion for Jack, but she was done with all that. She couldn't forget how ruthlessly he'd set Tim up, and hoped she would never cross paths with Eric Johnson, or anyone connected with 16 Cliveden Road, again.

As Mary passed into her new, enormous garden, her eyes couldn't help drifting to that of their new neighbours. She frowned, squinting. There was something odd about it – a shed with a key-pad lock on the door, and what looked like a ventilation system on the wall outside. Who'd need a shed with ventilation, and such a sophisticated alarm? Was it a bit odd? It looked like the kind of place you could keep someone, and . . .

Stop it, Mary, she told herself firmly, and, holding Leo tighter, went to stop her daughter eating pebbles.

BOOK CLUB QUESTIONS

1. Mary is a keen watcher of true-crime documentaries, which fuels her interest in the Samantha Ellis case. Do you think true crime has a positive or negative impact?

2. Mary sometimes feels she is a bad mother and compares herself to Francine and Alana. Did you agree with this, or think she acted badly at times?

3. Mary feels she can't do anything well, either her job or taking care of her family. Do you think society does enough to support working mothers?

4. How much is Tim to blame for what happened to Mariam?

5. Did you judge Eric for using sites like Only Fans, or do you think this is a legitimate way for women to make money?

6. How much did Mary and Tim's actions actually cause harm to Samantha and her family?

7. What did you think of the character of Alice, Tim's ex? Was she right to leave him or should she have been more supportive?

8. How much of a role do insomnia and sleeplessness play in the story?

9. Have you ever seen something in your own neighbourhood that you thought was suspicious?

10. Mary and Tim try to report their concerns to the police but are rebuffed, largely because of resource issues. Were they right then to take matters into their own hands?

ABOUT THE AUTHOR

Photo © 2021 Donna Ford

Claire published her first novel in 2012, and has followed it up with many others in the crime fiction genre and also in women's fiction (writing as Eva Woods). She has had four radio plays broadcast on the BBC, and her thrillers *What You Did* and *The Other Wife* were both number-one bestsellers. She ran the UK's first MA in crime writing for five years, and regularly teaches and talks about writing. Her first non-fiction project, the true-crime book *The Vanishing Triangle*, was released in 2021. She also writes scripts and has several projects in development for TV.